THE STUFF OF EMPIRE: THE COMPLETE ADVENTURES OF BELLOW BILL WILLIAMS, VOLUME 2

The Python Pit: The Complete Adventures
of Singapore Sammy, Volume 2

BY GEORGE F. WORTS

A Queen of Atlantis

BY FRANK AUBREY

Four Corners, Volume 2

BY THEODORE ROSCOE

Galloping Gold: The Complete Tales
of Sheriff Henry, Volume 4

BY W.C. TUTTLE

Jades and Afghans: The Complete Adventures
of Cordie, Soldier of Fortune, Volume 3

BY W. WIRT

The Ledger of Life: The Complete Cabalistic
Cases of Semi Dual, the Occult Detector

BY J.U. GIESY AND JUNIUS B. SMITH

Minions of Mercury

BY WILLIAM GRAY BEYER

White Heather Weather

BY JOHN FREDERICK

The Fire Flower and Other Adventures:
The Jackson Gregory Omnibus

BY JACKSON GREGORY

THE STUFF
OF EMPIRE

THE COMPLETE ADVENTURES OF
BELLOW BILL WILLIAMS, VOLUME 2

RALPH R. PERRY

ILLUSTRATED BY

SAMUEL CAHAN

COVER BY

PAUL STAHR

STEEGER BOOKS • 2020

TABLE OF CONTENTS

MISSING

*Nobody but the brawny Bellow Bill could
hope to get fair play for that hunted, framed
American—and nobody in all the South Seas
better knew the risks in that underground trail*

CHAPTER I

THE MAN WHO WAS LOST

BELLOW BILL WILLIAMS was singing. Though half a mile of carving beach lay between the trading store which the big tattooed pearler had chosen for the scene of his spree and the residence of the governor of Tatorima, every word of the song was audible to the governor's distinguished guest.

> "Let me chant of the dusky maid
> Who wrecked the Polly's crew:
> A lissome, laughing, maddening maid
> Who sprawled by the sea in the cool palms' shade.
> Of sharks and the deep she was sorely afraid,
> But not of male men at all!"

Pitched deeper than the boom of the surf, with a rousing, devil-may-care lilt and swagger, the stentorian voice roared out a ballad of Rabelaisian frankness, informing all Tatorima how the maid was wooed.

The guest of the governor flushed. Back home in Akron, Ohio, fifteen per cent of his enormous income was given annually to societies opposed to liquor and ribaldry. Had the government allowed a larger deduction from the income tax, Mr. Hosea Sprude would have turned over a larger donation.

"Really, your excellency!" he protested. "Before I tell you any more of my son's—er—misfortunes, can't that man be arrested for—er—disturbing the peace? Really, he is indecent!"

The governor suppressed a smile. Maitland was a slender

1

young Englishman of twenty-five. The title of "excellency" amused him, and so did the request.

"You fella Fetia!" he said sharply to a native policeman who dozed on the steps of the veranda. "Sing-sing below Bellow Bill fella too much. You stop."

The native remained where he sat. Only rolling eyes and a wide-open mouth showed that he had grasped the meaning of the command.

"Bill be cross along me. Knock out seven bells. Me fright

along Bill too much," he answered emphatically, and crouched down where he sat like a dog that awaits a whipping from its master.

"You see, Mr. Sprude? Please go on with your story," remarked Maitland blandly.

"Do you mean that you can't maintain order—"

"Quite so. Bellow Bill Williams stands six feet four in bare feet," Maitland replied sharply. "He weighs somethin' over two hundred and twenty pounds, and his only flaw as a fightin' man is that he is not a particularly good shot. I agree with Fetia

A pail of water revived the horrified trader.

perfectly. It's disgustin' discipline, and all that, but if he tried to shut Bill up Bill would throw him into the lagoon. At present Bill is singin', but if he were annoyed he might decide to take Twemlow's store apart, and I doubt if all of Tatorima would stop him. The peace is bein' preserved remarkably well as it is"—the the smile which Maitland had suppressed appeared on his face—"and as for the song, your son made it up and taught it to Bill. So please go on."

"My son has a taste for evil companions," said Sprude in a way that made Maitland want to wring his neck. "Nevertheless he is the only heir to my fortune, which is—er—quite substantial. Because of his own stubbornness he compelled me to turn him from my house and disinherit him. Now I have learned that I was wrong, and I want him back." Sprude stopped as though he expected praise for his generosity.

MAITLAND'S FACE hardened. Young as he was, he ruled

a dozen islands as judge, legislature and executive in one, and he spoke as such.

"As I understand it," he said, "there was a shortage in the accounts of your firm and you called in accountants and the police, threatening to make an example of the culprit. Your son came to you and said that he was the guilty man. You turned him out of your house that night—without a shilling. Or since you are an American, perhaps I should say without a nickel."

"It was my duty. He was a thief."

"After he had disappeared you discovered that a pearl necklace which belonged to your wife was missing. You insisted that your son had stolen that, too, though your wife managed to find the courage to tell you that she had given it to the boy so that he would not be utterly penniless."

"I had paid for the necklace. It was mine. My wife had no right to give it away."

"Quite so," snapped Maitland in his official manner. "Your ideas of duty and of what is yours are remarkably rigid. Fanatical, if I may say so. However, learning of this new 'theft,' you then felt it your duty to offer a reward for the return of the necklace, and incidentally for your son's arrest. Did it occur to you that you were making a hunted criminal of him?"

"I thought he was a criminal," said Sprude stiffly.

"And then, after two months, after the police had followed a trail to pawned gems that led to San Francisco and thence via ship to the South Seas, one of your employees came to you with the money that had been embezzled," Maitland accused. "He was a poor man, young, newly married, but your son and he had been friends. He told you that he had taken the money because it had meant the life of his wife. She and the baby were still in the hospital when you discovered the theft, and your son and he believed that if she learned he had been taken to jail, the shock would have killed her. So your son confessed—falsely—to gain time. Time for a sick woman to recover her strength, and time for the friend to replace the money and assume the blame—as he did!"

"If my son had explained—"

"Probably he was afraid to. I've known you less than an hour, Mr. Sprude, but under the same circumstances I would lie to you myself. You are a hard man, and you take a perverse and cruel pleasure in doing what you are pleased to call your duty. As a result, you put your son in the position of a criminal. You made him him hate you and all that you represent; law, duty, and respectability.

"Then, because you learned you were wrong and repented of your own act, you wish him back—and you think you can get him back because you control millions. I hope you can, but the injustice you've done has had consequences that are going to make it difficult. And I can't help you. For a month my police have combed the islands hereabouts for your son. He remains—missing."

SPRUDE WAS silent, but a tremor ran through his rigid body, and an expression of agony grew upon his face. "The police? My boy has turned criminal?" he whispered so piteously that Maitland relented, in spite of his anger.

"This afternoon, before you landed from the mail steamer, I would have answered yes," he replied. "I believed he was guilty of burglary and murderous assault, but now that I have heard your story I am not so sure. A month ago your son was here, Mr. Sprude. He told us nothing about himself, not even his name.

"We didn't know that he was an heir to millions, or that he was persecuted. We didn't care. We liked a beach comber that we knew only as 'Pug' because he was a man who seemed to want to wring out all the fun that was to be found in life at one quick twist. To me it was a godsend to have an educated and sober white man on this island; but in spite of all I could do, Pug's greatest friend was Bellow Bill Williams.

"They were drinking together when he knocked Bill down in fair fight, which hasn't been done often. Bill got up and knocked

Pug half through the window of Twemlow's store. The glass cut your son's cheek to the bone from here to here—" Maitland's finger traced a line from the nose to the angle of the jaw. "Bill sewed up the cut, and after that the two were inseparable. Bill may know where he is. In fact, I think he does."

"But why would a dissolute, brawling thug know more than you?" Sprude demanded.

"Because, liking Pug as he did, he smuggled him off the island when he thought Pug had committed a murder," said Maitland grimly. "That makes Bill an accessory after the fact, if you please, but in the islands we expect a man to take a chance like that for his mate. The facts are these:

"My policeman, Fetia there, came to me one night a month ago with the news that Cockney Twemlow was lying dead on the floor of his store with a four-inch gash in his skull. Some one had been attempting to open the safe, and had felled Twemlow with a club when he was surprised. I hurried to the store, of course, and at first I thought Fetia was right. Twemlow was scarcely breathing, and his pulse was indistinguishable. He lived, but he had concussion of the brain.

"I rounded up all the white men on the island, but they all had alibis except Pug, who was missing. So I sent out the police launch. Now, a 'newchum'—as we call newcomers—can't hide in the islands, Mr. Sprude, because native gossip brings word wherever he goes. An old-timer, who knows which particular natives have reason to keep their mouths shut, can. Pug had vanished into thin air, so it was a moral certainty that Bellow Bill, who knows every native for hundreds of miles around, both inside the law and out, had hired a boatman and advised Pug where to hide.

"Sure enough, when Twemlow recovered, Bill sailed away in his schooner. I believe he went to bring Pug back to stand his trial, but he returned alone. For two days Bill has been scowling around the island, and this afternoon, just as the mail steamer dropped anchor, he went to Twemlow's and began a spree. That puzzles me, for Bill isn't a man to try to drown trouble in drink.

"However, if you want your son, go to that dissolute, indecent thug, as you call him, and tell him that you'll stand behind the boy at his trial to the full extent of your millions... On second thought," Maitland added, "I think I'll go to Bill with you. You'd probably offer him money, and in his present temper he'd throw you through the window. It will be far safer, and perhaps we'll get better results if you let me handle him. Is it understood?"

Sprude nodded, and rose. There was little hope on his face, and he lagged behind the governor as they walked down the beach toward the sheet-iron store that shimmered in the heat of the late afternoon, and from which the booming voice poured songs that made Sprude flush darkly. Even without the governor's warning, it is doubtful if Sprude would have opened the interview. For years he had not been face to face with iniquity, and he was horrified by a sight which gave Maitland hope.

WHAT SPRUDE saw was a giant in a ragged undershirt and ragged duck trousers which had been cut off at the knee, lolling in a chair with two empty whisky bottles beneath it. On huge arms that gleamed with perspiration, a mass of tattooing in green, yellow and crimson twisted and writhed as his muscles moved under the skin.

What the governor noticed, on the other hand, was that Bill's eyes were alert, and the huge head with its mass of curly, coppery-blond hair was held erect. Bill had consumed enough whisky to put two ordinary men under the table, but his maudlin singing was a blind. To the governor's experienced eye, he was not intoxicated.

Gayly he waved a half-empty bottle at Maitland.

"Thanks, no," said the latter. "Bill, this is Pug's father. He's come all the way from the States to say that the charges against his son have been withdrawn. He wants him back, and I'm going to help all I can. You don't have to play a lone hand any more."

"Don't stall, Maitland," Bill rumbled in his deep voice. "I'm for

Pug, all the time, and even now. I know what his father did." On one bare knee a huge fist clenched. "Pug's been double-crossed by his old man, double-crossed by Twemlow, the crook, and crossed by me. But not double-crossed, by thunder!"

"Really?" said Maitland quietly. "You seem to know as much as I do."

"More!" the echoes rumbled in the iron storeroom. "Governor, have you read the mail the steamer brought?" A bitter grin crossed the pearler's face at Maitland's stare of surprise. "I thought not," Bill added. "When you do, remember Pug figured he was disgraced at home, and would be hanged if he was caught here. Don't blame him too much, nor me. He's done about the only thing he could do, I guess."

"Twemlow stole the necklace?" asked the still puzzled governor.

Bill nodded, and shrugged. "Thought it safe to steal what was stolen," he rumbled. "The kid had spunk, and when he saw what Twemlow was up to, he slammed him. That's telling you too much. Twemlow's cook's here, keeping watch of me."

"Where is the necklace?" the governor whispered.

"Where Twemlow thinks it's safe," Bill growled. "That's a trifle—as you will find out. You're gumming my game, so beat it!"

"But I can force Twemlow to open his safe," Maitland persisted.

"How? I know something about your English law. You can't—unless he wants to, which he won't unless the necklace ain't in it." Bill glanced through the window. "Twemlow's coming now with an officer off the mail steamer," he growled. "You get out of here, read your mail, and draw your own conclusions. Your good will and his father's forgiveness ain't worth a damn to Pug; get me?"

"I don't like the look in your eye, Bill," Maitland objected.

"No? All the more reason for getting out," rumbled the huge tattooed man. "It was me that put the scar on Pug's jaw, and me that sent him—where he went. I ain't drunk, Maitland. Whisky just makes my blood run faster. I know what I've got to do, and, by thunder, don't make my job harder!"

"Come, Sprude," said the governor with decision. Halfway to the door he turned. "I trust you, Bill!" he whispered.

"You're wrong, then," rumbled the pearler for all to hear. He glanced through the window, and suddenly shifted his chair so that it was tilted against the safe. "Pug may be a killer if he's driven far enough, but he ain't dirty, and he ain't mean," he added, as though it were an afterthought. One huge hand motioned the governor to be gone, and the latter drew Sprude out of the door.

INSTANTLY BILL'S head sank on his chest as though the whisky had overwhelmed him at last. A bitter grin at the dirtiness of the tricks which chance and fate play upon men lurked around his lips. He had sent Pug to the den of the worst scoundrels in the Pacific in the belief that only there would he be safe from the police. Bill had meant well, but when he followed to bring Pug back the young man had been missing, and the half-breed gambler who should have been hiding him had denied that he had come at all.

The gambler had lied. Though Bill had not found Pug, he had heard rumors of his whereabouts. Among the pirates who prey on the pearl luggers which work out of Thursday Island a white man had appeared. A young man, blond, with a newly healed scar that angled from the nose to the right jaw.

That scar would hang Pug Sprude if the British caught him. A Japanese diver who had been the sole survivor of a murderous piracy had sworn to it positively. Such testimony could not be offset even by all the influence which millions of dollars and official good will might bring to bear.

As soon as Maitland read his mail he would know that the new pirate was Pug. He would hunt for the young American harder than ever—but only to try and execute him. Pirates were the governor's worst enemies.

Pug could clear himself of such an accusation only by proving that he had joined the pirate gang in order to destroy it. Bellow

Bill knew that this was not the case. Either Pug had decided in desperation that he might as well be hanged for piracy as for the assault on Twemlow, or, which Bill thought more likely, his protege had stumbled on the secret of the gang and had been forced to join them lest he reveal it.

Whatever the cause had been, however, Bill considered that he himself was responsible for the hopeless predicament which Pug Sprude was in. Pug had trusted him. His advice had been bad. Therefore Bill's job now was to restore a decent, impulsive kid, who had been double-crossed by fate, to the position which he deserved.

That was settled. The risks Bill would run he shrugged aside; but in all his adventures in the South Seas he had never faced a task so complex. First, he must persuade the half-breed gambler to take him where Pug was hidden. Bill's initial attempt to do this had failed, and as far as he could see he would continue to fail unless he put himself absolutely in the half-breed's power. The latter had somehow made a pirate of one white man who came with a price on his head, and he might do the same with the second. As a pirate, Bellow Bill, who knew every trick of the South Seas, would be more valuable than a new-chum like Pug.

So far Bellow Bill could see his way. To take this first step he had planted himself in Twemlow's store and pretended to be uproariously drunk.

For the second step in his task he could lay no plans whatever. He must extricate Pug from the midst of a gang of pirates commanded by a clever scoundrel. And third, hardest problem of the three, he must effect the rescue in a way that would make the authorities believe that he had sent Pug to break up the gang, and followed himself after his protégé had failed.

Success in such a program looked impossible. Bill refused to admit it. No halfway measures would serve. The battle would be both with wits and fists, but the tattooed, bull-voiced pearling skipper was not a halfway man.

CHAPTER II

WHISPERS

THOUGH BILL PRETENDED to be sprawled in a drunken stupor, a grin lurked at the corners of his mouth as Twemlow paused in the door of the store and swore aloud to find him still there. The officer from the mail steamer, who wore the uniform of a purser, scowled anxiously.

"The ship sails at high tide, in an hour," the officer whispered. "What do you mean by having things like that around?"

" 'E was drunk, damn 'im!" snarled Twemlow. "Hi couldn't do nothing! 'Ere—'elp me get 'im out! 'E was torkin' to the governor, damn 'is eyes!… Bill!" the trader shouted suddenly, and stepping to the pearler commenced to shake him by the shoulder. "Hit's closing time! 'Ook yer blasted freight!"

"Go to the devil!" Bill rumbled.

"Tyke 'is feet, for 'Eaven's sake!" whispered Twemlow anxiously. " 'E'll sleep if we lay 'im in the warm sand!" He caught Bill by the armpits. The purser captured the ankles, and, grunting because of Bill's weight, they started with him toward the door. Bill gave a twist and a kick. His bare heel caught the purser in the back, knocking him to hands and knees. Bill struck the floor with a mighty thump. He sat up scowling, tried to rise, but sat back, swaying. One huge arm reached out and captured the whisky bottle.

"Lemme be or I'll knock seven bells out of you, Twemlow," he growled, and then tilted the bottle. For ten seconds the whisky gurgled down his throat. Bill sighed with content and slowly stretched himself out at full length on the floor. "Go 'way!" he growled, and closed his eyes.

"Damn the stinking swine!" panted Twemlow viciously. "Hi'd as soon try to carry a wild helephant! 'Ere!" The trader crossed the store swiftly and returned with a thin cotton blanket, which he dropped over Bill's body and face. Bill brushed the cloth from his nose, but made no other movement. The whisky he had consumed made the blood pound in his veins. He could hear the two men breathing.

"'Ere! Tyke this bottle and bash in 'is conk if 'e moves!" Twemlow instructed. "'It 'ard, 'cause everybody 'll believe hit was self-defense, and bly me, hit will be if 'e gets started!"

Through half-closed lids Bill saw the purser crouch by his head. Twemlow tiptoed to the safe. The combination clicked, and the door at which Pug had battered in vain swung open.

Instantly Bill's left fist shot backward over his head, striking the purser in the chest and knocking him heels over head. With a bound Bill was on his feet. The half empty bottle in his right hand he flung at Twemlow's head. The trader swung the safe door shut, but he dodged instinctively. Bill was on him before he could twirl the combination. Two tattooed hands swept the trader from the floor like a sack of meal and tossed him upon the purser, who was clawing at a coat pocket.

With a satisfied grunt Bill dropped on the heap. In the kitchen Twemlow's cook yelled shrilly for the police. The rear door of the store slammed as he fled, screaming robbery and murder at every jump.

This, to Bill's mind, was wholly to the good. The more spectacular the robbery was, the better. He squeezed his victims till they gasped, shifted his grip to the throat, and bumped two heads together with a resounding crack. Twemlow and the purser relaxed, dazed rather than completely knocked out, but in no condition to move. Bill confiscated the purser's revolver and went to the safe.

THERE WAS a package, waxed and sealed and addressed to a firm of jewelers in Paris. Bill ripped off the paper and picked a two and a half foot string of matched pearls out of a bed of kapok fiber. These went into his pocket. The paper, with its telltale address, followed. For the rest, the safe contained a small bag, presumably of pearls, and a little heap of bills and coin. Bill pocketed both.

Twemlow had begun to blink. In the distance other excited voices were shouting answers to the cook. The village of Tatorima, warned of the robbery, was collecting its forces and its nerve.

Methodically Bill tore the blanket into strips. He bound and gagged Twemlow, smiling grimly at the terror that stared from the eyes of the half-conscious man, swung him upon his shoulder, and stepped out of the store. The night was not yet dark, and his figure was clearly visible against the sand. A shout went up as he appeared, followed by a second cry, in a different key, as the character of his burden was recognized.

Men were running toward the store. Not natives, for they wore white jumpers and trousers. Sailors from the mail steamer.

Bill crossed the beach to a dugout that was drawn up on the sand, tossed Twemlow into it like a sack, and paddled out into the lagoon. On the beach the pursuit stopped. A revolver shot lanced the dark, and a bullet skipped across the water. The range was far too great for effective shooting, but immediately afterward a shout arose that was like the yelp of a wolf pack which sees its quarry delivered into its jaws.

A few men ran forward to cut Bill off from the land. The rest turned and sprinted back the way they had come to find boats.

The lagoon of Tatorima has but one entrance, which is a pass in the reef less than a hundred yards wide. Near this the mail steamer was anchored, with Bellow Bill's schooner also swinging at anchor near by. The distance from the point where Bill had taken to the water was little less than that from the boat landing to the entrance, and to escape he must get his schooner under sail before a boat's crew could reach either schooner or harbor entrance. Apparently he was trapped, but though every ounce of his strength went into every stroke of the paddle, so that the dugout tore through the water, he was grinning.

From the mail steamer a searchlight swung across the lagoon

and settled upon Bill in a glaring finger of radiance, blinding him so that he could judge the progress of the race only by the sound. The shrill of a boatswain's whistle and the creak of falls aboard the steamer he discounted. Another boat could not be lowering in time to play a decisive part, but as he drove the dugout alongside his schooner the racing *thump—thump—thump* of oars against the thole pins of the steamer's shore boat was disconcertingly close.

"Halt, Bill! I'm goin' to shoot!" shouted Maitland's voice.

A tremendous paddle stroke by the pearler sent the dugout into the shelter and darkness afforded by the hull of the schooner.

"Halt and be hanged? Like fun!" he thundered. Over the rail that shielded him momentarily the searchlight streamed in a pitiless glare. Like a half empty sack, what must have seemed to Maitland to be the corpse of Twemlow, was tossed upon the schooner's deck. Bill followed—ducked as a revolver exploded. The bullet whistled past his head, but another leap put the mast of the schooner between his broad back and Maitland's gun. Bill ran to the bow, and slipped his anchor chain. Though the schooner began to drift before the night breeze, her speed could be measured in inches.

Bent low to take advantage of the scanty protection of the low rails, Bill darted back to the mast and took hold of the throat and peak halliards together. To hoist a schooner's sails ordinarily requires two men and several minutes. Maitland and the sailors from the steamer were counting on that fact—and so was Bill!

With both ropes over his shoulders, bent forward so that his finger tips brushed the deck, he struggled aft, dragging the sail up behind him as he went. Those on the steamer could see his leg muscles bunch and knot in that herculean effort, but to Maitland, in the boat, the sail seemed to rise to the masthead by magic, catch the night breeze, and draw flat. Foot by foot, yard by yard the schooner gathered way, to leap ahead as Bellow Bill, flat on the deck by the wheel, trimmed the sheets for a reach to the harbor entrance.

Maitland's revolver spat in vain. The oarsmen swore as the gap that lay between them and the stern of the schooner began to widen. Nothing is more maddening to the man hunter than to see a victim that he has considered as good as caught slip through his fingers. For a moment the searchlight continued to flood the deck of the schooner, revealing the limp figure of Twemlow, motionless in the scuppers. Then, as though to concede Bill's escape, the light was snapped off.

The pearler raised his head. "Twemlow's neck for Pug's— and to the devil with your British law!" he bellowed across the suddenly darkened sea. Mockingly his laugh boomed out. The schooner slipped through the harbor entrance and was gone.

BILL SLIPPED the wheel into the becket, so that the schooner would steer itself, and slipped a huge quid of fine cut chewing tobacco into his cheek. The reaction from the escape was upon him. He would have liked a drink. As soon as an angry governor could get to the radio of the mail steamer every official within two hundred miles would have orders to arrest him.

That was all right. He was wanted for robbery, and—what else? For murder, or only for forcible abduction? The searchlight had been very bright. Some one on the steamer might have noticed the bonds around Twemlow's ankles. Bill hoped not, though even a kidnaping, backed up by the theft of a two-hundred-thousand-dollar necklace, would be enough to set every tongue in the South Seas wagging. The gamblers and pirates of Thursday Island would hear and be awed by the magnitude of that theft! They would have two reasons to welcome Bill.

He spat over the rail, picked up Twemlow, and descended to the cabin. A pail of water brought the trader to, but when the cockney realized where he was he shrank back and stared at Bellow Bill as though he were in the power of a madman.

"Bly me, what do yer want to do wiv me?" he whined.

"You? Oh, you're a dead man," rumbled the pearler with a

grim humor much more menacing than a threat. "Unless you can make yourself useful to me, maybe. For example, did you tip anybody off that they would be safe in playin' Pug a dirty trick? Using him for a goat, say?"

"So help me, no! I just copped 'is necklace!"

"Then who was that purser?"

" 'E was my bruvver!" whined the trader in desperation. "So help me, 'e is! We took different names when we come 'ere, and many a trick we've been able to turn! 'E was just going to sell the pearls for me! Bill! Yer don't mean—yer ain't going to murd—"

"Shut up! Your dirty neck's worth less than Pug's reputation," Bill growled. "No, I ain't. Not right away. Here's what's going to happen to you: I'm going to sail to a little atoll I know of where nobody lives. Natives come there when the coconuts are ripe for harvest, but coconuts won't be ripe for a month, savvy?"

"I'll starve," Twemlow whined in misery.

"You won't, because I'm going to moor the schooner there. There's plenty of food and water aboard to last till the natives come," said Bill, and smiled at the spark of hope and cunning that leaped into the cockney's eyes. "But you won't sail away, because I'm going to sink every sail the schooner has in fifteen fathoms of water," Bill added. "A native diver can reach them, but you ain't swimmer enough. I'll leave your pearls and your money, and if I ain't back in a month, hire some of the natives to sail you back to Tatorima.

"But if you leave the atoll sooner than that," Bill went on grimly, "I'll break your dirty neck the next time we meet. And that's a promise, so don't be too gay about making signals or hailing any ship that happens to pass."

Twemlow drew a long breath of relief. "So help me, I'll stay where I'm put, Bill," he promised placatingly. "But w'at about the necklace? Yer won't say nothing to Maitland about that, nor my bruvver—"

"No," Bill rumbled. "The necklace goes with you. It'll be bait, and so will you be, missing on that atoll. You see, where

I'm going I'm liable to need plenty of help. While you and the necklace are missing, all the governors and the police in the islands will be following right on my heels, all ready and willing to oblige with clubs and handcuffs!"

CHAPTER III

SOUTH SEAS TRAIL

FROM TATORIMA TO Thursday Island is three hundred miles as the crow flies. Atolls and islands, large and small, dot the ocean like grains of pepper sprinkled on white paper, so that the choice of routes between the two places is almost infinite, and the task of police who seek to intercept a fugitive is comparable to that of stopping all the holes in a sieve.

Yet as the days passed after the escape of Bellow Bill, launches that searched through the islands received continual bits of information about the movements of the pearler. Though Twemlow and the schooner had disappeared, Bill was seen at the atoll of Fuvea—two days before the police arrived.

At St. Etienne they missed him by six hours; at Moorora he had increased his lead to thirty hours, but now his trail pointed unmistakably toward Thursday Island. The cordon of launches was closing in, and wireless warned the officials at Thursday Island to be on the lookout for the fugitive.

It is a small place, swarming with men of every color whose work in gathering shell is enough to kill the strongest, and whose pleasures are scarcely less violent. In the fishing season it never sleeps. The carousing and the fighting are as loud at dawn as at midnight, and the officials keep a close eye on the favorite places of entertainment—among which the Hall of the Five Beneficent Virtues, a gambling house, opium den, and saloon, run by a bronze-colored, poker-faced half-breed named Mitaki, is outstanding. Though Mitaki was only thirty, the cunning and the ambition of a Dutch father joined in his blood with the savage passions of a Papuan mother. He catered to every vice and seized every opportunity that would show him a profit. It was to Mitaki that Pug Sprude had gone. In the Hall of the Five Beneficent Virtues he had vanished; to reappear—once—as a pirate.

Bellow Bill landed on Thursday Island an hour after midnight. Though he swam ashore from a pearl lugger that was sailing by, and struck the beach at a comparatively lonely spot, the news that he had come reached the officials at once, through a native constable who took to his heels upon recognizing the formidable figure of the pearler striding across the beach from the surf.

For Bill the incident was a bit of good luck. He had planned that he should be seen, just as he had planned that he should be traced. He was glad that the strain of keeping just beyond the fingertips of the law was over, and the crisis at hand.

As the native constable disappeared, Bill slipped into a thick clump of palms and pandanus bushes. He emerged almost immediately, and hurried toward the town. To the fact that half a dozen people saw him stride into the maze of stinking alleys that formed the most disreputable section of the little town, he was indifferent.

He was relying upon the quickness of his movements and the reluctance of any one constable to encounter him face to face. While the officials were gathering a dozen of their most trustworthy men, he dodged into a great thatched building where lean-to had been added to lean-to until the patched roof covered half an acre.

NOW THOUGH the Hall of the Five Beneficent Virtues had been built piecemeal, it was peculiar among native structures in that Mitaki had taken out the interior partitions until the building was almost as open as a huge barn. Instead of a maze of passages, there was only one, which ran from front to rear.

On the right hand side were the dance hall, gambling room, and barroom, separated from one another only by the posts which supported the roof. In the center was a long corridor. On the left was a series of three opium dens, next, Mitaki's private office, with a private gambling room above it where he would occasionally entertain any one who desired to play for enormous stakes, and beyond this, the storerooms.

Through the office door Mitaki could survey his whole domain, and from any entrance a policeman could see every customer except those smoking opium. A strip of open land about ten yards wide separated the building from the harbor front, and the water here touched, not a beach, but an almost precipitous bank of coral more than ten feet high. Boats were moored near by, but the police found it simple to spot any one who climbed the steep bank and crossed the open space. Consequently, the officials tolerated Mitaki, despite his reputation.

Bellow Bill knew that the interior was not as simple as it looked. On the left-hand side the outer wall was double. The space between formed a secret passage, parallel to the corridor, which also ran from front to rear. This secret passage connected the three opium dens, Mitaki's office, which was between the corridor and the secret passage like the cross-bar of an H, and the storerooms. Mitaki or any man he chose to hide could thus pass from room to room unseen, and could escape through the tangle of alleys in the rear, but, as far as Bill knew, could not escape by water, owing to the open strip of land and the high coral bank.

Any one who wished to see Mitaki in private approached through the alleys, entered the opium den in the rear, and sent the attendant after the gambler. This the pearler had instructed Pug to do, and he was now following in the footsteps of his protégé.

A black Fijian who lit the pipes and rolled the pills took Bill's message, grunted at being disturbed, and disappeared behind a dirty curtain that covered one wall of the den. Bill backed watchfully against the opposite wall, which was bare and obviously solid. From this foul room, acrid with smoke, covered with tattered straw mats on which drugged men lay sucking at pipes which rendered them oblivious to what happened around them,

Pug had stepped to become missing to the world of men who are white, and clean.

Whether the new-chum had gone through choice or treachery, Mitaki would know. The gambler had denied all knowledge of Pug on Bill's previous trip to Thursday Island, but this time he would be forced either to speak or start Bill along the same route. The police would soon be on his trail.

THE CURTAIN parted. Mitaki stepped across the recumbent smokers to face Bill. He wore a Chinese jacket and trousers of grayish white, undyed silk, and the usually expressionless bronze face was clouded with anger.

"The police seek me. I was seen as I came," Bellow Bill began, sinking his great voice to a rumbling whisper. "I do not wish to be seen again by white men. I found fishing for pearls too slow. Perhaps you have heard?"

"I have heard. Even now a dozen men are coming with guns. They will spoil the gambling for the night." The thick lips sneered, revealing clenched teeth. "Let them find you, and shoot! What is that to me, painted liar? Go—the door at your back in still open!"

"Liar!" Bill rumbled. He was angry and perplexed. Was it possible that Mitaki had learned what had been done with Twemlow? Yet how?

"Yes!" Mitaki spat. He had the courage to insult a white man face to face. The revolver was visible in Bill's waistband. "You sent a man with a scarred face to me. He said he had no money, and you sent no word. You would have tricked me!" snarled Mitaki, carried away by passion. "In his own country he was a rajah! A prince—yet he came to me like any beach comber!"

"Oh, he did come to you, eh?" Bill boomed. "And he went—where? Come clean, black man!"

"No!" Mitaki refused. "Shoot and the police hang you!" he added defiantly.

Bill's gun was half-drawn, but he controlled himself. He pushed the gun back, nodded, and shrugged his broad shoulders.

"That would be a great loss—to us both," he muttered, and reached into his pocket. The palm of his hand pressed forward against the cloth, outlined dozens of small round shapes. "Those are pearls already matched—the choice of thousands," Bill growled. "Am I a big enough fool to kill even Twemlow for nothing?"

"Let me see!" But Bill shook his head.

"Next you will ask to handle them!" he mocked.

The gambler hesitated. Though Bill was playing his last card, it was the ace of trumps. Risk and crime were trifles before the force of Mitaki's greed, but along with the flame of covetousness that flashed into the dark face came a look of hatred and passion. Bill glanced at the opium smokers, and at the Fijian attendant. He was alert for a hostile movement. If he had been unwelcome before, Mitaki now had a far stronger motive for being rid of him.

"Come!" said the gambler at last, almost roughly, and dodged behind the curtain so suddenly that Bill had to leap forward to keep within arm's length. He had no wish to follow through a secret passage that was pitch-dark unless Mitaki were under his hand. While the latter opened the door behind the curtain Bill's fingers closed on his neck.

MITAKI TWISTED nervously, but moved ahead as far as his own office. Here he slipped through another door, to reappear with a tiny native lamp. The bit of burning rag floating in melted grease gave scarcely any light.

"No touch neck now," Mitaki snarled and moved on, past his office and into the storeroom nearest the harbor. The room was piled with barrels and cases of bottled goods. Bill was disappointed. Faint as the light was, he could see that no one was hiding here, and yet he had come to the end of the secret passage. The gambler observed the frown and grinned.

"Passage double," he remarked, stamping his foot. "One topside, one dug underneath. Goes out underneath—under water. You take boat."

"You mean you've dug one below this?" Bill rumbled. Here was news! The Hall of the Five Beneficent Virtues was provided with an egress on the harbor side after all.

"Coral rock is soft digging, but how did you get rid of it?" he asked.

"Dump under bank. Make shallow place. Not much digging. Cave there," Mitaki grunted. "You will see."

He set the lamp down and groped in the shadows. A section of the flooring rose an inch or two. He caught the board and tugged upward. The trap door was irregular in outline and planked on both sides so as to be fully a foot thick. Below was a square hole, three feet across, and black as a well. Mitaki gave a loud hiss of warning, waited an instant until it was repeated from below, and then motioned Bill to descend.

"When you are down I will shut the trap," he purred. "Later we will divide the pearls."

"Yeah," Bill rumbled.

With no visible sign of excitement or suspicion he reached for the lamp, and suddenly, before Mitaki could move or cry out, tossed it down the dark shaft.

There was a shrill cry of pain, and a flicker of light as the hot grease which spattered on the ground below was ignited by the blazing wick. Like a flash Bill covered Mitaki, crouched at the opening, and glanced below.

He saw planked walls, a plank floor—and a knife that lay in a pool of blazing grease directly under the trap door. As Bill looked, a brown hand snatched at the weapon.

Instantly the pearler swung his legs into the hatchway and dropped. He was too slow to get his foot on the knife, but not to thrust his gun against the ribs of the Melanesian native who had seized it. At the touch of the muzzle the man stiffened. He did not move even when the heavy trap door fell into place.

"What name belong you?" Bill growled.

"Yoshimo," the brown giant gasped, and the knife slipped from his limp fingers. Bill smiled grimly. To have shot Mitaki would have taught him nothing, but this henchman seemed made of stuff less stern.

"One white man—scar-face fella," Bill growled. "Take me him, or you be dead fella."

THOUGH THERE was no answer, Yoshimo shivered. He straightened, and started to move down a planked passageway that extended in both directions into darkness.

In that airless place, however, Bill was not going to leave a fire burning behind him. He crowded Yoshimo to the wall with a thrust of the gun, ripped off his *pareu,* and was beating at the flames, when a light showed in the passage. Other men had smelled the burning grease and smoking wood—four of them, all Melanesians, and all armed. They moved forward, uncertainly, and Bill swung Yoshimo's body between them and himself and waited, his gun pressed against the bare brown back.

"No kill—me chief fella! They go!" Yoshimo whined, and called to the others in a dialect which Bellow Bill understood well enough for all practical purposes. It was well for him that he did, for Yoshimo, it developed, was much more the prudent man than the coward.

Though the native had wilted at the touch of a gun, his orders were bloodthirsty. His men were to come and put the fire out first, and then go back, the man with the light leading the way. Not until they were in the room from which they had come, out of the white man's sight, were they to draw their knives and stand in ambush on both sides of the door. He, Yoshimo, would throw himself flat as be entered, and they must drive their knives instantly into the white man's body before he had time to shoot. Mitaki had hissed when he opened the trap. Therefore this white man was to be killed.

It was a very pretty plan, and a credit both to Yoshimo's nerve and intelligence. Bellow Bill could not help grinning, but before he answered he flung the *pareu* around the big brown man's throat and suddenly twisted it tight. Yoshimo could no longer dive away from the gun, or escape in darkness.

"Now tell them to drop their knives—where they stand," Bill growled, in a variety of the same dialect.

A concerted gasp was testimony to the fluency of his speech. The knives fell to the planks.

"Put the lamp on the deck and go to your room," Bill commanded. "When I am past the door you can come out again and put the fire out."

He was obeyed. The natives retreated in a sullen mass. "You, Yoshimo"—Bill pressed the gun in the bare back—"go to the room of the white man whose cheek is scarred."

"It is locked," said Yoshimo, with the fatalism of the native who yields to superior force. Nevertheless he stepped forward obediently.

WHEN THEY came to the knives, Bill shifted his gun to the hand that held the loin cloth and picked them up, slipping them into his belt until his waist bristled like a pirate's. They had almost reached the lamp, which he meant to order Yoshimo to carry, when the fire behind him went out!

The suddenness of the thing made Bill jump. He had heard a sound, as though a pailful of sand had been dumped on the flames, yet the opening of the trap door had been noiseless. A shot streaked the dark behind Bill and a bullet ripped into the planking by his shoulder.

He fired, and knowing that he had missed, as usual, he pushed Yoshimo forward with all his strength, snatched up the blazing lamp wick, and extinguished it in his hand.

"Shoot again, Mitaki!" he boomed. "I'm waiting for the flash of your gun!"

It was a bluff, but it worked. There was no answer, and no second shot. Bill had been forced to drop his revolver to extinguish the light. He groped for it, found it, and rose, expecting every second to hear a rush of bare feet and feel the impact of Yoshimo's men.

"Go on!" he growled into Yoshimo's ear. "We kill one fella seven bells, savvy?" A punch with the revolver indicated what "fella" he meant. Yoshimo stepped out, noiseless in bare feet. Bill followed as silently, straining his ears for the sound of a rush from behind.

There was none, yet even to the pearler's iron nerves the walk up the passageway seemed endless. Actually, he went some forty feet before he caught the sound of a door being shaken vigorously, and twenty feet more before Yoshimo stopped beside it.

"Pug!" Bill whispered.

"For God's sake!" was the answer, startlingly loud.

"Shut up!" Bill whispered. "Which way does your door open?"

"In!"

UNDER A thrust of the pearler's shoulder the lock burst. He twisted the *pareu* around Yoshimo's throat until the native gasped, pushed him through the door, and followed, shutting the door with his foot.

"How much farther does this passage go?" he whispered.

"This is the last room—this way. The other way it leads out to the water—"

"The deuce with the other way! I don't crave to crawl up against a gun in the dark!" rumbled Bill grimly. "I'll let them try that! Talk quick, Pug, and low! Why the devil are you locked in? And why the deuce did you turn pirate? The truth came out at home and your old man showed up all ready to pardon you—"

"I didn't!" Pug whispered indignantly. "Mitaki double-crossed me! When he found out I didn't have any money, he asked if you were going to bring him some, and I said I didn't know."

"The devil! Why didn't you lie?"

"I didn't know, did I?" Pug whispered. "You were broke, and you'd have to get the necklace away from Twemlow first. Well, Mitaki said he'd get me away, anyhow. This underground passage leads to a big cave on the water's edge. There was a boat waiting outside, with a bunch of natives in it. We rowed out to a lugger and got aboard. Everything was O.K. till another lugger was sighted. Then a man they called Yoshimo put a knife to my back and told me to stand up. I did. Wouldn't you?"

"Yeah."

"They boarded that lugger and killed every man on her but one. I know that one saw me. The moon was bright."

"He did," Bill growled.

"Then they brought me back—here, underground. Mitaki came and told me—told me, mind you, the devil!—that when a reward was offered for the white pirate, dead or alive, he'd turn me in dead and get it."

"Which was why he claimed he hadn't seen you," Bill reflected. "But a dead or alive reward is never posted for just one pirate. That was a month ago, too. Mitaki must have changed his mind. How did he find out you had money back home?"

"From a newspaper," Pug groaned. "My father offered a reward of ten thousand pounds for any one who could tell him where I was. Before he came out to the South Seas, I guess. I don't know why we never saw the ad in Tatorima. My scar must have fooled Mitaki, but when he did recognize the picture in the newspaper he was wild. He locked me down here—I don't see what for."

"To let the excitement about the white pirate die down, of course. Well, that's that," the pearler muttered. For a moment he was silent, and then began to chuckle.

"What's funny about breaks like that?" Pug demanded.

"Nothing, for you. But it's sure a heck of a joke on Mitaki and me," Bill rumbled. "He's double-crossed himself out of your father's big reward by killing you for a little one, and I—gosh! I figured I had three things to do; find you, fly the coop with you, and alibi you. I think I'm good because I find you. Yeah—I make a monkey out of Maitland and the police, just to let a half-breed gambler coop me up like a rat in a hole. Yeah, I'm a swell guy—not. And the next two stunts are harder." Bill chuckled. "I did just one thing that wasn't dumb. I double-crossed Mitaki about the pearls.

"He thinks I've got them, but I buried them in a pandanus thicket near here, and showed a handful of small sea shells through the cloth of my pants. I think I'll put him wise to that before he decides to get the necklace and let the rewards go. Here—take my gun and hang onto this native. I'm going out."

"Shall I shoot if Mitaki fires at you?" snapped Pug.

"No. There'll just be one tattooed roughneck less," Bill whispered calmly. "We've got to eat and breathe, and Mitaki can stop us from doing both. I don't think he'll shoot after I talk to him. Too many shots might bring the police down into this hangout of his, even if that trapdoor is thick. And what's more, buddy, Mitaki's just as sore about this mess as we are!"

Bill handed over his revolver to Pug, and the cloth that restrained the now sullen Yoshimo.

"Mitaki! Come look at these pearls before you throw that reward away!" he called into the dark. "You'll have to strike the light, because all my matches are wet!"

CHAPTER IV

THE SMEAR OF BLOOD

NEITHER BILL NOR Mitaki was reckless enough to make a light before obtaining some assurance of the intention of the other. After a discussion, spoken with the length of the passage between them, one of the natives set a lamp before Bill's door, and took back a handful of the sea shells. Bill gave the gambler plenty of time to examine these, and then stepped from his concealment confidently. He would never have had such shells in his pocket by accident.

He was without a revolver, and Mitaki thrust a small automatic into the pocket of the gray silk jacket when they met.

"Trying to have me knifed was a bum idea," said the pearler

gravely. "Don't snarl, man! You want to get Pug back to his father, don't you? Well, so do I!"

"How?"

Bill picked up the lamp and led the way to the trapdoor. He motioned Mitaki to open it, and when the planks overhead moved back, climbed out and reached down one huge, tattooed arm to the gambler. A gun was pressed against his chest, but he only grinned and lifted the other gently. When the trap was shut again he sent Mitaki for a lamp, and squatted, facing the suspicious half-breed across the tiny flicker of yellow flame.

Bill was in no haste to begin. He must rescue Pug and clear away the charge of piracy. Only the cleverest stratagem would outwit Mitaki—unless he were made an ally. Characteristically Bill took the straightforward, honest course.

"Unless the real pirates confess, the evidence against Pug is enough to hang him," he began quietly. "There is no way around that, so you will have to betray your gang to earn the ten thousand pounds. If you object, say so."

Mitaki licked his lips like a stalking cat. "Yoshimo brings me little money," he said frankly. "Yet to kill him and his four men would not be easy. The Japanese diver I cannot find."

"You enjoy a double-cross, if it's safe, eh?" Bill growled. "That's what I figured. You didn't want to kill Yoshimo. You want him to confess, only you're afraid he'll accuse you of complicity in the piracies. Right?"

Mitaki nodded.

"O.K. Now suppose Yoshimo and his men were caught, not by any deed of yours, but because I was with them when they attacked a lugger. Suppose you went to Yoshimo in the jail and told him to turn king's witness. Tell him that if he confesses he will save his neck. He will thank you, and when he has explained how the white man with the scar was taken by force—didn't want to be a pirate—you will be able to collect the big reward. Yoshimo's men will be hanged, of course."

Bill smiled grimly. Their execution will be a good riddance.

"However, if Yoshimo confesses first, anything they say will be put down for wild talk, uttered by ignorant savages who are trying to save their necks. Yoshimo clears the white man, savvy, and still goes free himself."

Mitaki looked thoughtful. "Yes, but the white man with the scar knows who I am."

"Before he can talk the reward is paid to you," said Bill promptly. "Fifty thousand dollars is enough to pay you to disappear."

"Suppose you fail," said the gambler, conceding that point. "Yoshimo sails with four men."

"Then you are rid of me," Bill grinned. "You risk nothing, for Yoshimo will not suspect you."

"But if you succeed, I am not rid of you," the gambler snarled. "You turn Yoshimo over to the police, and escape. Swiftly you go to the father and claim part of the reward."

"I have never broken my word," said the pearler simply. "I'll swear to do nothing of the kind. Besides, the police want me—and for my share, I keep the pearls."

MITAKI WAS silent. He could see that to kill the two white men would gain him nothing, and years of successful piracy by Yoshimo would not yield a profit of ten thousand pounds. Such a sum was beyond his wildest dreams. Greed fought with the suspicion characteristic of the savage half of his ancestry, for he could not conceive that Bill, once free, would keep faith. Mitaki had many irons in the fire. He sought for a way to use this white man, balancing risk against profit. Both were great. For many reasons Mitaki was ready to leave Thursday Island.

"Why do you care what happens to the other white man, since you have his pearls?" said Mitaki at last.

"Because I must leave the Pacific, and need your help. You will not help me escape for nothing." Bill was aware that Mitaki was seeking some scheme for getting the pearls, too, and answered in the way that would appeal to the warped mentality of the native. He knew he was playing a desperate game, but unless

Mitaki did help he could never get Yoshimo's testimony before the officials. He was taking the third step before the second. The rescue of Pug must come last.

"There are oaths no man dares to break," he suggested:

"Will you swear on the sharp edge of steel?"

"On a knife blade or a stack of Bibles," grunted the pearler.

"The oath on the knife you will not break," said Mitaki with cold relish. Again he licked his lips. He had thought of something. "You tell your friend to release Yoshimo. I will give him orders to go to sea, at once, and take you along as a prisoner. I will tell him to attack the first lugger he sees. You must be bound, of course."

Bill grunted.

"Only with cords," said Mitaki. "Here is a small knife which you can hide in your belt, and free yourself when you wish. Before you leave I will bring you gold for the trip, for you must not return here. The police might follow you and find your friend too soon. Do you know the godown of Ali Khan?"

"By reputation," Bill rumbled. The Malay was a pearl buyer and as great a scoundrel as Mitaki.

"He will hide you until to-morrow night and then send you to sea on one of his luggers," Mitaki promised. "Once you have sworn, I will trust you not to come back. Is it agreed?"

"Yeah," Bill rumbled, wondering what the other was up to. To give away hard money was suspiciously generous. Bill called to Pug, however, and waited till Yoshimo was released and had received instructions for the trip. Here at least Mitaki had kept faith. He whispered his orders, and seemed to take care that Bill should not overhear, and yet he managed to make his instructions audible to the pearler.

"Come," said Mitaki, after Yoshimo had turned away to get his men. He led the way down the secret passage to his own office. Silk curtains covered the door leading to the big gambling hall. Bill could hear the click of Mah Jong tiles and the clatter of a roulette wheel.

Mitaki, however, stepped to a chest and picked out a Chinese dagger without a hilt, hollow-ground and razor-sharp and with a handle of ivory. His eyes glittered as he stuck the knife into a table, where it stood quivering.

"Hold the hilt loosely and slide your hand down on the blade. You will cut yourself," he commanded.

Bill obeyed. He took care not to cut himself deep, but instantly the palm of his hand was covered with blood.

"Grab the hilt," chanted Mitaki excitedly, "and say: 'May all knives do this to me and more if I betray Mitaki! May I not touch hilt without spilling blood, and may my own knife slip from my fingers into my heart.'"

"—slip from my fingers into my heart," Bill intoned, repeating the oath word for word. The curse that turned a man's own weapons against himself was old in the South Seas, though he had never heard it in exactly this form. He stepped back, and Mitaki caught up a square of silk and wrapped the knife carefully.

"The steel will remember," said Mitaki gravely, and put the knife down carefully on the top of the chest. "Now, go back! I will come soon; I have been long away from the gambling tables. My players will cheat me."

Before Bill could object, the gambler strode out—into the full light of the gambling hall, where Bill could not follow without being seen by those who would carry news of him to the police.

He did not like having Mitaki out of his sight. He eyed the stair that led to the gambling room above. There was not a sound from that direction. Empty, probably. He shrugged, and stepped into the short, straight secret passage at the side. He had to trust Mitaki a little.

Perhaps for a minute after his departure the private room was empty. Then the curtain at the door stirred, and Mitaki tiptoed back. Furtively he listened to make certain that Bill had retreated, then opened the chest. With a satisfied smile he lifted a knife that was a twin to that upon which Bill had sworn, slipped it into his left sleeve, and tucked the first knife, still wrapped in silk, under his arm. Without a sound he ascended the stair to the private gambling room overhead.

A MIDDLE-AGED Chinese sat with unconcealed impatience before a poker hand face down on the table. Five high stacks of gold coins were at his elbow, and beside them half a dozen slips of paper. In marked contrast, in front of the chair that Mitaki took were less than half a dozen scattered gold pieces.

"Is your honorable luck improved, Unfortunate One?" the Chinaman asked sarcastically. "Write another chit, and let us go on. Long have the warm winds of fortune blown from you to me, but never as on this night."

Mitaki leaned far over the table to sign another chit. "My luck has changed, Yun Sing," he declared. "The five hundred taels I owe you will soon be repaid."

The Chinaman smiled, glanced at the seventh promissory note, and with both hands began to push the stacks of gold across the table. As he did so Mitaki whipped the knife from his sleeve and struck.

The razor-sharp blade sank to the hilt in the Chinaman's left breast. He quivered, sighed, and toppled forward across the gold.

Swiftly Mitaki snatched his chits from a spreading pool of blood. Stuffing them into his sash, he tugged the dagger he had used from the heart of the Chinese.

Next, he unwrapped the dagger on which Bill Bellow had sworn. Selecting a clean corner of the silk, he covered the hilt upon which the print of a huge hand was marked in dried blood and, with care to leave no traces of his own fingers, pushed it into the wound.

The print of Bill's fingers stood out exactly as though he had gripped the knife when the fatal blow was struck. Mitaki grinned like a satisfied cat. Already the pearler had saved him five hundred taels, and that would not be all. He filled his pockets with gold from the table, closed the door on the corpse, and glided down the stairs.

Carefully he hid the blood-stained knife and the telltale piece of silk behind the hangings. If Bill failed to overpower Yoshimo on the lugger, Mitaki would be perfectly safe in accusing him of the murder of Yun Sing. If he succeeded and escaped to Ali Khan, the knife would be evidence enough to support the accusation. But while Bill was at sea Mitaki intended to warn Ali Khan to turn Bill over to the police as soon as he came to the godown.

Bill could say what he pleased to the police. The latter could believe the story or not, for Mitaki meant to be gone. He would take the man with a scar with him for a hostage, and from a safe hiding place he would send natives to arrange for the ransom. When the ten thousand pounds were his, he would give the scarred man up, or kill him, as seemed best, but meanwhile—when Bill was brought to trial for the murder of Yun Sing, Mitaki planned to send an emissary who would offer to turn over the second dagger and the silk wrappings—when Bill told truthfully where he had hidden the pearls.

Swiftly Mitaki hastened after Bill. They had been separated less than two minutes.

"Here is the money I promised," the gambler said, offering a handful of coins. Bill was squatting beside the tiny lamp. He reached out and took the coins without looking at them, though his eyes never left the gambler.

The pearler slipped a quid of fine cut tobacco into his cheek. On the lower part of Mitaki's right sleeve there was a smear of blood, dark against the silk. Mentally Bill reviewed the scene of the oath. He was positive that the gambler had not touched his hand, and that the sleeve had been clean when the dagger was driven into the table top.

"Any trouble in the gambling room?" he rumbled.

"No. Why?"

"Nothing. Just curious about the police," Bill rumbled. "Yoshimo's ready. Let's go."

CHAPTER V

KNIVES

IN THE DIRECTION of the harbor the underground passage ended in a cave in which the tide rose and fell. The four natives, who were in advance, walked confidently into the water, dived under the surface close to the opposite wall, and vanished.

Bellow Bill hesitated, for his hands were bound. Yoshimo's knife pricked his back.

"Swim. Five feet beyond is the sea," he snarled, delighted that the tables were turned on the big man who had captured him.

Bill dived, kicked out with his feet, and rose among the four natives, who seized him.

They stood shoulder deep beneath the steep coral bank, in deep shadows for the moon was about to set. The entrance to the cave was evidently under water at all stages of the tide, which explained how Mitaki had been able to construct a hideout under the very noses of the authorities, but to Bill's amazement there was no boat near by except a fragile dugout totally unfit for use at sea.

Into this, however, all six men climbed, though their weight sank it until the gunwale was only an inch higher than the water. Like any group of natives out to fish at night, they paddled along the shore as far as a lugger that was moored alone. They embarked in this, set the sails, and steered out to sea. As they cleared the harbor another lugger, black against the silver path of the moon, sailed into view. It was hardly a mile away, and Yoshimo promptly trimmed the sheet to intercept it. The four natives stationed themselves forward, and Bill, lying by the tiller felt the prick of Yoshimo's knife.

"Stand up!" the bronze pirate snarled. Bill cut through the cords that bound his hands before he obeyed. He kept his hands clasped together before his body. Yoshimo crouched behind his back, close to the deck. To those on the other lugger it must have looked as though the white man was steering.

The two boats were drawing together rapidly. On the deck of the other but one man was visible. He would be disposed of in the first rush, and any one below could be killed at leisure when the pirates had won the deck. Already the four natives were crouched in the bow, tense as sprinters awaiting the gun.

Bill loved danger for its own sake. To match strength and wits against odds, with life or death hanging on the issue of a split second, was the breath of his nostrils. He must let the pirates attack in order to take them red-handed. Though the lugger was small, they were closer to their victim than he to them. That was their advantage.

Yoshimo's knife-point touched Bill's back.

"Be still!" he threatened.

The pearler looked over his shoulder. Yoshimo was steering left-handed. He was on his knees, his head just behind and on the level with Bill's left hip. Evidently the leader meant to take no part in the attack except to keep the white man from interfering.

Slowly Bill inflated his chest. He had planned his escape. In the bow of the lugger was a four-foot capstan bar, stowed handily in a rack. There was his weapon, if he were quick enough on his feet to reach it. He tensed, and thought of the blood on Mitaki's sleeve—not Pug's blood, and not his own. You couldn't trust Mitaki.

THE TILLER went hard down. The bow of the lugger veered and crashed into the other boat. With a wild yell the four natives sprang to their feet and leaped like tigers for the other deck; but Bill had started with the swing of the tiller. His left fist crashed back in Yoshimo's face; he leaped for the bow before the knife could be driven home. The stab spurred him, and his bellowing roar drowned the shriller yells of the pirates. Three leaps took him up the deck. He snatched up the bar, and sprang onto the other lugger on the heels of the pirates. A two-handed swing of the club smashed the skull of the hindmost.

The other whirled, knives raised, but Bill caught his bar by the center and bored in. The butt jabbed into the face of the nearest native, a short-arm swing stretched the other senseless. Thrust and blow, thrust and blow, another swinging, full-armed smash that crashed down, an upflung arm that landed heavily on the woolly skull beneath. Four half-naked men sprawled in the moonlight. Two would never rise again.

"Finish them up!" Bill thundered at the Japanese steersman, and sprinted back along the deck, leaping the gap that had opened between the luggers. He thought that Yoshimo was trying to escape, but the brown pirate crouched low to slip under the swing of the club and sprang to meet him. His knife streaked for Bill's throat, but the shortened club struck the wrist, and the steel clattered to the deck. As Yoshimo caught his broken arm, Bill swung his fist to the unguarded jaw.

Bill leaped for the tiller to bring the two luggers together.

"Hi! Don't kill those men!" he roared, just in time to prevent the Jap steersman from stabbing the two unconscious pirates.

The Jap straightened, and uttered the hiss with which those of his race indicate polite respect for the commands of a superior.

"They are pirates, honored sir!" he protested. "Pirates kill my uncle's cousin, but they are steered by a white man with scar here!" he touched his right cheek.

"Listen, you!" Bill thundered. "That white man came to help you—to catch pirates, like I did, savvy? He couldn't do it, though."

"No savvy," said the Jap stubbornly.

"You savvy you kill pirates you hang all the samee them!" Bill shouted. "You take to the governor. Let him put in jail. Hang later, savvy?"

A hiss of acknowledgment.

"That's better," Bill rumbled. "No mistakes now. I want those pirates turned in. Here!" He twisted a rope around Yoshimo's feet and tossed him over into the Jap boat alongside the others.

"You come governor?" called the Jap.

"No. Come later. There's others in this gang," Bill answered. "I'm going—" he paused, shrugged, walked to the tiller, and put the lugger before the wind. Where was he going? He was supposed to escape to Ali Khan. And yet, why?

Pug would be cleared. Whether Yoshimo turned king's witness or not, the pirate would reveal the truth when he was cross-examined, nor would Mitaki be liable to harm a man whose life was worth fifty thousand dollars. Bill himself had little to fear from the police. He might be arrested, yet he could clear himself. The police around the Hall of the Five Beneficent Virtues might help him, even. They could get Pug out of that black underground hole.

BELLOW BILL steered the lugger toward the harbor, gradually distancing the Japanese. All these ideas were very logical, but none of them accounted for that smear of blood on Mitaki's sleeve. A jinx had hung over Pug Sprude from the beginning. Everything done to help him seemed to make his situation the worse. Was the jinx still at work? Back in Tatorima Bill had resolved to find Pug, clear him, and rescue him. Two of the problems Bill had solved single-handed. Why not all three?

Once in the harbor Bill pointed the lugger for the high bank that marked the entrance to the cave. To avoid attracting attention he slipped over the stern as he passed, letting the boat sail on, and swam under water to the shore, groping around until he found the hole in the bank. No fish could have risen more silently inside the cave. Only Bill's head was above the surface of the still water. He exhaled slowly.

He had been gone, he judged, less than three-quarters of an hour. The tiny peanut-oil lamp still burned beside the pool, but there was no glimmer of light from the room where Pug had been left. That was strange. To be confined in a dark room is a form of torture, and Mitaki had every reason to treat his prisoner well.

"Pug!" Bill called.

Though there was no answer in words, a dull knocking began in the far end of the passage. Bill's suspicions redoubled. A bound man might make such a noise by pounding with his heels on the plank floor of the den.

"Pug! That you?"

Thump—thump—thump in measured cadence.

"Are you all right?"

Silence.

The flicker of the tiny lamp at the edge of the pool only made darkness visible, but in the black mouth of the passage there was a stir.

"Where is Yoshimo?" said the voice of Mitaki.

"Going to the governor—in irons," answered Bill.

"Ah!" whispered the gambler smoothly. "I tied your friend, for fear the police would follow you, or him. You may come out, Bellow Bill. I am alone."

Thump—thump—thump—thump. Bill needed no warning from the frantic noise from the rear of the passage. Again he remembered the blood on Mitaki's sleeve. Things were not as they seemed here, and wade into the light he would not. In darkness his bare hands would be a match for any weapon that Mitaki might have. A thrust of his palm sent a sheet of water splashing at the lamp.

The flame spluttered, and recovered. Beyond it, a pistol spat, and a bullet barely missed Bill's head. He laughed sneeringly.

"Your life will pay for Pug's, Mitaki!" he called. "Treat him right, for the police and I are going to pull this place down around your ears!"

The answer was a second shot, but the pearler had ducked under water and was swimming through the hole in the bank.

"AHOY!" HE roared at the top of his lungs as soon as his

head was above the surface. "Here's Bellow Bill! Come on, you cops!" The echoes rolled across the water, and, with a promptness that delighted the pearler, a head peered over the high bank.

"Put up yer 'ands!" cried a voice shrill with excitement. "I arrest yer in the king's nyme—"

"Sure, O.K.!" boomed the pearler. "That'll be all right, constable. Listen, there's a white man down here that's been kidnaped. Jump down and go in after him with me. I need a shot or two fired to scare off a guard."

"You're balmy!" snapped the constable. "Put yer 'ands up! I arrests yer for the murder of Yun Sing!"

"Who?" Bill gasped.

"Yer knows blamed well who! Mitaki told us 'ow yer knifed 'im across the poker tyble and took 'is sovereigns. Yer shouldn't leave knives in a bloke's chest—not when yer hand print is clear on the 'ilt! Why, there's a bandage on yer duke now!" the constable snapped indignantly. "Tellin' fairy tales erbout kidnaped white men an' all that rot!"

Bill's head sank in the water until only the top of his head was visible. So. Hence the oath, and the blood smear. Mitaki was smart; the jinx still at work.

"Surrender, nothing!" Bill snarled at the constable. "Come and take me, you yellow bum!"

With the taunt he ducked under water. He had not misjudged his adversary. Any constable on Thursday Island had to be all clear grit, and this one leaped feet first off the bank after Bill without the slightest hesitation. As he struck the water Bill caught him around the knees and dragged him under.

The struggle was brief. For half a minute the water boiled with thrashing arms and legs while Bill wrested the revolver from the constable's grip. When that was accomplished the fight was won. The pearler was the heavier by fifty pounds, and by far the stronger. He twisted an arm back into a punishing hammerlock, crooked an elbow around the throat, and rose, holding the other to his chest like a struggling child.

"Listen, you!" Bill rumbled. "I didn't kill Yun Sing, but right now I can't bother to prove it. I'm going under this cliff. Your gun I'll need. Don't follow me. Yell for your mates, surround the place, or do anything else you like. That 'll help me." The constable stopped struggling.

"Also, there's an underground passage. You'll find me in it," Bill continued. As briefly as he could he gave directions by which the police could reached the trap door.

Meanwhile he was feeling on the bottom with his feet for the constable's revolver. When he located it he stooped, snatched it up and shoved himself through the hole under the cliff, not caring much whether the constable understood his directions or not, and ready to smack him on the head if he did follow after all. But he did not.

BILL ROSE quietly in the underground pool. The lamp still burned at the water's edge, with darkness behind it. Mitaki might be there, might not. Bill eased to the side of the pool, so that any shot he fired would strike the side of the passage close to the water, instead of ranging along the corridor to the end, where Pug might still be lying bound.

He shook the water out of the revolver barrel and whirled the cylinder to insure that no sand had worked into the action. Most modern cartridges are water-tight. After such a brief immersion these were probably O.K. At random he fired three shots across the mouth of the passage.

Flame streaked from the dark in answer. With a roar of delight that Mitaki had not retreated, Bill charged out of the pool, firing once as he came. He was hit. His leg burned as though a cigarette had been pressed into the flesh. He sent his fifth shot below that lance of flame that leaped toward him and lunged forward in a flying tackle.

His arms wrapped around a silk-clad body that did not struggle. Mitaki shivered and groaned.

"Pug!" Bill shouted anxiously. Bound feet thumped in the distance. Pug was where he had been.

The pearler felt a spurt of blood against his arm. It jetted from the left side of Mitaki's chest at every heart beat.

"Got you, eh, Mitaki?" Bill rumbled. He relaxed his grip. "Tell me how you killed the Chinaman," he demanded.

The gambler only moaned feebly, but with a sudden inspiration, Bellow Bill felt in the sash of the dying man, and found it full of coins.

"There'll be blood on these— The Chinaman's blood," he said firmly. "Tell the truth for once, man! You're done for!"

"You—a devil," Mitaki whispered. Blood was rising in his throat and he coughed weakly without being able to dislodge it. His voice was thick, choked. "Another knife—behind hangings—my office." Feebly the dying man caught at Bill's wrist. "Yun Sing—cheated—won all—"

Though Bill waited, that was the last word. Mitaki was dead.

THE PEARLER picked up the lamp. Though his own wound was bleeding freely, the bullet had not touched the bone. A bandage and a little rest would fix him up, and he was quite able to limp down the passage to Pug, to fling open a door that Mitaki had closed on the prisoner, and cut the cords that bound him with the tiny knife. Pug sat up, blinking, and rubbing arms and legs to restore the circulation.

"We're done, buddy," Bill grinned. "One—two—three, and out! The jinx is laid, and you're once more in the clear."

He paused. This had been the most difficult, the most complex task he had ever tackled. Of all the white men he knew he liked Pug Sprude the best. A clean, gritty kid—whose duty now would take him back to the States. The heir to a great fortune is like a ship captain. He cannot honorably evade his responsibility.

"I wish you really had been nothing but a beachcomber. Then we could be pardners," Bill added.

"We'll be pardners back in Ohio if you'll come," said Pug swiftly. "Come along with me, Bill. You've earned it, and you'll like it—"

The big, tattooed skipper shook his curly head. "Don't let's kid ourselves, buddy. I belong here, where life is rough—like me," he refused. "Fact is, I like it that way, even at the worst."

MORE THAN MILLIONS

*Bellow Bill Williams, pearling shipper, knew an
SOS in the South Pacific spelled trouble—even
without the ruthless greed of salvage hunters*

CHAPTER I

S O S!

JOHANN VAN TAL was a desperate, embittered man. On the island of Toaara, in the South Pacific, he was all-powerful. He was the official resident, and the only white inhabitant. He was the legislator, the judge, the executive, and the policeman. He made what laws he wished, and carried them out as he willed. To support his power there was a nation in Europe which would send a gunboat to deal with any one who opposed him, and yet, despite his unlimited authority, he was an outcast.

For Van Tal was too surly and too hard to rise in the ranks of colonial administrators. His government had sent him to a lonely island on the rim of an empire in order to get him out of the way. To his government he was a pawn and a failure, fit for nothing better than to rule a handful of Melanesian savages only three generations removed from cannibalism and the taking of heads.

If they killed him, the government would suffer little loss. If he killed them, or a few of them, the government would never know. Whether he lived or died, no better post would ever come to him, and he knew it.

He was fifty-eight—a raw-boned giant whose flesh had been sweated into stringy muscle and sinew by the heat, with a jutting lower jaw and cavernous, smoldering brown eyes beneath tufted reddish brows.

He cared nothing for the future. He had none. He did not fear death. He had been ordered to Toaara to wait for it. He snapped

his fingers at disgrace. The worst that could happen to him was preferable to obscurity, loneliness, and the inevitable oblivion to which he was destined.

Such a man is ripe for crime, but though Van Tal brooded and studied over means of using his official position for personal advantage, Toaara offered no opportunity. The spoils of the South Seas are simple: pearls, and dealings in slaves. The profit to the criminal is comparatively small, and a resident who turned pirate or slave blackbirder would certainly be caught. Therefore Van Tal waited for some stroke of luck, some unforeseen event which would enable him to improvise a scheme where the profits would be huge.

With a hard and bitter recklessness he resolved to let no such opportunity slip, however trifling it might appear in the beginning. And when the time came he did not.

HE WAS sitting with head phones over his ears at the wireless which was the only link between Toaara and the civilization which had cast him out to rot. Outside a gale of almost hurricane force was blowing. Flying coconuts torn from the palms boomed on the sheet-iron roof of the residency, and two

Bill was one against many.

schooners which had taken shelter from the storm tugged at their anchors. The time was noon, but the darkness of rain and storm wrack had compelled Van Tal to kindle a lamp. The light flickered and smoked in the drafts that pressed through doors and windows, so that the faces of the schooner captains who sat with the resident seemed to writhe in alternate light and shadow.

Bellow Bill Williams, the pearler, rested huge forearms on the table. Every square inch of his skin was covered with tattooing. A shirt, open at the neck, revealed the topsail of a ship tattooed on the tremendous breadth of chest, hinting that Bill's body was a living picture gallery to the waist.

That was the fact. Bill's skin was covered with outlandish designs inked by the tattoo needles of a dozen nationalities, but about the man himself there was nothing bizarre. He was an American, about thirty-five. His hair was curly and coppery blond, the eyes blue and steady. More noteworthy than the tattooing was the sheer size of him—two hundred and forty pounds of quick, hard muscle, a height well over six feet, shoulders to match.

The other skipper, Squeegee Ryan, was much slighter. What his means of livelihood was no one could say definitely, not even

Van Tal, who knew Squeegee well, though he was acquainted with Bellow Bill only by reputation.

The resident suspected that Squeegee pirated pearls, black-birded, picked up what quick profits the sea gave to the reckless audacity of a laughing, black-headed, wild young Irishman. Mentally Van Tal had marked Ryan for a useful tool that would leap at a daring opportunity.

"S O S!" said Van Tal suddenly. He tensed and reached for pencil and paper.

Bellow Bill caught up a large-scale chart of the ocean around Toaara and spread it under the lamp.

"S O S—the Wayfarer!" muttered Van Tal, translating the signals. "Damn the fools! They keep repeating that over and over. Why don't they give their position? I've listened in gale after gale for an S O S on the chance of salvage, and now that it's happened a fool operator has to get panic-stricken!"

He threw a switch and commenced to pound out an answer on his feeble battery set. His hand was shaking with a fierce eagerness.

"My batteries are six months old!" he snarled. "The gunboat is overdue now with the fresh set. She hasn't answered the signal, though. Maybe the chance will come to us—"

The deepset brown eyes blazed at the two skippers.

"It ain't blowing so hard I can't put to sea," Bill answered in a voice the depth and timbre of which matched his size.

"Nor me!" snapped Squeegee. "Divil a wind can keep me ashore when there is salvage afloat! The Wayfarer—that must be a yacht, which means a sight-seein' millionaire. If he's sinkin', our fortune's made, eh, Van Tal?"

"Shut up! I got him!" Van Tal concentrated on the signals. "Sinking fast," he translated. "Bottom ripped by a coral reef." He paused, head thrust forward and teeth bared, glaring at the chart.

"The position, ye loon!" Ryan roared. "First come, first served it is! Bill and I race for it, eh?"

"The position is—three degrees and forty-one minutes south," said Van Tal distinctly, "east one forty-three, ten."

Squeegee leaped for the door. The blast of wind that entered the residency as he dashed for the beach made a cloud of smoke spurt from the lamp and spread thickly over the ceiling. Bellow Bill followed, though with less haste, for his strength would enable him to hoist anchor and raise sail more quickly than the younger man.

Van Tal was in no hurry at all. He turned the lamp out, and stopped to close the door of the residency. He was smiling. The chance he had longed for had not only come, but luck had been with him. The S O S had been very faint, and no one but himself had answered. What he could squeeze from salvage and resell would be his alone.

NOT THE resident of Toaara, but Johann Van Tal, walked down to the beach, launched a dugout, and paddled to Ryan's schooner. Already Bill had loosed his mainsail and was straining to raise the anchor.

"Let him get under way first, Squeegee," Van Tal commanded. "Don't hurry. Better pretend your anchor is foul."

"Let him go?" demanded the Irishman in a howl of protest.

"Exactly," Van Tal nodded. "He'll find no yacht sinking at the latitude and longitude I gave him." The resident smiled at the shocked, incredulous face of the Irishman. "Why, did you think I told the truth, too? I must be a better actor than I figured," he added, well pleased. "I looked at the chart and gave a position near the dot of an island. Why should I throw a good thing in the way of a roughneck pearling skipper who wouldn't drive a bargain, or share it? Bellow Bill would bring that yacht to the harbor and leave his pay to the courts. So I sent him north. The Wayfarer lies—in a place I'll mention if you'll play with me."

"How much?" asked Squeegee.

"Only half. You're lucky, and I believe in helping luck."

"Half ye get—if that's, anything, ye divil!" Squeegee grinned. He glanced toward the harbor mouth, out of which Bellow Bill was racing, sail flat to the water, already half concealed by driving rain and flying storm wrack. Something more than chicanery or luck would be needed to rescue a yacht from that ugly sea, but he was pleased with the trick played on his rival.

"The Wayfarer lies east—and less than twenty miles away," said Van Tal.

CHAPTER II

SCENE OF THE WRECK

EVEN TWENTY MILES meant more than two hours of weary, storm-beaten sailing; when the conspirators arrived at the position actually given in the SOS they found pitiful reminders that they were too late floating on the surface of the sea. They passed a spar, a shattered hatch, a life preserver, an ornate mahogany dining table spewed from the hull of a lost ship as she sank.

Squeegee put the schooner before the wind. He was grave, as any sailor would be, and because Van Tal sat like an image he believed the other man shared the same mood.

"They may have put over boats," he shouted hopefully. "Our salvage is gone, but what the hell! We'll be heroes!"

"What of it?" Van Tal answered sourly. He stared under the sail and pointed to starboard. "Anyway, you'll get your wish," he added sarcastically. "There's a boat!"

"Only one boat? Three-quarters of them are drowned, then!"

"Just one," Van Tal muttered. "Still, if the owner is there he'd pay—"

"Holy saint, forget loot!" Squeegee snapped. "That boat's undermanned! Only two at the oars—two women—yes, and a man bad hurt! I can see him lying in the bottom! Just five left out of the ship's company. Stand by with a line, Van! I'll have to pick them up on the fly, and I'm as like to drown them as save them."

He crouched over the helm, eyes dancing with sheer reckless love of a difficult piece of seamanship. In the sea that was running the impact with the schooner would shatter the lifeboat. When its occupants jumped, their movement would thrust the broken hull under water. There would be but one moment to seize. Failure of judgment or loss of nerve on either side would be irretrievable.

Bareheaded, shirt plastered to his body by the rain, Squeegee did his part superbly. The schooner hove to just to leeward of the drifting boat. He lashed the helm and ran forward to join Van Tal, who stood in the bow with a line coiled and a bowline ready knotted. That rope would snatch one of the five persons from the sea.

"Get the girl!" Squeegee ordered.

She was in the bow. Her face was slightly tanned to the smooth tint of old ivory, her eyes a light blue. She wore a linen blouse and trousers. A light blue ribbon bound her dripping hair close to her head. She caught Squeegee's look, and smiled.

"I'm ready, and I'll take care of myself!" she seemed to say.

At her elbow was a stout and imposing woman of fifty. The rain had washed the powder from her face, and the rouge on her cheeks stood out in hard, circular patches, but she sat on the thwart like a duchess, stoutly indignant at danger and discomfort. Clutched to an ample bosom was a leather box half the size of a suitcase. Around her throat was a necklace and even in the gloom fully a dozen rings on the pudgy fingers revealed themselves as precious stones.

STRAIGHT INTO her face Van Tal threw the rope. She glared at him, as though he had meant to strike her, and caught the line. But instead of using it herself she slipped the noose over the head of the elderly man who lay unconscious in the bottom. The two sailors picked up the limp figure by shoulders and feet and prepared to toss it aboard the schooner.

"Don't let my husband drown!" the woman commanded in a lusty scream. "It's J. Carson Snyder! Do you hear me?"

"Stand up, ma'am!" snarled Van Tal. The lifeboat poised on a wave crest and crashed at the schooner like a battering ram.

The girl leaped like a deer. Squeegee caught her outstretched hand and swung her aboard. She never lost her feet. J. Carson Snyder was hurled onto the deck like a sack. Not till he was safe did the sailors jump, and that half-second delay cost one his life. His clutch on the rail slipped, and he fell between boat and schooner as the wave threw the two apart. As they dashed together again he vanished without a sound.

The other sailor squirmed over the rail, across which Van Tal and the woman with the jewels were locked in a grim tug of war. Mrs. Snyder had jumped as far as two hundred pounds could. One smoothly fleshed and undoubtedly powerful arm was hooked over the rail. With the other she clung to the leather case. Twice as the schooner rolled she was doused deep into the sea, but no bulldog could have held more stubbornly. Van Tal had her by the shoulders, but her weight was too great for him to lift her inboard.

"Mother! Drop the case!" cried the girl.

Mrs. Snyder dipped under water and rose with the schooner. "No!" she spluttered.

Three times she had been ducked. To her and to Van Tal the struggle must have seemed long, though actually not more than fifteen seconds elapsed before Squeegee and the sailor sprang to her aid. A concerted pull brought her aboard, case and all, but though she tumbled ludicrously on the deck she sat up instantly, panting, half-drowned, but with a dignity which was impressive even though it resembled that of a large and bedraggled hen.

"Can't you rescue a woman decently?" she demanded of Van Tal, and then glared at her daughter. "Drop my traveling jewels? And the Snyder emeralds, Claire? Why, the idea!" she panted. "Losing the yacht was bad enough—and your father knocked senseless—"

"Gregson's drowned, ma'am," muttered the sailor.

Mrs. Snyder's commanding features softened.

"I saw it. He was very faithful," she murmured.

The sympathy was genuine. Mrs. Snyder was simply a robust and thorough-going egotist. Shipwreck and death were all viewed in connection with herself and her family. Her courage sprang from the conviction that she was too important to be hurt. She clung to the jewels because they were hers, and what was hers she would not relinquish even to an angry sea.

Van Tal stared at her speculatively.

"Will you come below, ma'am?" he said. "I know enough of medicine to look after your husband. He must be a very important man."

"Gracious, haven't you heard of him even here? Mr. Snyder is Wall Street," said the wife, so blandly that her daughter looked embarrassed.

VAN TAL gathered the unconscious man, who could not have weighed a hundred and twenty pounds, into his arms. The hard, embittered face of the resident was blank, but the brown eyes burned.

He led the way into the tiny cabin. Claire Snyder followed, and her mother, still carrying the jewel case with the Snyder emeralds, whatever those might be, brought up the rear. The sailor remained on deck with Squeegee.

Briefly he told of the disaster. The Wayfarer had broken her back on an uncharted pinnacle of coral. She had lasted less than an hour. The boats had been handled well, but the storm had been at its height when they were launched. The owner and his wife and daughter had gone first, as a matter of course.

There were no guests. Snyder was a big shot, trying to get away from business strain. That was why the Wayfarer had avoided the usual sailing tracks.

"Anything that guy says about money is important," the sailor remarked. "Him and Morgan is buddies. He can even boss his wife. Yeah. Fact."

The lifeboat had carried a crew of eight when it was launched, but it had capsized. Five got back. The big shot had been knocked cuckoo, but Miss Claire saved him. She was a swell dame. Swam like a fish. The other boats, with less skillful sailors, had never got away at all. All the survivors of the Wayfarer were on the Schooner.

Van Tal returned to the deck before the tale was done, and listened to the end in silence.

"There's whisky below. Go pour yourself a drink and come back," he said.

The sailor scrambled down the companionway. Van Tal pulled the slide shot to keep out the spray, and gave Squeegee a long look.

"**WE'VE NETTED** some queer fish," he said.

"What the divil is queer about her? A prettier colleen never—"

"I'm talking about the old woman and the man, you wild Irishman. Forget a pretty face. Think of millions. Even the jewels in sight are no trifles—and we've got the man that is Wall Street."

A reckless light flashed into Squeegee's eyes, only to die.

"It's impossible," he grunted. "We could swipe the jewels and run, but the police would pick us up when we tried to pawn the stones."

"Forget the jewels," said Van Tal evenly. "I don't see thousands in this, but millions. More than millions. We'll hold Snyder for ransom."

"You're crazy!"

"Never less. I'm king of Toaara. The natives are mine. What would a multimillionaire pay to get himself and his family out of the hands of a crowd of Melanesians? He don't know they're not cannibals. In fact, neither do I."

"Holy saints!" breathed Squeegee, appalled. "He'd pay, but the risk—"

"To hell with the risk! What have I got to lose?" retorted Van Tal fiercely. Then he recovered himself. "Risk?" he repeated. "Where is the risk? We land at the back of the island, not at the residency. We take them up the trail to Mohu's village, and leave them there while we sail the schooner around to the harbor—"

"Leave a woman and a girl with a bunch of head-hunters?"

"Why not? Are you going to be squeamish when there are millions—"

"No-o," Squeegee muttered doubtfully. "But there's the sailor, and that woman's as strong as a man. They'd start something and get knocked on the head."

"No, they won't," said Van Tal grimly. "They'll go like lambs."

"Then there's Bellow Bill—"

"He suspects nothing," Van Tal snapped. "Think, man! God, my head is racing, and this idea is perfect! Luck has worked for us every second. The S O S was faint. There were no other survivors. The lifeboat from which we rescued these five was crushed. Any one finding it will think them drowned. All we have to do is to deny we found them at all, and hide them with Mohu till we've got the money. We've got months to collect, and what can any one do? I'm the resident—the government. Suppose Bill does suspect something? We catch him flat-footed, and he can't fight the whole island, can he? He's nothing but a big, overgrown windbag anyhow!"

"Hm-m!" Squeegee grunted. "I've heard tales about Bellow Bill. Still, he could be handled if we could get the Snyders into the interior. They are practically two to two, and my guns are in a locker that they are sittin' on. If it wasn't for that, a fifty-fifty split on a millionaire's ransom looks good."

"Go below and get a revolver!" snapped Van Tal impatiently. "You aren't as hot as I'd like, but maybe I can warm you up. Go below. That girl wanted to thank the handsome young captain who saved her mother."

SQUEEGEE ROSE with alacrity. Van Tal watched him disappear with a sour smile. The sailor came on deck, and the resident, who was at the wheel, motioned him to come aft.

"Is that sail drawing well?" he demanded, stooping behind the wheel as he spoke.

Unsuspiciously the sailor looked upward. Van Tal straightened. He had picked up a brass belaying pin. From behind he struck. The heavy club thudded where the back of the sailor's head joined the neck, crushing the skull and spine. Van Tal caught the body as it fell and hurled it over the rail into the sea.

"Man overboard!" he shouted, and flung the helm over, despite the gale. He ducked as the boom swept over his head and brought up with a crash that shook the schooner from stem to stern and snapped the main sheet like a thread. A sea heaved over the rail and buried the deck knee deep. For a moment the schooner was on its beam ends, then it recovered, fell into the trough, and rolled like a mad thing, the boom flailing from side to side.

Squeegee leaped out of the hatch, slamming the slide after him. With a snarling oath he flung himself at the boom, secured it with a rope and brought the schooner into the wind.

"I gybed her, and the boom knocked the sailor overboard," shouted Van Tal loud enough for those in the cabin to hear.

"He's too far astern to pick up now!" Squeegee raged. "Even if you're no sailor you should have steered better than that!"

"I know it," Van Tal answered,. He looked the other in the eye and slowly raised the belaying pin. Squeegee's face went white at the sight of the blood stain, half washed away by the sea water. The weapon was held ready for a blow. The Irishman looked back into a pair of brown eyes that seemed to burn into his backbone. He swallowed a lump in his throat, and shrugged.

"Well—nothing can be done now. It's too bad," he said aloud.

Van Tal smiled. A jerk of his wrist flipped the belaying pin into the sea.

"You'll be hotter now, I think," he whispered. "As an accessory after the fact… Get hold of yourself, and quit staring! This is our chance for millions—and I told you I believed in helping luck!"

CHAPTER III

THE SUCKER

DURING THE AFTERNOON and the following night the gale blew itself out. Morning dawned fair over a Toaara that was bright green and dripping with moisture. As the heat of the day increased the volcanic cliffs in the center of the island gave off steam. Late in the forenoon Bellow Bill Williams sailed into the harbor.

Squeegee's schooner was at anchor, and as he rowed ashore he cast a sailor's eye over the damaged rigging. There was no sign of her owner, and Bill wondered idly whether Van Tal or the Irishman had been injured by the accident. Ordinarily an incoming boat, particularly a rival in a search for salvage, would have been met at the beach. Here there was not even a man on the veranda.

Bill mounted the steps and entered. Van Tal sat bolt upright in a straight-backed chair beside the table. Squeegee was on the opposite side of the room, fully twenty feet square. He was slumped in a wicker armchair with his feet stuck so far out that he was resting on his shoulders and the back of his neck. Both men wore coats, despite the heat. Neither was smoking.

"Well, she sank," Bill rumbled in his deep voice.

He filled his cheek with fine-cut chewing tobacco from his hip pocket, chewed vigorously for a moment, and crossed the room. He half sat, half leaned against the table at Van Tal's elbow and looked directly over the resident's head to Squeegee.

"I didn't find a floating stick," he announced. "I cruised wide, too."

"Tough luck," the Irishman grunted. "We got wrecked just outside. Never had a chance to look."

"Gybed, didn't you? Squall catch you from aft?" Bill boomed. "Puff of wind, eh? I had the wind for'ard the whole way out."

"You did?"

"Well, you both got a night's sleep, anyhow," Bill retorted. "You both look plenty wide awake."

"Yes," said Van Tal.

He started to move his chair aside. Bill hooked a huge foot in the rung, holding the other motionless.

"I don't mind being played for a sucker once," he rumbled, "but damned if you can work me constant for a plain green fool! Your eyes are red and you've both been up all night. Squeegee, there's grass stains on your shoes you never got between the harbor and here!

"And Van Tal! Next time you lie about a position, pick a local chart that shows details. The only coral anywheres around the island you sent me is the barrier reef. If the Wayfarer had hit that she'd have been high and dry. I didn't find that out till morning because I was too busy to look at a chart, but when I did I came right about. That was a damned dirty trick, Van Tal, and I've sailed seventy miles to tell you so."

For a moment neither of the others spoke. Squeegee eyed Bill like a cat. The lip of the resident curled.

"All right, Bill, I lied," he admitted. "We got nothing out of it because we never found the yacht either. That's that. You've bawled me out. Now take a drink, and forget it." He started to rise. A huge tattooed hand on his shoulder swung him around.

"A lie and rotten bad seamanship cost that yacht a chance for rescue," Bill growled. "Forget it? Not me!"

"Then what?" challenged Van Tal nastily.

"Why, if you'd found that yacht I was going to smack you one in the nose. Since you didn't, and particularly since you lied about turning in and have been tramping in the back country, I'm going to stay here and made a report to that gunboat that's due—and smack you in the nose anyhow!"

"There's a fair wind out of the harbor," said Van Tal softly. Over his shoulder he exchanged a glance with Squeegee. "Better sail, Bill. I'm the resident and the government here. You're heading right smack into trouble."

"Better take off your coat," Bill said.

VAN TAL shrugged as though he were yielding to an unavoidable misfortune—which was exactly the way he felt. There was a gun in his coat pocket. Squeegee's attitude in the chair had been chosen so that he might keep a gun in his hand. To kill Bill would be awkward. It would leave a body and a schooner to be disposed of, but the big pearler had left no other course open. Van Tal jerked free of the grip on his shoulder and took one step backward. The two were scarcely an arm's length apart. To miss was impossible. He reached for his coat pocket.

A trigger must be found and pulled. A ready fist moves instantly.

Bill slapped his face. The smack of the open hand was sharp as a pistol shot. Iron fingers closed on Van Tai's wrist. The coat ripped as hand and revolver were torn from the coat pocket together. He cried out as his arm was twisted behind him. The gun clattered on the floor and he was flung across Bill's hip, head down, heels flying.

Into that whirling mêlée Squeegee hesitated to shoot. He sprang up and dashed in, revolver raised for a blow at Bill's head. Bill flung Van Tal at the new enemy. The hurtling body stopped Ryan, but he managed to keep his feet. Bill snatched a chair and hurled it at his head. Squeegee promptly ducked.

Poised to follow the chair in a headlong dive, Bellow Bill saw that his chance for a hand-to-hand fight was gone. Like a cat that twists in mid leap, he whirled around. A sweep of his arm sent the heavy table careening across the floor. Then he ran. He was bent double. He did not stop to work the door latch. Squeegee fired one shot, hastily aimed, as the impact of Bill's shoulder burst the flimsy fastening from the wood. The bullet ripped a hole in the panel a foot over his head. He tumbled outside and ran along the wall of the building.

To his left, fifty yards away, was the harbor. Directly ahead was a grove of coconuts, the slanting, foot-thick trunks of which would confuse a marksman. Bill sprinted into that shelter.

SPEED OF foot and his choice of cover saved his life. Squee-gee proved to be an amazingly good shot. Bill was a hundred yards away when the Irishman opened fire. A dozen trees were between them, and Bill was leaping erratically from right to left.

Yet the first bullet thwacked in a trunk directly behind his back. In front two spurts of sand shot up. A bullet droned past his head. The limited accuracy of a short-barrelled gun rather than poor aim, was behind those missed, and an instant later the crash of the thirty-eight was joined by the sharper crack of a rifle.

Bill made a flying dive into a thicket of pandanus at the edge of the grove. Here was real cover at last, temporary safety, but his huge chest was pumping like a bellows and his back was crawling in anticipation of a flying bit of lead. He wished he were a rabbit with a handy burrow, and at the same time he was mad at himself because he wanted to hide. To run away shakes the coolest nerves.

Out of the residency charged Van Tal and Squeegee. Both had rifles. The resident fired as he came, but Ryan was charging in workmanlike silence.

"Man-hunt, huh?" Bill panted. His face flamed. "The bums had it rigged—waiting for me!"

He was at the edge of the uncut jungle, a tangle of vegetation in which he could have hidden for a long, long time.

Yet he chose the scantier cover and greater risk involved in a slanting retreat that had for its objective the shore of the harbor.

Bellow Bill was unarmed, and hunted, yet it was characteristic of him that when he saw the full extent of the danger he should shift from headlong flight to a retreat which might become an offensive. There were two schooners swinging at anchor, with firearms on both, and the open water was scarcely an obstacle to a man who could swim and dive with any native of the South Seas.

For a hundred yards through the thickets it was a foot race between Squeegee and himself, in which he held his own. He bounded across the open beach while his pursuer was still hidden by the undergrowth, then splashed through the shallows, and dived. He left a circling ripple in the smooth water as the only target for the rifle. Squeegee squatted on the beach, rested his elbows on his knees, and took aim.

"He's got to come up," he said as Van Tal joined him. A hundred feet out the surface was broken by a swirl like that of a rising fish. There was a glimpse of a nose and mouth. The rifle bullet skipped from the surface of the water.

"You missed!" Van Tal snarled.

"Hell, I'd no time to sight!" Squeegee spat. "Say! the son of a gun is makin' for my schooner! What's the idea?"

"Get him as he climbs the rail!"

"I'm too low down to get a shot if he boards from the far side. The cabin will cover him," Squeegee growled disgustedly. "Hell, I figured you were good at murder! Bill breezed in just like you expected, and then spun you like a monkey!"

"He's boarding!"

"I saw the mast quiver, myself," granted the sailor. He moved back into the undergrowth. "Watch me nail him when he sticks up his head," he boasted.

BILL MADE no such childish blunder. He was an indifferent shot, and he would have been at the mercy of anyone who fired from concealment. First of all, Bill was a sailor. He was grinning as he crawled across the deck and squirmed below. Without a glance he passed rifles and a revolver, on his way forward. He found a towing hawser, made it fast, and tied a hundred yards of thin rope to the end, making all clear to uncoil. Then he unshackled the anchor chain. The chain whipped through the hawser pipe with am echoing rattle, and the schooner began to drift.

Bill crawled on deck, and squirmed over the rail. He held the thin rope. Filling his lungs, he ducked under water and started to swim toward his own craft, which was not far away. Though he did not break the surface, the rope trailing after him, revealed his movements.

Squeegee, who was a sailor, too, swore aloud.

"The divil is trying to maroon us on the island!" he exploded. "He'll slip his own anchor chain and take my boat in tow. He can set his jib while he's layin' flat on the deck!"

"Won't he have to stand up to loosen the after sail?" asked Van Tal desperately, for his perfect crime was crumbling to ruins.

"That's our only chance!" the Irishman snapped, but with very little hope.

The chance was one that Bill never gave. Flat on his back on the deck in the shelter of his own rail, he cut the lashings that furled the sail with a sheath knife lashed to the end of a pole, set the jib and hoisted the mainsail. The wind was scarcely a breath. Very, very slowly the schooner gathered way. The towing hawser tightened.

There was not a sound in the harbor. Bill watched the tops of the palms.

The conspirators, gripping their rifles, lined the bowsprit against a huge block of coral on the opposite shore. A minute passed. Neither perceived a movement.

Something that neither attacker had counted on was proving decisive. The tide was running in. The current was setting both schooners toward the beach. From the undergrowth sounded an oath of delight.

Bill, as quick to recognize the facts, glanced at the towing hawser with a wry grin. By cutting loose from the tow he could sail out. He could blockade the harbor until the gunboat arrived, whenever that might be. No one knew better how elastic the schedules of such a vessel were.

With a shake of his head he slipped the wheel into the becket and crawled below. He slipped a revolver into his pocket and strapped a Winchester and tied both onto his back. Though he could blockade the harbor in comfort, he preferred to take the risk involved in carrying the war ashore.

Several facts were yet wholly unexplained. His enemies had been up all night. There were green stains on Squeegee's shoes. Both had been waiting for him with guns very handy, and would attempt murder to conceal a lie that had proved harmless.

"They found that yacht, and wrecked her," Bill rumbled. "Her fittings would be worth ten or twenty thousand bucks. That must be their game. O.K., gents! Try and collect—and see how you like being bushwhacked!"

Without a sound he squirmed over the rail. For a hundred yards the hull of his schooner, drifting slowly backward in the current, protected him. Thereafter he swam under water, and though Squeegee shot and shot accurately, whenever he twisted out his mouth and nose, Bellow Bill reached the opposite shore unhurt and crawled out behind a block of coral. His plan was to stalk his enemies and deliver the beating he had promised, then to wait in the comfort of the residency for the gunboat.

Across the harbor Squeegee blew the smoke of his last shot out of the rifle muzzle.

"Bill is just a bag of wind," he quoted mockingly. "Hell, so is a hurricane!"

There was no humor in Van Tal.

"It's him or us now," he stated. "Sail his schooner out of the harbor and set fire to her before you jump overboard. We'll claim he was lost in the gale, and we'll get out Mohu and his trackers to make sure we're right. He's got a whole island to fight, and he still don't know it."

CHAPTER IV

A NECKLACE FOR A HEN

THE SNYDERS SAT close together in the center of a large native hut thatched with grass and floored with dirt. Around the wall extended a rack with wooden pegs, on each of which hung the fleshless jaw of a pig—a common South Seas religious symbol. The prisoners shuddered as they looked at the naked fangs.

High in the peak of the roof were other objects, not altogether fleshless. Father, mother and daughter had all noticed them, and remained silent. The things were human heads.

An old crone, three-quarters naked and wrinkled and brown as a coconut husk, was stirring *poi* near by. The idea of another meal of the sour, ill-tasting, evil-smelling stuff nauseated them all, but there seemed no help for it. To refuse to eat might not please their jailer.

The latter crouched ten feet away with a paddle-shaped war club across his knees, silent, and unwinking. Claire Snyder had never seen so powerful a man, or a face so devoid of pity. She remembered professional wrestlers who were bull-necked, round-headed, knotted and rugged with muscle, but this brown giant was thewed strongly enough to tear such giants apart, and scowled as though he would enjoy the opportunity.

One side of his face had been tattooed in a solid mass of ink which time had faded to a livid green. All expression save ferocity was lost. The name of the savage, she knew, was Mohu. He had obeyed Van Tal, but when he moved an eye the other natives in the hut shrank away. Claire glanced at her father, who lay on his back, still feeble from shock and exposure.

"What price wild men?" she smiled at Mohu.

She had to say something, and why be serious? If she were serious she would go into a blue funk and scream.

"Do you think that Mr. Van Tal means to leave us here? He lied when he told us his house was in this jungle. This place is all native."

"Why didn't he rob us?" complained Mrs. Snyder bitterly. "The jewels are nothing compared to your father's health—"

"Or mine?" asked Claire.

"Or yours, of course. You take after my side of the family, however, and you are not delicate," retorted Mrs. Snyder severely. In her prominent blue eyes came a glint of humor. "Sometimes it's an advantage to be descended from a pioneer grandmother. When the Sioux attacked the wagon train in which mine was traveling, she split one brave's head with an ax."

"Great grandma'd be quite at home here."

"Well, you needn't shudder, Claire. She did it. People had to do things like that in those days. She was the quietest, gentlest old lady. A little stout, to be sure. I inherited her tendency to put on flesh... Carson!"

"Yes!" muttered the recumbent man.

"If that Van Tal wants ransom, don't haggle. You're always the business man."

"Business is always business, too," said Snyder positively. He tried to sit up, but failed. "You're the man of the family, Ada," he muttered to his wife, mocking his own physical weakness. "Nevertheless, a petty white official and a tattooed savage ought not to be too difficult to outwit. Give your necklace to Mohu there."

"Give it to him, Carson?"

"Exactly. A gift calls for a return. And Van Tal may be indiscreet enough to try to take it away from him. I hope so."

Reluctantly Mrs. Snyder unclasped the necklace, walked over to Mohu, who scowled at her without moving, and clasped the glittering stones around his corded throat.

"Let him see how he looks—in your vanity case!" called Claire.

MOHU LOOKED into the tiny mirror. He grinned, and suddenly grunted out an order in the native dialect. A half-grown boy lounging near the door of the hut disappeared as if shot. Mohu sat playing with the jewels, turning them in a ray of sunshine that came through the roof so that the hut was filled with flying gleams of colored lights. Outside a chicken squawked as its neck was wrung. Mohu grinned at Snyder, and made a motion of carrying food to his mouth.

"Business is always business," murmured the financier. "Savages or bank presidents—"

"A ten thousand dollar necklace for a stringy pullet is nothing to boast of," snapped Mrs. Snyder tartly.

"Mohu is in a position to make terms, my dear. For a savage he has a clear understanding of the fundamental principle of trade... I'd give your vanity case to the cook, Ada. By the time Mr. Van Tal returns we'll have his dividends distributed among his employees. We'll sow the dragon's teeth, and at least we'll be amused and fed."

A shadow fell across the doorway. Van Tal stepped inside.

Snyder grew red as a small boy caught in the act of putting chewing gum in teacher's chair, but although the resident noticed the necklace at once he only greeted his captives by a curt and sardonic nod and spoke to Mohu in the dialect. The savage uttered a shout and leaped up with flashing eyes, brandishing his club.

On Van Tal's lips explanation changed to command. Mohu listened, grinning wolfishly and nodding after every staccato sentence. At the end he hurried out of the hut and began to shout for the men of the village. They answered, loud and eagerly. Bare feet pattered on the hard ground. A man ran in, caught a club from the wall of the hut, and hurried out.

"Head hunting was their national sport once," Van Tal remarked in English. "They appreciate an opportunity to indulge in it." He paused, relishing the cruel suspense in which he had put the Snyders. "You're not the victims, yet," he added.

Claire came to her feet.

"And who is? Your accomplice?" she retorted. "That would be like you! Don't try to make cowards of us, for you can't! Good heavens, can't you even go wrong with some fire about you? If I were a man—"

"Squeegee might be less interested in you!" retorted Van Tal icily.

"Bah! Old stuff!" snapped the girl. She strode toward the door.

"Come back!" Van Tal grated.

CLAIRE TURNED. Not in obedience to the command, but because half a dozen armed savages were clustered in front of the hut. She had no wish to step from frying pan to fire, but she was too stubborn to yield altogether. She remained near the doorway, looking over the tops of the trees down the hillside toward the sea. She was like a small, sulky child who tries to show independence.

Van Tal smiled.

"Just as you please, my dear," he remarked mockingly and turned toward Snyder.

"Giving up that necklace was simple—and foolish," he accused. "I expected something better from the man who is Wall Street."

"Lift me up, Ada," remarked the other. "I fear you have been boasting of your husband... Ah! That's better. So hard to talk flat on one's back." He looked hard at the resident, and old and sick though Snyder was, the habit of authority and unlimited resources made his glance one before which a weak man would have quailed.

Van Tal bore the stare unmoved.

"I noticed you let Mohu keep it," Snyder said.

"Why, I can trade it away for a broken musket and a hand-

ful of powder any time! Give away the lot if you like," said Van
Tal indifferently. "These people of Mohu's both fear me and
love me. Very like dogs, Mr. Snyder. A trained pack of wolves.
They'll take your scraps of meat, but when I snap my fingers—"
Van Tal shrugged, leaving the threat unfinished. "Their loyalty
is the corner stone of my advantage," he resumed easily. "I have
gone over every detail, provided for every contingency with
my—er—partner."

"Mohu?" Snyder interjected.

"Ryan," Van Tal contradicted. "You'd be pleased to see us
quarrel. We haven't. My head hunters are to track down a notorious pearl pirate who was driven in to take refuge from the
gale. A man who'd cut all your throats for one of Mrs. Snyder's
finger rings."

"Oh, indeed?" bristled that Amazon.

"Whereas, such trifles do not interest me—"

"Please don't try to fool us, Van Tal," Snyder broke in. "I'm
aware that you are playing a game in which you won't stick at
murder. We are the goose that lays the golden eggs, but that
goose was killed, you'll recall. I've no wish to fall a victim to
your stupidity, or a quarrel among your accomplices, or an ill-ad-
vised attempt to rescue which might force you to be rid of three
awkward witnesses. Anything that is possible I will pay in any
way that is practical. I would advise you, and not selfishly, to be
moderate. Well, sir?"

"You assume that I am in a hurry," retorted Van Tal grimly.
"On the contrary. Your yacht is already reported missing. In a
month or two it will be posted as lost. When your office has
believed you dead for five or six months I doubt if they will be
so anxious to investigate, or rescue."

"You'll keep us here for months!" exploded Mrs. Snyder.

Van Tal bowed. "I will. My demands might not seem moderate now, but when I make them you'll be glad to give up half you
possess to get free," he flashed out with a sudden fierce blaze of
smoldering passion. "Meanwhile, I've given orders for the boys

of the village to guard you. There is a club or spear at every door and window, and they know their lives will answer for yours. I would advise you"—Van Tal mimicked Snyder—"wholly self-ishly, to be satisfied!"

"He's right about the boys, mother," called Claire from the doorway. "I can see them. There's something on fire down near the shore, though."

"A schooner. At my orders," explained Van Tal, who was unable to resist the opportunity to show his captives how completely they were in his power. "Even if you should escape from this hut, there would be no escape from the island."

"I see the schooner, and it's not the one we came on, either," Claire answered with repressed excitement. "I am talking of the other smoke down near the water front, hidden by the trees."

Van Tal ran to the door. As he peered out, his back grew rigid and his fists clenched. The smoke could only rise from his residency. The only explanation possible was that Bellow Bill Williams had set fire to the building in retaliation for the destruction of his vessel.

Food and supplies, trade goods to reward the natives for the man-hunt, the very paper and ink on which Snyder was to have written the agreement Van Tal had in mind, were going up in the smoke. Bill might have meant only to force his enemies to keep near their schooner, or to take to the bush as poorly equipped as he was himself, but the stroke had been shrewder than he guessed.

Van Tal swore aloud.

"That wasn't at your orders, was it?" said Claire sweetly. "That pearl pirate you mentioned seems to be enterprising. I'd really like to see him. Know why?"

She paused, but Van Tal only glared.

"Because you hate him—and because you're afraid of him!" she challenged. "We're not alone here after all!"

"You'll see his head!" Van Tal threatened fiercely. "I'll roll it

through the door to teach you manners—and before sundown,
too!"

CHAPTER V

HOUNDED

BELLOW BILL DESPISED the native of the South Seas
as a fighting man. Though expeditions ashore in Borneo and
Matalia had given him considerable experience in bushcraft,
he was in no mind to pit his cunning against that of the brown
trackers, but rather to lure all his enemies into battle. He set fire
to the residency that the fight might be prompt. The sight of
the smoke ought to bring Squeegee Ryan ashore, ought also to
anger Van Tal into hurrying to the attack.

Once the building was well alight, therefore, Bill took to the
woods with no attempt to cover his trail, and went no farther
than was necessary to find a locality suitable for setting a trap. In
a grove of huge trees about a quarter of a mile from the beach he
stopped in his stride, and stood with legs apart that there might
be no footprint to indicate that he had halted.

High overhead dense foliage almost shut out the sunlight.
Underbrush there was none. He stood in a greenish gloom on a
sodden carpet of rotting leaves. The tree trunks, forty and fifty
feet apart and thicker than he could span with both arms, rose
like dark columns supporting a green roof. The gigantic branches
that radiated from each trunk resembled rafters. Orchids grew
from the bark in green, bushy masses, and vines festooned from
tree to tree, thick as the towing hawser of a ship.

Bill searched that living network until he found a vine that
grew from the earth. He walked straight to the root and cut it
through, pulled on the vine to make sure that it was anchored
solidly above and then climbed up. He was a heavy man for
monkey work. He was glad to reach a limb as thick as his body

and lie there, panting. Looking down, he could see how his trail crossed the grove, and stopped short. The severed vine would indicate he had taken to the air.

Thus far his stratagem was an old one. His next move was one which a pursuer would be unlikely to anticipate. He worked his way out along the limb, trailing the vine by which he had climbed. Crossing from one tree to the next was a bit of ticklish work, for the ground was thirty feet below, but he made it without mishap and crawled onward until the new limb grew thick and he could conceal himself in a clump of parasitic plants.

The severed vine now stretched from tree to tree, indistinguishable from a mass of similar vines, but hanging lower than any. Bill looked over his arrangements with a sailor's eye, and stretched out on the limb to wait.

MORE THAN an hour passed before a huge brown body glided into the grove. Mohu was bent over the trail like a questing hound, following it at a trot. The gems around his neck sparkled, and Bellow Bill, a pearler by trade, knew jewels.

"Women's gear!" he rumbled deep m his throat. "Van Tal did more than wreck a yacht. He's robbed a body, or—or—"

That problem could wait. Mohu was at the end of the trail. For a moment he paused, then glanced upward swiftly and uttered a low whistle that imitated the call of a bird. From right and left brown bodies drifted into the grove until eight men were gathered around Mohu. They were silent as ghosts, but fingers pointed to the severed vine, beady eyes searched the foliage overhead. Bill lay motionless. Though he dared watch no longer, he used his ears.

There was a faint grunt from below that had a triumphant ring. Bill gripped his rifle. Had the savages noticed the twigs broken in his route from tree to tree, or had they located him? The limb shielded him from spears and war clubs and would enable him to fight against a rifle on fairly even terms, but he did not wish a siege or a protracted duel. This was the crisis of his stratagem. He held his breath until he heard the noise of a white man's shoes coming on the run across the sodden leaves, and then peered downward.

Van Tal had joined his trackers, and stood looking upward, his gun-half raised, trying to see what Mohu was pointing out. The huge arm of the savage was extended straight in line with Bill's face, but now that Van Tal was in the crowd, the pearler no longer cared. Gripping rifle and vine together he rolled from the ring and swung down in a hurtling arc into the midst of his enemies.

He came as an acrobat swings downward on a trapeze, legs stiff before him, a human battering ram that split the group and knocked it sprawling. Even to Bill the impact was terrific. He rolled over and over with an impetus that carried men along with him, staggered to his feet and clubbed his rifle.

The first blow broke the stock short off against a woolly head. Bill lashed out with the barrel. Clubs swung at him, but the half-hearted blows failed to stop his rush. The natives yelled in panic as he charged back from their midst. He smashed a fist into Mohu's face, knocking the chief sprawling.

Then a native gripped him by the knees. Bill clutched the native's throat in his powerful fingers till the man lay still. Then he broke through the ring.

Van Tal was up. With a bellowing roar Bill rushed. Between the two were three natives, in flight. Van Tal was being carried backward when he fired—into the brown of the mass—shot after shot aimed indiscriminately at Bill and his own men.

A native dropped. The rest scattered, and Bill ran with them. The revolver seemed to spit in his face. He leaped for the shelter of a tree, tossed away his useless rifle, and jerked out his revolver.

Van Tal, however, was retreating in the rear of the panic-stricken natives. Bill fired at him and missed, cursing the invention of firearms which make all men equal. Six of the savages lay unconscious on the earth. Only the chance that Bill's rush had been checked, the ruthless fire into the midst of his own party, had saved the resident.

"Damn you, shoot it out!" the pearler roared.

There was no answer except the crackle of branches broken by precipitate retreat. Bill swore and started to pursue. He could stalk if he had to. Most of the natives would not fight again; and for Van Tal alone he was more than a match.

Nevertheless Bill was not reckless enough to charge blindly through the underbrush and offer a target. Indeed, within a hundred yards his chase ended because of an occurrence that he might have anticipated, but which he had forgotten. The gunboat had reached the harbor. The woods echoed with blast after blast of a steam whistle, calling, Bill decided with a grin, for Van Tal.

The gunboat changed the whole situation. In the eyes of the officials, Bill's fight with Van Tal would be an attempt at murder to be severely punished, instead of a war. Since to capture the resident was impractical, Bill was eager to lay his accusation before the naval men before Van Tal was able to cook up some plausible lie. Therefore he turned and ran toward the water front.

AS HE came in sight of the sea and the blazing embers of the residency, he found that events had taken a course which pleased him highly. Squeegee had been captured. The schooner was anchored near the gunboat in the harbor, and on the beach a squad of bluejackets in command of a lieutenant was advancing, with Ryan in their midst.

"Ahoy, landing party! Fine work, sir!" Bill roared. His head was bleeding from a blow that he had not felt in the heat of the fight. His shirt was in shreds. His trousers were foul with bark and leaf mold, and a revolver was stuck in the waistband. Bill forgot such trifles.

"What's the news from the yacht Wayfarer?" he bellowed.

The squad halted. Rifles came to the ready, but Bill raised both hands high. The lieutenant in command stepped forward.

"There's wrecking or worse afoot here, sir," Bellow Bill began. "We received an S O S from the Wayfarer. Your resident sent me to a false position, and I suspect—"

"*Ach*, so?" interrupted the lieutenant phlegmatically. He was a chubby, middle-aged man whose tunic wrinkled over his belly, and whose round blue eyes swam in his head. "Der Wayfarer? Dot iss a yacht. It iss strange our wireless hear noddings, no?"

"You'd have heard it all right if your operator hadn't been asleep or seasick!" Bill rambled.

The round blue eyes grew hard. At a nod from the lieutenant, a sailor stepped from the rank and took away Bill's revolver.

"We hear of der Wayfarer and odder t'ings," said the lieutenant implacably. "From him." He motioned at Squeegee. "How you are drove ashore mit slaves, und der resident attack—"

"From him? Didn't you capture him?" asked Bill quietly.

"He does not run away. When he sight us he sail right oudt. Mit der story, und a letter from der resident. I take you by der ship and der resident find. Den we have der trial."

"I'm to be tried by Van Tal, for blackbirding?" said Bill slowly. "Well, damn his brass-bound nerve!"

"*Jah!*" confirmed the lieutenant. "Dot iss der law. He der governor of der island iss."

He gave an order, his squad divided and surrounded the pearler. Bill eyed the eight rifles and spat on the sand in disgust. Squeegee was grinning. Bill itched to wring the lieutenant's fat neck, but he grinned back.

"I've got to admire Van Tal's nerve," he boomed. "He's a cold-blooded bum, but he don't overlook any bets. He's smart, particularly since he set fire to my ship, which makes a trial come down to my word against his. If I hadn't seen that necklace—"

"Vot's dot?" demanded the lieutenant, who had caught the last word.

"Necklace, I said," Bellow Bill growled. "A woman's necklace on a Melanesian's throat. But you'll never find that, of course. I'm beginning to savvy something."

THE HUGE shoulders of the pearler squared. He stood quiet, mentally testing the meshes of the net that Van Tal had woven, and into which he had plunged. In a trial, even if these naval officers meant to be fair, Van Tal's word would outweigh his. The resident had built upon that fact very cleverly.

And yet for Bill to escape, which was the only alternative, seemed impossible. He was surrounded. If he knocked a couple of sailors down and took to his heels he would be shot.

He looked toward the water front. The party had landed in a cutter, a six-oared craft too heavy and broad of beam to be capsized by one man. If he dived overboard without capsizing the boat, it would be rowed two feet for every one he could swim.

Bill walked on with the party and took his place in the stern of the cutter. The officers before whom he would be tried might be shrewder than the lieutenant who faced him. Then again, they might not be.

"Lieutenant, there's two sides to every story," said Bill suddenly. "The S O S is the only fact that would enable you to check up between me and Van Tal, and if your ship didn't hear that, I'm beaten. Perhaps it was too faint to be heard except here in the island."

"Perhaps dere wass no S O S, no?"

Bill shrugged. "The government can do no wrong," he quoted grimly. "Believe what you like, and cover up your own inefficiency all you please, but remember that I accuse Van Tal of wrecking a yacht and probably of kidnaping a party of her passengers—including one woman who is rich enough to give a native a valuable necklace. Remember that, and find that necklace, will you?" Bill's voice rang across the water.

"*Pfui!*" grunted the lieutenant in contempt. "You accuse Van Tal, who has a resident thirty years been! His honor iss proven. Und why must I worry, *hein?* You will Van Tal see, and yourself accuse him—"

"Oh, yeah?" said Bill gently.

The cutter was gliding into the gunboat, all oars trailing. Bill leaped up. His fist smashed to the point of the lieutenant's chin, and as the latter pitched forward, cleanly knocked out, Bill caught him up and leaped with him over the stern.

IN THE clear water every move of the pearler could be seen both by the oarsmen in the cutter and the sailors near the rail of the gunboat. Bellow Bill swam straight down, dragging the unconscious officer by a hand fast in his collar. Both disappeared in the shadow of the gunboat hull.

There was a babble of orders. A junior officer leaped from the ship into the cutter. Sailors on deck ran for rifles, for life preservers, only to stop, unable to use either. One volunteer dived overboard, but for ten or twenty seconds there was no sign of Bill or his victim.

Then the figure of the lieutenant became visible in the depths, rising slowly upward by the natural buoyancy of the body. The cutter dashed around the gunboat to the rescue, but still there was no sign of Bellow Bill.

"Damn you, look behind the stern of the schooner!" screamed Squeegee. "He can swim like a divil-fish!"

No attention was paid to the yell. Prisoners could be recaptured, but if the lieutenant sank a second time he might never rise. A boat hook caught his collar, and he was drawn, limp and dripping, into the air. Two sailors held him up to let the water run from nose and mouth. Artificial respiration was begun instantly and very soon he coughed, groaned and stirred.

Not until then did the pursuit for Bill get under way, and by then Bill was almost across the harbor, swimming under water toward the rock which had protected him before. He was seen the last time he came up for air, shot at when he leaped into the brush, but the bullets went wide.

His escape was only temporary. The cutter was racing toward him to avenge the assault on their officer. Another landing party was getting away from the gunboat. Sixteen men would comb the island until they found him.

In the meantime, if Bill were lucky he might tear a woman's necklace from the throat of a savage and then face his accusers with evidence which even perjurers would find difficulty in accounting for.

CHAPTER VI

BILL'S SQUIRREL HUNT

BELLOW BILL RETURNED to the spot at which he had abandoned the trail of Van Tal, as fast as he could run. Every second counted, for although the resident had foreseen that the gunboat might come, its actual arrival had surprised him with his natives scattered and in panic-stricken retreat. He could not be sure that Squeegee had lied with success; could not be sure that the armed sailors were not seeking him.

As far as Bill could guess, the return to the shore and the escape had been accomplished in less than a half hour, and he judged than Van Tal would find that interval a scanty one in which to conceal the evidence of his undertaking. Somewhere on the island must be either the hull of the Wayfarer, the wreck of some of her lifeboats, dead bodies, or living prisoners. Any of these things are hard to hide. Which of them the resident was concealing Bill did not care in the least.

In the moist leaf mold of the forest, the trail of Van Tal was not difficult to follow. First widely spaced footprints indicated headlong flight. Then Van Tal had stopped suddenly. He had hesitated, for there was a trampled space in the soft earth. Probably he had stood here when the whistle of the gunboat blew. Afterward he had set out toward the hills.

Two hundred yards farther along Van Tal had been joined by a native. They had trotted up the slope of a hill and turned into a path.

Here footprints were no longer visible, but since Van Tal had been heading inland, Bill also followed the path uphill, watching the sides to see if the resident had turned aside. Van Tal had not. After a mile of rapid walking Bill heard the clucking of a hen, and entered a grove of breadfruit trees.

Both signs indicated the proximity of a native village, but the pearler hardly slackened his pace. He caught up a stick from the ground to use as a club and charged in grim silence into an open space of bare earth surrounded on three sides by long, grass-thatched dwellings.

At the sight of him, women and children screamed and scattered like ants. Most of them were quick enough to escape, but one withered old woman stumbled. Bill caught her. She gasped and hung limp in terror.

"Where one fella Van Tal? Where one fella chief?" Bill growled.

The woman was dumb, paralyzed by fear, but she pointed— toward the path by which Bill had come.

That was a lie, obviously, but Bill wasted no time in threats. Greatly as the old woman feared him, her terror of Van Tal and the chief must be equally great. Though the village was silent and unpeopled, the pearler knew that some of the natives were watching him from the bushes. They would carry the news that the old woman had been a traitor, and though vengeance would be delayed it would be terrible.

There was a chance that in lying the old woman had pointed in a direction exactly opposite from the true one, but Bill wanted facts.

IN THE afternoon hush he caught the faint clink of metal against metal. The sailors had followed him, and were coming fast; amazingly fast, unless they had found and impressed one of Van Tal's natives for a guide. They were not over a quarter of a mile behind. Probably less.

In grim haste Bill pushed the old woman into the nearest of the thatched houses. Mats and cooking pots were scattered over the big room. The flight of the women would not have caused so much confusion, but nevertheless Bill could see no signs that the place had been occupied except by natives. There were no shreds of cloth, no tin cans, which are the sign manual of the white. Nothing at all, except a greater terror manifested on the part of the old woman.

Something had happened here. The crone stood rigid. Her eyes were tightly shut lest she reveal the secret.

Carefully Bill examined the mats, the walls, the floor. The sound of metal against metal became clearer and clearer, but at last he saw something which was not native. In the center of the earthern floor were two parallel gouges. Some one had stood there with feet braced, and had been dragged forward. The marks were narrow. From French heels.

Near by were drops of blood, indistinguishable against the brown earth until Bill knelt above them. He could visualize the scene. A woman caught by the arms, who had resisted the efforts to drag her into the open. The sudden swing of a club; a white woman, bleeding, dead perhaps, flung over a shoulder. Then the retreat.

Bill strode to the nearest door. There was a drop of blood there.

Across the open space he quartered like an eager hound. The woman had been bleeding badly. The blood drops became a trail which led to a faint path that wound into the forest, pointing toward the high hills in the center of the island.

Once sure of that, Bill let his prisoner go with a feint at a blow which made her leap screaming into the bushes. He watched her disappear, grinning. The sailors would learn nothing of his movements from her, at least. He hoped they would be delayed in the village as long as he had been, for he could actually hear the thump of their feet.

He ran up the path. The drops of blood had been fresh. He was not more than five minutes, not more than ten at most, behind Van Tal.

The path led through another grove of breadfruit trees, and then into a forest. Always it climbed. The trees became scattered with patches of sunshine alternating with shadow, and what had at first been a broad ravine became a cañon with walls of black lava drawing closer and closer together. Bill's dread lest Van Tal hear him and turn aside vanished. If the resident were still ahead, it would not be impossible for him to climb the rocky walls or to come back unseen.

Therefore Bill pressed on. He did not care whether Van Tal or the sailors could hear the sticks that snapped under his running feet. He was gaining. He would overtake a man burdened by the weight of a wounded woman within a half mile at most.

HE WAS panting halfway up a steep slope, sparsely covered with large trees that grew in the canon bottom, when he caught sight of Van Tal.

The resident was alone, and coming down hill at a swinging walk. He carried a revolver.

For an instant Van Tal stared in amazement. Then he took aim. Bill promptly stepped behind the nearest tree.

"Come out of that, Williams! I saw that you haven't a gun!" called Van Tal softly.

Instead Bill made a leap that took him to a much larger tree—a three-foot trunk more than broad enough to conceal his entire body. He had exposed himself only momentarily, and the resident did not fire.

That was lucky. The pearler did not want to call in the sailors. He set his hands against the trunk and peered cautiously around it, alert to dodge in either direction.

"Ever hunt squirrels?" he taunted.

"*Dummkopf!* Come out!" snarled Van Tal.

The resident had an eye and a bit of a cheek to shoot at. He leaped ten feet to the right. Bill barely shifted position—and still exposed only the eye and cheek.

"Come and get me—woman killer!" he purred. "Only way to get a squirrel is to walk right up to the tree. I'm waiting!"

He was. When Van Tal advanced within ten feet he meant to throw his stick and rush. A man who dives at the knees is hard to stop with a bullet. The fight was not unfair; its end uncertain. Van Tal, however, was no fool, and he had learned his lesson in Bill's hand-to-hand tactics. He sat down.

"Bill, I don't want to kill you," he said. "I want you out of the way. That's all I've ever wanted."

The pearler was silent.

"Do you believe in luck?" Van Tal went on. "I do. I've had bad luck all my life. I was a failure, sent here to rot. Yesterday, with the S O S, my luck changed. Everything has worked for me. Everything is still working for me. You've put up a good fight. What has it got you?"

"There's a woman brave enough to put up a scrap against a club-toting savage. And smart enough to give that brute of yours a necklace," Bill growled. "She's stood enough, if she's living. Bring her out."

"The fat old hell-cat is living. So is her husband and her daughter," retorted Van Tal coolly. "Whether they keep on living is entirely up to you."

Bellow Bill was silent.

"To you!" Van Tal emphasized with a touch of anger. "The gunboat captain believes the letter I left with Ryan, or doesn't believe it. I don't know which and I'm not asking you. Since you're here, unarmed, I figure they did believe it. Lieutenant Brandenburg has a single-track mind. I'm a fellow official, which is enough for him."

To this Bill agreed heartily, but he made no reply.

"I've done murder. I'll do it again rather than lose this chance," said Van Tal icily. "There are millions—more than millions that my luck brought me! Do you hear? Speak up!"

"I think you're mad," Bill rumbled. He was careful not to expose more than a bit of his face. "What was it you said about your prisoners and me?"

"Go up this trail a hundred yards and you'll see. They lie on the ground, bound, with Mohu standing over them with his club. I told him to kill them if a white man should lay hands on them. He will do it."

"I guess he would," Bill admitted. "But I am not the only white man."

"You're the only one here! I'm going to the others. I or my natives will come for the prisoners. You'd better stay away," snapped Van Tal.

He rose and began to circle down the slope, keeping a wide interval between Bill and himself.

"Life is worth more than millions to those three," the resident said bitterly. "Leave them alone. Follow me down the trail, and then hide. If the sailors find you, little damage will be done. The charges against you will be dismissed later."

"You're going because you're afraid to fight it out with me," said Bill suddenly.

"Why should I fight? I have too much to lose," Van Tal shrugged.

He made a dash that took him past Bill. Down the trail he ran, faster and faster, looking backward to menace Bill with the revolver in case of pursuit.

THE PEARLER did not follow. A shot would bring the sailors and precipitate the worst. In his mind the dilemma was whether to advance or to hide as Van Tal had suggested. Millions were worth less than life; but only a man callous to human risk and suffering would trust a Melanesian savage with three lives. Mohu would only kill if necessary. He might kill though no real need arose.

By choosing to keep his prisoners at any cost, Van Tal was exposing them to the fatal consequences of a blunder or an accident which was almost certain to occur. A sailor might blunder on this path, an officer might insist upon following it despite the advice of a guide. Mohu might grow tired of waiting.

Bellow Bill tightened his belt. Thoughtfully he threw away his stick, and opened and shut his empty hands.

"Luck!" he rumbled in disgust. "Any guy that's willing to double-cross the human race can be lucky!"

He turned up the trail. He walked slowly, like a weary and discouraged man. His shirt had been half torn from his tattooed body. Obviously the pockets of his duck trousers concealed no weapon. He did not look formidable, and no forlorn hope was ever undertaken in a more lackadaisical fashion.

Bill limped and hung his head on his chest. Mohu must have no reason to fear him. He was playing the part of an unarmed white man who plodded like an ox to slaughter. He was gambling that a savage chieftain would be unable to resist the temptation to gain much honor by slaying the white man who had routed the entire tribe, when that honor could be gained by a single stroke of a war club. Orders are seldom followed literally. By savage races, almost never.

Bellow Bill had made his decision, but he was afraid. Not of the unequal contest he meant to provoke, but of a blunder. His heart thumped as the cañon walls drew together. He had plodded to the end of the trail. He stopped and drew a swift breath of relief.

THE UNDERGROWTH parted. Mohu stepped out. He carried a heavy wooden war club, paddle-shaped, sharp-edged as a sword. Suddenly he swung a vicious blow at the pearler's neck.

Bill leaped back with a grunt of triumph. Mohu jumped after him. The war club flashed in a sweeping circle, waist high. It was the stroke that disembowels the enemy not equipped with a shield.

Bill dodged again, bent double to escape the whistling point. Like a flash Mohu recovered. The point of the war club streaked at Bill's throat, and for the third time he saved himself by yielding ground.

They had moved twenty feet down hill. With war club held vertically like a broadsword, Mohu weaved as a boxer does, maneuvering craftily to work Bill's back against a tree. The white man was almost caught.

Again he sidestepped as the club hissed by his head. Mohu recovered too quickly for a rush. There was no chance to spring within the swing of his blows. He swung the club like a sword, striking from the wrists, with both hands always close to and level with his chest.

The trees were now Bill's salvation. Except for the brief respite they gave him, he could have been cut down by the relentless advance and the quick, chopping strokes of the club. For an instant the duel was a pursuit rather than a fight. Bill dodged behind a tree, stooped, and sprang away. In that instant's respite he had pulled off his shoe, the last resort of a cornered sailor, and the weapon which has settled a thousand fo'c's'le brawls in every port of the world.

Mohu gave a grunt of contempt, but Bill neither threw the shoe nor struck with it. He slipped it onto his left hand.

As the club came down he parried the sharp wooden edge with the leathery sole. The smack of the impact was like a pistol shot. The shock tore the shoe from Bill's hand, but he was within the sweep of the club at last. His right fist smashed to the tattooed chin and he stepped in, breast to breast.

For a minute of vicious fighting Bill had never been nearer death. Yet that single blow, the only one to reach its mark in the whole fight, ended the struggle. The club dropped from Mohu's hands. Bill held a limp body that dropped to its knees, then to its back, unconscious.

Bill snatched up the club with a haste which brought a shamed grin to his face. He had scorned the native as a fighter, and for once he had been very wrong.

"Ahoy!" he called softly. "Ain't no one around?"

THOUGH THERE was no answer, a step into the brush from which Mohu had charged revealed three figures, bound and gagged, who lay side by side. Bill untied Claire Snyder first, but the girl was too exhausted to speak. She smiled at Bill, and commenced to sob from sheer excitement.

Not so Mrs. Snyder. There was a three-inch gash on the scalp of that redoubtable lady, caked with dried blood, but her spirit was unbroken. As the cords of the gag were loosened she spat out the wad of dirty cloth.

"Help Carson first!" she commanded. "He's fainted, and no wonder! And who, and what might you be? Can't you have something done for that tattooing? It's savage."

"Mother! He rescued us," murmured Claire, but Bellow Bill only threw back his head and laughed.

"Ma'am, you and me are going to get along swell," he boomed. He reached into his pocket, slipped a quid of fine cut much larger than any need called for into his mouth, and squatted, blue eyes twinkling, and making no attempt to release either husband or wife.

"Ma'am, you and me together could run the South Seas," he muttered. "Even including each other, maybe."

"That would be too much for either of us. We're not used to it," said Mrs. Snyder crisply. "Do you know whom you have rescued?"

"In a general way," grunted Bill, busy with knots. "Names don't matter much."

"Sometimes they do," snapped Mrs. Snyder. "Sometimes it is pleasant to have things like influence and millions to reward, and to punish. You and I do understand one another, I think. I don't want to pay you, but is there anything you want?"

"A pearling, schooner, with a motor," Bill rumbled. "Which of you thought of giving that Melanesian a necklace? You, ma'am?"

"My husband," said Mrs. Snyder proudly. She could not be switched from the subject.

"Only a schooner? Our name means much more than that, really. I've a blunt tongue and a strong will, young man, but I really do appreciate—" She stopped. "As for Van Tal—"

"There's the crew of a gunboat wandering around this island and Van Tal has joined them. Wait till you see his face when I ask him about his luck before you go to thinking up punishments, ma'am," interrupted Bill grimly. "He figured on every-thing except people, which is always a mistake, if you ask me."

The pearler cleared his mouth and rose.

"Ahoy!" he bellowed in his tremendous voice. "Ahoy, the gunboat! This way, lads!"

Faint in the distance came an answering shout. To Van Tal it was the prelude to a hangman's noose; to Squeegee a jail sentence. For Bill it meant an apology from an angry lieutenant, a new schooner, and a chance to know a new friend better. For Mrs. Snyder could not be denied. Bellow Bill was her ship captain for the remainder of her cruise through the South Seas.

THE STUFF OF EMPIRE

"It isn't gold like this that builds empires," the little South Seas Dutch commissioner said, "It's roughnecks like Bellow Bill Williams!"

CHAPTER I

THE TOKEN

"**YOU BLACK FELLA,** stop along me!" shouted the voice of a white man. "Wait! Stop! Hell, where's my gun?"

All but the last words were in the native dialect of New Guinea, and Bellow Bill Williams, who understood the language perfectly, waited calmly for the sound of the shot. He could not interfere. He was sitting on the veranda of the Dutch commissioner's house, at least a hundred yards from the scene of the murder, if murder it was to be.

The commissioner himself sat with him. Bill wondered what the little official with the round pink face would do to a trader who fired at a native. Nothing, probably. Leyden was very young. The trader, Pollard, was the only other white resident of this little cluster of huts which are the last outpost of civilization in fifty thousand square miles of tangled, heat smitten, insect ridden South Sea jungle. Pollard was a hard bitten South Sea bully, and he could always explain that the native had been stealing.

The shot, however, seemed long delayed. Leyden, who had jumped up at the alarm, suddenly gripped Bill's shoulder. Up the path that led to the jungles of the interior trotted a native so utterly savage in aspect as to be remarkable even in such a place. Bushy headed like all Papuans, he was uncommonly tall. Smears of white clay outlined every rib so that the lean, sinewy body recalled a skeleton. He wore a G-string of bark cloth. At every step knee bracelets of human bones rattled. At a businesslike angle he carried an eight-foot spear.

"Catch him—alive!" whispered the commissioner fiercely. "He is from the bush. Perhaps he knows!"

"Knows what?" Bellow Bill rumbled, but instantly he vaulted over the veranda rail into the path like a huge cat. Bill was six feet three in his socks, but the breadth of his shoulders and the depth of his chest were such that he did not look tall when he stood alone.

"Wait, friend!" he snapped at the native in a voice that had the booming crack of a mainsail jibed in a gale.

The native stopped, though the spear point dropped into line with Bill's chest.

"Shall I knock him out?" rumbled the latter coolly. "I've handled plenty of his kind on my pearling schooner."

"No, no, no!" Leyden babbled excitedly in English, and then shifted to Papuan. "Ask him if he knows where the white woman is lost in the jungle."

"You hear, friend? Speak!" Bill boomed.

The native understood. He grasped even that he was no longer threatened, for he lifted his spear, though he was still tensed for flight at the slightest hostile move.

"Tell him the white woman went into the jungle two years

Bellow Bill lunged with the spear.

ago to live with people like himself," Leyden babbled more excitedly. "Tell him I want to find her. Tell him I will equip an expedition and start at once to bring presents to his tribe, and if he can guide me I will give him more tobacco than he can carry!"

The eyes of the native widened at such a princely offer. He hesitated.

"I am a priest," he said mournfully. "Varema is war chief. Varema would kill me. I—have spoken."

He whirled, like a deer that leaps from a standing start he was in full flight before Bellow Bill could move. Two leaps took the native across the path. He plunged into the underbrush, and was gone.

"Donnerwetter!" Leyden roared. "He knew! She is alive! I was sure of it! If you could have held him—"

"Man, I offered to knock him cold for you," Bill grinned. "And if I'd had any idea what this was all about I'd never have taken orders." The pearler reached into his pocket and filled his mouth with fine-cut chewing tobacco.

"What kind of a white woman can live two years in bush where white men have never gone?" he demanded. "She's dead."

"An ordinary woman, yes," Leyden conceded. "But this woman is one of your scientists of America. Her name is Miss Joan Saunders of your Smithsonian Institution, and she is still alive, maybe, *because* she is a woman!"

"Meaning a tribe that would kill a white man because they were afraid of him might let a strange woman live among them?" rumbled Bill. He had heard of female ethnologists before, and his vast practical knowledge of South Sea natives made the scheme plausible.

"*Ja,*" Leyden nodded violently. "She is a strange woman, unmarried. The tribe guards her as it guards its own unmarried girls. While she observes the woman's tabus, no one could be more safe. The older women protect her from the men. But— she leaves for one year of study, and she is gone for two! Perhaps she has broken a tabu. Perhaps she is a prisoner, but where can I go to find her?"

Leyden swept an arm behind him at uncounted square miles of matted jungle. "I ask every native from the bush," he explained sadly. "That medicine man was the first who seemed to know. He has heard of her—"

"He's come from her," interrupted a surly voice. "If I could have found my gun I was going to shoot him in the leg to hold him. He just gave me a message, and skipped."

POLLARD HAD walked up the path so slowly and quietly that he had attracted no attention. He was a huge, unkempt man with a thick brown beard that hid his features. He scowled at Bill and mounted the veranda toward Leyden. When the big pearler sent a jet of tobacco juice close to his heels and followed, he turned with a darker scowl. Bellow Bill grinned.

"Commissioner, that medicine man said his name was Ohaea," Pollard reported. "He comes from a village that lies in a circular mountain—he must mean an extinct volcano, and there can't be so many of them—back there." Pollard pointed eastward into the heart of the jungle. "He says a white woman sent him, and that he slept eight times coming here. Eight days' march. Call it fifty miles. I can find the place," the trader boasted. "I savvy the bush, and the natives. Get your porters and I'll guide you."

"Ja," Leyden assented. "We start to-morrow, though the directions are very vague. If I could only be sure he was not lying, or understood why he would not wait to guide us—"

"Was that *all* Ohaea said?" Bill purred.

"Yes. And who the hell might you be?" Pollard scowled.

"A Yankee pearling skipper that stopped for fresh water," Bill retorted evenly. "Now that I've heard this white woman is an American, I'm going to join your expedition. I speak the lingo, and know something about natives myself."

Bellow Bill looked at Leyden, who nodded a confirmation.

"Three men are better than two," the latter remarked sententiously. "Even so, our party will be small, and weak. I am puzzled that Ohaea would not guide us, and that Miss Saunders would trust her message to the mouth of a native I do not understand at all. If she had sent a letter, or a map—"

"Did I say she didn't?" Pollard growled. "What I said was that the native didn't tell me nothing else, and he didn't. But he gave me this—and it's something no native ever made."

Sullenly the trader reached into his pocket and produced a cross about two inches long. On it was scratched with a knife-point:

HELP ME QUICKLY.   J.S.   2/19/31.

"Dated just eight days ago! To-morrow we start!" exclaimed Leyden.

Bellow Bill looked hard at Pollard. The cross had been rudely hammered out of soft, raw, placer gold.

CHAPTER II

AMBUSH

IN THE VAN of the expedition six naked brown porters were chopping a path through a matted tangle of vines and underbrush which covered an all but precipitous slope. In the rear the three white men cursed the heat which they had endured for eight days, the wood leeches which crawled through the tiniest gap in their clothing and, most of all, the thickness of the jungle.

The path they were cutting was like a tunnel walled with solid green. They could not see ten feet high. They could not tell whether the slope they were climbing was the side of an extinct volcano or only another hill. They had climbed dozens of hills, only to find a higher ridge just beyond.

Bellow Bill had climbed a tree an hour before and reported that a flat topped mountain ahead looked like an extinct volcano. Not far behind the expedition was a crumbling cliff of lava, with a talus of broken lava blocks below it. Every sign pointed to the fact that the expedition was near the goal, but meanwhile they must struggle with more heat, more jungle, more insects, and an oppressive silence that was broken only by the noise of their own brush-knives slashing through the lush foliage.

For two days the party had not encountered a native. It seemed to them all that they had worked their way into country too rough and mountainous for natives. Bellow Bill was guiding the party because he was a sailor who could read a compass better than the others, but he had special reasons for doubting whether the course he set would bring them to Joan Saunders.

Therefore the ambuscade was wholly unexpected. The attack was made utterly without warning, and with a silence that was both horrible and paralyzing. At one instant the porters were chopping a path into a green wall. The next, out of that green wall white specks darted from a dozen different points.

Suddenly, in the bare bodies of the porters quivered two-inch thorns, the butts wrapped in white kapok fiber to fit in a blowgun, the points smeared dark with sticky poison. The white men, further from the ambuscade and protected by clothing, fared somewhat better, but they were hit.

Bellow Bill jerked a poisoned thorn out of the breast of his khaki jacket before the point could scratch his skin. The porters had dropped their wood knives. They stood stock still, rigid and speechless with terror. Leyden's mouth was open. Pollard was gasping curses and clawing for a revolver jammed in the holster. Another moment would bring a second volley of arrows.

"Run, you fools!" Bill thundered. "Damn you, run! Back to that rock slide we passed!" His booming voice broke the spell of horror. With a shriek the porters turned and fled. Leyden ran. Pollard ran, but Bill stood his ground.

SIX TIMES he fired into that blank wall of green as fast as he could pull trigger. He aimed at nothing. He wanted noise, and as the gun clicked on an empty shell he shifted it to the left hand and snatched up a bush knife.

"Shoot, pigs!" he bellowed in that enormous voice, using the Papuan dialect. "Shoot! I'll reach one of you!"

The thin powder smoke drifted back into his face. He was crouched for the charge. The two-foot knife blade whirled around his head. There is no antidote for blowgun poison, but not one pinprick, not a dozen, could have stopped his rush. The Papuans in ambush knew it. There was not a sound from the wall of green. Not a leaf quivered. They were hunters. They knew better than to attack a tiger at bay.

"Pigs! Women!" Bill snarled. For him the moment of greatest danger had come. Cool as he was reckless, he hurled the brush knife into the tangled underbrush, whirled on his heel and ran, head drawn low behind the shelter of his spreading shoulders.

The white-tipped darts flew around him as he turned, but

he felt no wound, and his stand had covered the retreat of the others. Fortunately the rock slide he had mentioned was close at hand, and once in the open, the firearms of the survivors would be more than a match for the blowguns. What was left of the expedition could fight.

There was, however, very little left. The poison acted fast. One by one Bill ran past the porters struck in the first volley. With them lay the food, the water, the spare ammunition of the expedition, but Bill dared not pause even for such necessities. Ahead was the rock slide.

He plunged out of the jungle onto a slope where the heat of the sun, gathered by the sharp volcanic stones, scorched his feet and rose against his face like the breath of a stove. A cliff of seamed and jagged lava about forty feet high afforded a scant strip of shade, and here Pollard and Leyden had made their stand. They menaced the jungle with drawn guns.

"Save your lead!" Bill boomed warningly. He scrambled up the slope to join the others, wiped away the sweat that had runneled out on his face, and filled his cheek with tobacco.

"Well," he announced conversationally in his deep, rumbling voice, "we're a hell of a rescue party! Are either of you carrying a canteen, or any spare shells?"

They weren't, and Bill had seen that at a glance. Nevertheless, though eight days of jungle travel had taught him much about his companions, the manner in which they reacted to a defeat which was at the very least stunning disaster, and in all probability a prelude to death, would reveal far more. Bill's own mind was made up but he wanted the next move to be suggested by the other two.

"There is a dart in your sun helmet. In the back," said Leyden.

Bellow Bill grunted with approval. The politeness of manner was unforced. The childlike blue eyes in the flushed pink face were round and wide, but there was no trace of panic or dread. Though Leyden was too frail to be of much physical assistance in breaking through a cordon of savages, his nerve could be relied upon.

BURLY, BEARDED Pollard stared sullenly at the jungle edge and at the waves of heat rising from the rocks. He said nothing. He was not afraid, either. Yet, though the unkempt brown beard concealed the exact character of his emotion, he was evidently strongly moved.

"I am sorry for the porters," said Leyden soberly. "Though even if they were here, we could do nothing for them."

"Nothing," Bill rumbled.

"As for us," the commissioner went on hesitantly, "we cannot stay here; is that agreed? We should die of thirst. Since we must go, I think we should go ahead. This is an extinct volcano we are on, not so? Perhaps the village, and Miss Saunders, are not far ahead. We should go on. *Ja!*"

"What do you say, Pollard?" Bill demanded.

"What good is a revolver in thick brush against a blowgun? None!" growled the trader sullenly. "We might as well push on as far as the village, if it's beyond this cliff. That woman may have these blacks eating out of her hand after all. Might be able to help us—"

"Why?" Bill rumbled.

"Why, just because a woman yells for help don't prove she needs it," Pollard growled.

"That so? Did you ever hear of a native attack on an expedition as strong as ours absolutely without warning or any offence given?"

"No," the trader conceded.

"Neither did I. The thing ain't in Papuan nature," Bill rumbled. "I've made up my mind to go on, but—I'm wondering. Somehow we've given these Papuans offence. Damned serious offence. Every bit of the dope that guides this expedition has come through you. You know the bush, and the natives. So I'm asking you: *what offence?*" the booming tone of the last two words echoed from the cliff.

"Think you're the big boss, hey?" Pollard retorted dangerously. The bearded lips parted. His eyes narrowed, and both hands hooked in his belt, bringing the right close to the butt of his revolver.

"All right—and the hell with you, you damn hell-for-leather Yankee!" he snarled. "I'm as good a man as you any time, even if I can't make so much noise, and you can put that in your pipe! We were attacked because we are *here,* that's why! This is the volcano we were looking for, all right, because the native that come to my store warned me that no strange warrior goes in or out of them cliffs. It's a tabu."

Bellow Bill took a quick forward step that brought him breast to breast with the trader.

"But why did you not tell us before?" Leyden exclaimed indignantly.

"What for? What could we do about it in the damned bush?" the trader retorted with brutal sarcasm. "What do you suppose I brought you along for? I couldn't go poking in here alone. Your damned Dutch red tape wouldn't have given me permission to explore, and I couldn't equip an expedition anyhow. Gawd, you're dumb! All you looked at was the cross. *Where did the gold it was made out of come from, hey?*"

"You came for the gold, and not for a helpless woman—" Leyden began bitterly.

"Sure. Why not?" Pollard retorted, with brutal defiance.

"But *donnerwetter!*" the commissioner exploded.

"Shut up, Leyden. As he says, why not?" Bill cut in. "I guess you don't savvy roughnecks. There was two colors of placer gold used in makin' that cross. I saw that." The pearler's left fist suddenly doubled. He was standing close enough to knock Pollard down before a gun could possibly be drawn. Bill grinned. He reached out with his right hand, palm up, fingers open.

"You got nerve, but I'll trouble you for your gun," he purred to the trader. "You'd better carry mine, which is empty. I ain't sure that we've got the whole truth out of you yet."

Pollard weighed the chances, and shrugged. Though his expression was ugly he handed over the revolver without a word. With equal calm Bill turned to survey the cliff.

"Then—then it is the gold with you, too!" Leyden burst out.

"I don't hate the stuff. Still, you better learn to size up rough-necks," Bellow Bill answered. "I can climb that cliff—"

He stopped. All three men started. Over the edge of the cliff, fifty feet above their heads, a blowgun was being thrust.

CHAPTER III

BETRAYAL

FOOT BY FOOT the slender wooden tube was projected until almost its entire length was extended over the cliff. Bill caught a glimpse of a slim brown hand.

"You fire, Leyden. Lead's scarce, and I'm a rotten shot," the pearler whispered. "But wait till I give you the word! That native's careless, or—"

The blowgun began to swing from side to side in wide arcs, as though it were a fishpole moving an invisible bait on an invisible line. Timidly the huge, bushy head of hair of a Papuan poked over the cliff-edge, and was drawn back. A slim brown hand beckoned to the men below.

"A girl! Let's go!" Bill boomed. Instantly he began to climb the cliff.

"A savage!" whispered Leyden. "Suppose it's a trap?"

"Suppose it ain't," the pearler rapped out. "There'll be a warrior there soon enough anyhow!" With a sailor's agility he climbed by the seams and cracks in the lava cliff. More slowly Leyden and Pollard followed. The blowgun was withdrawn.

As Bellow Bill crawled over the edge of the cliff the girl was not in sight. Ten feet away the underbrush grew like a green wall. He started to draw his gun—and the leaves parted. A brown hand beckoned to him and vanished. He heard the snap of a twig as the girl retreated.

"Hurry, lads—and don't follow me too damn close!" he whispered grimly to the men behind, and pushed into the thicket after his guide, whom he could follow by the stirring of the leaves. Experienced in the bush though he was, he could not avoid tripping over vines. Gain he could not. Always, just ahead, the disturbed leaves were slipping back into place. The sweat rolled off Bill. Behind him Leyden and Pollard were gasping and stumbling.

For a long distance the way led through the jungle. The opportunity to ambush or capture the white men was perfect. Then, unexpectedly, Bill found himself on a native trail. It was little more than a crevice in the dense jungle where no vines grew, but he grunted with relief. Even a few feet of clear vision was preferable to none, and on his left, half concealed by a twist in the trail, the girl was beckoning excitedly.

Bill began to run. So did she. They crossed a level plateau, and descended a slope that was almost a cliff. The trail became broader. Once on the level ground again Bill passed a breadfruit tree, and then another. He slackened his pace enough to let his companions overtake him.

"We're getting into a village, all right," he panted. "The girl's on the level, but don't follow her into the community house. I've been into one of those big grass-walled barns. They're traps."

More slowly, to save what little wind he had for a sprint or a fight, he ran on, and suddenly the three white men were at the edge of a clearing which was roughly a quarter of a mile in diameter. Involuntarily Bellow Bill halted. Before him spread a Papuan village which was typical except for one structure. The leaf-thatched grass-walled community house, fifty feet long and nearly thirty broad, dried and yellowed by the sun, raised above the ground on piles to the height of a tall man, with chickens scratching for garbage in the space beneath, was what he expected. A brook which angled across the clearing, cutting deeply into the gravelly soil, was not extraordinary. The naked children playing in the sun, the two women bearing fruit from the jungle, the warrior who dozed on the veranda of the long house with a spear across his knees, might have been duplicated at any Papuan village in all New Guinea.

BUT AT the upper edge of the clearing, built directly across the brook, was a small, boxlike, loop-holed stone fort such as Bill had never seen before except in the Marquesas Islands. Before the whites came to the South Seas powerful native tribes had built such forts. This one was still in good repair and still occupied, for a thread of smoke rose over the flat roof. Toward it the native girl was running like a frightened doe.

The sentinel at the long house sprang up with a wild yell. The children scattered. In the distance the women dropped their burdens and scuttled for the forest. Before Bellow Bill and his companions had covered fifty yards warriors were rushing one by one out of the long house like ants from a nest. At least twenty must have been waiting with blowguns and spears in hand. In a yelling mass they raced to intercept the white men, and though the girl, with her head start, was able to pass them and reach the stone fort, it was evident at once that the white men could not.

"Let 'em have it, Leyden!" Bill boomed. "Shoot, man! We're swamped if they close in!"

The pearler had stopped. His gun was drawn, but it was pointed at the ground. With head and chin outthrust, a fixed grin on his face, and golden flecks dancing in his eyes, he was judging the character of the attack. Fifty yards away the band of savages drove toward him Spears were leveled. Clubs waved. They were charging home.

"Break them apart, Leyden. I'll get you through," Bill boomed.

The little pink-faced Dutchman took a forward step, and a deep breath. With arm rigid he raised the revolver high, and brought it down slowly. At fifty yards a black body racing at the gunsights behind a flashing spear, with, other spear tips, other bodies, other faces to left and right, is not an easy target.

The revolver spat. A Papuan pitched on his face, dead. Two more pitched over the body and the spear he dropped. Another shot. The leading spearsman crumpled. Leyden's pink face was mottled with white patches, but there was a different note in the yells, and at twenty-five yards the charge had slowed to a trot. Twice more Leyden fired, each shot a bull's-eye. The charge wavered.

"Now!" roared Bill in his tremendous voice. Straight at them he dashed. Ten feet away he fired twice into the mass. They broke. One desperate spear thrust Bill knocked aside with one sweep of his revolver barrel, stretching the warrior senseless with a second. The others were scattering before these white men who sent death with every bullet.

Through the mob and toward the door of the fort the three sprinted. The heavy wooden barrier was swung back and they plunged into a room that was gloomy as a cellar, with only two bars of sunlight shining through loopholes for illumination.

"Well done," said a girl's voice in English. The door slammed shut and a heavy bar thudded into place behind it. "You're safe now, for the moment. I'll bring you some water, and food." She paused. Her voice was low, almost husky; controlled, and yet shot through with a thrill of excitement like the high note of a violin that rises above the deeper melody of an orchestra. "I'm Joan Saunders, of course," she went on. "I knew my cross would bring you if anything would, but I was afraid Tina wouldn't be in time to warn you of the ambush. This tribe can fight like white men, almost."

The thrill of excitement rose more clearly. "You won't mind that! This brook is full of placer gold! You can dig out a fortune from the gravel here in this cellar!"

"And get it to the settlement—how?" rumbled Bellow Bill.

"That has puzzled me for more than a year." Joan Saunders stepped back, so that a beam of sunlight fell upon her face. Bill's mental picture of a female ethnologist underwent a transformation so abrupt that he grunted. He had visualized a woman of forty, scrawny and plain. He saw a girl browned by the sun, hardened by jungle life and primitive diet as was to be expected, but to a man who prefers good looks without powder and rouge, beautiful.

JOAN WAS certainly not over twenty-six. Her chin was round and determined. Under straight, rather heavy brows, brown eyes sparkled with a reckless challenge. That she had come to a spot where men had been hard put to follow no longer seemed so extraordinary. Rather the mystery became why so competent and forceful a personality should have called for help at last.

"With this tribe gold is tabu," she explained. "Their god is a nugget as large as your head, shaped roughly like the head and face of a man. They worship that, and they believe that the smaller nuggets in the brook are the children of the god, and that he will be displeased if they are disturbed. When I saw that nugget-idol I forgot that I was a scientist, I'm afraid."

"Ja," Leyden nodded gravely.

"How big was it?" whispered Pollard.

"Oh, seventy or a hundred pounds. Naturally I haven't been allowed to lift it. It's in the long house on top of a pole, with a most interesting arrangement of human heads above it. I've a sketch of the whole thing in my ethnological notes. Well, I soon found smaller nuggets in the brook, and I was almost speared on the spot.

"I was too excited to observe the tabus governing the women, you see, and that's what a woman must do. I learned that even the men must not lift or keep a piece of gold, and that no strangers were allowed to leave the crater." Joan smiled, and shrugged. "But I kept two of the nuggets that I picked up. That's what made the cross."

"Kept them over a year?" Bill asked.

"Trying to persuade one of the more daring warriors to take them to the settlement to trade," Joan nodded. "Honey to bring flies, and gold for adventurers. I failed, but I lingered on. I couldn't give up—"

"And you liked the game of it," Bellow Bill rumbled.

The brown eyes flashed emphatic agreement.

"Though I don't see how you guessed that. A scientist isn't supposed to love risks. Of course they all do. Matching wits against a suspicious, timid people who can and will kill you for a whim. It's earth's greatest sport—"

" 'Ow thick is the gold?" Pollard breathed.

"Thick enough to pick up with your fingers. I never dared to dig again," said Joan briefly. "Well, I lingered too long. You see, my position with the tribe is exactly that of one of the tribe's own unmarried girls—who are guarded very carefully by all primitive peoples. But even savage girls do marry. The chief of the tribe, who is called Varema, decided to marry me. He had a perfect legal and moral right to do that, while I had no right whatever to refuse."

"Donnerwetter!" Leyden gasped.

"Just one of the risks, though the greatest," Joan smiled. "I'd prepared for it, somewhat, by making myself useful to the medicine man. I'd given him a few handfuls of effervescent salts, so that he was able to make cold water boil up. And a few grains of dye that he could tuck under his lip, so that he could spit first green, and then blue. I won't bore you with the rest of the tricks. You seem to know about them!" Joan exclaimed to Bellow Bill.

The big tattooed pearler nodded and filled his cheek with a generous portion of fine-cut.

"Then you can realize how they increased Ohaea's prestige. He was my friend, and he made the nugget idol say that the chief must not marry me. That was my ace, but Varema trumped it. He defied Ohaea and the idol, and got the warriors to support him. That meant open war between the chief and the medicine man. Ohaea took me in here, where even two girls and an old man could stand off a siege, and I was able to persuade him to go to the settlement with my golden cross. I told him that the result would prove that the idol had prophesied correctly," said Joan dryly. "But I expected a stronger party."

"It was, till Varema met us in the bush with blowguns," said Bill. He shifted his quid. "So we're six altogether. I've four cartridges left, and Leyden has two. Pollard ain't got any, on account of a misunderstanding."

"Aw, shut up!" snarled the trader. He was on his knees by the brook, trying to pan the gravel in his sun helmet.

"How many warriors has Varema got?" the pearler went on.

"About forty," Joan answered.

"Some Papuans are scared of wood devils and won't fight at night," Bill reflected aloud.

Joan swept away that hope. "Not these," she reported.

"And they're wise to all the usual tricks."

"Yes. I'm sorry—"

"Hell, what for? Damned if you ain't done better than a man so far!" boomed the pearler with a sincerity that made Joan's eyes drop. "Only we ain't got much to fight with and we got a hell of a long ways to run. I've got to figure a bit."

WITH AN oath Pollard leaped up and thrust a dripping hand into a beam of sunlight. His beard quivered as his jaws worked and his eyes glared.

"Look at that! Out of a hat—a *hat!*" he shouted.

In his palm was a streak of coarse gold dust, and a nugget half the size of a grain of rice. "I wasn't down to bed rock!" he babbled hoarsely. "That stuff ought to run fifty dollar pans!"

"Sure. Now go spend it," grunted Bellow Bill sarcastically.

Pollard stiffened. In another second he might have struck the bigger man out of sheer blind rage, but from the upper floor of the fort the girl Tina called out warningly in the dialect.

"Malita is coming—without blowgun or spear. He wants to speak to the white men!" she called.

"Who's he?" Bill whispered to Joan.

"Varema's younger brother, and the sub-chief," the girl whispered back.

"Then let him in," Bill decided.

The sub-chief, however, was too cunning to enter a trap so obvious as the open door of the fort. He stopped in the sunshine and demanded to see the chief of the white men.

Before Bellow Bill could move, Leyden crowded past him and stood in the doorway.

"I am the chief," the little Dutchman declared importantly. "I rule this land, under the queen who rules us all. I am angry at you—"

"You are ruled by a woman?" the savage marveled.

"Yes!" Leyden snapped. "I said I was angry because you killed my porters. Therefore send your chief to me now—at once—that I may judge him and fix the price of blood. This land we stand on is forfeit to me until the blood is wiped out!"

"Ah!" muttered Bill in the shadow of the door. "That's the game, eh? It's a swell bluff, even if it ain't going to work."

"Be still!" Leyden whispered over his shoulder. "So great a gold field must be controlled by the Crown. I must impress this chief."

Malita looked puzzled; then he spat. "With us a woman is a little thing," he declared. "The chief, my brother, says you fight well. The big man whose body is painted fights best. We could kill you all—"

"Hear him!" Joan whispered. "Bluffs are older than civilization! He means he's afraid he can't!"

"But why should great warriors fight over a trifle like a woman?" the savage continued blandly. "My brother wants the strange woman, as is right. He is sorry he attacked you, and if you leave he will attack you no more. He is not your enemy—"

"The woman leaves with us," Leyden snapped. "As for your brother, if he dares to attack us I will come with many men and burn his long house to the ground! Send your brother here himself. A chief talks only to a chief."

Defiance began to gather on the dark face of the savage.

"Step aside. I'll run out and grab him for a hostage," Bill whispered sharply. He leaned forward for the rush. He had forgotten Pollard, standing behind him in the semi-darkness. "Now go spend it," Bill had sneered at the trader, and left him standing with a pinch of gold dust gripped in his left fist, and his brain maddened by greed.

Softly Pollard drew the empty gun that Bill had forced on him. Suddenly he brought the barrel crashing down upon the exposed back of the pearler's head. Bill pitched forward on his face. Pollard stooped with a snarl and snatched the loaded revolver from his belt. Joan cried out, and Leyden, whirling, wide eyed, tried too late to pull a gun.

With a bound Pollard was on him. A gun butt crashed through the little Dutchman's sun helmet and struck heavily on the skull beneath. With a moan Leyden crumpled across the threshold. Pollard turned to snatch at Joan, but from the shadows where the girl stood streaked the flame of a shot.

Pollard staggered from the shock of the bullet. He swayed against the door jamb. The revolver dropped from his right hand, which he pressed against his ribs. From the shadows came a click as Joan recocked her weapon.

Pollard sprang outside the door and dodged out of her sight.

"I am a friend—a friend!" he shouted to the sub-chief in the dialect. "Quick! Come take your woman!"

CHAPTER IV

NIGHT MAGIC

PAINFULLY BELLOW BILL recovered consciousness. He lay in darkness. Therefore he had been out a long time. That was bad. He stirred, and found his limbs free; opened his eyes, and discovered he was still in the fort. That was good.

Leyden lay prone beside him. Beyond, a thread of rag burning in a dish of grease gave a mere glimmer of light.

"What happened?" Bill muttered.

"Why—I got the door shut in time," Joan answered crisply. Her voice was a vast relief to the pearler.

"Oh!" he rumbled.

"You see, I had a revolver of my own," she continued quietly. "I'd kept it—for emergencies. You understand?"

"Sure. The last cartridge and all that," Bill rumbled. "Pollard slugged me. You shot him—"

"Not seriously, unfortunately. Then he ducked out of the door and called to the natives. They rushed the fort, but after a few more shots they went back. Pollard called them back, in fact. I was shooting at him, mostly. They seemed to accept him as a leader, or at least as an ally."

"So?" Bill grunted. "Leyden dead?"

"Just knocked out."

The pearler sat up and touched an enormous lump on the back of his head.

"I guess Pollard decided we couldn't get away," Joan continued. "He was right to figure the natives would accept him. If he'd overpowered us he'd have been solid with the tribe and could have developed this gold field for his own, at his leisure."

"Chance he took wasn't much bigger than the one he was running," Bill growled. "I'm—I'm sorry, Miss Saunders. I don't often pull a boner."

"I imagine not. Well, it's done," the girl answered with a grim calm. "I'm sorry I sent for you, for that matter. I shouldn't have done it, but I guess if Pollard could go over to the natives, you and your friend can. You see, the brook—"

Bellow Bill started. That was the sound he had missed—the gurgle of water running through the fort.

"While you were out Pollard took all the natives upstream and dug a ditch to divert the water," Joan reported. "They're still busy, though the current has ceased flowing. I've filled every pot we had, but there weren't many of them. Enough for two or three days."

HERE, THEN, was the full measure of the disaster, and of Pollard's cunning. Unerringly and decisively he had struck at the weakest point. Bellow Bill was silent. Mechanically he mouthed a fistful of free cut. His big jaws worked for half a minute, and then he began to grin.

"As for surrendering the hell with it!" he boomed. "Pollard has got to kill Leyden and me first, and you later. Then he blames the job on the natives, so a punitive expedition takes care of them. He tells a yarn of how he made a miraculous escape to the under-officials at the settlement, and registers his gold claim. He's a damn straightforward, practical, treacherous bum," said Bill cheerfully. "So nix on sacrificing yourself, sister. It's die dog or eat the hatchet for him and us, too, and that's a help!"

"How?"

"Why, a big roughneck like me that's been slipped a ticket for his own funeral can get tough like you'd never believe!" Bill grinned. With narrowed eyes he stared at the glimmer of light.

During the last attack on the fort a blowgun dart had entered a loophole and now lay on the damp sand near what had been the edge of the brook. Thoughtfully the pearler picked up the thorn and wiped the poison off on his trouser leg. He played with it, rolling it between finger and thumb. Suddenly it disappeared.

"Careful! What became of that?" Joan cried out.

Bellow Bill grinned and opened his hand, revealing the thorn palmed between thick, muscular fingers. "Poison's gone, anyhow," he rumbled. "I'm going out to raise a little hell while Pollard and his buddies are busy with the brook." He leaned forward and blew out the light.

"Do you want the gun?" Joan whispered. "Still, its empty."

"I might use it to work a bluff with," Bill grunted. "Listen. Stand by for half an hour—savvy? Never mind the yelling.

There'll be plenty. You *wait*. You may think you can slip out, too, and make a run for the settlement, but that's too slim a chance. They'd be sure to catch you in the bush—savvy?"

"I suppose so," Joan agreed dubiously.

The door of the fort opened and shut. Bellow Bill was gone, belly down in what had been the bed of the brook. No wolverine, no tiger, could have moved with less sound.

The night was starlit. The sky seemed blue, almost light by comparison with the ink-black shadows cast by the banks of the stream. Inch by inch Bill crept in the direction of the long house. The gabble of savages at work came to his ears from the upper edge of the clearing. He could identify the voices of warriors, and also the tones of the women who were performing the actual labor.

Once, unmistakably, he overheard a command from Pollard. Most of the Papuans seemed to be gathered upstream, but Bill was positive that some sentinel would be posted to warn the warriors of just such a sortie as he was making. He was right. Soon he glimpsed the bushy head of a Papuan outlined against the sky. The sentinel was squatting at the bank of the stream, ten yards or so away. There was a spear across his knees. A blowgun pointed in a thin black line at the stars above.

ADVANCE FURTHER Bill dared not. He knew the keenness of savage ears, but that same sharpness of perception could be twisted to his advantage. Soundlessly he groped for a small pebble and snapped it like a marble down the stream bed beyond the savage. It fell with the faintest click of stone on stone, but instantly the bushy head turned. The blowgun snapped promptly into line with the sound.

Like a sprinter from a crouching start Bill rushed. The thud of his feet on the sand betrayed him. The sentinel yelled shrilly and swung the long blowgun to bear on the actual foe. But Bill had closed in. A sweep of his arm knocked the unwieldy weapon aside. His left fist smashed to the jaw. The sentinel dropped.

Bellow Bill knelt on his stomach, groping in the loin cloth

for the gourd of poisoned darts, snatching at the blowgun. There was a chorus of yells from upstream, echoed by the shout of a second sentinel posted lower down. The Papuans were charging.

In the shelter of the high bank Bill slipped a dart into the blowgun and placed the spear to his liking. Let them charge.

It was the misfortune of the other sentinel to arrive first. A dart from Bill's blowgun pricked his body as he rushed in. He screamed, but kept coming. Bill rose from the lower ground before him. All the vast strength of the pearler's back and shoulders went into a lunge with the spear.

There was no cry—only a horrible thud and gasp. Struck low in the body, the charging Papuan stopped as though he had collided with an invisible wall. For an instant he stood before the eyes of his fellow warriors, his arms up-flung, the head of the spear which transfixed him projecting a yard beyond his back. Then he toppled and lay kicking.

Already Bellow Bill was back behind the bank, the blowgun raised. A charging warrior cried out at the prick of a thorn. Already the front rank was too close, in the dim starlight, to stop. But none of the leaders cared to be the man to receive a second spear thrust such as the one which had toppled their comrade.

The charge divided. On Bill's right and left warriors leaped into the stream bed and crouched in the shadow of the banks. In front, the less venturesome flung themselves down to fight at long range. For a second Bill lingered. He gripped the spear dropped by the sentinel he had transfixed; he hoped to catch sight of Pollard, but the trader kept well back.

With a curse Bill flung himself out of the stream bed on the side opposite his enemies, rolling over and over on the ground, and keeping flat, for darts were beginning to fly. A Papuan raised his body above the stream banks, and was struck by a random missile. The cry of the warrior was music to Bellow Bill.

"Shoot, fools!" he bellowed. "Me you hit in the bush, and I am still here! Shoot, and kill yourselves!" The echoes of the great voice rolled back from the edge of the clearing. Bill puffed a dart at the head of a warrior, missed, and pushed himself backward. Life and death hung on the movement of that half visible, bushy head. If the warrior advanced, others would follow. They would surround Bill in the open. They would spear him like a cornered wolf. On the other hand, the bravest warrior might hesitate to leave the shelter afforded by the stream.

For an eternal second the bushy head was motionless. Then it disappeared, and Bill pushed himself backward again, faster and faster, until he dared to rise and run, bent double. He kept the blowgun and the spear. The warriors would follow, of course. There was no escape for him, but he sought none.

"SPREAD OUT!" bawled Pollard in the dialect. "Varema! Malita! Send your warriors into the bush! Don't let him escape! He is a night devil! We will kill him easily in the day!"

Bill grunted, and turned sharply to his left. He was running in a half circle, flanking the warriors who were spreading out, he hoped,, to flank him. He could not see them, but not far away was the dim bulk of the long house, which was his objective. He circled to get in the rear of the building, the side on which there was no veranda. He shifted blowgun and spear to his left hand, reached up and gripped the foundation beam and drew himself up.

The wall of grass and thatch against his face was thin, and dry as tinder. Within he caught a gleam from the embers of a fire. He thrust his body forward, bursting the wall, and tumbling into the huge main common room. An old woman screamed. Children yelled and scattered. An old man, crouched by the embers of the fire, stared, thunderstruck at the enemy who had dared to invade the stronghold, then reached, too late, for a blowgun.

Bill leaped across the floor and set his foot on the tube. He had guessed correctly. The fighting in the clearing had drawn the last warrior from the house. He grinned, and menaced the old man's throat with his spear point. Dozens of eyes were on him. The women he could neglect. Savage women do not fight, but there was danger that some half-grown boy would muster up courage to shoot from a door or through a chink in the partitions of the interior.

"Would you shoot me, grandfather?" Bill boomed in the dialect. The grin widened. "That would not hurt. See!" Bill stooped, and from the old man's gourd of darts pulled a freshly poisoned thorn. He held it high in his fingers where all could see. Suddenly his hand came down, slapped against his leg, and was slowly withdrawn.

There was a moaning gasp of astonishment from many voices. The thorn was stuck in his trousers, the point buried deep in his flesh.

Bill grinned. To the savages the thing was a miracle. They waited for the first symptoms of the poison to appear on his face, breathless, silent, though outside men were yelling as the warriors seeking Bill drew nearer and nearer to the long house.

"Have you seen enough?" Bill rumbled. Suddenly the grin was gone.

"Go!" he boomed, sweeping an arm at the women. "Hide your heads and hold your brats close! You"—the spear point darted near the old man's throat—"find Varema and your new white chief. Tell them the great chief wants them—here!"

Wide-eyed, the old man rose and moved toward the main door of the long house, which opened on the veranda. Bill looked swiftly around. Against the rear wall, about thirty feet from the door and directly opposite, was a thick post. An object the size of his head was mounted upon it, reflecting the firelight in golden gleams.

The post was thick enough to protect a man's back, even a back as broad as Bill's. He walked to it and turned, slipping a dart into his blowgun. The spear he laid on the floor, carefully placing the shaft across his right foot.

The women had vanished. Outside the yelling had ceased. A single voice was talking rapidly, almost incoherently, falsetto with excitement and awe.

"Go on, grandpop! You tell 'em!" muttered Bellow Bill.

CHAPTER V

THE TEST OF A CHIEF

HE WAS BRACED for an attack through the doorway. He hoped, even expected, that Pollard would head it in order to reestablish his leadership over the tribe. But there was a delay—a complete, sudden silence, only a second or two in duration, yet endless to Bellow Bill.

Two revolver shots broke the calm. They were fired *outside* the long house. Two more shots echoed them, followed by a shout from Pollard and a howl of triumph from the Papuans. The rush was coming—but in its van there dashed through the doorway, not the trader, but Leyden; white-faced, desperate, a smoking revolver swinging in his hand.

The little Dutchman was too intent, too hard pressed, to notice Bellow Bill. In the very doorway he whirled and whipped out matches to set the thatch alight.

"Belay that! One side!" Bill boomed.

The command came too late. The match had spluttered. A tongue of flame licked up the side of the door, caught on a projecting tuft of leaves, and leaped toward the roof above. Only then did Leyden seem to hear. He stepped aside, turning a strained and piteous face.

"I missed!" he gasped. "I tried to shoot Pollard, and I missed. Twice. I—I—"

"One side!" Bill snapped. The flaming doorway framed Pollard. Behind the trader were two warriors with spears. He leveled his gun, crouched, peering to locate Bellow Bill. Leyden he ignored. At the sight of him the little Dutchman dropped an empty revolver and drew himself up proudly, as though to die well.

All this was in the catch of a breath. As Pollard sighted,

Bellow Bill flipped his spear into his hand with a quick jerk of his foot. The sweep of his arm, the flash of the spearhead as it sped, were simultaneous with the report of the revolver.

A bloodstain started out on the pearler's jacket—but the spearhead was deep in Pollard's chest. The bearded face jerked back. Pollard dropped the gun and caught with both hands at the shaft of the spear. The wound was mortal. He swayed and fell.

With a deep pitched roar Bellow Bill followed the spear. Pollard had barely touched the floor before the pearler was astride his body. One wrench jerked the spear free. A huge warrior with feathers in his bushy hair was first to recover. He shortened his spear for a thrust. Bill knocked the point aside and gripped the Papuan by the body. For an instant they were locked. Then the pearler caught his own spear a foot back from the point and struck with the unwieldy weapon as though it were a dagger.

The thrust did not travel ten inches, yet the spear point showed red behind Varema's throat. Like a sack Bill threw the warrior across his hip, swung him into the air and hurled him at the heads of the other Papuans.

"Is that your chief?" he thundered. "Or *that?*"

Bill stooped. He caught Pollard by both ankles, and with a sweeping heave flung him at the mob. Two warriors were knocked down. The rest gave back. One slipped on the edge of the veranda and fell to the ground. Malita, foremost now, gaped at Bill across the two bodies. The warriors who had been knocked down crawled right and left like snakes, leaving their spears.

"Or am I the chief?" Bill thundered at Malita. The pearler held a spear gripped for a cast. Flames were roaring in the roof overhead. A thin shower of red-hot leaf stems was falling around him like burning snow. If he felt the burns nothing showed it.

Malita dropped flat on his face. Then shoved himself backward, falling rather than crawling from the veranda edge to avoid the threat of that ready spear.

"Go!" Bill bellowed after him. "Go hide in the bush with your women, or I will kill you all!"

Already the women had fled. Already the bulk of the warriors were on the run. Last of all Malita darted from the shelter afforded by the veranda into the firelight. He was bent double, running his best, and he was headed straight for the bush. Cowed, overawed, gripped by superstitious fear, the last bit of fight was out of the tribe.

"Leyden! Outside and get Joan!" Bill ordered in English. "We'll hit the trail back. They'll never follow before sunrise—if then."

With arms shielding his head and his jacket blackened by falling embers the commissioner dashed into the open. As he passed, Bill turned and walked without haste into the blazing interior of the long house.

YET AS Leyden was rapping at the door of the stone fort Bellow Bill came striding across the fire-lit clearing, his shadow enormous before him. A blowgun and a spear were across his shoulder. His jacket, wadded into a thick bundle, was held against his side.

The door opened and Joan uttered a low cry of pleasure and relief.

"I heard the shots," she began. "Leyden wanted me to run, but I wouldn't until I was sure—"

"He's wounded," the commissioner interrupted.

"A scratch along the ribs. It'll stop bleeding of itself," the pearler rumbled. "That's nothing. I'm glad—"

"But of course!" Leyden broke out volubly. "How can I—how can my government thank you? I did what I could, and it was nothing. But I will write a report, you shall see! To the governor! To the queen herself in Holland, God bless her. You will be rewarded—"

"Buddy, will you shut up?" Bill boomed. "After a fight some guys take to drink, and some to conversation. Damn if you ain't gone and spoiled the only highfalutin' speech I ever come near making in my life."

"I—I am sorry. I do not understand."

"No, you don't savvy roughnecks," Bill growled. "Your head is full of governors and queens. You mean well, and you got nerve, but you just don't savvy. You're seeing yourself the commissioner of a district with a gold field in it right now, ain't you?

"The road to the coast is clear. We could make those Papuans act as porters to us now, I reckon, though I figure it would be better to fade before they get their nerve back. More mysterious, and besides their god might tell them to make one more try to keep strangers from violatin' the tabu of the valley. You'd better come back with a big expedition, Leyden—"

"Which you will command, *ja!* In my district you are the great man!" the little Dutchman insisted. "I do savvy, as you say. I am not so foolish as to think that gold is the stuff that builds empires. No! It is what you call the roughnecks, men like your-self—"

"And Pollard. He'd have built the empire, and Holland would have had it just the same," Bill grinned. "No, you'll never savvy. But there's one that does!"

"Thanks, Bill," said Joan quietly. "I think I do. I came in here to learn the songs that Papuan mothers sing to their babies. That sounds almost silly, now, doesn't it?" She paused. "I'd like to hear your highfalutin' speech," she suggested.

"Too late," Bill rumbled. "And what of it? We're wise, you and I. I'm the skipper of a pearling schooner on the loose, with a tattooed hide and a taste for chewing tobacco and hell raising. I can't stay in one place anyhow, and the only place except the South Seas for me is a circus. But," the big voice boomed out, "I rate you a hundred per cent. And if you ever need help from me again you won't have to send a gold cross to get it."

"You may not be such a roughneck as you think, Bill," the girl answered quietly. "But—you seem to know yourself, and what you want. So that *is* that. And what in the world have you got in your jacket?"

Across the face of the big pearler flashed a mocking, reckless grin.

"That?" he chuckled. "Oh, I just took what I thought I could get. That's the nugget the tribe used for an idol. Seemed like a pity to leave it to melt, and it 'll be a souvenir worthy of the game. Let's march, buddies! It's a long road back to the coast."

SPEARHEAD

Bellow Bill Williams, South Seas pearler,
was too good a sailor to wreck his own ship
if there had been any other way out

CHAPTER I

SHIPWRECK

BELLOW BILL WILLIAMS left his own pearling schooner moored to the government dock in the harbor at Port Denison, Australia, and sailed alone in a rotten unseaworthy old craft that he bought for ten pounds.

The exchange of ships was peculiar, but if Bill's subsequent maneuvers had been observed—he took great care that they were not—the kindest and the most logical explanation would have been that the big, tattooed sailorman with the booming voice had gone absolutely and hopelessly insane. He had a habit of doing everything backwards.

In the first place, he hurried along the coast of Cape York for five hundred miles as fast as he could drive; and then, for no apparent reason, and with a fair wind behind him, he dodged into a little bay where there were neither pearls, nor white men, nor anything save silence, heat, and a grove of mangroves which screened him from discovery.

Here he remained four days, all his hurry forgotten; fishing, sleeping and whetting a ten-inch deep-sea diver's sheath knife. Not until the sky clouded over and every sign indicated that one of the dreaded Australian busters was about to break on the coast did he bestir himself—and then he removed a wire backstay which was the strongest part of the standing rigging of his rotten old ship. He replaced the wire with a jury rigging of manila rope.

Even this did not satisfy him. He arranged a draw knife on

The wild dogs showed their wolf blood as they attacked.

a cord at the foot of the backstay so that he could cut his jury rigging without leaving the wheel, and then, in the teeth of a storm which would have made any sane sailor thankful for shelter, he tacked out to sea.

A few miles up the coast, however, the method in his madness began to appear. As he rounded a little promontory the dark green forest of brush and mangrove trees which stretched for hundreds of miles to the south and extended, as Bill knew, as far to the north, was broken by a square patch about a hundred acres in extent where the foliage was a lighter grayish green and the trees were coconut palms, hitherto unseen along the coast.

Two houses, one big, and one small, with red sheet-iron roofs became visible; a copra drying shed, and at the mouth of a small river, a pier. The place was an oasis of cultivation in the heart of a wilderness.

Bill's old ship had begun to make heavy weather of the storm. Nevertheless he held his course, refusing to luff even when the mainsail was all but flattened to the seas, apparently striving with all his seamanship to weather the next point.

A white woman ran onto the pier, her white duck skirt flying

in the wind, and beckoned him frantically toward the land. A white man followed by a dozen half naked black fellows dashed out of the coconut grove and lined up at the edge of the surf.

Bellow Bill nodded with approval. Norcross was evidently no fool, and neither was the sister. The wind was increasing in force. A ship caught on a lee shore, as Bill seemed to be, must either come about and scud for the mouth of the river or beat its way out to sea. The line of black fellows ready at the edge of the surf was evidence that Norcross had both the imagination to anticipate a danger and the force of character to lead savage plantation laborers into an unfamiliar task.

Bill waved reassuringly toward the shore, swung the bow of the ship to seaward—and pulled on the drawknife. Like a flash the backstay parted. The mast, unsupported, snapped off a foot above the deck. For an instant the old vessel survived. Then a comber rolled her bottom up. In that last second, however, Bill dove over the rail. His head reappeared, well beyond the wreckage, and he struck out, swimming strongly as a duck or a pearl diver, for the land he had seemed to disdain.

The distance was less than half a mile. Bill was in no more

danger than a man must run who elects to wreck a vessel in the open sea in the midst of a gale. There was a human chain waiting for him in the surf, but he managed to make the mouth of the river and to climb the piling of the pier without assistance. His would-be rescuers had gathered at the spot. The bush blacks, who hate and fear salt water, were chattering and staring open mouthed at the sight of a feat which to them bordered on the miraculous.

"I say, bully swimming!" Norcross applauded. He was a tall, sandy haired youngster of twenty-five, burned red by the sun, with the quick, bright eyes of the enthusiast.

"When your boat turned over I gave you up," said the sister. Although four years younger than her brother, Evelyn Norcross possessed the more mature character. She was small, graceful, and quick, though Bellow Bill noticed those qualities later. At the moment he noticed she was beautiful, and found himself speaking, without knowing why, as though to a man his equal in courage and resolution.

"Why, no," he boomed in a voice deeper than the note of the surf. "I crowded my luck and trusted too much to my ship, that's all. I didn't want to land, but I'm here now till a trader takes me off."

"Yes, your boat has already broken up on the beach. Traders won't pass with the hurricane season coming on. You're here for three months at least." She looked up. "You would trust too much in the strength of the things around you. Naturally. I don't blame you. I wish I could."

Bellow Bill stood six feet three. He tipped the scales at two hundred and forty, with not a pound fat. He would have been judged handsome anywhere, except that from wrists to neck and from neck to waist his skin was covered with tattooing. The dragon on his back was Chinese work, the ship on his chest had been pricked in at Hoboken, for he was American born. Some may consider tattooing a blemish, yet for a man whose life is spent among primitive peoples it has uses.

"I SAY, you'll live with us, of course," Norcross interrupted hospitably. "Eh, Evelyn? Losing ship and cargo like that! Quite a facer, eh? But there are opportunities here. Marvelous! Really! All the land you want, and jolly good labor. Blacks are lazy, but not vicious. Eh, Evelyn?"

"Yes, we'll be glad of company." The girl was looking past Bill. The pearler turned. The third, and the most important white resident of this oasis in the wilderness was walking calmly down the pier.

HE WAS a small, wizened man on the threshold of old age, buttoned to the chin in snow white, stiffly starched ducks. Hair and beard were cut close, probably with sheep clippers, and were of a peculiar grizzled yellow color like the coat of a dingo—the Australian wild dog. He walked stiffly, moving his legs from the hips and his arms from the shoulder, and turning his head whenever he wished to glance to right or left. His eyes were fixed constantly straight ahead.

Both of these physical peculiarities gave an impression of set, predetermined purposefulness. By reputation Bill knew Dingo Trelawney. To read into his appearance the characteristics which Dingo was known to possess was natural, yet though the pearler was prepared to encounter an exceptional man, he was more than a little startled.

A back handed slap would have knocked Dingo down, but Bill would as soon have thought of striking a pane of glass. Dingo was hard, rigid; and therefore not a man to handle carelessly.

"Come to my house," the planter commanded.

"But I say!" Norcross protested. "I've already invited Mr.— er—"

"Williams," said Dingo. "Even I have heard of Bellow Bill Williams. Even here. There can't be two men that big, and tattooed like that." Every word was bitten off. The bearded lips scarcely moved. "He goes where most men won't. He never asks to see a profit in advance, and he falls on his feet, like a cat. I'm flattered to have him call on a stick-in-the-mud like me."

"Call?" Bill rumbled.

"Come to my house," Dingo repeated. "Later you may come back."

The planter turned, all in one piece, and walked away as though a refusal were inconceivable. Bill shrugged vast shoulders, grinned at Norcross, and followed. He was guided for a short distance through a grove of coconut palms which were superbly cultivated and loaded with green nuts. Beyond was the big house the red roof of which had been visible from the sea.

The broad veranda commanded a view of the river mouth and the ocean, and though the wind was cold and unpleasant Dingo motioned Bill to sit down in the open and handed him a pair of field glasses.

"You'll see your ship is a complete wreck," he stated.

Bill looked.

"Those are the best field glasses you ever looked through."

"They're good," Bill boomed.

"They cost the value of twenty tons of copra in Germany before the war," said Dingo categorically. "They're worth the price. For instance, I watched you through them." The planter smiled. "Bill," he directed, "let's leave lying to new-chums. That wreck of yours must have looked very convincing—to the naked eye. But I haven't survived thirty years in the bush to be caught napping. What did you come to get from me?"

BELLOW BILL handed the glasses back.

"I'm not sure," he rumbled—which was the truth.

"Your trick was smart," Dingo declared with relish. "If you'd sailed into my harbor in the ordinary way I'd have filled your vessel with cargo and sent you off inside of twenty-four hours. Now I'm compelled to treat you as my guest, even though you're an enemy. You've got to stay here a couple of months, and I'm not foolish enough to think I can control you by force. I'm sixty years old, and I've just one faithful body servant to back me up. The rest of the laborers would scatter like mice if you shouted at them. So you've succeeded. Whatever you want you can take. I can afford to be robbed, but by God! I'm too old and too proud to pretend to be hoodwinked!"

"I don't like tricks either," said Bill as calmly as though his plans had not been completely overturned. "I'm no thief, and I'm not your enemy—I hope. You've suddenly become important to the world, Dingo."

"What?"

"Straight goods. You turned up here out of nowhere thirty odd years ago, Dingo, and started to clear the bush and plant coconuts—though a coconut tree had never grown on York Cape before. Everybody prophesied you'd be eaten, get sick, or starve. Nobody gave a damn. You were just one more fool pioneer trying the impossible."

"Who told you all this?"

"The Governor of Queensland, no less. You're famous, Dingo. As a matter of fact," Bill continued with complete sincerity, "your name has been well known ever since I came out to the South Seas. Even a sailorman like me heard about you—even hundreds of miles away in the pearl lagoons," he added ironically. "The stories weren't altogether to your credit. Dingo Trelawney was the queer customer who developed a plantation where no one else would go on a bet, and then stayed right on his land. As one old-timer to another," Bill grinned, "you were and you are considered a bit balmy. You haven't shown your nose in a town—any town—for thirty years."

"That's no reason to wreck a ship," Dingo answered stiffly.

"It wasn't, but it is. Little by little you put a problem before the Governor that's worth more than a ten pound ship to have answered. Maybe that surprises you. I figured no one would be much interested in me until you hauled out those field glasses. Maybe you've been figuring the same—but the Governor has a memorandum of every yarn that has been told about you for thirty years, a copy of your advertisements for settlers, and the letters you wrote to the applicants."

"I'm flattered," Dingo sneered.

"I hope so," Bill replied gravely. "Because this is what the Governor said to me: 'Williams,' he said, 'up on York Cape is one of the greatest pioneers Australia has ever produced. He's a man I'd be eager to help and to honor, except that there's evidence that loneliness has driven him insane. I'm afraid he's done murder, and I'll have to put him in an asylum. Go there and live with him during the hurricane season, and report to me which step to take.'"

BELLOW BILL delivered the ultimatum impersonally, in a level tone. Dingo's eyes closed for an instant. Not another muscle moved. He might have been prepared both for the praise, and the accusation.

"You've the devil's own impudence—and courage—to force yourself into my house and tell me that," he stated.

"Why, no. As you've said, I'm not afraid of you," Bill answered honestly. "It's the honors that we want to give you, if possible. I'm not here as a policeman, Dingo. This game is bigger than justice. Let me ask you another question: what is a fair price in human lives for the prosperity and happiness of a couple of million people? Six lives? Six have died already. Would nine lives be too much? I don't think so, even though mine were the ninth."

"That's crazy talk."

"It would have been. It isn't any more," said Bill earnestly. "We're a pair of South Sea roughnecks who can get along in wild country. Governors never used to give a damn about us, but to-day there's millions of people all over the world crying out to their Governors for work. There aren't jobs enough to go around in the old countries, so the Governors are trying to find new. There's new land enough here on Cape York to keep a million people busy and prosperous for generations—if the conditions are right. Isn't it worth an old ship and a pearler's tattooed hide to find out? I think so."

"And how will you and your precious Governor find out?"

"You've proven that *you* can settle on York Cape and prosper," Bill boomed. "Once the Governor is convinced that other men can do as well he'll throw this country open to homesteaders. Little by little the millions will settle here, and bring prosperity with them. The point is, are you the rule or the exception? You've lived. The first six men who followed you died."

"Therefore you suspect I killed them. That's logic. Quite like a colonial Governor," Dingo sneered. The stiff arms and legs stirred. "For what reason?" he snarled. "Williams, you and your damned Governor are going too far! This *is* a white man's country! Twenty years I spent proving it, and ten more trying to develop it, and as a reward I'm to be dragged off to an asylum and pawed over by doctors! When I'd cleared all the land I needed myself I advertised for young, patriotic Australians. No riffraff, no city spoiled Englishmen, but younger sons of good Australian families who knew something of the back country. I offered them free land, seedlings, the use of my labor—"

"More than any government could offer settlers," Bill cut in with the big voice that drowned argument. "You did all that, and one after another six good men died. Six deaths in ten years. Norcross is the seventh, his sister the eighth, and I'm the ninth. Six settlers don't disappear by accident in a country fit to be settled by white men."

"Who claims they did?" Dingo shouted. His voice rose to a falsetto and cracked. "After the first death, didn't I warn the other five that they must stay on the plantation, as I did? The Governor has my letters. Didn't I insist they must develop the *land?*"

"You did, and that very thing hints at a secret, or worse," said Bill calmly. "Tell a young Australian of the right spirit that he's got to stay, and he's going to go, in spite of hell. You wanted me to leave the lying to new-chums. I'm agreeable. I was sent here to prevent any more accidents during the hurricane season. After- ward my orders are to take you to Port Denison—either as the honored guest of the Governor, or as a material witness in the death of six settlers. Just as you prefer. We're going to check the possibilities of York Cape as a country for white settlers once and for all. The Norcrosses are distantly related to the present Governor, and are the children of a former Governor. Nevertheless they are to be left here alone to live or die. That will show you how much in earnest we are, and how far we're willing to go."

For a moment Dingo was silent. Then he smiled bitterly.

"On your heads be it," he said. "I shall go to Port Denison, if I must, but I think Norcross will die."

"From what?"

"Folly!" Dingo affirmed. "You insist on learning the secret I have tried to keep. Learn it and be damned!" From the breast of the starched white jacket he produced a large quill, stripped of the feathers and stoppered with a wisp of cotton. Into Bill's hand he poured a few yellow grains.

"Gold?" rumbled the pearler.

"Quite so. Gold," Dingo sneered. "When I came here thirty years ago the natives used to wear these quills stuck in their hair. That's not the worst. For a few pounds of tobacco, which is far more valuable than gold to them, they'll take any white man to the spot where they find the stuff. As fast as my settlers learn the native lingo they head into the interior and never come back." Dingo snapped his fingers. "Folly!" he snarled. "In thirty years I haven't seen five hundred dollars' worth of gold dust altogether, but the sight of a pinch or two is enough to drive a young man mad. They could stay and raise copra and get rich, like me. Will they? None of them have yet!"

"And you've never tried to find the diggings?" Bellow Bill rumbled deep in his broad chest.

"I'd other fish to fry," Dingo snapped. "I'll admit I've been tempted, but I kept sane enough to weigh the values. Something slow and sure and safe is better than a wild goose chase." The grizzled, yellowish beard twisted savagely. "I shall be delighted to supply *you* with a guide," Dingo challenged. *"But keep the secret from Norcross.* I want to make him a planter, if I can!"

CHAPTER II

YELLOW DUST—AND BLACK

HAD BELLOW BILL been a free agent he would have demanded the guide on the spot. He had prospected before— for gold in Borneo and for diamonds in Papua, and though he was well aware that a man may find gold and still remain poor, the lure of the unknown fired his blood.

Here duty and inclination were one. Nothing would bring settlers into this land so quickly as an important gold strike. Even if the gold deposits were scanty, as Dingo intimated, proof of the fact would hold new settlers on the plantations.

Bill was ready to dash off at a tangent when to his intense annoyance Norcross appeared at the edge of the coconut grove and advanced swiftly to the veranda, where he seated himself in the full sweep of the wind facing the other two men.

"I say, this is a rum spot for old bones," he remarked. He was embarrassed, for both Bill and Dingo showed that he had interrupted them, and that they didn't like it.

"Sixty isn't old," Dingo retorted.

"Oh, I say. No offense meant. You scarcely look sixty. Tougher than whipcord, eh what?" Norcross hastened to reply. The open, ingenuous face flushed. "Awfully sorry. I say! Evelyn sent me over to keep you from monopolizin' the guest, but we'll never have a better time for a little conference, eh? Men's talk." He beamed at the two old-timers. "A partner is what this bally land has needed. I'm goin' to violate my contract, Dingo, and take a *dekko* into the interior with Williams."

The yellowish head turned as though on a pivot.

"No, you're not!" Dingo refused.

"Oh, you can take back your plantation," Norcross answered pleasantly. "Sorry no end to break my written word and all that, but I've a theory about the mystery, you see. That's the important thing, eh what? Here's an empire hangin' in the balance and all that deuced rot, all because nobody knows what's happened to six settlers. I've guessed, and now I can make sure."

He fished out a briar pipe and struck a match, which the wind extinguished instantly. "No use, I guess, eh?" He remarked pleasantly and stuck the unlighted pipe into his mouth. Dingo was leaning forward from the hips.

"A *dekko* looking for what?" Bill rumbled. He wanted to speak casually, but no American can acquire the airy manner with which those of English training discuss matters of life and death, any more than their deadly sober earnestness in telling jokes.

"Oh, gold. I've been pickin' up the lingo fast," Norcross beamed. "There's been a bit of gold brought to the coast, though Lord knows how long it's been collectin'. You can have all we find, Williams. You'll earn it, for what I'm looking for is treachery." Norcross waved the pipe in the air. "Six men don't die in the bush by accident, any more than on the farm. Two or three might have gotten lost, or been pulled under by the crocodiles in the river, or been caught by a pack of dingos out huntin', but six out of six is too many, what? Those are all the dangers there are. Dingo here is just hipped on the notion of staying on the land. Carstairs, now, could handle himself in the bush a bit."

"You knew Carstairs?" Dingo demanded. "He was the fifth," the planter explained aside to Bill.

"Knew him well," Norcross nodded. "Knew all your settlers in a way. Rum thing. All six came from families that were acquainted. That came out in the early days. I'd rather clear up the mystery than prove the country. Selfish of me, but that's the way I am. Smoked pounds of tobacco thinkin'. No accident. Therefore men murdered them. Must have."

DINGO FROWNED. "Meaning I did?" he challenged.

"I say! Really, old chap!" protested Norcross, genuinely

shocked. "No, indeed! Talking to you because you're as anxious to clear up the mystery as I am. You've no motive whatever, and murderin' six young, active men isn't so easy by half. I thought you might be guilty before I settled here. Watched you at first like a hawk. You're an eccentric old blighter, but you're not crazy. Just opinionated. What's true for you is true for everybody. No argument. You can treat the natives like dirt. You've got 'em scared to death, and that's that. But your black fellows have killed your settlers. Must have."

"Nonsense!" barked Dingo.

"Australian black fellows aren't dangerous," Bill boomed out of long experience. "Though you may be right that six deaths in the bush are too many to be explained by accident."

"Wild bush fellows, yes," Norcross agreed pleasantly, "I'm referrin' to the half tamed ones. Dingo's got 'em scared, but a strange white man might be fair game, eh? They've been taught the value of property. The tobacco, the weapons and the gear a white man carries into the bush are a fortune to them, and grubbing up weeds from sunrise to sunset gets to be a beastly bore. They've got a double motive, what? Knock a tyrant over the head and escape to a lazy life with all his oof. Revenge, and gain, eh, what?" Norcross stuck the pipe back into his mouth and beamed.

"Two men can protect themselves. Needn't sleep at the same time," he argued. "Come on out with me, Williams. It'll be more interestin' than to sit here and watch the nuts grow. If the black fellows jump us we'll catch them in the act. If they don't, we'll prove the country is safe for partners workin' together. There's never been a pair of partners on York Cape before."

Dingo twisted his whole body in his chair—the quickest, most involuntary movement Bill had observed so far. Watery blue eyes fastened on the pearler with mute appeal.

"Bill is a free—*agent*," he declared. The emphasis on the last word gave the sentence a double meaning which escaped Norcross, while Bill was reminded whose agent he was. "An accident to another settler will give a bad name to this country, and to me." He paused. "I have worked a lifetime for one—purpose. I have reached my limit. The future is in the hands of—others."

"Oh, but I say! I can't agree with your advice, you know, but you shouldn't take a little thing like that to heart!"

"Have I said I was sorry?" retorted Dingo bitterly. "You are the seventh man to propose an expedition. The story is old to me, though in the past the reasons given were more plausible. Your theory is nonsense, Norcross. You've never been in the bush and you know nothing of black fellows. However, if Bill wants you for a partner my refusal will be a waste of breath. Your sister will be safe here, at least."

"The theory is not nonsense," Bill rumbled. "But a country where a white man can't travel the bush alone is no damn good. Besides, Dingo had already offered me guides, and I don't want to bother with a new-chum."

"But I say! Already?" Norcross snapped. "There's something behind this I don't understand—"

"Plenty!" Bill boomed in his big voice. "For one thing, your sister is worried. No time for you to leave her."

"What guides did you give him?" Norcross demanded curtly.

"Tam! Etyo!" Dingo called out. "My best men—with far too much to lose here to ambush a stranger in the bush," he added with a sneer.

"Your native spy and your black shadow!" Norcross retorted angrily.

In answer to the summons a withered little bushman, gray as an ape, sidled onto the veranda. Behind him strode an enormous man, whose front teeth were filed to points and whose bushy head all but touched the veranda roof.

"Tam's no native," Bellow Bill muttered. The big black bore the tribal marking of a Fijian—the meanest and most savage race of Melanesia.

"Would you prefer another guide?" Dingo asked.

Bill grinned exasperatingly.

"Why should I?" he inquired mildly—too mildly.

CHAPTER III

FLOAT

WITH ALL THE other suggestions which Dingo made regarding the expedition—and there were many—Bellow Bill agreed as readily. He was perfectly willing to start as soon as an outfit could be collected, lest a postponement until the following morning give Norcross an opportunity to follow him and join him in the bush.

He accepted the rifle and revolver which Dingo provided, and made no comment at the rather scanty supply of provisions furnished. By the middle of the afternoon he was standing by the bank of the little river, calmly chewing fine-cut tobacco, while Tam and Etyo packed the outfit in a dugout. When everything was ready he shook hands with Dingo and seated himself in the center of the little craft with his back to the Melanesian body servant. Norcross's warnings and Bill's own suspicions might never have been uttered.

Superficially the attitude of the pearler was careless; under the circumstances, foolhardy. Actually he was refusing to weary himself either mentally or physically over details. Bill was alert, but his watchfulness was that of the veteran campaigner rather than the raw recruit, of the old sea dog who keeps his eyes open for the first unusual thing on the horizon, instead of peering and staring like a landlubber, with such intensity that the overstrained retina begins to see dangers which are not there.

Bill was puzzled. All his experience had taught him that problems and motives on the frontier are simple. Greed, passion, and madness are easy to recognize and swift to act. But Dingo was neither mad nor poor, and whether the planter was playing some obscure and complex game himself, or was the victim of the folly of his settlers and the cupidity of his laborers, the drama had been prolonged for years.

Dingo had had a dozen opportunities during the collection of the outfit to give Tam and Etyo detailed instructions, but Bill had never encountered the native who could overpower him. Though his back was toward Tam, the space between them in the dugout was sufficient to prevent the Fijian from striking him with a paddle or stabbing him with a knife without moving from the stern seat, and the first abrupt movement from the rear would have brought out Bill's revolver.

That Dingo had never investigated the source of the gold himself was scarcely credible. That he should have been so prompt to reveal the secret and so eager to pack Bill off into the interior certainly had a significance of some kind, but these facts were no evidence of either insanity or crime, and might spring from the very natural desire on the part of a proud, egotistical man to get rid of an unwelcome investigator as quickly as possible.

At any rate, Bill had forced Dingo to act, and for the present the pearler was satisfied to get things moving and let himself be borne along with the current.

THE RIVER which the dugout ascended was narrow, but comparatively deep. The banks were muddy, heavily wooded, and swarming with crocodiles. Near the sea the most noticeable sound had been the wailing of curlews along the beach, but as twilight came the bull crocodiles began to bark gutturally, and far away in the forest the dingos howled.

"Better we stop. Dark too much," Tam growled.

"Catchee long way little bit," Bill contradicted. He estimated that the dugout had covered ten miles or so, but for the guide to dictate the camping spot would be bad discipline. A half mile farther along he motioned toward the bank where a small creek entered the river, and leaped out as the dugout touched the bank. Both natives followed. A few minutes' work with wood knives cleared a space in the tangle of vines large enough to sling Bill's hammock. Etyo dropped on his knees and kindled a fire.

"What name you *kai-kai?*" Tam inquired.

"Soft bread while we got it and bully beef while there's plenty of water," Bill decided. Both natives went toward the dugout for the food. Bill was alert—but not for what happened.

Tam got into the dugout. Etyo stopped by the bow—and suddenly gave the boat a mighty shove, leaping into it as it shot out into the stream. Tam threw himself flat in the bottom.

"Come back along me! I shoot seven bells!" Bill thundered. He fired with the word. A splinter flew from the gunwale, but the dugout continued to glide out of the circle of firelight like a low black shadow. Bill dashed along the bank. A vine tripped him and he fell elbow deep in the soft mud. When he scrambled up, the dugout was gone into the darkness. By straining his ears he could hear the swift dip of two paddles heading downstream. Almost at his feet a crocodile slipped into the water, and far away a single dingo howled and was answered by the howl of a pack.

Bill swore under his breath. Then the humor of the situation got the better of his anger. He threw back his head and laughed with a deep throated roar that was audible at a half mile.

He was marooned, and he was very neatly outwitted. While he watched against a deadly attack, he had fallen the victim of a crude practical joke. Ten miles of vine tangled wilderness were impassable during the darkness. The river was no road for a man without a boat. Some crocodiles could be frightened off by splashing in the water, but others were more courageous. He'd have a supperless night, and on the morrow he'd tear his clothes to ribbons getting back to the coast. The joke was on him, all right, but what did they take him for? A new-chum that would get lost? An impulsive fool that would leap in the water and swim after the dugout?

The roar of laughter died. Bill threw more wood on the fire and examined his surroundings in the light of the leaping flames. Dingo had not been a man to relish second-rate practical jokes.

If Dingo had gone to all this trouble to keep him away from the plantation, the plantation was the place for Bill to be—considerably earlier than he was expected.

The forest was full of dead wood, but to make a raft without an ax is difficult. Fallen trees are liable to be held to the earth by a root, or to be too big for one man to move. Perhaps Dingo and Tam believed a raft impossible, but by the aid of a torch Bill found one trunk eight inches through at the butt and nearly forty feet long that had been broken clean off. He smashed the branches off with a club, stooped, seized the log and worried it to the water's edge. With limbs and poles and vines he lashed together a rude catamaran—enough to keep the half-trimmed tree from rolling over in the water.

He cut a long pole, and within three hours was headed down stream. He could only drift with the current, using his pole to shove the unwieldy raft back into the river when it grounded on the bends, as it almost invariably did. The sun had risen before he heard the sound of the surf, and saw the first coco palm of the plantation. Nevertheless he estimated that he had gained at least five hours. He leaped to the bank.

"Coo-ee! Coo-ee!" a black fellow shouted warningly from the underbrush.

BILL SCOWLED and started to run through the grove toward Dingo's house. Any effort to conceal his movements was useless now that the black laborers were beginning to come out of their huts, but he could still burst in on Dingo and choke an explanation out of Tam in the presence of the planter. He took the veranda stairs at a leap and rushed into a bungalow—which was empty.

The sleeping hammock of the planter was still stretched. No breakfast had been eaten. Dingo might have been gone for hours, or minutes. Again Bellow Bill felt like a fool, and this time he could find nothing at which to laugh. The veranda shook to his heavy stride as he started for the Norcross house. The stares and grins of the laborers in the doorways of the huts behind the bungalow exasperated him.

"Coo-ee! Coo-ee!" rose a cry of warning.

"I'm bein' paged!" Bill rumbled. "Ahoy, Norcross!" he bellowed.

The shout brought the settler out on the veranda. Evelyn was close behind, still holding a napkin. Bill walked up the steps, conscious of his ripped clothes and the mud that smeared him to the knees.

"What's gone on here during the night?" he snapped.

"Oh, I say! You were attacked, what?" demanded Norcross delightedly.

"Nothing's happened here," replied the girl. "Even the laborers are going out to work as usual, and they are always glad of an excuse to chatter."

"Well, Dingo's vanished," Bill growled. Curtly he related the circumstances. Norcross stepped inside and returned with a revolver buckled around his waist. He looked at his sister, and kissed her.

"Dingo's never disappeared before. Must find him, what?" he inquired.

"You'll be careful, Evelyn? Keep watch, eh? I'll ask among the laborers first. They'll know where Dingo went, and whether Tam came back. Fortunately I can speak the lingo. Though I've never been able to get a word out of the black fellows about that pair. They're feared like devils."

"You'll keep cool?" Evelyn replied steadily. She spoke to her brother, but she looked at Bellow Bill. "Dingo's never been entirely frank. He must have chosen to disappear—"

"Naturally. Cool as ice, what?" snapped Norcross, who was wildly excited. "Don't worry about me, Sis." He hurried down the steps and led the way toward the grove.

THOUGH THE laborers had started toward a newly cleared field where their work was to grub up the weeds around the seedling coconuts with heavy brush hoes, the knowledge that a crisis impended had spread among them with the telepathy characteristic of primitive races. Norcross could obtain no coherent answer to his questions. He pressed on to interview the overseer, and the blacks trotted behind him in a crowd that gathered numbers with every step.

Within a hundred yards more than twenty of them were at Bill's heels. They ran ahead, man after man, for a look at Bill's face, only to dodge aside when he glared at them. They were voluble and noisy as a flock of crows.

Shouts in the distance and the appearance of a second milling crowd that swirled out of the old coconut trees at the edge of Dingo's plantation completed the confusion. In the center was Dingo, a revolver in his hand, prodding along Tam and Etyo. Blacks with waving hoes circled the three, and though the dread of Dingo and the threat of the revolver sufficed to keep a small space clear, even the planter seemed unable to obtain silence.

The two mobs came together. In an instant a ring of blacks four men deep was packed around the three white men and the two prisoners.

"Steady!" Bill boomed, for Norcross was fingering his gun. The deep toned voice brought a sudden silence as the blacks pushed closer to hear what was said.

"Tam claims you kicked him out of camp," rasped Dingo. "I figured he lied. Here he is. Knock seven bells out of hi—"

The breath of the laborers was on Bill's back. In front the ring was stirring—the quick ripple of tensing muscles that precedes a mob movement. By a split second Bill took the initiative. Before the cue was given him he swung from the knee. The upper-cut lifted Tam clear off his feet and hurled him backward, staggering the circle at Dingo's elbow.

A hoe handle thrust out of the crowd wavered. Meant for Etyo's hands, the black fellow had to reach out to grasp it. He swung the six inch, earth stained steel at Bill's head, but the pearler, having struck, was back on guard. He ducked under the blow. Etyo leaped past him, straight for Norcross.

Bill dove. A huge tattooed hand closed on Etyo's ankle, jerking him to earth. The hoe flashed past Norcross's face, but as he snatched for his gun black hands seized his arms. Dingo fired. The bullet smacked into the earth an inch from Bill's head, missing Etyo—if Etyo was the target—by more than four feet. Bill rolled aside, pulling the little black fellow over him as a shield just as half a dozen laborers flung themselves upon him.

For a moment he was pinned down by sheer weight, held not only by the blacks who had seized him, but by those who tripped over the heap as the bulk of the crowd scattered in panic. Few of the blacks had orders. Fewer any heart to fight. The flash of the revolver stampeded them.

The weight on Bill lessened as men rolled off the heap and fled, screaming. He twisted under the pile, got a hand on his own gun, and pulled the trigger. The flash burned him, but the bullet wounded a laborer and the wild scream of pain that followed the muffled crash of the report broke up the pile as though a bomb had exploded.

BILL SCRAMBLED up. There was fight left in Etyo, but a left handed shove sent him flying head over heels. Ten yards away Dingo, carried back by the rush of his laborers and tripped by some fanatic black, was scrambling to his feet. He snapped a shot at Bill, turned and ran, twisted to fire again, and then took fairly to his heels. He was holding his head as he ran, and made no effort to aim.

Something strange had happened to him in the mêlée. The back of his head gleamed in the sun, and though Bill's fore sight was lined between the shoulder blades the pearler hesitated to press the trigger. It was partly a disinclination to shoot down an enemy in full retreat, partly the cool recollection that even if Dingo was a scoundrel the authorities would prefer to have him alive, but chiefly curiosity.

Dingo's stiff legs would not carry him rapidly. He hobbled rather than ran. The grizzled, yellowish mop of hair drew further and further away from his neck. Suddenly he snatched off the wig entirely and sprinted with all his poor speed, both arms pumping, and his head shining bald as an egg.

Bill holstered his gun, and kicked the last black off Norcross. The wind had been knocked out of the settler, and it was a moment before he could rise.

"Evelyn?" he gasped with his first breath.

"She's okay. In fact she's coming on the double with a rifle. Heard the shots, I guess," Bellow Bill rumbled. "Say, what the hell does a white man livin' alone among blacks want with a wig?"

"Wig? But I say! He shot at you deliberately. I saw him!" Norcross panted. "The blighter's an outright cold blooded murderer!"

"Yeah—but we suspected there was some kind of murderer around here," said Bill gravely. "He's a foresighted old beggar. He figured that I'd get back to the plantation as mad as a wet hen. I swing on one of the blacks, and the whole tribe jumps on me. He shoots a black or two, but he's mobbed himself before he can protect us. That would have been a logical kind of accident, Norcross. I savvy that kind of fighting, and I hand it to him for doping white men and black fellows out to a T. But why does a man as smart as that bother with a wig? This is a hell of a hot climate, and he ain't wearing anything so uncomfortable for fun."

"Didn't you know he wore a wig?" called Evelyn sharply. She had come close enough to overhear Bill's last speech. "Any woman would. I suspected it from the first, and a month ago I was sure. He caught me staring at him, and realized I knew. Why, I told you about it at the time, Neale! I said it must be some sort of disguise—"

"Disguise! When he's been here alone thirty years!" Norcross scoffed.

"Just when did you first hear from the natives that there was gold in the interior?" Bill rumbled.

Norcross thought a second, and then looked up, startled.

"About a month ago! I say! You think there might be some connection—"

"I think Dingo has got a secret that he hasn't blabbed yet," Bill nodded gravely. "He's responsible for the disappearance of the settlers, but if he killed them because they'd recognized him, why in the devil did he bring them in here in the first place? I think we better round him up and keep him a prisoner until a schooner comes to take him to Port Denison. For it's a cinch he didn't want to go there."

Bill took the rifle from Evelyn.

"Better come along, but keep far enough behind us to be out of the line of fire in case Dingo makes a stand at his bungalow," he ordered calmly.

CHAPTER IV

THE SKELETON IN THE SHAFT

THE PEARLER DELAYED the pursuit only long enough to bind Tam, who was still unconscious, hand and foot. Etyo had scuttled into the bush, and so had the blacks who had abetted the treacherous attack by thrusting out the hoes and seizing Norcross. That seemed of small consequence. The fight was between the white men.

Cautious scouting through the grove and up to the big bungalow, however, disclosed that for the second time that morning it was deserted. Dingo had not even stopped there for arms. Both his Winchesters—and Norcross was positive he had but two—were still in the rack. Evelyn examined the food supplies. All the canned goods and the metal boxes were in perfect order. Nothing had been snatched up hastily. The inference was that the planter had fled with nothing but a revolver from which three shots had already been fired.

The guess was confirmed by Norcross's foreman, who had

taken to the bush with the others, but who now summoned up courage to approach the whites. Dingo, the native insisted, had run to the river bank, still holding his wig, pushed the dugout which Bill had used the previous day out of a little creek where it had been hidden, and paddled off alone.

"Ask him how he knows. All that is too much for one man to see," Bill growled.

One black laborer, the native explained, had told another. A dozen had seen Dingo, some here, some there. The foreman had been a chief. He had pieced all the gossip together and brought it to his master, as was his duty.

"He's always been friendly. I don't think he's lyin'," Norcross commented.

Bellow Bill stuffed a handful of fine-cut into his cheek.

"Dingo didn't leave that dugout as a means of retreat," he rumbled. "No man is as foresighted as that. He's running. Point is, Etyo and half a dozen of his nerviest blacks are running, too. They'll join, and then they'll be strong enough to come back some dark night. We've got to stay here till the end of the hurricane season, thanks to my own damn foolishness."

"But I say! We've got to catch him, of course."

"Ain't that simple!" Bellow Bill grinned. "Here's what bothers me: if I chase him alone, he can slip around me and shoot you some evening by the light of your own lamp. If I take you two with me, we're liable to walk into an ambush every ten yards—for that's what a chase up a narrow river and through thick bush always means. I was sent by the Governor of Queensland to find out what was queer about this country. I can admit that now.

"If Dingo can get rid of us in any way nothing has been learned. He's still got the lead in the game. He claims that the settlers died when they went upriver after gold, and at the first reverse he flies upriver himself without stopping for an outfit or a gun. All we know is that he's willing to do a murder, and that he wears a wig."

"You keep returning to the wig," said Evelyn.

"Because it's the most unusual thing about a situation that's unusual all through!" Bill boomed. "The wig's part of the answer. Get all the facts and the strangest situation knits itself together into a pattern. You're a woman. What's a wig worn for?"

"To make a man look younger, or handsomer, or to hide a scar. Dingo's head might be scarred. If he were a criminal—an escaped murderer—who could be identified by that means—"

"I says to myself he's an escaped convict and then I'm stopped short," Bill retorted. "He's a smart man. With the pioneering he's done and his real importance to the state he could ask for a pardon, and get it, too."

"Oh, I say! Easy to see you're a Yankee. Not under English law, old chap! My civil service ancestors would turn over in their graves at such an idea!"

"Some crimes are never pardoned," Evelyn agreed. "They are too awful. Kidnapings, and child murder. Though I don't remember any such *cause célèbre* in which the murderer escaped. Not in my lifetime." She shrugged. "However—I'm not going to be left on this plantation alone. Consider that settled."

"Much easier to ambush one than three. Our duty to go, for the sake of the country," Norcross insisted lightly. "Still insist the danger is halved by havin' a partner. Shall we take my foreman to trail and paddle?"

"I can do both and I'm leary of guides," Bill countermanded. "We'll borrow Dingo's rifles, and his grub. He won't have more than an hour's start, and I can shove a dugout along three feet to his one."

BILL WAS not boasting of his ability in bush craft. Less than a half mile up the river he noticed a spot where the branches had been disturbed. The muddy bank bore the prints of shoes and naked feet. Here Dingo had beached the boat. He had walked down stream for twenty yards and squatted behind a fallen tree for some time. The prints of his heels in the mud were deep. Here two natives had joined him. The three had shoved the dugout off.

"He hid where he could ambush us if we came before his

blacks joined him, savvy?" Bill explained. "We're close behind now, though we won't gain much against two paddles. But I think if Dingo'd meant to fight, he'd have tried it here. You better lie flat in the boat, Evelyn. Your brother and I will drop to the bottom at the first shot. The sides of these dugouts will stop a revolver bullet, as I've proved."

The pursuit was resumed, but noon and afternoon passed without an attack or another trace of the fugitives. At dusk, however, Bill swung around a bend—and backed water. On a pebbly bank by the mouth of a small creek which entered the river from the right hand side lay Dingo's boat. The absence of any attempt at concealment was insolent.

Though the river banks up to this point had been wooded the creek ran through a natural clearing an acre in extent, formed by an outcropping of rocky ground in which only shrubs could find root. Back of the clearing was a semicircular belt of brush in which the trees were smaller and younger, so that the bank of green rose from the clearing to the forest in the rear like the sloping seats of an amphitheater.

"Pick up your rifle. There's been timber cut here," Bill ordered. "Dingo left that dugout so that we'd be sure to follow him ashore, but damn it, I don't see what else we can do!"

A quick paddle stroke brought the three to the bank, The supplies were gone from Dingo's boat, and this time the footsteps of his party in the pebbles had been carefully smoothed out. Bill began to circle, his rifle ready, scrutinizing the undergrowth as carefully as the ground. An irrepressible grunt made Norcross and Evelyn hasten to his side.

More than timber had been cut. The gravel in the bed of the creek had been shoveled aside until the water flowed over bare rock, seamed with quartz. Stones were piled in heaps, and as the three advanced they came to the rotting planks of a gold rocker.

"Six settlers never did all this," Bill muttered. The low tones had the threatening boom of a thunder shower far away. "Unless they spent all their time here, one after another. Maybe Dingo needed white miners, and killed them rather than divide the dust. We'll see." The pearler stepped to a cut bank where the placer operations had ceased. "Get me the frying pan from the boat, Evelyn," he instructed. "And you, Norcross, for Lord's sake keep your eye peeled. Dingo *wants* us here, even though it catches him in a thundering lie!"

With the frying pan he began to wash a sample of gravel taken from a crack in the bedrock. Pebbles and sand sloshed over the rim until nothing remained. Bill squinted dubiously at an almost microscopic yellow speck.

"Maybe that's color, but the pans ain't worth a nickel each," he rumbled. "I'm still working the creek bed… Norcross, this placer never did amount to a damn! Nothing to kill a man over. The gold must have all been in one pocket, or the pay'd be more widely distributed."

"Even with black labor, nickel pans wouldn't pay as well as copra," said Evelyn. "Some one did a lot of work. But Dingo has been here for thirty years."

NORCROSS POINTED upstream. "I say! That heap of stones! They're sharp edged!" he exclaimed. "Looks like a shaft dump."

"Can't be!" Bill boomed.

Yet it was. A cautious advance revealed a circular hole five feet across in the center of a ledge of rotten quartzite. The workings were old. The winch had been removed or had entirely rotted away. The depth of the shaft was hidden by the gloom.

Norcross struck a match.

"Oh, my bally soul!" he gasped.

"How deep?" Bill demanded.

"Oh—thirty feet. But my word, there's a human skeleton in the bottom. A big skeleton—too big for a black fellow!" The settler twisted around excitedly. "Carstairs was big—and he used to grouse about goin' to the dentist. I'm going down. I can tell if it's him by the teeth!"

"Steady!" Bill muttered.

"You can't trail any further in the dark!" Norcross snapped. "Carstairs was my chum! And—if the shaft touches rich ore isn't it the answer to the riddle? My oath, Bill, you aren't getting the wind up?"

"I'm always leary as hell until I can see the guy I'm fighting," Bellow Bill admitted with cheerful honesty. "That shaft's in solid rock, and the walls further down looked mighty smooth—"

"I'll cut a vine for a rope and a pole to hold the end fast—"

"Cut 'em, then," Bill growled. The back of his neck was prickling. He did not have the wind up, but he had a hunch. Some danger was closing in, but all his experience could not suggest its nature. An ambuscade was less likely in the dark than during the day.

His hunch had no rational basis, and yet he could not rest until he had scouted around the mine shaft. He glided into the bush, moving with a silence the most expert black tracker would have envied, and worked forward until he came to the big trees. His ears and his nose were alert. A black fellow smells.

He was compelled to move very slowly. He heard Norcross chopping in the brush, heard him tell his sister in what was meant to be a low tone that he was ready to descend as soon as Bill returned. With the coming of night the crocodiles had begun to bark and the dingos to howl, but not a sound, not an odor was abnormal.

Bill commenced to work back toward the shaft. "It's me coming—don't shoot, Norcross!" he whispered clearly.

From the river bank resounded a snarling, savage howl that raised the hair on Bill's neck. No skulking, yapping dingo, that, but the bay of a hound hot on the trail. And not one hound, but two, three, four, a dozen, as beast after beast gave tongue. Close at hand, and closing in with every leap, gaining in numbers every second—and cutting through the cry of the pack, the blast of a whistle, the falsetto *"Hi-yah! Hi-yah! Sss! Sss! Sss!"* of Dingo, urging his dogs to the kill.

CHAPTER V

PARTNERS

"BILL!" NORCROSS CRIED uncertainly.

"Coming—don't run!" the pearler thundered. He crashed out of the brush into the open, throwing his rifle aside and whipping out knife and revolver. The pack was too large to be stopped with bullets, too close to make flight practical. To run was only to become separated in the bush, to be pulled down one by one while searching for a tree large enough to hold the weight of a man.

Bill had been taken utterly by surprise. He had only a split second to decide, and yet, as far as was within his power, he attacked. He leaped across the mouth of the shaft.

"Down, Evelyn!" he snapped. "Kneel, Norcross, and shoot as quick and straight as you can." Bill made two steps forward, towering over the others. He braced himself. He was standing. The dogs would leap for him—he hoped.

Across the little clearing the pack came charging like a low, snarling wave. In the dusk individuals could not be seen clearly, nor a target singled from the mass. Norcross's rifle streaked fire. A dog yelped, but the pack came on. As a breaker gathers, rises, and bursts against the breast of a bather brave enough to dare its shock, the pack hurled itself at Bellow Bill.

Two leaders sprang at his throat, side by side. Cold steel met one. The knife drove to the hilt in a shaggy chest. A carcass was slung aside from a reddened blade. The smashing blow of a revolver barrel met the second, which dropped, half stunned, at Bill's feet. There were more dogs. The shock of the impact staggered him. His hands could not be quick enough to strike all. In an instant he was bitten in the arm, and the ankle. His shirt was slashed to rags, for the dogs—big beasts with rough yellow coats, half hound, and half wild dingo—fought with the snap and leap aside tactics of their wolf blood.

"Climb down the shaft, Evelyn!" Bill thundered. "I'll hold them off!"

The death of the leaders divided the first rush. For an instant the pack circled, teeth snapping, bodies weaving in and out. Instantly Bill also changed his tactics. He reversed the revolver and fired point blank. He dropped two dogs, which were attacked by their companions. Norcross, shooting straight and fast, accounted for two more.

The men were hard pressed. It was thrust and swing as fast as the hand could move, yet Bill was fighting now in a semicircle of bodies over which the dogs fought, as eager to devour their mates as to drag down the men.

"Reload for me, Norcross! I'll hold them!" the pearler bellowed. The knife swung right and left in a glittering arc. One dog, leaping in, had its throat slashed. The rest were hanging back—snarling, threatening, yet loath to press the attack home while food lay between them and the men. One animal, bolder than the rest, did leap across the shaft toward Bill's shoulders. The knife met it in midair and pitched it, disemboweled, far outside the circle.

With amazing coolness Norcross was shoving cartridges into Bill's revolver. The battle was on the turn when Dingo opened fire. Undoubtedly he aimed at Bill. If he had aimed straight it would have been better, for unless the pearler had been fatally wounded he could still have kept the dogs at bay. Dingo's bullet, however, grazed Norcross across the top of the head. The settler slumped upon the half loaded revolver.

Bill thought him dead. It was defeat. Bill knew it, even as the thought of charging through the pack at the flash of the gun crossed his mind. By himself he might have reached Dingo with the knife, despite the dogs and the two bullets which the planter had left. Such would be the proper end for a fighting man. It would be revenge—but a sally would leave Norcross to be worried by the pack, and Evelyn at the mercy of the black fellows.

GRIMLY BILL knelt. The knife swung in swift arcs while he pushed the revolver down the shaft and slipped his left arm under Norcross's waist. Defeat was bitter. Once at the bottom of the shaft he was trapped, yet if he could not save Evelyn he could die with her. Bill flung the knife at a dog leaping in to attack, caught the cross piece which spanned the shaft with one hand, and hung, holding the limp body of Norcross, until he found the vine which served as a rope with his feet. The dogs snapped at his fingers, but dared not leap into that black hole.

"Look out below!" Bill rumbled with desperate humor, and slid to the bottom. There was just room to lay the settler down. Beyond one quick involuntary gasp Evelyn made no comment. She touched her brother's chest.

"He's alive! I feel his heart!" she shouted above the tumult made by the dogs.

"Good!" Bill boomed with a cheerfulness he was far from feeling.

"Your revolver fell on the stones. Better take mine. I'll be too busy with Neale to use it myself." There was a rip of cloth as Evelyn tore her waist to make a bandage.

"Good! Damn good!" the pearler rumbled. Now he did feel better. His big hand closed on the girl's shoulder with firm, steady pressure. "You're a pardner, and so is he. Take it from me, that's the most that *can* be said!"

Bill took the gun and raised his eyes to the circular patch of sky thirty feet overhead. On his face there was a fixed grin. Had there been light, Evelyn would have seen his eyes fill with dancing specks.

"Dingo! Here's your badger! Come pull me out of my hole!" he shouted at the top of his enormous lungs.

A wild hope that Dingo would be rash enough to peer down the shaft was not fulfilled. There was a crack of whips as the planter and the black fellows set about beating off the dogs, which was neither a quick nor an easy task in the ravening condition of the pack. Dingo finally accomplished it by having the dead dogs hurled to one side. The pack followed, but snarls and the cracking of bones continued to be audible.

The reddish glow of a camp fire spread across the mouth of the shaft, kindled, as near as Bellow Bill could judge, some thirty or forty feet away. Norcross's head was bandaged before the dry, precise voice of the planter sounded from above—and still Dingo was too wise to show his head. Bill had the revolver ready.

"You may climb up, Williams," said Dingo. "I'll not harm you. On my oath. I've no quarrel with Americans, or you."

"In God's name what's your quarrel with my brother and me?" Evelyn called out.

"I speak to Bill Williams. Four of the others walked into my trap and climbed down the shaft greedy for gold. The dogs drove two down the shaft, but you were not fooled, nor beaten altogether, Bill." Dingo laughed dryly. "Dogs are a weapon, but who would guard against them—on Cape York? Breeding the pack was the smartest thing I did, save one."

"You can go to hell!" Bill boomed.

"As you please," Dingo retorted. Without showing a finger he pushed the cross piece down the shaft. The sapling and the vine tumbled on Bill's head. "Stay down, then! The shaft walls are smooth. Thirst and sun will work rather quickly. I would have preferred that the Governor of Queensland should know at last who I was, and why I am neither mad nor a murderer."

"And what do you call yourself?" Evelyn cried out bravely.

"A judge, applying the law of an eye for an eye and a tooth for a tooth," said Dingo with even, matter of fact positiveness. "As you did to my brother and me, I do to you. Punishing the children for the sins of the fathers even to the third generation. A hard law, but just… more just than the punishment meted out to me."

BELLOW BILL gripped Evelyn by the shoulder. "Keep him talking," he whispered. "Mad or not, he means to leave us here.

The shaft walls are too far apart for me to touch both sides at once, and they are smooth, all right! While there's noise, though, I might do it… don't get your hopes up."

"Punishment? Then you are a criminal! We thought so!" Evelyn called.

"My brother and I were not criminals," Dingo snapped, "but we were sentenced to be hanged by the neck until we were dead and every official in Australia applauded. Your grandfather and your uncles among the rest. Do you recollect the Taber brothers—the doctors of Kalgoordie?"

Bellow Bill was notching the sapling with a jackknife, all his strength behind the blade. He felt Evelyn start.

"The Doctors Taber? Why, dimly. That was a notorious case," she ejaculated. "They murdered more than a dozen children, but—"

"We did not!" Dingo shouted. "We experimented! That was our crime! There was an epidemic, and the black babies were dying like flies. No remedy published in Osier was any good. 'Brother,' I said, 'the germ is in the spine. If I puncture the spine with a needle and inject an antiseptic the germ may be destroyed, and the disease cured.'

" 'That has never been done,' he warned me. 'We cannot explain such drastic treatment if it fails. Yet if you dare—'

"I dared," said Dingo. He was back in the present. His voice was precise and matter of fact. "I was almost right, but not quite. The antiseptic killed the patient as well as the germ. Yet I operated only on the dying. Not one of the children lost more than an hour—at most a day—of life. Yet your stupid official justice maintained that I had done murder and that my brother—God rest his gentle spirit—who never approved, who only helped me—must be hanged, too!"

"The courts were right," said Evelyn. "The murder of one to save others is murder still."

"So?" Dingo snapped. "Bellow Bill claimed that the death of six pioneers was not too high a price for a continent. I think a dozen lives are cheap for the conquest of a disease. It does not matter. My brother and I escaped. Eventually we came here and found natives wearing quills of gold. I dreamed of enough gold to let me leave the country, to work in a medical laboratory until I had proven that my treatment would cure the disease. I dreamed of returning to Australia a famous doctor, under another name, saying to the officials, 'You sentenced me to hang. See! I was right! Your stupid justice nearly robbed the world of a great physician.'"

Bellow Bill placed the sapling across his knee and broke it into three pieces, each about a yard long. Softly he began to rip his clothing into strips.

Overhead Dingo laughed.

"Gold!" he sneered. "Thirty years ago we came here first. We mined like madmen. There was only a pittance of dust in the placers, but here there was a thread of ore leading into the hard rock. With the blacks to help us we followed it down until it pinched out in worthless quartz. The disappointment killed my brother. I was of tougher stuff. I gave up my dream. I saw this country was worthless except for planting, and revenge. I planned.

"The officials who ruined me I could not reach, but their sons, nephews and cousins should suffer all the privations, all the horrors of loneliness, all the irony of frustration and the bitterness of being crushed unfairly which I had endured in my life within a span of a few days. As you will suffer," Dingo promised. "Nothing without wings can escape from that shaft."

"Tie this knot—and keep him close by!" Bill whispered.

EVELYN FUMBLED in the dark. A section of the sapling was bound to Bill's left forearm with strips of cloth. It projected back of the elbow. Another section, tied between ankle and knee, stuck from his right leg. "Tie the third piece to my right arm—quick," the pearler commanded. "I'm afraid he'll go away and leave the black fellows. Tam may like long pig."

The girl obeyed.

"Then that gold yarn was a stall?" Bill boomed.

"No. I never harmed a settler on my plantation," Dingo stated contemptuously. "If they could stick in the mud, they could live. What I punished was imagination—theories—the itch to improve and test new ideas."

Bellow Bill slipped a little finger through the trigger guard of the revolver, gripped the sticks bound to his arms, pushed the ends against the wall of the shaft, and drew up his legs. For an instant he hung supported by the thrust of his arms alone. Then one foot touched the quartz and the pole bound to the other leg found a tiny crevice.

The straining body straightened. There was a quick *bump bump* as he shifted the arm poles upward, and he hung again, supported by the thrust of his arms alone, with a foot and a half between his feet and the bottom of the shaft.

Evelyn caught her breath. An active and powerful man can climb the angle of two stone walls by the pressure of elbows and knees. Bellow Bill had used the sections of sapling to lengthen his arms and legs, but instead of the angle between two walls he had to deal with the rounded bore of the shaft, instead of pressing flesh against the rock he must rely on the friction between a wooden stick and slippery stone. The girl could only guess at the strength required. Yet Bill was ascending. He grunted warningly. Regular thumps marked his progress.

"Oh—oh—but I say, Dingo!" Evelyn called. Though her voice was loud, it was unsteady. There is a limit to the best of nerves, and she was waiting at each instant for Bill to slip and fall. "That story of yours may amuse you, but it's quite impossible, you know. Young as I am, I've heard of the Tabers—but they were both elderly men when they escaped thirty years ago. You're scarcely sixty now."

"Poor, literal minded official's daughter!" said Dingo with savage sarcasm. "I may *look* sixty. Did you think a Taber could show his face, even here, with a hue and cry all over Australia? Quite impossible for Trelawney to be Taber. Much too young, eh, what?" he added mockingly. "Oh, I can hear the officials—but my brother and I were surgeons, and I had other ideas that had never been tried. I was fifty-eight when I escaped. I'm eighty-eight now. You little fool, *I lifted my face to get rid of the wrinkles.* Like a vain old woman. Women lift their faces, but not men! Oh, dear no!" Dingo laughed. "When I grew bald I had to wear a wig, but even you never suspected the wig was to hide the scars of an operation."

"Jolly clever!" the girl cried, shrill with excitement. Bellow Bill was at the top of the shaft. He must raise his head into sight before he could hook his elbows over the edge of the shaft and free his hands to shoot. The big body swaying above her gave a convulsive lunge upward.

A shot rang out. Flame streaked from Bill's gun in answer. There was a chorus of snarls from the dogs, a shout of alarm from a black fellow. Twice more Bill fired.

"You fellow Tam! Whip back those dogs, or I'll shoot you seven bells too much!" roared the pearler.

TAM HAULED Evelyn from the shaft. She found Etyo whipping back the dogs, which snarled over the two animals dropped by Bill's last shots. Dingo lay on his back near the shaft mouth, with a bloodstain on the left breast of his jacket. Bill covered the two blacks, alert for treachery, but the shooting of Dingo had taken the fight out of them.

The pearler was bared to the waist. His tattooed skin gleamed in the firelight, and the figures of ship and dragons and snakes seemed to writhe as his chest rose and fell from the terrific exertion of the climb. With the saplings still bound to his arms and one leg stuck stiffly in front of him he was an incongruous and a menacing figure.

Norcross had been lifted out first and lay beside the fire, breathing easily. Evelyn started toward her brother, but overpowering curiosity drew her to Dingo. She lifted the wig, and touched the thin white scars that seamed the temples.

"His face was lifted," she said. "That part is true, at least. I—I think all his story is true. What a horrible thing, and what a horrible, mad vengeance. Do you suppose he really was insane? To live and plan to punish the innocent—is awful. How he must have gloated when he watched a new settler tire of the land and begin to be lured by the tales of gold."

"I'm no expert on insanity," said Bill slowly. "Maybe a doctor could tell us, but—shall we ask?"

It was a question. The girl looked up, puzzled.

"Dr. Taber is dead—officially," Bill rumbled. "Dingo Trelawney's dead, too. Officially, he's a great pioneer. I'm a sailorman, and personally I like the plain damn truth, even if it's ugly in spots. I'm only wondering if you want to tell it. Here's Cape York, white man's country without even gold in it to get any one into trouble. Land so rich that a pair of elderly doctors could scratch out a livin' from the start. First settled by the notorious Taber brothers, one of whom hid at a mine in the interior while the first, pretending to be alone, started a plantation on the coast to which he lured—"

"Stop it," snapped Evelyn half hysterically. "Really, Bill, just because I haven't broken down and screamed you mustn't remind me of all that. Some things can't be told to the people: It just isn't done, eh?"

"It's your country," Bill boomed. "Well, we'll bury Dingo, then, and go back and raise copra till a schooner comes. I'll tell the Governor that Dingo died, breathin' his faith in the land to the last, and that the country'll be perfectly safe for settlers now that the Norcrosses pulled through." The pearler reached for fine-cut.

"Bet you," he muttered with his mouth full, "that the Governor builds Dingo Trelawney a monument."

"Well? Even if his aim was vengeance he proved a continent, nevertheless," said Evelyn sharply. "He deserved a monument—and your bullet, too!"

THE ACCOMPLICE

*Skipper Bellow Bill Williams had his job
cut out for him when he went after the most
dangerous crook in the South Seas*

CHAPTER I

SENT BACK

RONTONGA IS THE headquarters of the second largest pearling fleet in the South Seas, but the harbor is small. The entrance is a narrow gap in the center of a coral reef that extends along the shore for twenty miles, and onto which the trade wind drives the surf in thunder and foam. Behind the reef is an inner beach about two hundred yards wide, and then comes the harbor proper—a deep circular basin some nine hundred feet in diameter.

Though the inner haven is safe for ships, even in a hurricane, the coast is dangerous for a sailing vessel. To miss the gap in the reef is to be on a lee shore. Therefore, when the pearlers idling in Rontonga sighted a lugger driving toward the land before a fresh breeze, close to the surf and fully a mile to the north of the channel, a crowd gathered swiftly.

There was a man in the lugger. The crowd could see him plainly; he was slouched over the tiller, but he seemed bent on steering straight to destruction. From the moment when the lugger was sighted, he had not altered his course; and though the harbor entrance was unmistakable, he did not so much as raise his head to look.

Such unnatural disregard of danger fascinated the crowd. Jap suit divers, Polynesian skin divers, Chinese and East Indian pearl buyers, Australian, French and English lugger owners came on the run to watch either a wreck or an exhibition of reckless seamanship.

Yet out of fifty men, but one was quick-witted enough to

The four men were marooned on the atoll.

snatch up a pair of binoculars. That one towered over the others like a liner among a crowd of tugs. Six feet three in his socks, weighing two hundred and forty pounds, with every ounce hard muscle, he dominated the mob the instant he joined it. His coppery blond hair gleamed in the sun; his huge arms, exposed by a cotton singlet, were covered from wrist to elbow with tattoo marks, crowded so closely there was scarcely an inch of undecorated skin. A bullet scar made a white welt on the left shoulder, and an old knife slash cut through the tattooing on the forearm.

"Is 'e going to chynge course, Bellow Bill?" sung out an Australian.

"By Barney's bull, no!" boomed the big pearler. "You fella! Run to that lugger!" he roared at the nearest Polynesian skin diver, in a voice that thundered like a mainsail caught aback in a gale.

Bellow Bill Williams's ordinary conversation was audible at a hundred yards. His shout made the black fellow leap in the air and set off at full speed before the command was half uttered.

"Hurry up plenty too much, or I'll knock seven bells out of you! Swim out to her and put that tiller hard up! Sail her back to the harbor here!" Bellow Bill commanded.

"Why, wot's the matter, Bill?" demanded the irrepressible Australian.

"Murder," Bill rumbled like the growl of surf. "That helmsman's dead."

He turned on his heel. The binoculars slipped through fingers like wooden marlinspikes and dangled against the immense, tattooed chest. Bellow Bill was not easily shocked. He had hunted pearls the length and breadth of the South Seas. The jungles of New Guinea and the wastes of the Australian bush had echoed to his booming voice. By preference, Bill went to the places and on the expeditions from which weaker men held back. He had seen violent death and murdered men often enough. But this—this was different.

It was not the sight of the corpse that shocked Bill, but the fact that the corpse was there for all Rontonga to see. This was not merely a murder, but a crime that flaunted itself, brazenly and unashamed. For the binoculars had revealed that the helmsman of the lugger was held erect by ropes, and that the tiller was lashed fast in the crook of a bent and stiffened arm. The breast of the duck coat was dark with blood. The binoculars had brought the dead face close; the lips were tight shut, but the open eyes stared horribly, and straight ahead, as though they still gazed at the muzzle of a rifle.

To kill the man had not been enough. The murderer had deliberately and skillfully sent the corpse sailing back, advertising the crime instead of concealing it.

"**YOU GO** get Sergeant Fisher, of the water police," Bill commanded the Australian. He looked the crowd over and selected the cashier of the Rontonga Bank. "And if you would be good enough to ask the commissioner to come to the beach, sir, a lot of time would be saved," he requested. "This isn't a routine case. It's queer."

As the messengers departed, Bill ran along the beach after the diver, the crowd trailing at his heels.

Though he had acted promptly, the task he had set the Polynesian was impossible. Before the black fellow could run a mile, the lugger struck in the surf, capsized, and bumped across the reef into the deeper water beyond. The best the diver could do was to cut the body free of the wreckage before the lugger began to pound itself to pieces.

By the time Bellow Bill and the crowd reached the spot, the sand was strewn with broken bits of planking. The body, however, still bent in the position into which it had been bound, lay in the dry sand above the high tide mark. The Polynesian squatted beside it, cringing in terror of a beating.

"You catchee plenty soon. My word, you no fright along me," Bellow Bill rumbled reassuringly.

The man had been dead a long time; *rigor mortis* was far advanced. In the coat were two large bullet wounds, at the center of the chest and less than three inches apart.

"Who knows this chap?" Bill asked.

To judge by the silence in the crowd, no one seemed to.

"I think he stopped here for a couple of hours about three days ago, Bill," an Englishman answered at last. "I met him coming out of the Residency. My oath, Bill, how could he be sent back like this? It's uncanny!"

"Easy enough to lash the helm of a lugger, when the trade wind is steady as a compass," the pearler retorted. "What the helm is lashed with doesn't make much difference. It would be a smart way to get rid of a corpse, if there was open sea to leeward.—Only here," Bill added significantly, "Rontonga lies across the path of the trade winds, twenty miles from end to end. I'm betting the lugger was aimed to come ashore near the harbor, where we'd all be sure to see it."

From a hip pocket Bill pulled a wad of fine-cut chewing tobacco. He chewed slowly, frowning.

The crowd surrounding the body gabbled. The commissioner and the sergeant of police were coming at a rapid walk. Fisher was a lean, phlegmatic old-timer with a sandy mustache shot with gray, and the mournful brown eyes of a hound. The Australian trotted beside him, talking thirteen to the dozen.

The cashier had returned to the bank; but Carruthers, the commissioner, was accompanied by a man whom Bill knew only by reputation, despite a far-flung acquaintance among the pearlers and copra planters of the South Seas. Not that Frank Harren was either mysterious or secretive. Quite the contrary. Rather, he was English, and well-to-do, and intimate only with officials and executives. He had arrived at Rontonga a year before, sailing his own yacht on what he admitted he had planned as a cruise around the world. He was fair-haired, red-faced, with an athletic body which had put on fat. His age was about forty-five, and though he bragged in a reserved way about his yacht, the craft was nothing more than an old pilot boat.

Later, Harren admitted that he had picked the sloop up cheap in France, and that he had taught himself navigation to save the wages of a shipper, after he decided to retire from business and spend the rest of his life in travel. What his business had been he never mentioned.

He had fought in the infantry during the War, and retired with the rank of major. He gave the impression that he had fought hard all his life. Business was a battle. The Germans were tough foemen, and England after the Armistice became a grimmer battlefield than the Ypres mud, for a business man whose business had gone west while he was in uniform.

But Harren had made his pile all over again, and now he meant to jolly well enjoy it. Always had been fascinated no end by the tropics—nice to lie under a palm and listen to the surf—after thirty years of clawing for shillings and hugging the mud to keep your skin whole, eh, what? And so the world cruise had ended at Rontonga. Harren had purchased a copra plantation five miles from town, and settled down to bask in idleness and drink stengahs with the commissioner—though according to his own account, he had never been idle before in his whole aggressive life.

AT THE sight of the body on the sand, he hurried forward and examined it with the calmness of a veteran soldier.

Not so Carruthers. The slender, wiry figure of the commissioner seemed to shrink and then recover, as a steel spring might adjust itself to a heavy burden. For a long, tense minute he stood with his head bowed, in silence.

His chin came up at last. "This is my brother, gentlemen," Carruthers informed the crowd. "He was a member of the secret service. I sent for him—unofficially, and as a favor—to test a theory I had formed as to the identity of the pearl pirates who have been harrying your luggers this season."

Carruthers's lips quivered uncontrollably. "I think my brother found the guilty man, and that this is the answer. But I know the man my brother went to arrest, and within the hour I shall take the police boat out myself. Perhaps you know the person I suspect—a man crazed by drink; a gentleman going to the dogs; a man whom you have heard accuse me of sentencing to prison unjustly, and of being responsible for the death of his wife. I—I shall bring him back for a fair trial," Carruthers promised bleakly. "Meanwhile, will you help me carry my brother to the Residency? I must bury him within the hour."

The crowd murmured. Four men stooped to lift the stiffened, twisted body, and in the hush the surf roared on the beach.

Pitched in a lower, deeper note the voice of Bellow Bill broke the silence. "You mean More Fathoms Todd, of course.—And I think you're wrong, commissioner," he boomed.

CHAPTER II

THE MAN EVERY ONE KNEW

FOR THE MOMENT the statement went unanswered. Carruthers merely inclined his head and began to walk back toward the town.

Even the crowd realized that there could be no further discussion in public. Government, in the person of Carruthers, had announced a decision. Bellow Bill, the most experienced pearler present, and representing unofficially but none the less definitely the old roaring days of the South Seas which antedated law and officials and wireless and police, had challenged it. Personality and individualism had taken issue with organization.

During the long walk back over the hard beach sand, the history of More Fathoms Todd was uppermost in every mind. Todd was a broken and embittered man, but among the pearlers he was liked. His crimes were against the new code—and not the old.

Three years before, he had arrived in Rontonga with a pretty wife and a three-year-old boy. He had bubbled with enthusiasm in the shy, apologetic way of an Englishman who is the younger son of a good family, and who has his way to make in the fringes of dominion. He had half-a-dozen guns of all sorts, in pigskin cases. In a straight-stemmed briar pipe he smoked tobacco that came packed in vacuum tins; and he announced that he had purchased the copra plantation on Cooke Island, thirty miles to windward of Rontonga, together with the pearling rights in the water around it.

Old-timers grinned behind their hands. During the previous season the coco palms on Cooke had been girdled by rats. Its pearling grounds were in the area where suit diving was prohibited, and the shell had been stripped as deep as the average Polynesian diver cared to go. The Honorable Mr. Todd, in his enthusiastic ignorance, had been most beautifully swindled. He had bought on the basis of the balance sheet of the previous year, in a land where plantation profits and pearling revenues vanish overnight.

The swindle was traditional, and not especially frowned upon. New-chums must get their experience somehow. Poor men sweat for it on sun-blistered decks or in the bush. Rich younger sons pay for it, and the lesson is usually cheap at a few hundred pounds.

Unfortunately, the few hundred pounds was every shilling Todd had. He had looked forward to a career in the consular service, and had planned to learn about the South Seas at first hand while he waited for his appointment. A month after his arrival he was flat broke, and Bellow Bill had found him trying to feed his family on fish and breadfruit, like a native. *Poi* is no food for a white man. It tastes and smells like paperhangers' paste. Todd and his wife, however, had no other diet, and no other place to go save back to England—self-confessed, laughable failures. In the consular service there is no place for a failure or the butt of a joke. Something, Bill decided, had to be done.

"Of course, there's plenty of pearls left a few more fathoms down," Bill remarked.

"Oh, I say! Really? And I thought I was jolly well flattened!"

"You are," Bill rumbled. "There's limits even to Polynesian diving. But I happen to be able to swim a damned sight better than the average native. Come out, and I'll prove it."

THE BIG man moved his schooner far from the shore, into twenty-five fathoms. He dove and swam, down and down. For three minutes he was under the surface, and when he rose he was at the end of his enormous strength. Bill's face was blue, and a thin stream of blood trickled from nose and ears, but he carried three large shells. While he rested on the desk, gasping, Todd opened the shells. Bill sat up at a cry of delight.

"Yep, it's a pearl. Worth about five pounds," he panted. "They are there, all right—just a few more fathoms down, if you can get them. I've gone as deep once before, but there ain't going to be a third time! It's man-killing work. The thing for you to do is to get permission from Carruthers to hire divers wearing suits. Then you can scratch out a decent living."

"Really? Just a few more fathoms?—Oh, I say!" Todd stammered.

He was bubbling with enthusiasm, oblivious in his ignorance of diving that Bellow Bill had risked his life. Bill didn't tell him. There was a law against skin divers working deeper than twenty fathoms. Todd would find that out in time.

Bill sailed the next morning for his own pearling grounds, wholly unaware that he had initiated a ghastly tragedy. The developments were swift. Carruthers, bound by red tape, refused to lift the restriction on suit diving. He refused also to shut his eyes to what was going on there. He said—and perhaps it was true—if he did so there would be suit diving in restricted waters throughout his whole district. That was just what white pearlers like Bellow Bill wanted.

Todd returned to Cooke Island and a diet of breadfruit. There, the knowledge of the pearls, a few more fathoms down, mocked him. Quietly, he hired three native skin divers, bribing them by enormous pay to risk the pressure of the depths. Within a week, all three divers were crippled for life by the bends. Carruthers had Todd arrested, and sentenced him to two years in the jail at Sydney.

That was bad enough; native justice was worse, however. The brother of one of the crippled divers sought Todd with a spear. Learning that the white man was safe in jail, the native turned for revenge to Todd's family, according to the queer and perverted justice of the Polynesian, by which a man's family and tribe are equally responsible with him for his acts. The spear was plunged through Mrs. Todd's breast. Fortunately, the avenger was shot before he was able to kill the baby. That was More Fathom Todd's only bit of good luck.

The tragedy on top of the wreck of his future, and the disgrace of it, broke him. When he returned to Rontonga with his son, he was drinking hard. He had been heard to mutter threats and accusations against Carruthers, lips slack and eyes bloodshot, but he had done—nothing. At the beginning of the pearling season, he had returned to Cooke Island with a load of trade goods purchased with the pittance given him for hard labor in the jail. The bulk of the stuff was trade gin; and as the pearlers knew, he had made no attempt to trade. Whoever called at Cooke Island found him haggard, unshaven and ghastly pale, a bottle of gin before him, no matter what the hour.

Bellow Bill had wondered then how long Todd would last, and what would become of the boy. He wondered now if dissipation and brooding had indeed driven Tod mad, or roused him to a brief, murderous frenzy at the news that he was to be arrested again. That was possible. It would even be the comprehensible and logical climax of Todd's fate. The charge of pearl piracy, however, Bill simply could not credit. Unwittingly, he had initiated Todd's downfall. To stand by the poor devil to the end was only fair.

THROUGHOUT THE long walk back to the Residency, Carruthers moved like an automaton; but once through the door and out of sight of the crowd, he dropped into a chair. Harren handed him four fingers of neat whisky, which he drained at a gulp.

"Sorry," he said. "I'll be all right in half a mo'.—Sergeant, get the smaller police boat ready. Take one of the wireless operators—Brown will be the best man—and his portable set. I must keep in touch with things here, and be able to give orders. You'll go along, of course; and as for the others—"

"I'd like to volunteer," Bill said.

Carruthers frowned. "You're abler than any constable I've got, but you're an American," he objected.

"I've helped British commissioners before, though," Bill purred. "It's not that, sir. I'm the nearest approach to a friend that Todd has. I can handle him easier than any one else. According to your idea, he's insane, or at least mad drunk. Arresting him won't be any cinch, while if my hunch is right and we have a sane criminal to deal with"—Bellow Bill's enormous shoulders shrugged and he grinned—"the job will be just that much harder."

"I agree with Williams," Harren interrupted. "You've admitted to me that you've been criticized by the pearlers for dealing with Todd too strictly according to the letter of the law. Naturally, you want to avenge your brother. If anything should—er—happen, I think there ought to be a pearler along. It'll stop gossip, and all that sort of thing.—In fact," Harren added thoughtfully, "I think I'd better go along with you myself. I'll follow in my yacht, in case there's no room in the police boat."

"For what possible reason?" Carruthers snapped, flushing darkly.

"Because I was your guest when the crisis arose, and because you've done me the honor to call me your most intimate friend," Harren explained imperturbably. "I haven't forgotten how to handle firearms of every kind, or how to stand still under fire, either. You're not quite yourself, Fordyce."

"Why should I be? No reason for both of you to treat me like a bloodthirsty navvy," retorted the commissioner irritably. "Very well! You can go—both of you. I don't like to strip Rontonga of constables, at the end of the pearling season. We'll need no more men, sergeant."

Fisher saluted and withdrew.

"But understand me, both of you," Carruthers swept on, "I'm

not looking for vengeance." His bright brown eyes fixed on Bellow Bill. "Last year, only one lugger was attacked by pirates. This year, a dozen have been gutted, and their crews murdered. I made a careful record of every case, and I have discovered one point of similarity in every case: each time, the lugger was separated from the pearling fleet. Now, if the pirates operated in a sailing vessel, they couldn't hang around the edge of the fleet without being seen, and if they worked in the fleet, they couldn't very well follow a straggler, attack it, and be back in their place by morning."

"That's sound, sea-going reasoning, even if it never occurred to me," Bellow Bill agreed.

"I inferred that the pirates had a motorboat, so low in the water that it could see a sail before it was sighted itself, and fast enough to return to its base during darkness. There aren't many motorboats in the islands. Petrol is too expensive. None of the boats I knew about could be used by the pirates—usually because they had been seen in harbor at the time of one of the attacks. Therefore, I appealed to my brother to find out if a motorboat had been shipped to this district secretly. He learned that there had been—and to More Fathoms Todd!"

"Personally?" Bill rumbled. "Where'd Todd get the money to buy a motorboat?"

"From some one he met in jail," Carruthers retorted confidently. "Naturally, he didn't take delivery of the boat personally. We traced it to an unscrupulous trader, who delivered it to a stranger he described as a damn' ugly Samoan. I sent a trustworthy native to Cooke Island, under pretense of diving for pearl, and he reported that a damn' ugly Samoan was hanging about."

"OH.—IN OTHER words, you suspected Todd from the first, eh?" Bill rumbled. "Did your agent see the boat?"

"My brother was to have found her," Carruthers snapped. "And see here—I won't have you impugn my motives—"

"I'm not! You're straight as a string," Bill answered gravely.

"But if you'd have been a little bit crooked three years ago, it would have been better for Todd. All I wanted to point out was that you were working on a hunch—and so am I. You're putting too much weight on the fact that your brother was shot, and not enough on the fact that he was sent back here."

"What do you mean?"

"I've seen Todd beastly drunk since he came back; but no matter how bad he might be, I never found his kid hungry or dirty. A man who will look after a kid is a long way from the bottom—and the criminal who lashed your brother to the tiller was a cold-blooded brute that the devil himself would have disowned."

"That's sentiment! When an Englishman goes to the dogs, he goes all the way," Carruthers answered.

"Maybe.—Here's another point: a lugger can be sailed before the wind, but it will jibe from one tack to the other. To have that boat strike near the harbor here it must have been set adrift only ten or twelve miles away—not thirty."

"That's perfectly possible, if Todd had a motorboat," Harren pointed out.

"Sure. But while he was sailing or towing a lugger twenty miles, he'd have had time to sober up, no matter how mad drunk he was to start. Carruthers claims he was mad drunk, and out for a madman's revenge. I'm sure that before he could have finished this job he must have been sober enough to realize what he'd done—and he'd either have tossed the body overboard or put a bullet through his own head."

"You may both be right. Todd may have done the shooting and ordered his Samoan to dispose of the body," Harren objected.

"That's the queerest of all!" Bill boomed, indifferent to the fact that the crowd lingering outside the Residency could hear. "For I dropped by to see Todd a week ago, and he told me that since the time when his wife was speared he couldn't bear the sight of a brownskin!—Native accomplice, my eye! What accomplice would put his neck in the noose for a broken down, drunken has-been!—You're wrong, Carruthers! Todd may have shot your brother—those bullet holes looked like the work of a double-barrelled express rifle to me, and Todd's got one—but the man who sent the body back was sane! He wanted to get you away from Rontonga, and he did devil's work to make sure!"

"But—for what possible reason?" Harren asked.

Bill's jaws clamped on the tobacco in his cheek. "I'm damned if I can figure out," he growled. "Some one knew that a certain stranger was the commissioner's brother, and who wanted the commissioner at Cooke Island—But right there I bog down. I can't figure why or how, unless that some one also had a fast motorboat! But I'm damned sure we'll find out. The crime's unnatural, but we're setting out to solve it in the natural way. We're doing just what the criminal calculates we'll do, and sailing into his trap!"

"Yet you want to go along," said Harren thoughtfully.

Bellow Bill grinned at the thickset, middle-aged planter. "Guess you ain't heard much about me. That's *why* I want to go along!" he thundered.

CHAPTER III

TWIN BARRELS, CALIBER .50

THE SMALLER OF the two police boats based at Rontonga was a thirty-five-foot gasoline launch with an open cockpit aft and a cabin forward, armored with sheets of boiler-iron thick enough to stop a rifle bullet. The cabin windows were large, for the sake of coolness, but they were equipped with sliding steel shutters instead of glass.

The armament consisted of a Lewis machine gun with two gun mounts—one inside the cabin, for use at sea, and a second on top of the cabin roof, to permit the gun to be fired in any direction when a native village was to be punished or overawed.

Despite the weight of the armor, the launch had a speed of twelve and a half knots, and by completing the funeral within an hour, Carruthers and his party were able to reach Cooke Island by two o'clock in the afternoon.

Todd's bungalow was on the leeward side of the island, close to the beach, and Carruthers ordered the launch to approach slowly, ready for an emergency. The neglected plantation was a scene of desolation and decay. The dead palm trees were still standing, but the bare trunks were stark as a forest of telegraph poles. Around the bungalow, weeds grew shoulder high, with only a narrow path broken through the tangle between the beach and the rotting, sagging veranda. The roof was thatched with palm leaves which had split in the fierce sunlight and were far from watertight. A green patch here and there showed where Todd had made half-hearted efforts at repair since his return from jail. His lugger, however, was not at the mooring in front of the beach, and the bungalow seemed to be abandoned.

To Bellow Bill, who hoped that Todd was not only innocent but ignorant of the murder, the silence was like a blow. Apparently Carruthers's inference that the crime had been committed here was correct. Todd had no reason to be away from home. On Bill's last visit, little Livingston Todd had come flying down that weed-grown path, shouting with delight, while More Fathoms himself had staggered out onto the veranda. The contrast was sinister.

Carruthers pushed forward to lead the party ashore, but Bill refused to step to one side.

"If you don't mind, sir," he rumbled, "I'll go first—and go alone. If Todd planned to bring you here, he could ambush you mighty easy in that path.—Whereas I'm his friend."

"Bill's right!" Harren approved. "If you were hurt, Fordyce, it would be small satisfaction to us to arrest the madman who did it."

"But I've no right to let him run the risk," Carruthers snapped.

"The real point," said Bill smoothly, "is whether Todd's alone or working with an accomplice. What would you do when you got ashore, sir? I can read tracks like a bushman—and if I do draw a shot, you can support me from the launch. Take my word for it, sir, when you can't see an enemy, the important thing is to be able to duck into some place where he can't get at you.—The launch is our base. You hold that while I scout."

"Those are sound, cautious tactics," Harren drawled sarcastically.

"Which ain't my habit," the pearler retorted grimly. He vaulted over the side of the launch, though the water was waist deep, and was across the beach examining the head of the path before the others were even aware that the discussion had ended.

"I'll cover you with the machine gun, Bill!" the sergeant called. He climbed to the cabin roof, and began to swing the barrel right and left over the expanse of weeds.

"That's the stuff, Fisher!"

BELLOW BILL crouched, alert as a stalking lion. Though his immense physical strength made him reckless by habit, he was no bull-headed fool. A murderer at bay may be forced to kill a friend in self defense, and of the men in the launch he trusted none but Fisher.

Brown was a twenty-year-old kid who might do anything in a crisis. Harren, and to a lesser degree Carruthers, were cool enough, but either one might have almost anything in mind. Bill could not forget that the identification of the murdered man rested upon the commissioner's unsupported statement. Harren might or might not have known that a brother in the secret service had been summoned for special duty. Neither man had mentioned the point during the long run to Cooke Island.

Nor had Bill. Even British commissioners and retired British majors may stoop to murder. These two were friends; they might be accomplices. Or either one might be present now to shield the other. Harren's excuse for joining the expedition was pretty thin. He might have suspected that Carruthers had a scheme, or might be pursuing one of his own.

But what scheme? What motive was involved, if revenge was not? Bellow Bill could not even make a guess—except that the crime must be more profitable than pearl piracy. For the latter, though grandiose in sound, yields only a small return in cash. The typical pearl pirate is a bloodthirsty native to whom a hundred pounds represents riches.

Bill advanced up the path slowly, watching the weeds as well as the ground. In the loose sand were many footprints, but all were so badly blurred that he could only guess at their age. Only the prints of Livingston's small feet could be identified, and all of these lay beneath more recent imprints. Halfway up the path was a hollow in which grains of sand were still moving.

"Some one is here, Fisher!" Bill called.

He drew the revolver he had taken from the arms chest on the launch, and ran swiftly up the high veranda steps and into the bungalow. The big room was empty, but the floor was easier to read than the path. Todd had merely swung a pair of hammocks for his son and himself, dragged out cases of bottled gin from his stores for tables and chairs, and tacked up a new ceiling cloth overhead to keep the cockroaches from dropping out of the thatch and into his food. All these things were undisturbed. The big room was squalid—but the floor had been recently scrubbed with soap and water.

Bill swore aloud. No bachelor ever scrubs a floor except from bitter necessity. Scrubbed! Poor Todd! Hadn't he known that soap and water cannot remove bloodstains from wood? Better— so much better and so much easier—to have touched a match to the thatch and sent the bungalow roaring up in flame.

The dark patch in the center of the floor which the scrubbing had failed to erase was a death warrant. Even the trail of dripping blood where the body had been carried out of the door was revealed by pale brown stains.

But perhaps Todd had wanted the police to be able to reconstruct the crime? Poor, futile, gin-crazed devil!…

Grimly Bill filled his cheek with fine-cut. He had liked Todd. But facts were facts.

Todd was lurking somewhere in the weeds, waiting to be arrested, or to complete his revenge.

The pearler opened his mouth to bellow a demand for surrender when he started violently. In the doorway, where the light was strongest, the cleanly scrubbed planks revealed footprints, faintly traced in the dust and sand from the path. There were the marks of Bill's big feet—and other marks almost as big, but printed by naked toes; the footprints of a native who had never worn shoes. The toes pointed into the bungalow—and no trail led out!

"Stand by, Fisher!" Bill roared. "There *is* an accomplice, damn it—"

OVER THE head of the pearler the ceiling cloth swayed. Bellow Bill fired upward at random as the cloth bellied downward, swathing him in its folds as though a tent had collapsed upon him. He struck right and left, trying to tear through the cotton with the front sight of the revolver.

Some one leaped from the rafters to the floor behind him, and a club crashed against his head. He staggered and fell.

The revolver slipped from his fingers.

He was not quite knocked out, though his head rang and his arms and legs were leaden.

With characteristic coolness, he lay still, simulating unconsciousness while his strength returned. Only his fingers moved, groping cautiously under the cloth for the gun.

From the launch Carruthers was shouting his name. He heard a splash in the water.

"Harren—Brown—come back! Let the commissioner go!" Fisher ordered.

The men he addressed only shouted incoherently. They were charging up the path to rescue Bill.

"Back—all of you!" Bill shouted.

Outside the bungalow a heavy rifle exploded. Simultaneously, a club landed on Bill's head and consciousness snapped out like a light....

He came to slowly. Many minutes—it might have been hours—had passed, for the ceiling cloth which had covered him was gone. A native was squatting beside him with a short club. Dully, Bill identified the man as a Samoan. He was big and ugly enough for two.

"My word, you want to break head belong me?" Bill rumbled thickly. He sat up. His head was spinning, but in dealing with a native, a white man must speak first and act first.

"S-s-steady, Bill!" commanded a chattering voice that banished any idea of a desperate counter-attack.

Bill turned his head stiffly. More Fathoms Todd sat on a case of trade gin, with a double-barrelled express rifle across his knees. The twin muzzles were pointed at Bill's chest. Todd's fingers trembled around the triggers. He was unshaven, ghastly pale, and shaking as though he were on the verge of delirium tremens.

Nor was this the worst. Bill saw that Harren now lay senseless on the floor, bleeding from a cut scalp. Brown and Carruthers sat beside him, their hands tied behind them. Another native, also a Samoan, but slender and light yellow of complexion, stood guard above them with a revolver. Fisher was missing.

"Who killed the sergeant?" Bill asked quietly.

The unshaven features writhed. "I—I did!" Todd answered in a gasping snarl.

"He was a good man," the pearler rumbled. "It was a neat little trick, Todd.—It worked. Well, you poor damn fool, you've put your scheme over. Now what?"

The last words boomed like a revolver shot.

Todd gave a nervous start.

"Here I am! Go on—shoot!" Carruthers interrupted bitterly. "If you'd had any manhood except what you got out of a bottle, you might have shot me on my own veranda at Rontonga.—Go on! I'm ready, but for God's sake don't sacrifice any more innocent men!"

Todd did not answer. His fingernails beat a louder, more erratic tattoo on the stock of the big rifle. The bloodshot eyes never left Bill's face. "Y-you'll s-see w-what's next," he threatened hoarsely. "M-Moju, you take him. K-Kaleka can watch the others."

The big Samoan seized Bill's wrists and tied them with cord. Kaleka motioned for the other two to lift Harren.

"**I SAY,** where are you takin' us?" Brown burst out.

"To hell! To hell with you and all of you!" Todd screamed shrilly.

He sprang across the room and struck the wireless operator savagely in the face. Then he recoiled and stood, ashen faced and shaking, as Kaleka thrust a revolver against the youngster's back. Bellow Bill wrenched at his bonds; but though he pulled the skin from his wrists, the cords held. Moju jabbed him in the back with the point of a knife.

"G-go on!" Todd gasped.

He remained where he stood while Harren was carried out, but the two Samoans needed no orders. They herded the prisoners onto the launch, and threw the body of Fisher off onto the sand with callous brutality. Bill observed that the sergeant had been hit just over the heart.

Moju took the wheel and Kaleka started the engine expertly. Bill sized up the big Samoan as a stupid thug. The slender yellow native, however, was obviously of a much higher order of intelligence. The two might be responsible for the recent pearl piracies. Yet if so, why had they embarked on an infinitely more dangerous game? Had Kaleka discovered that piracy did not pay?

"I say! Are you going to send us *all* sailing back?" Brown ejaculated.

Bellow Bill shrugged.

Nevertheless, he gave a grunt of relief when the launch swung to starboard, at right angles to the course toward Rontonga.

Gradually the boat drew away from the shores of Cooke Island. Harren recovered consciousness, and was immediately bound. The launch went mile after mile into the open sea.

A frown gathered on Bill's forehead. The two natives had not exchanged a word, but Bill knew the waters intimately. On the course the launch was steering, there was no land for more than sixty miles. No habitable land, this is. About ten miles away there was a tiny coral atoll which rose a few feet above the sea. That tiny ring of sand was swept by every storm. No palm tree had been able to take root. There was neither water nor shade there. Turtles came to the atoll to lay eggs, for at noonday the sand was hot to the touch. This, however, was not the turtle season; and pearling luggers and native dugouts were unlikely to visit the atoll for several months.

Bill's frown deepened. The sun, beating down on that ring of sand, would kill the strongest man within a day or two—even with food and water, the heat and the glare would madden any one marooned on the atoll. Within a week at the most. There is a Chinese torture which consists in forcing the victim to stare at the sun. This would be much the same. A little slower, a little more tantalizing, but in the end only the more cruel.

Two men had died. Were four more to be marooned and tortured for the sake of revenge upon one? The idea was fiendish—and strange. For there was a flaw in the scheme, whereas the ambush had been flawless in plan and execution.

Nevertheless the prisoners were to be marooned. Moju conned the launch up to the atoll, and with a vicious grin hurled a gin bottle full of water out onto the sand—a pint of water for four men!

With his knife he then motioned to the white men to jump ashore.

Carruthers, his face dead white, sat still. "I'll be damned if I do!" he announced.

Without a word the two natives picked him up by the arms and legs and tossed him out of the boat.

Harren rolled over the side before he could be touched, and Bellow Bill did the same. Brown was hurled after them, screaming. Kaleka instantly shot the launch off shore, and headed at full speed back toward Cooke Island.

"WHY DIDN'T you fight?" Carruthers raged. "My God, Williams, have you ever been thirsty? Is that water, or did those devils leave us gin?—Not that it matters! What's an hour more or less?"

"Easy now!" Bill rumbled. "Stand back to back with me and untie my hands. A pint of water may be enough."

As soon as the cords were loosened, Bill picked up the bottle and tasted the contents. It was water, though the heat of the sun gave it a flat and earthy taste.

He buried the bottle deeply enough to be cooled by the dampness under the sand; then he released Carruthers and Brown.

"You three can have all of that," he rumbled. "Better go easy with it, though you're not going to die of thirst. I'm just waiting for the launch to get out of sight."

"Are you mad?" Carruthers snapped.

Harren's prominent eyes popped. "Waiting?" he questioned.

"Only that," Bill answered calmly. "This is a good place to maroon four white men—ten miles from the nearest land. And I see a couple of shark fins out there.

"It would really be a smart, devilish idea—*except that I swim better than most Polynesians, and Todd's one of the few who've seen me do it!* It's true that I hire divers to get my pearls, but Todd knows that I can go deeper and stay under water longer myself than they can. Did you know that?" Bill barked at the commissioner.

"I say! I'd forgotten!"

"But diving isn't swimming!" Barren objected.

Bill grinned. "Any man who can go down in twenty fathoms can swim ten miles," he purred. "Ain't it a bit queer that Todd should try to maroon *me?*"

"He might have planned to maroon us, and failed to change his plan out of friendship," Harren replied. "We can't swim."

"Carruthers, who knew that your brother was going to cross-examine Todd?" Bill demanded.

"Why—Brown, here, relayed the message. And I discussed the matter with Harren. I really don't see the connection—"

"Couldn't you see that Todd's hands were shaking too badly to sight a rifle?" Bill roared. "He had the jitters—and he hit Brown when his nerves snapped.

"But he didn't forget! An accomplice he may be—he may have helped a pair of pearl pirates get a boat—but he never bargained on murder. I'm his friend, but would I have mercy on him after this? Not I—nor he on me, if he's guilty!"

"He may be planning to separate you from the rest of us," said Harren sharply. "You've just accused Brown or myself of complicity in this crime. That's going too far! I insist on knowing what grounds you have for saying that.

"I did miss my shot at Kaleka. He stepped out of the weeds and tripped Carruthers. I fired, and he smashed me over the head with the barrel of his gun. As I went down, Brown fell over me—and Kaleka had a cold drop on us both."

"So?" Bill rumbled. "Things like that happen, Harren. I've missed a man with all six shots when he wasn't ten feet away. But I'm thinking of the queer things. You and I claim to be fighting men. Were you ever outguessed more neatly? I wasn't. Who led the charge to help me?"

"I did," Carruthers admitted. "And I'd do the same thing again. Only a coward would let you be attacked without trying to help you."

"It seemed to me that Fisher could defend the launch,"

Harren argued angrily. "Furthermore, I'm not the kind of soldier to let his officer charge alone.—As to your accusation, Williams, it's too ridiculous to deserve an answer. I was with Carruthers the day his brother was shot, and I'm here now."

Bellow Bill smiled bleakly. "If it wasn't a ridiculous accusation, I'd be wringing your neck right now," he rumbled. "Just the same, I've a hunch I'm right. You haven't done a thing—but some one is planning every one of these damned queer moves like a game of chess! No dead man in the lugger—and no police boat leaves Rontonga. No police boat—no ambush. No ambush—no marooning. And now comes what?"

The pearler stripped off his trousers and tossed the cotton singlet onto the sand. The white skin of his legs was in startling contrast to the full-rigged ship on his chest and the tattooed snakes that twined around his hips.

"I'm a roughneck!" Bill boomed proudly. "I don't pretend to be able to outsmart a guy who has been planning a crime for weeks and months. But by Barney's bull, I can swim ten miles and try to raise hell!"

He strode into the water.

"But the sharks?" Brown cried excitedly.

"Youngster, mighty few sharks will attack a swimmer," Bill growled. "I'd go through a hundred of them for the chance to do something unexpected."

CHAPTER IV

MAN NAKED

AND INDEED, THOUGH the triangular fins cruised slowly toward Bellow Bill, they sheered off when he began to splash with his hands and feet. He waved an arm gaily back at the little atoll, and settled down to the long swim.

Despite suspicions and uncertainty, Bill was in a grimly

cheerful frame of mind. The afternoon was half gone, and he could not hope to reach the island until long after sunset. Darkness, however, would be in his favor. The criminals had been so completely successful thus far that Bill doubted if they would take the precaution of guarding their boats, and he anticipated little difficulty in stealing either the police launch or the craft in which Moju and Kaleka had reached the island.

Alas for anticipations! He had been swimming four hours, and was near enough to see the bare palm trunks around Todd's bungalow, like sticks against the starlit sky, when the police launch got under way. Bill turned on his back as the sound of the exhaust came nearer and nearer. The boat passed within a hundred feet of him—on the course for the atoll!

Nevertheless, a light continued to burn in the bungalow, and Bill swam onward. His suspicions against Harren were redoubled. The fact that the launch was returning to the atoll was almost proof that Todd was the victim, and not the accomplice, of the criminals. Yet to Bill's utter amazement, a second boat swung at the mooring in front of the beach. This craft was low and lightly built, and unless appearances lied, it would be three or four knots an hour faster than the police boat. Bill touched the hull, and felt the smooth surface of varnished mahogany. Here was the motorboat which Carruthers had traced to Todd!

All that concerned Bill, however, was the boat's speed. Whoever was on Cooke Island could remain there. No third boat in the district could match speed with the police launch and this craft. It was even possible, Bill calculated swiftly, to beat the launch to the atoll, to rescue Carruthers and demand an explanation from Harren.

Bill was about to climb into the cockpit when his ear caught a low, confused noise that was as continuous as the wash of the ripples on the beach. He let himself slide back into the water. In a flash he understood why Todd had shouldered the guilt of a cold-blooded killing. In the bungalow a terrified child was sobbing uncontrollably.

Small wonder that Todd had drugged himself with gin against horror, and that he had posed with the double-barrelled gun across his knees. The two natives had his son. If he had given the show away, young Livingston's life would have been forfeit as well as his own.

BILL CRAWLED noiselessly across the beach. There was not even a stick on the sand, and he dared not search through the high weeds for a weapon. If a snapping twig warned the man in the bungalow, the fellow had only to put a revolver against the kid's head. Risk harming the child Bill would not, even—even though the criminals must plan to kill Livingston in the end. For they could not let a witness survive.

Like a shadow, Bill tiptoed up the path. The veranda floor was almost level with his head, but through the doorway he could see Livingston, lying face down on the floor. The thin shoulders shook with racking sobs. Between the boy and the door sat Kaleka.

Bill crouched, and moved forward. At the bottom of the veranda steps he paused. Kaleka had a revolver. He was an expert shot. The steps were warped by the sun, and would surely creak beneath a weight as great as Bill's. To get into the bungalow… To give the kid a chance to escape, whatever the outcome… To hurry Kaleka's shot… A club would be no weapon for such a job, even if he had one. He must rely on his hands, and he must manage to get close enough to use them.

The lowest step leading to the veranda was formed by a slab of coral fully two feet long and almost a foot thick. Bill lifted it. The weight was thirty pounds or more. It was heavier than he liked, but he dared not take the time to search for a better missile.

Above the veranda the thatched roof slanted upward. The ridgepole was twenty feet or more above the ground, and fully thirty feet from the edge of the veranda. Too high, and too far—yet there was no alternative. Bill filled his lungs and bent low. He swung the coral slab back and forth between his knees. He was considered abnormally strong. He must heave the slab over the ridgepole—and startle Kaleka by an attack which would seem to come from above.

The great naked, tattooed body snapped erect as Bill flung the slab upward as he would have flung a medicine ball. It failed to clear the ridgepole, but only by a foot or two; and as the heavy stone tore through the sun-dried palm leaves, Bill took the veranda steps in two jumps and charged through the door.

Involuntarily, Kaleka leaped up at the crash. He snatched out his revolver, staring upward. He turned too late. Though he fired, it was as Bill dove headlong at his knees. They went down together, but a second after the coral slab thundered to the floor beside them. Bill's huge hand closed on the yellow wrist which held the gun. Kaleka fired, but the revolver was pointing harmlessly into the air. Bill pinned the native down with one knee, and swung once, to the point of the lean yellow jaw. Kaleka lay still.

Young Livingston had scarcely had time to move. With round eyes the boy stared, the tears still sliding down his cheeks. "Bill!" he sobbed. With a wild leap he was in the pearler's arms. "They took Daddy away in the boat."

"They?" Bill rumbled. "Son, did this yellow devil hurt you?"

"Oh, he just tied my hands and my mouth," the boy answered. "But I mean Moju, the ugly one, took away Daddy. He came here day before yesterday. I ran out to see them, and they grabbed me. I—"

"Aye, aye, son!" Bill rumbled. "Never mind that. Get me a rope, and we'll tie this fellow up and stick a rag in his mouth. I'm in a hurry!"

"He made the wireless go!" Livingston insisted. "I saw the sparks."

"He what? Oh, he sent a wireless message with the set on the launch, eh? All right. Hurry up with that rope!"

WHEN KALEKA was bound and gagged, Bill made a hasty search for more revolver ammunition. He found none. The double-barrelled rifle was also missing. The revolver he had taken from Kaleka still held three cartridges, and since he had no intention of going up against a machine gun with small arms, Bill did not lose more than a minute in carrying Kaleka to the motorboat.

The launch had too long a start to be overtaken. Bill steered for the atoll, but not by a direct course. He suspected that Harren meant to return to Cooke Island.

From Livingston he could learn little except that no white man had appeared at the island since his own visit. As far as the boy knew, the two natives were acting independently, but Bill did not believe that.

"I choked the truth out of Harren," he growled as soon as Kaleka recovered consciousness.

"Which was Harren? The fat man?"

"Belay that stuff!" Bill threatened. "Who did you send that wireless message to?"

"If you live, I hang," Kaleka answered.

"You were a fool to commit murder for a white man." Bill abandoned the attempt to frighten his captive. Kaleka had courage.

"Not this man. If he told me to jump into a shark's mouth I would do it," the native answered simply. "I have killed many for him; and because he is wise, I can laugh at the water police. You have not choked him. I can see what course you are steering by the stars. You are afraid to meet him, and you are right."

"So it is Harren? He got you this motorboat for pearl piracy, didn't he?"

"We are not children!" the native retorted scornfully. "Yes. He got this boat for us, and we took a few pearls." Kaleka spat into the starlit water. "Perhaps I shall die, but I shall not hang. You will try to trick him, as you did me. *I* was fooled, but he—"

"Why didn't Todd escape with his kid when you left him alone?"

"Because I handcuffed the boy's arms and legs around the trunk of an ironwood tree," Kaleka sneered.

He rolled over on his side. Bill shrugged his shoulders. The pearler's respect for Harren had increased tremendously. Then he gagged Kaleka.

By steering a rather circuitous course, Bill succeeded in avoiding the launch. In a little less than an hour, he arrived in sight of the atoll. On the ring of sand, pale in the starlight, two dark figures lay sprawled and motionless. Even before the keel grated on the beach, Bill recognized Carruthers and Brown; but when he bent over them, expecting to find two bodies riddled with bullets, he was startled to discover that both were breathing.

He lifted Carruthers by the shoulders and shouted his name. The commissioner's eyes remained shut, and when Bill released him he dropped limply to the sand. He was not wounded, but he was hopelessly, helplessly drugged into a stupor so profound that it would endure for many, many hours. Brown was in the same condition. Between the two lay the gin bottle—empty of the water it had contained.

"They could swig the stuff or go thirsty," Bill muttered. "The damn clever devil! And yet—why didn't he kill them? He didn't drug that water out of kindness."

Bill stuffed his cheek with fine cut, then picked up his trousers and put them on.

"Todd's still in the launch," he reflected aloud. "I think I begin to savvy." Deep in thought, the pearler carried Carruthers and Brown to the boat.

"Your daddy's all right so far, son," he rumbled. "Harren's got a brain, all right—and nerve! *What* a scheme!—with an alibi for himself at every step, until the whole thing was set up and ready to go! But he knows I've got his boat and his accomplice now, son, and therefore—"

—Therefore Beliow Bill pointed the motorboat toward Rontonga, and nursed the engine to its utmost speed....

CHAPTER V

GUNS ARE TRUMPS

FROM COOKE ISLAND to the gap in the long, straight coral reefs at Rontonga was thirty miles. The launch would arrive in about two hours and a half. From the atoll, Bill estimated, the distance was thirty-five miles. He could cover it in two hours.— But Harren had a head start. If he arrived first....

Bellow Bill shifted his quid. That wouldn't be so good. A sailor to his finger tips, he tingled to the rising suspense that grows in the race for position which precedes a battle between two ships at sea. For a landsman the dark, starlit water would have been without menace or excitement. Bill peered ahead for the white blur that is made by a racing propeller, which differs from the white, evanescent streak of a breaking wave.

He had no longer any doubt that Harren had engineered the murders, and the ultimate purpose of the planter was almost as obvious. Since he bore no grudge against either of the dead men, he must have turned criminal for money; and the only considerable sum in the district was in the bank at Rontonga. In those old-fashioned vaults, unprotected by time locks, were all the pearls collected by the whole fleet, during an entire season— and most of the cash shipped in by steamer for the purchase of pearl shell as well. Half a million dollars in unset gems, and in notes and gold that could never be traced. Loot enough to kill for, and to plan for.

Despite Harren's cold-blooded ruthlessness, Bellow Bill could not repress a feeling of grim admiration. The pop-eyed, fleshy ex-major was a man—hard-bitten as any soldier produced on the Western Front, and desperate as only a retired capitalist who sees his competency shrink in a world's wild depression can be. But none the less cunning and brave.

The immense distances among the South Sea Islands, and the slow means of transportation available to an escaping criminal, which had been sufficient in the past to preclude even an attempt at a major robbery, had only whetted Harren's cunning. Before he could rob the bank he must lay it open to attack. He had done that. To escape with the loot he must set the pursuit on a false trail and provide himself with an alibi. He had done that, too. He had to drill native accomplices to stand in the foreground while he guided them, unseen. He had also done that. And finally, he must trick the law into thinking that the case was closed and all the criminals dead. And he would probably do that, even now.

One small miscalculation had destroyed the fruits of his cunning, but there remained the hard-bitten courage which had enabled him to run coolly into an ambush which he himself had arranged. He was not beaten yet. He was only unmasked. He must bring off his *coup* now, or hang; and the steps preliminary to the crime had succeeded so well that he could bring it off if he reached Rontonga first. He had an armored launch, armed with a machine gun, and he had sent a wireless message.

Had that message gone to confederates in Rontonga? Or was it a message to the police, in Carruthers's name, ordering the other police launch to put to sea on a wild goose chase? Bill shifted his quid. Either way, that radiogram wouldn't be of any help to him. He splashed water over the two drugged men, but without the slightest effect; and he tightened the bonds and gag that secured Kaleka. If he won the race to the harbor, he could arouse the bank manager and alarm the town....

RONTONGA WAS in sight before he knew that he had lost. He made out a white streak and a black shadow, on a sea that elsewhere was violet-blue. Almost simultaneously a tracer bullet *z-zipped* overhead. The hiss of the bullets was followed by the *rat-tat-tat* of the machine gun.

Bill spun the wheel hard over. The boat veered to port, with bullets flying all around it in short bursts. Even with tracers, the range was too long for Harren to get on the target; but he drove the boat faster away from the harbor and to the shelter of the night.

Bill did not turn tail. When the firing stopped he reduced the speed of the engine and swung slowly back to starboard to keep in touch with the launch. Livingston crawled aft and nestled against him, and Bill gripped the wheel, to run again in case the launch turned to attack.

At the speed both craft were making, the reef and the surf of Rontonga drew near rapidly. The launch, Bill guessed, was making for the harbor. Within a minute or two he must either follow, or change course to avoid a wreck. To stop and wait for the other boat to come out, and then follow it at a safe distance, never occurred to him. The resourceful Harren might have prepared a hideaway on shore.

"Kid, do you want to help me get your daddy?" he rumbled.

"Oh, quite!" The answer, in its plucky English idiom, was so sturdy and so unexpected to American ears that Bill laughed. "Then get me the water breaker, son, and some more rope," he chuckled. "We'll make a sailor of you yet! Here—take the wheel and steer for that tall palm tree, straight ahead."

Bill poured the water from the five-gallon keg and screwed the plug tightly into place. "Kaleka," he rumbled, "I'm going into the harbor, and I know damn well that Harren will riddle this boat with the machine gun as soon as I'm within a couple of hundred yards. Of course, I can leave you where you are—"

"My God, no! Please, sir—throw me overboard! Let me go—I can reach shore," protested the native violently. "I am afraid—if a bullet hits the tank, the boat will catch fire. I cannot stand that!"

"Say—I never thought of it. That's an idea!" Bill growled. "Or, as I was going to say, I can give you the chance to save Carruthers and Brown, here. Maybe they'll be grateful enough to commute your sentence."

While he spoke, the pearler cut off a length of rope with a pair of wire-cutters from among the engine tools, and unlayed the strands. With the fine cords thus obtained, he lashed Kaleka's left hand to Carruthers's left hand—not only by the wrists but by the thumbs—and knotted the twine again and again. Kaleka's right hand was secured to Brown's right hand in the same manner. Swiftly, Bill laid the three men in the bottom of the boat, breast against back. Brown was on the bottom, Carruthers next, and Kaleka on top. With a rope passed under their arms, the pearler tied them together, and then he unfastened the bonds which had secured Kaleka's feet.

"You won't untie those little knots with your teeth in a hurry, even if you can reach them," Bill rumbled. "But you can tread water with your feet, and you got use enough of your arms to hold their heads above water.—You better do it, for if they drown, they'll pull you down, too."

"I savvy," the native assented eagerly.

"Not the half!" Bellow Bill contradicted. He passed a rope through the handles of the water breaker, and fastened it against Brown's chest. "That'll help hold them up, but it won't keep your nose high," he said.

He lifted the three men onto the narrow deck at the stern, and with one hand held them from rolling overboard.

"I'll drop you as near shore as I can. You better take them the rest of the way. Tide's coming in, and that'll help you."

Kaleka nodded.

The boat rushed for the narrow gap at the harbor mouth, through which the launch had already passed.

"WHEN I say 'Jump!' Livingston, you jump," Bill ordered calmly. "I know you can swim like a little fish. Then get to the beach and yell as loud as you can for men to come and pull Mr. Carruthers out of the water."

"Will that save daddy?"

"It'll help," Bill answered solemnly. "Is there a pet-cock for draining the gas tank, Kaleka?"

"Forward, under the deck," the native answered.

"And my pants ain't been in water, so my matches are dry," Bill reflected aloud.

A twisted but altogether joyful smile was on his lips. He reached forward and thrust the largest wrench from the tool kit into his belt, thought for an instant, and coiled what was left of the rope loosely around his neck.

"I was in the War myself," he rumbled. "Soldiers can plan—but it takes a sailor to improvise. Stand by, lads!"

He threw the throttle wide open. The boat swung around the reef at the harbor entrance and pointed straight down the narrow gap through the inner beach and toward the harbor proper, which was a circular basin about three hundred yards in diameter.

"Jump!" Bill thundered to Livingston as he passed the sands.

The kid sprang over the side, and with a mighty push the pearler thrust the three men bound to the cask clear of the propeller. Then he leaped forward, opened the gas cock and went back to the wheel.

"Turn out!" he roared with a bellow fit to waken the soundest sleeper. "Turn out, you mugs! The bank's afire!"

From the beach in front of the slumbering town a machine gun stuttered into action. Harren had had the impudence, or the cunning, to lay the launch alongside the official police dock. The first burst was low. The bullets churned up a patch of water ahead, through which the boat must pass.

Bellow Bill tossed a lighted match into the bilge and rolled overboard. As the water closed over his head a stream of bullets ripped into the bow. The motorboat seemed to explode into flame. It yawed, and ran crazily, unsteered, to crash onto the beach. The fire which enveloped it cast a reddish sheen over the water in the harbor.

CHAPTER VI

THE DEADLINE

WHILE THE ATTENTION of the machine gunner was centered on the burning boat, Bellow Bill Williams had swum to the beach, mostly under water. The spreading circle of fire-light found him in the shelter of some native dugouts drawn up on the sand.

The larger police boat, he noted swiftly, was no longer in the harbor. Evidently the forged radiogram had succeeded in its purpose; but a pearling town is never completely stripped of constables. Nor were the pearlers of Rontonga ever all asleep. Already men were astir, though, sailor-like, the first thought of each was for the safety of his own ship. The burning motorboat was a menace to every lugger in the harbor.

A Jap ran across the beach and launched a dugout. A native, more excited, sprinted stark naked down the street and dashed into the water. Behind him came a constable, buckling on a revolver belt as he hurried toward the police launch for orders.

"Never mind the launch—watch the bank!" Bill roared.

The constable glanced across the harbor, but he did not stop. Discipline came first with him, and who the hell was a tattooed Yankee that he should give orders?

"I s'ye, Bill—wot's the matter with the ruddy bank? It's top hole!" yelled the irrepressible Australian.

From the cabin of the launch came a staccato roll of drum fire—a full magazine fired in the single burst. The constable, halfway across the beach, spun around and pitched on his face. A man wounded by the stream of lead that swept the front of the town, uttered a gasping scream. Sailors running toward the harbor flung themselves down—to leap up and scurry like ants for the flimsy shelter of the nearest hut.

The hush of consternation which followed that murderous blast was so complete that the shrill yelling of a small boy was heard over the whole harbor.

"Help!—I say, *help!*—Pull Mr. Carruthers out of the water!"

The machine gunner had profited by the death of Fisher. No one was on the cabin roof. The gun which commanded the town was thrust through a window at the bow; the gunner was shielded by a half-inch of boiler iron.

There were brave men on the beach, but they were stunned by the attack and they were bewildered by Bill's shouts. The tank was all right. Here in front of them, on the police launch which had so amazingly changed sides, was the menace.

The pearlers, unorganized and but half armed, each man of them flat on his belly behind such shelter as he had been able to reach, recognized defeat.

So did Bellow Bill. The deadline established by the machine gun could be maintained until the launch chose to put to sea. Any attempt to rally the town would only result in a futile loss of life.

Bill fingered the rope around his neck, and shook his head. There wasn't enough of it. He groped in the dugout, and found a small fishing net and the wet gunny sack the owner used for carrying pearl shell. Wrapping these around his body, he ducked under water and swam toward the launch.

THREE HUNDRED yards is a long swim. He knew that he would have to rise five or six times, and he cursed at the shout and the confused murmur which filled the air as his head broke the firelit water for the first time.

He risked a hasty glance. He had not caused the alarm.

Out of a side port in the cabin of the launch poked the head of More Fathoms Todd. A gag was in the mouth. His eyes rolled desperately, and the whole head wagged from side to side— mutely, yet in a pantomime of helplessness that was eloquent. The message lasted only an instant. Then the head jerked upward spasmodically and disappeared within the launch, as though Todd had been struck down from behind.

"I s'ye! 'E *asn't* swiped the boat!" screamed the Australian. "And mytes! Look there in the 'arbor!'"

Bill ducked. When he rose again it was with all his skill, turning on his back and breaking water with a puff and gasp almost as quick as the leap of a fish. Nevertheless, two heavy bullets smacked the surface within a yard of his face. Not the machine gun, this time, but the elephant rifle. A heavy weapon for snap-shooting in such tricky light, as the man behind it seemed to realize.

Bill drew revolver fire from the launch on his next emergency for air, but to his delight the pearlers on the beach did not fire upon him.

The last fifty yards was the most dangerous part of the swim, but he managed to locate the dark bulk of the dock, and worked his way along the rough blocks of coral of which it was constructed so that when he rose at last his head was beneath the overhanging stern of the launch.

Shouts informed him that he had been seen from the beach. Some pearler, more quick-witted than the others, opened fire on the launch with a rifle. A short burst from the machine gun drove the riflemen to cover, but Bill needed only those few seconds to wrap the fishnet and the sack around the propeller blades and to tangle the rope in and out around the rudder post and the shaft.

A gasp and a roar from the town warned him to be swift. The machine gun fired a long burst. Bill, hidden under the overhanging stern, did not understand the cause. He hoped that no one was fool enough to charge; and indeed, but one man charged the launch, and he was not a fool. The hail of bullets was fired to aid him, not stop him.

"Follow me! Come on, lads!" Harren was shouting.

He came into sight at the end of the street, with a heavy canvas bag under each arm and a revolver bouncing at his hip.

"Follow me! Come *on!*"

No one followed. The machine gun saw to that. If the pearlers thought at all, they thought that Harren had gone mad. Where had he come from? Was he crazy enough to carry bombs, instead of throwing them? In five seconds—while the pearlers waited for the withering fire to cut him down at every stride—Harren was across the beach. He leaped onto the launch, over the roof and down into the pocket. He disappeared. But the fire of the machine gun kept on.

Then the pearlers knew that they had been tricked, and they began to yell with impotent rage.

Bellow Bill Williams did not recognize the voice, but he heard the thud of Harren's feet on the deck. An instant later the engine coughed and the launch slid away from the dock with a speed that was abruptly checked as the cordage jammed around the propeller blades. The engine pounded, and the launch barely made steerageway. Nevertheless it moved, and the machine gun continued its domination of Rontonga.

The wash of the propeller forced Bill from beneath the stern, where there was nothing to which he could cling. He slipped along the side of the launch, too close to the planking to be seen or fired upon by any one in the cabin. A short plunge beneath the water would have taken him around the corner of the coral dock; but as the launch continued to move and the engine to turn over, he twisted in the water and swam with it for a few strokes.

On the beach the shouting ceased. Bill's arm reached up. He caught the anchor chain, where it looped from the hawse pipe to the deck above, and drew his body half out of water to keep his legs close to the boat.

"Oh, I s'ye!" yelled the Australian.

Some one on the beach clapped a hand over his mouth.

The launch turned slowly, and headed for the entrance to the harbor. Bill made no attempt to climb aboard. He now held the chain with both hands, and his feet dragged along the side, throwing up ripples that streamed unnaturally across the fire-reddened water. Across the basin and past the inner beach; past the reef and into the open sea, the launch moved at a snail's pace. Bellow Bill clung to her like a barnacle.

CHAPTER VII

CLEARED

EVEN A LUGGER could outsail the crippled launch. Once beyond rifle shot of the shore, the engine was stopped.

"Near thing, that!" said Harren crisply. "How'd it happen?"

"That Bill, he swim," Moju growled.

"Quite!" Harren agreed without animus. "I should have judged him by the markings on his skin instead of the color of it. He's tattooed like a Polynesian. Where'd you see him last?"

"I see no one," Moju growled.

Harren was silent.

"Well, jump overboard and cut that propeller clear," he ordered at last. "I'd give half the pearls to know how he knocked Kaleka out with that rock—*if* he knocked him out with that rock.—In fact, I'd give all the pearls to have him helping me instead of fighting me. I need a man who knows the South Seas like a chart. There'll be a wireless sent out about us—and together Bill and I could rob the Bank of England… Half a mo', Moju. Better take a knife in each hand. That stuff may be tougher than you think."

"You see one fella Bill?"

"No, I didn't see him.—Now don't get the wind up," Harren retorted. "You were scared to death about the bank; and I did the job alone, didn't I?" Harren laughed. "It worked out exactly as I told you it would. You and Kaleka would have had less trouble than I. The manager was asleep in the bungalow next door, with nothing over the window but a piece of mosquito netting." Harren chuckled. "Two feet of steel around the cash and pearls—and nothing but a veil around him! You should have seen him blink when I leaned through the window and shoved my gun against his ear. The old blackguard! It was on his advice I put every shilling I had into unsound investments....

" 'Come and open the vault for me or I'll blow your head open!' I said to him.—'Oh, Mr. Harren! Are you mad?' he said. Blatted like a sheep, when he saw I meant it.—Two feet of steel around the vault—but he couldn't work the combination fast enough. Shook so much that I hit him over the head only when the last door was open.—A bag of pearls, and as much currency as I could get my arm around."

Harren stopped talking. A breaking wave dashed softly against the bow of the launch.

"What's the matter, Moju?—Get over the side before those luggers start after us!" he ended in a cold snarl.

As the big Samoan dove over the stern, Bellow Bill lifted himself high enough to peer over the bow. Harren stood in the cockpit. He had a revolver raised over his head, and he was facing—forward. Bill let go the anchor chain and permitted himself to sink deep. The sea water was like ink, but a phosphorescent glow indicated where Moju was. Bill rose directly beneath the native.

Gently as he moved, he made enough stir in the water to betray himself. Moju set both feet against the keel of the launch and dove to meet him, outlined in gleaming silver. A knife bit into the pearler's scalp, but he caught the wrist and flung his knee upward. His other hand hooked in Moju's armpit, and the arm broke across his knee. A great bubble of air burst from the native's mouth. The knife, slipping from limp fingers, scraped the pearler's chest as it sank.

Bill shifted his left hand to the throat, but shock and pain had wilted Moju. When the pearler located the other hand, there was no knife in it. Moju's legs were still. His head lolled; yet when Bill released him there remained enough air in the lungs to make the body rise. The lines of the hull above were outlined in silver phosphorescence. Bill swam for the stern, rose silently beneath it; but Moju floated straight upward.

AS THE Samoan's head broke the surface a shot came from the launch. The body quivered and sank.

"Moju?" Harren rasped. A pause. "Oh—then it *is* you I hear breathing under the stern? Eh, Bill? I wasn't sure you'd stuck along.—But my motto is, 'Leave nothing to chance.'"

Bill braced himself against the rudder post. Both hands were ready to snatch at the revolver as soon as Harren leaned over the side.

"You might have waited to make sure, you double-crossing murderer."

"Why? I meant to shoot Moju anyway. Kaleka, too," Harren retorted indifferently. "After the event has taken place, accomplices know too much, don't you see? So I shoot them, knock Todd in the head, and scuttle the launch near the atoll. Then I swim ashore and bury the swag in the sand—the tide would be rising again to smooth out the marks—and lie down by Carruthers. In the morning, when they come to, there I am—complaining of a headache as bad as theirs.

"I never meant to show my nose out of the launch at Rontonga—as long as I wasn't recognized. I had a perfect alibi with the commissioner himself to vouch for it; and the police would have had a perfect case. When the bodies rose, wouldn't it be obvious that the thieves had fought over the loot? Even if I had been forced to show myself in Rontonga, the police would have been apt to hunt for the commissioner first, and—I've made a pretty good run for it, as it stands."

"So far," Bill rumbled. "Belay the gab, Harren! It's an old trick, and I'm wise to it. Take a gun or a knife and come on overboard!"

"Fourteen years ago and I'd have done it, Bill," Harren retorted. "But I've lived soft, and I'm pretty fat. My weapons are men—men with brains enough merely to obey orders to the letter. I'm sorry, Bill, but you'll have to come after me if you want me."

In the silence the waves splashed against the hull.

"You're strong," said Harren grimly. "But I wonder if you're strong enough to hold onto the anchor chain all night? I'm going to steer in the trough of the sea and duck you at every roll. I sent that other police boat to Thursday Island. They can't recall it inside of twelve hours, and nothing else can face a machine gun.—So you see, I'll be waiting for you to climb the side, Bill."

Bill grinned, remembering that Moju had failed to unfoul the propeller.

The launch rolled gently. Bill tensed for an attack. He was almost caught in the open as the engine started; and he swam desperately for the bow to seize the anchor chain before Harren could get from the engine to the deck. He succeeded, and clung with one hand as the boat moved slowly ahead. He had to watch the starlit sky. He must be ready to throw himself around the bow in case Harren leaned far out of the cabin window. The ruthless, scheming intellect above had hit upon the correct strategy. Sooner or later, Bill must attack—and the bigger the man, the bigger the target.

Nevertheless he was gathering himself for the forlorn hope. He did have a gun, though it had been under salt water so long now that he did not trust it. His fingers were hooked over the rail when the launch yawed widely, as though no hand were at the wheel.

BILL HEAVED himself on deck. The cabin windows gaped but two yards away. He expected the flash of a gun as he hurled himself at the opening. His shoulders were too broad to enter the cabin quickly, so he wriggled rather than dove through, striking right and left with his revolver in the dark, and wondering why the shot did not come.

He tumbled, heels over head, onto a fat writhing body. He gripped the throat. He smacked the head with the barrel of the revolver. The writhings ceased.

The pearler stood up. He was shaking so that he could not get his wet fine-cut out of his pocket. He did not understand.

Had Harren had a fit? Had he been hit by a bullet and failed to notice the wound in the excitement?

Bill fumbled until he found the switch of the cabin light. Harren lay like a log. Beneath him, still bound, still gagged, but with eyes that rolled and blazed, More Fathoms Todd was struggling to get his legs from beneath the unconscious body. Bill pulled him clear and untied the gag.

"I kicked him!" Todd gasped. "I inched across the deck while he was talking to you, and when he stood by the wheel I kicked him! Like this!" The bound feet raised in the air and shot forward savagely, both heels together. "I heard Livingston shouting at Rontonga; and after that I could do something. I didn't much care before—except for him. That is—I'm down and out. I didn't much care what they did—to strangers, or even to the commissioner. I got the shakes when I saw you—but they'd only have killed us all, right there, Bill."

"By Barney's bull, are you apologizing to me?" the pearler boomed. "Shut up! Ain't it enough to down the most dangerous crook that ever worked the South Seas?"

"I'll never convince the commissioner I wasn't Harren's accomplice—at the start, at least," Todd protested. "And it's true. I did hate Carruthers."

"Shut up! He's a man, even if his neck is too damn stiff," Bill rumbled. "I doubt if you know all that Harren did, Todd. Carruthers isn't going to look any further than those heel-prints you put in Harren's back; and as for bein' down and out he'll see to it that that's ended—and so will I!"

Bellow Bill spun the wheel and the launch turned slowly toward Rontonga.

TERROR ISLAND

*That South Seas island was a place of mystery
and danger—so Bellow Bill Williams was
in all the more hurry to get there*

CHAPTER I

THE CRIPPLED LION

BELLOW BILL WILLIAMS had been loafing in the little port of Marobe, on the southwestern coast of New Guinea, for three weeks previous to the arrival of the mail steamer. Nothing whatever happened, which was altogether usual and right for the port and the season of the year. Nothing ever did happen in Marobe except sunrise and sunset.

Even the coming of the mail steamer served merely as an excuse for all white men to get drunk, which was customary and normal. And yet—three hours after the ship docked a trader offered Bill full steamer freight rates to take a cargo of hardware to the Marshall Islands, twelve hundred long sea miles away.

A pearling schooner, such as Bellow Bill owned, isn't ordinarily chartered to carry cargo. Not at steamer rates, and there was no more market for hardware in the Marshall Islands than in Marobe. It looked to Bill as though some one had suddenly decided it was worth money to get him out to sea, which for Bill was the best of all reasons for staying right where he was. He told the trader he couldn't possibly sail before sundown, as demanded, and sauntered over to the nearest bar to ponder the wherefore and the what-the-hell.

He had barely tasted his stengah when a beach-comber came reeling through the door and jostled against his elbow.

"Who're you pushin', you big blighter?" screamed the drunk. He snatched Bill's glass from the bar and hurled the contents into the pearler's face.

The Kanaka was trying to slip up on him silently.

Half blinded, Bill twisted his left hand in the breast of the drunk's coat and lifted him off the floor. A huge, tattooed right fist snapped back—and paused. The drunk had shut both eyes. His face was pallid and drawn with terror as he awaited an annihilating blow. Held like a puppy at the length of Bill's great arm, his punches and kicks were ineffectual, half-hearted.

Bellow Bill stood six feet three. He weighed two hundred and forty, every pound sea-hardened muscle. From neck to waist and from wrists to shoulders tattooing covered his skin in designs that were Polynesian, Melanesian, Chinese, and European—a record of his travels and his experience at sea and in the jungles. A bullet scar, one of many, was visible on his arm.

And yet a drunk, with a roomful of men to pick a fight with, had selected him? Not likely. Not naturally, nor out of liquor or bravado. Rather to earn a five-pound note by taking a beating.

The pearler lowered the drunk to the floor.

"Run along, bozo!" Bill rumbled in the deep voice that had the echoing growl of distant thunder or of storm-driven surf. A constable was peering through the barroom door, a truncheon

gripped in his fist. Marobe, on mail ship days, is well policed. Barroom brawlers land in jail.

Bill grinned, and thrust his cap farther back on curly, coppery blond hair.

"No trouble, constable!" he boomed mockingly. "Nothing but an accident—as this gentleman will explain!" Bill tossed a sovereign to the beachcomber. "Buy yourself a drink you'll be able to enjoy, bozo!" he rumbled, and strode out past the constable. Some one, he reflected, would be as well pleased to have him in jail as at sea.

With a trace of a grin Bellow Bill filled his mouth with the fine-cut chewing tobacco he carried loose in his hip pocket. Marobe might seem as dead as ever—but it wasn't. Indolently and carefully Bill looked over the harbor. Near the mail steamer a small, dirty trading sloop was preparing to put to sea. The blocks squeaked as the sails were hoisted.

Bill's own pearling schooner was moored alongside a long, rickety pier three hundred yards farther up the beach—and there was a stranger already aboard it! Over the taffrail projected a yachting cap, snowy white and ornamented with gold. Bill swore aloud. Not even an admiral had the right to board his vessel uninvited. He set off at a run.

As his feet pounded on the loose planking of the pier the intruder rose. The man was tall. A close-cut Vandyke beard, white as wool except near the lips, where it was stained with tobacco, concealed his features. Dark-brown, level unwinking eyes stared at Bill. In his prime the interloper had possessed Bill's breadth of shoulder, and almost his depth of chest. Though age had wasted the muscles, the set of the shoulders and the indomitable lift of the chin were unaltered.

The man was lionlike—and against his hip pressed the most enormous dog that Bill had ever seen. The shaggy gray head was leonine, and despite the heat the tongue did not loll. The dog was as calm, as masterful and self-possessed as the man.

"Bellow Bill Williams?" he inquired.

"That's me. And what the devil are you doing on my schooner?" Bill rumbled as he leaped to the deck of the boat.

The dog growled. The bearded man reached under his coat. Into sight flashed a double-barreled pistol, a foot long, the barrels chambered to shoot shotgun shells loaded with buckshot. The man held it level at his waist.

"Watch him, Puck! Watch!" he commanded the dog with icy calm.

Again, more urgently, the beast growled. The shaggy gray head turned slightly.

It was that movement more than the almost noiseless rush of bare feet along the pier which warned Bill. He whirled, crouching with a fighter's instinct. Almost at his shoulder he glimpsed teeth bared in a snarling black face, the bushy head of a Papuan, the gleam of a heavy wood knife drawn back to strike.

BELLOW BILL threw himself backward. The wood knife hissed over his head. The black stumbled over his body, and fell. The dog uttered a blood-curdling growl as Bill rolled upon his assailant. A huge tattooed fist smacked against the back of a sinewy black neck. Bill snatched the wood knife from black fingers that were suddenly limp and swung it like a scythe—against thin air.

Though the dog's teeth were bared, it still crowded against the hip of its master. Though the buckshot pistol was leveled at Bill's head, the man did not fire.

"Bellow Bill?" he demanded, fierce and urgent.

"Me!" Bill boomed. "Damn you, stranger, if you ain't after me, why the hell didn't you pop off that black?"

"Down, Puck!" the man commanded. "Because I'm blind," he added icily. "You're lucky that I didn't blaze away, I think. All I knew was that the dog warned me a man was running toward me threateningly. Did you knock out that Papuan?"

"How'd you know he was a Papuan?" Bill boomed.

"I smell the grease in his hair. The same old stuff." The double-barreled pistol was lowered. "You don't recognize me, I perceive. I'm Atterson. The blind hulk that used to be Nick Atterson!" He spoke with the quiet irony of the strong man, accustomed to power, who has become a helpless cripple.

"Golden Nick Atterson, eh?" Bill rumbled. "If we've never met, we've worked together!" All the pearler's preconceived ideas underwent a sudden and violent alteration. He had nearly—he grunted to think how nearly—hurled the knife point-first into Atterson's chest.

Only the cool head and the quick wit that Bill carried into a rough and tumble fight had saved him from cutting down a man who had not come to attack him, a blind man who had drawn a pistol only to defend himself—and who, with a murderous struggle in progress, had possessed the courage not to shoot at random, who had even restrained his dog. Ninety-nine men out of a hundred would have filled Bill with buckshot.

"Is it in the Marshall Islands you want me, or jail?" Bill snapped.

"What? I don't understand. Neither," Atterson replied. "I

want you to take me to Utuoa and be my eyes and my right hand and my bodyguard, Williams.

"I heard a sloop hoisting sail. Is it standing over this way?"

"About two hundred yards off."

"Then duck below. Get your head down!" Atterson commanded. "Down, Puck!"

In his voice was urgency and the thrill of imminent clanger. The big dog flattened himself against the deck, and Bill, too good a leader of men himself to refuse to take an order, was as prompt.

Atterson, however, remained erect, merely turning to face the sloop. The bearded lips parted in a snarl. The Papuan, unguarded, rolled off the deck and swam feebly toward the oncoming vessel.

"Let him go," Atterson whispered. "He was a tool, sent by his master to kill you because I wanted you. No more responsible than Puck would be if I told him to tear the throat out of a stranger. Do you see a white man on that boat, Bill? A small man with a hooked nose and a scar on his forehead, shaped like a cross?"

"Nothing but Papuans," Bellow Bill reported. "There's a woolly headed black as big as a house, and a shriveled-up witch doctor."

"Then Clipper Clarke is hiding behind his natives—as usual," said Atterson savagely. "Don't get up, Bill. He's likely to have a rifle aimed through a porthole in the hope of a shot at you or the dog."

"And you?" Bill boomed.

"Not me. He's waiting for me to bring him a hundred thousand in gold—and my worn-out carcass," Atterson replied calmly.

A ROPE was tossed from the sloop and the Papuan who had attacked Bellow Bill was hauled aboard. The sails caught the breeze and as the sloop drew out of rifle shot Bill rose—eagerly, with his hunch become a certainty. Clipper Clarke he knew by reputation—the sole trader on a lonely island which was all green jungle and savage, splintered black volcanic rock. An island which white men called Utuoa, but which the Papuans, who knew better what went on there, termed Terror Island, and avoided like the plague.

Of Golden Nick Atterson, Bill knew far more. Atterson had been one of the first adventurers to come to the South Seas. Besides courage, he possessed a gift for organization, the instinct for trade which makes a great business man, and a sense of fair play and a loyalty toward those whom he hired which drew and held men like a magnet.

Though Bill had never seen Atterson before, he had worked off and on for years for Atterson, Inc. Atterson's company had given him the tip that a new pearl bed had been discovered in York Bay. Atterson's company, when his schooner had been wrecked, had let two years go by without pressing him for the payment of principal or interest, without even insisting that he work for them, like an ordinary shell diver. Bill had eventually repaid the loan with New Guinea gold. Atterson, Inc., was a white concern.

Bill glanced at the blind man. He understood why.

"Some one wearing shoes is coming down the pier," Atterson muttered. "A constable, I suppose. I'll send him away. Being owner of a big concern does have a few advantages."

A few words were enough. Atterson seated himself slowly on the taffrail. The huge dog Puck laid its great head on his knee.

"I came to Marobe to meet Clipper Clarke because I learned you were here, Bill," said Atterson at last. "A good many hundred in cable tolls that information cost. But I had a hunch—which has proven true. Clipper Clarke seems to share my opinion. Not a man in the South Seas can bring this stunt off. Except, possibly, you. Others would just try. And get themselves—and me—killed."

Bellow Bill spat over the rail.

"Long ago," said Atterson, "I pistol-whipped Clipper. I cut

that cross on his forehead with the foresight. It's a mark of Cain. Some crimes are too foul and too mean to punish by death. Clipper's was the worst sort, and so is he. There's no need to go into details. I branded him and kicked him out, and in the course of time I forgot him. But he didn't forget me."

"He's boss and witch doctor and god to the Papuans on Terror Island," Bellow Bill rumbled. "They're afraid to spit without his say-so."

"Exactly. There's no limit to the evil a clever, vicious white man can accomplish among savage and superstitious blacks on a lonely island," Atterson agreed. "He's like the master of a pack of dogs. Remember that. For years I've been too high for him to reach, but six months ago he had my only son kidnaped."

"Kidnaped him, you mean," Bill grunted.

"No, I don't," said Atterson grimly. "Clipper was too clever to act himself. My son Tom disappeared. A month later—after I had failed to trace him—Clipper sent me word that the wild natives on his island had a white boy imprisoned among them. It might be my son and might not. Oh, he was damn innocent—and helpful. He thought he could ransom the boy—if I would send him five hundred dollars to buy gin and tobacco."

"Not much ransom," Bill rumbled.

ATTERSON HELD up his hand. "Wait! Of course I sent the money. Nothing happened. Next month he informed me the natives wanted five hundred more." Atterson leaned forward and the pointed white beard bristled as he set his teeth. "I'm no fool. *I knew then that he never meant to send my son back.* He couldn't torture me, but he knew that I knew what happens to a seventeen-year-old boy in the hands of savage blacks. At best, hardship and disease and a quick death. At worst, a slow descent into bestiality.

"So—I burned the cables to locate you, Bill. I told Clipper to meet me here. He came. He knew I dared not touch him. My son's life was hostage for his, as he reminded me at the first word. I demanded upon what conditions he would release my son at once. And he laughed and said that if I would come to Terror Island with one companion and one only, with a hundred thousand dollars in gold, he would do—what he could."

"Frank scoundrel, ain't he?" said Bellow Bill calmly. "Implies he's going to give you the double cross, and dares you to come. To get the pistol-whipping repaid with interest, and bringing him gold enough for a getaway. Are you going, Atterson?"

"I must."

Bellow Bill looked up swiftly, and his blue eyes flashed in admiration of courage. Nevertheless, he spoke doubtfully.

"The wildest native on Terror Island would walk through fire if Clipper so much as crooked a finger, if half I've heard is true," he said. "If you fail Clipper won't give up your son. Easier to kill you both, and blame the 'wild' blacks."

"Exactly," Atterson nodded. "But could a gunboat or a regiment find my son before he was speared?"

"Why, no!" Bill boomed. The great, voice rolled across the harbor and then dropped to the lowest whisper it could compass. "No, the job's for one man, but at that, Atterson, we've only the chance of a snowball. We can't shoot Clipper, or the kid will be speared. We can't plunge into the jungle, or we'll both be speared. I'll take a chance on ambush by unorganized natives, but I'd be a damn fool to expect to get through broken lava hills with a white man planning the ambuscades. And we can't just hand over the gold, or both of us will be *kai-kai'd*, and the kid too!"

"I've no plan," said Atterson. "I must go, that's all. I hoped— but—never mind. After all, we never met before. You've no children of your own—"

"I've a head on my shoulders, thanks to that dog of yours, and no buckshot in my hide, thanks to you!" Bill thundered. "Hell, I've never welshed on a brave man yet, but I'm not fool enough to trust altogether to the off chance! I'm not going to sail up and be killed. He has spies here; we've got to fulfill his conditions or he'll murder the boy. Clipper's afraid of me, and hungry for gold, but that's not enough to unstack the cards. Is there anything about you that he doesn't know?"

"I'm not absolutely blind," Atterson answered. "That is, I can tell where the sun is if I stare at the sky, though more by the feeling of the sunlight on my forehead than by sight. I can shoot straighter than one might think by sound, and Puck here is beautifully trained. His nose might be worth more than eyes—"

"Clipper's seen the dog. Puck ain't long for this world," Bellow Bill rumbled grimly. "But if you can locate the sun—now *that*, Nick, may let us hit at Clipper from an angle he doesn't expect!"

CHAPTER II

THE JOINT IN THE ARMOR

FOR FOUR DAYS after returning from Marobe, Clipper Clarke sat in his bungalow on Terror Island, like a spider in the heart of a web freshly strengthened to ensnare important prey. He did not drink, and he ate sparingly. He was a tall, sinewy man without small personal vices. His teeth were white and small and set far apart. His lips were cruel, and the knobs and seams of the old scars left by the pistol-whipping seemed to belong upon his countenance, as though a Torquemada had inflicted one of his punishments upon himself in order to wither his last impulse toward mercy.

Through the huge Papuan named Tetio, who was his war chief, his last instructions went out to the hundred-odd bushy-headed savages who peopled the jungles and cliffs and pocked and riven slopes of black lava which was Clipper's empire. If a gunboat came, go here. If a schooner, a dozen spearmen must gather at this defile, another dozen there....

With the old witch doctor, Haupu, Clipper talked far into the still, hot nights. He was preparing to fight, not with crude force only but with craft. Occasionally the cross scarred on his forehead turned crimson at the memory of the failure to keep Atterson and Bellow Bill apart. They were both big men—big in more than body, and Clipper hated men who were successful, who possessed in their make-up a touch of grandeur, with all the venom of a mean, warped soul. That the trader feared Bellow Bill was not precisely true. He would merely have preferred an antagonist less redoubtable, an easier victory without the need of strengthening his web or perfecting his plans.

It was dawn of the fifth day when Tetio roused him with the news that the big tattooed man was sitting on the beach.

Clipper snatched up binoculars. His throat was hot and his brain raced at an announcement so unexpected. Three hundred yards from the bungalow Bellow Bill sat in the sand, calmly chewing tobacco. The pearler was naked to the waist, barefooted, the belt of his thin duck trousers empty of weapons—and there was no ship of any sort in sight by which he might have arrived.

Like lightning Clipper thought of a wreck, and discarded the theory. The trade wind had blown steadily for days. Yet the nearest island was fifty and more miles distant.

Clipper buckled on a revolver.

"Come with me, Tetio," he rasped. "You, Haupu, be ready—with the others."

Bellow Bill grinned lazily at the sinewy trader and the huge black who advanced toward him. There was a wood knife in the Papuan's loin cloth, and he also carried an iron bar, slightly longer and heavier than a poker, with its end hooked and sharpened. Casually the pearler glanced toward the sea. Nothing was visible above the curve of the horizon, but far out the schooner was hove-to, drifting before the steady trade wind with Atterson and the dog.

Bill had fulfilled Clipper's conditions to the letter. Atterson and he had come alone. In the night the pearler had swum to Terror Island. At sunset Atterson would hoist sail and steer for the setting sun. The blind man would come near enough to the island for Bill to paddle out in a canoe and steer the schooner in if all went well. If not—if Atterson failed to hear Bill's hearty bellow—the plan was for him to put the schooner before the wind and run at full speed until some passing vessel answered his signals of distress.

"HOWDY!" BILL boomed at the tense, suspicious trader. "I've got three hundred and forty pounds of gold ingots consigned to you, Clipper! Better not cut off my head premature-like. I'm a living bill of lading. Show me you can produce Tom Atterson, alive and well and on the hoof, and I'll be back with the *dinero.* You can't really expect old-timers like Nick and me to take your word you've got the kid, now can you?"

"Move over. Sit down on the sand—there!" Clipper ordered harshly. He pointed at random to a spot twenty yards distant.

"Why, Clipper! I'm surprised!" Bill rumbled mockingly. "You don't suspect I've got a gun buried in the sand, do you? Not me! I'm a rotten shot!" Grinning, Bill moved to the spot requested and sat down, huge tattooed forearms across his knees.

"I've never said I had young Atterson," retorted Clipper bitingly. "But I think you'd better decide that I can get him and signal for the gold to be brought here. If you know what's good for you." The thin lips hardened. "Come out!" Clipper shouted in Melanesian, which Bill understood perfectly. "One man drive a pig past this big tattooed pig—quickly!"

In Melanesian there is a play on words between big pig and "long pig," which is roast human flesh. A score of savages stepped from the underbrush, headed by Haupu. A half-grown pig appeared almost at once and was driven, squealing, between Bellow Bill and Tetio. As it passed, the huge Papuan swung the iron bar like a golf club.

The sharpened iron hook ripped through the pig's belly. It squealed horribly and dropped by Bill's knees, kicking and spouting blood, not dead, not even to die quickly, yet too fearfully wounded to rise. A cold breeze seemed to blow against Bill's spine. Tetio swaggered and swung the sharpened hook within a foot of his face.

"That is the punishment I order for men who displease me slightly," said Clipper. "I think you'll agree I can produce Tom Atterson when I choose."

Bellow Bill's right hand moved. Not swiftly enough to threaten, yet quickly enough to seize the iron bar before Tetio could withdraw it. With a twitch of his shoulder Bill pulled the bar from the Papuan's grip, catching the handle in his left hand.

"Let's understand each other, Clipper," he rumbled. In the tattooed forearms muscles leaped up like the ridges in the trunk of an oak. The iron bar commenced to bend in his grip. From the savages came an awed murmur. Bill's voice went on, deep and unhurried, unaffected by the tremendous exertion he was putting forth. The bar had become a loop.

"You can shoot me or have me speared, of course. I didn't come here unarmed because I'm a fool. The stakes are big enough on both sides to take some risk—and you don't see Nick Atterson or the gold until I see Tom."

The iron bar had become a spiral. Indifferently Bill tossed it at Tetio's feet.

"Bend it back, little man!" he boomed in Melanesian. "In Samoa men try which is the stronger by seeing which can knock the other down, but your master fears you are too small to face me—even though you strike me first." Bill grinned at Clipper as the savages murmured. "You can cheat, but you've got to play!" he added in English too swift for Papuan ears. "I'll see a hope of getting the kid back—or he and I'll be all you get. You're king here. Prove it."

"Break the jaw of the big pig, Tetio. Or go—you know where," said Clipper bitingly. His hand was on his gun. Bill, leaping up and bracing himself to receive Tetio's blow, saw the dark face turn greenish and then flush jet black with desperation. The contest was not one of boxing. Bill must stand with his arms at his sides and take a blow fair to the head or chest. He could only hold the point of his chin out of the way.

TETIO WAS immensely strong, and nerved by terror of failure to a supreme effort. In a hundred fights Bill had never absorbed such a punch. He kept his feet, but the beach whirled around him. For an instant the sky was black. He was conscious that he had staggered two yards backward, of the awed murmur of the savages. Tetio waited the return blow, the dusky head lowered to take the punch on the cushion of hair, six inches thick.

Like a wounded lion Bill gathered himself and leaped, shoulder and body lined behind his fist. He aimed for the jaw, but as Tetio ducked Bill's knuckles crashed against the temple. The punch lacked neither strength nor timing, but only an inch or two in direction.

Tetio's knees sagged. A gush of blood colored his lips, and he crumpled in his tracks. Panting, Bellow Bill stood over him, waiting through ten and twenty seconds for him to rise. The savages did not breathe. Clipper stood rigid, staring.

"You smashed his skull! He's dead!" the trader gasped, and jerked his revolver clear.

The cold wind blew down Bill's spine. He had hoped to master Tetio; to shake by a feat of strength Clipper's hold upon the natives. To rescue Tom was possible only if the Papuans learned to fear Bill himself but little less than their master. They feared him. Their eyes rolled, but none the less he had succeeded too well. The death of Tetio was too great a blow to Clipper's prestige. He must assert his ascendency at once, and at any cost.

Bill looked the trader in the eye.

"Is it worth a hundred thousand gold?" he challenged over the level of the revolver.

He won. Clipper did not fire.

"Want to see the kid? You'll see him!" the trader snarled. Passion was shaking him. "Stand still, or I'll drill you and to hell with the gold!" he gasped hoarsely. "Haupu—make the curse—the Great Curse!"

The Papuans caught their breath, and the sound was like the hiss of a gust of wind through palms. The witch doctor ran forward with a thin, shrill scream. In front of Bill he dropped on hands and knees and commenced to crawl in a circle that grew narrower and narrower. The muscles of the sorcerer's back began to twitch. He writhed on his belly, like a snake, round and round.

This was all mumbo-jumbo. But—was it? The Papuans who stared at Bill expected him to die. He could read the conviction that he was doomed in eyes that were all whites and the greenish-ashen pallor of the circle of faces. The witch doctor believed he would die, and over the leveled gun Clipper was planning death—at the proper time and place. Native magic, Bill thought steadily, had—seldom had—any effect on a white man. But there was no mumbo-jumbo about Clipper... A young boy in the jungle. An old man, all but totally blind, tossing at sea....

The spasms that shook the witch doctor ceased. He lay at Bill's feet rigid, like a dead man.

"Now—will you signal in the gold, or do you want to go find Tom?" Clipper whispered softly.

"Tom's what I came to find!" Bill boomed. The nerves in his back crawled, but his face and voice were unmoved, defiant, as though he felt able to smash menace of any sort by one blow of his fist.

CHAPTER III

THE JAIL WITHOUT BARS

AT A SIGN from Clipper the savages converged upon him from three sides. None of them touched him. Despite their clubs and spears, they kept beyond the reach of Bellow Bill's arms, but they drove him toward a path that led away from the sea as they would have driven a fierce animal of which they were individually in terror.

As soon as Bill guessed where they wished him to go he strode ahead without compulsion, neither slowly nor in haste. Clipper and the revolver were never far behind, and the pearler saw neither the opportunity, nor the use, of making a dash for the shelter of the jungle.

The path climbed steeply up an ancient flow of lava that was like a road of rough black glass. Five hundred feet above the sea Bill came to a narrow gap in the rim of the ancient crater. The walls of dark obsidian rock on either hand were hardly twenty feet apart, and the creek which had flowed along the left hand side of the path all the way from the sea was no longer visible, though he could hear its murmur as it dashed through a subterranean channel.

Brush grew in the cleft between the cliffs. A dozen men might have held the pass against an army, but there was no reason which Bill could perceive why the savages should suddenly halt in their tracks and stare at him as though he was as good as doomed. With a thin smile Clipper raised the revolver to urge him on.

Bellow Bill looked doubtfully at the ground ahead. The flow of lava upon which he had walked thus far broke at the inner rim of the crater. To go farther he must jump down about five feet and cross a funnel-shaped pit about a hundred feet in diameter and fully forty feet deep which seemed to have been scooped out of a loose soil composed of volcanic ash, grayish black in color, and filled with blocks and bowlders of porous, steam-blown pumice.

Directly opposite him was the lava flow, about five feet thick, also broken short off. The lava must have flowed across the soft soil before there was a pit. The ground had dropped away, leaving a bridge of lava, which had broken—and disappeared, except for a section about ten feet long which was visible in the very bottom of the funnel, tilted sidewise, as though it were sinking too. Beside the black stone was a hole no wider than Bellow Bill's shoulders.

Not a blade of grass grew on the sides of the pit, though the murmur of the creek was still audible. As Bill looked, a bit of the dark gray ash broke loose halfway up the slope and slithered to the bottom. More ash and a stone or two joined the slide—but the ash rose no higher against the tilted black stone and the hole beside it was not closed!

"Tom Atterson's just beyond!" Clipper shouted raspingly. "I don't deal with the savages who've got him because I don't like the looks of their front gate. Go call on him, big pig, or run back through us! We're lining the path!" He raised the revolver and fired near Bill's feet. The bullet ricocheted from the lava with a banshee wail.

The shot was echoed by a shout from the opposite side of the pit. The bushes were parted by a white boy, blond-haired, and naked except for a loin cloth.

"Go back! Go back, stranger!" he yelled. "I've seen one man jump in there! I tell you—go back!"

"Back, hell!" Bill thundered. He made a running leap, as far toward the side and as high up the slope as he could manage. The boy must be Tom Atterson, and he was unguarded. To conquer the sliding ash Bill relied upon his enormous strength. Better that risk than a shot or a spear thrust if he tried to run the gauntlet behind.

HE STRUCK the ash, and plunged knee deep. A pawing hand only scooped up dust. He fell, and all the earth around him commenced to move. He could not rise. He could not crawl. Hands and feet found no purchase. Inexorably he was carried downward, not swiftly, but he was utterly helpless. His feet touched the tilted block of lava. He twisted and seized the edge with his hands, but beneath his body the ash continued to sink. He was in the small hole which he had seen from above, hanging by the grip of his hands in an upright position. The sound of flowing water was loud in his ears.

Too late he understood that it was the creek, flowing beneath the roof formed by the bridge of lava fallen from above, which carried the loose ash away as fast as it slid from the sides. Bill kicked out with his legs, hoping to bring down tons of ash and choke the current. All his strength could barely stir the soft stuff around him. The ash continued to slide slowly, inexorably seeking an angle of repose.

The top edge of the tilted block was higher than he could reach, though the lava was rough enough to afford handholds by which he might pull himself up. To what? To stand in the sun, to be bowled over by the rocks which Clipper would roll down the sides of the pit upon him. In a flash Bill comprehended the diabolical sport afforded by the man-trap, and the awed stares of the savages who had realized what was in store for him.

Any poor devil whom Clipper disliked had the choice of running a gauntlet headed by Tetio and his iron hook—or of dodging about on a tilted, ten foot oblong of black lava until a pumice bowlder crippled him, knocked him off into the sliding ash which dragged him slowly beneath the block to drown in mud and water.

The bottom of the block was almost level with Bellow Bill's eyes. It was rough, like the sides, forming a roof about a yard square where the ash could not rest. Grimly and carefully Bill felt with his toes for the other blocks of lava which must lie beneath this one. He could touch nothing.

He looked up. Tom Atterson had gone. That hurt. The boy might at least have watched, even if he could do nothing. On the opposite side of the pit Clipper stood where the lava broke off. He held a bowlder in his arms.

"Climb up, Bill! You're strong enough!" he shouted. "The last fellow kept dodging half a day!"

"You go to hell!" Bill boomed.

"Well, you've got strong arms. You can spin the fun out if you like to hang there," Clipper taunted. He paused. "And, Bill—maybe I don't get the gold this time. But when you don't come back Atterson will come again, if he loves his son. With another companion. One that will give me less trouble than you did—and more fun. Think about that!"

"I am," Bill rumbled. "You win, Clipper. I'll take your regards to the devil!"

The huge shoulders twitched as Bill released his grip. His coppery yellow head vanished beneath the tilted block in a swirl of sliding, grayish-black ash. The men above saw the pit engulf him. They could not see his fingers hook into a crevice in the lava roof. Bellow Bill hung by his fingers alone. The ash was as high as his mouth. He had seemed to surrender, to choose the quickest death, and yet as long as his strength held out the choice had only moved him some three feet nearer the abyss.

CHAPTER IV

TUPAPAKU

THE STRAIN UPON his arms and fingers was steady and extreme, considerably greater than would have been the case if he had been hanging in mid-air. He heard Clipper shout across the pit, threatening to shoot if Tom Atterson did not go back. Grimly Bill reminded himself that neither friend nor enemy could reach him, yet the fact that the boy had at least made an effort heartened the pearler.

Tom Atterson did not persist. There was no second shout, no sound except the whisper of the ash sinking around Bill's body. His fingers ached. The temptation to pull himself back into the sunlight before his muscles cramped was all but irresistible. He would have to reach for the edge of the lava block and hold himself by the pressure of his fingers against the rough stone while the ash dragged at him.

Bill wondered whether he could hold on with a lack of emotion and a detached impersonality which surprised him. Another man might have been hanging by his finger tips with sunlight and clean air and life a foot or so away while Bellow Bill Williams looked on.

Under his breath he counted. One—two—three—four. When he got to a hundred he would make a snatch at the edge.

To emerge too soon would be fatal. Clipper must have time to go, convinced that Bill was dead, but the passage of time was slower, infinitely slower for the pearler. He reached one hundred, and began again at one. Counted to two hundred, trying to measure seconds; began at one, and got to sixty... Six minutes since he had vanished.

At sixty-two Bellow Bill snatched at the edge of the block. He had reached the limit of his physical endurance.

For a moment the sand covered his face. He thrashed desperately with his legs, for his arms could only hold him from sinking, not lift him. The ash dropped past him more swiftly. By inches his head neared the sunlight. He reached up, flattening his hands against the face of the lava. With his elbows hooked he could lift himself. Like a huge mole that paws into the open through dry earth, scattering the dust right and left, Bill clawed himself onto the top of the tilted lava block.

On one side of the pit a black Papuan leaped up with an amazed cry that was choked in the dark throat by the clutch of superstition and horror.

"*Tupapaku! Tupapa*—"

"Aye, *tupapaku!*" Bill roared.

He shook the dust from his hair and scowled threateningly. Though he was all but exhausted and still trapped, he felt a quick, fierce stir of hope. The savage whom Clipper had left behind as a sentry had believed him dead—and had seen him drag himself out of the earth.

Of all the horrible monsters in Melanesian demonology the most fearful are the *tupapakus*—the spirits of dead men who return to earth. These possess human malevolence, supernatural strength and cunning, and lack any soul or life principle that can be touched by weapons, because the spirit which animates the *tupapaku* has already been dispatched to the hereafter. The most vicious sharks, the devilfish that kills fisherman after fisherman and cannot be hurt by spears, are *tupapakus*. In animal form they are deadly, but the worst reappear in human shape.

At Bill's shout the Papuan flung down the spear that was useless against a spirit. He turned and ran headlong down the steep trail which led to the sea.

"Tupapaku! Tupapaku!" he screamed, fainter and fainter, to warn his fellow warriors against the menace from which he fled.

Bellow Bill grinned and reached for a mouthful of fine cut. Wanted to dominate Clipper's savages, had he? His lips twisted sardonically. Well, he dominated them right now—but Clipper's power did not rest altogether upon the natives, and Clipper wasn't going to go ga-ga from superstition. When that panic-stricken savage brought him the news that a *tupapaku* was loose, Clipper would guess what had happened and come running.

FROM THE opposite side of the pit came a gasp of incredulous joy. Tom Atterson leaned through the bushes. His face was working. He had been fighting to hold back tears, but in his hands he still held a long vine to the end of which he had attached a block of pumice. The vine was too stiff to throw accurately, but the stone, sliding down with the ash, brought the end within Bill's reach. Tom twisted the vine around a sapling, and the pearler hauled himself up the slope.

Even with the support of the vine he was unable to stand near the bottom of the pit. He had to haul himself along by the strength of his arms. Higher up, though the ash still slid, it was a little stiffen.

"I ran to get the vine when I saw you were caught," Tom explained excitedly. "But when I got back with it you were gone, and Clipper was going to shoot me—"

"Aye, aye, kid. You did fine," the pearler snapped. "You're fit to be Golden Nick's son, and that's enough for anybody. Think fast, now, kid. Clipper will be coming back. How'd you get across that pit?"

"I didn't. They lowered me from the cliffs on a rope. There's no place where I can climb out, either."

Bellow Bill glanced at as much as he could see of the circle of glassy obsidian, and nodded.

"You're alone?"

"They lowered an old woman to cook for me."

"And they could lower a couple of blacks to cut your throat too, eh?" Bill rumbled. "I could stay here with you and stop that, of course. But your old man's sailing back to the island." The pearler glanced at the sun, which was not yet at the zenith. "I gotta go back, kid. If Clipper hasn't hurt you so far, I don't think he will. You'd be a damned sight more apt to get hurt with me. You ain't a *tupupaku*, savvy? Stand by and keep cool and obey orders."

"But you can't go back!" the boy objected. "A vine will only reach halfway across the pit—"

"Halfway is enough, kid," Bill boomed. "I got an edge on Clipper that I won't have long, or again!" The big man stepped into the thicket. The muscles on the tattooed back bunched and writhed as he bent a sapling as thick as his wrist back and forth until the tough wood snapped. With vicious jerks he stripped the side branches off, and snapped the top over his knee. In less than a minute he had made himself a pole about ten feet long.

"I've a knife," Tom offered.

"So've I, kid!" Bill boomed. His face was set and his under lip out-thrust. His eyes never left the opposite side of the pit for long. "This is faster!"

He broke and stripped a second sapling, and strode toward the pit with a pole in each hand.

"Have that vine handy!" he rumbled—and drove the right hand pole into the loose ash with all the enormous strength of his arms and shoulders. The tip sank three feet into the soil. Bill threw his weight against the pole, found it solid—and stepped out onto the treacherous slope. The ash slid from around his feet, but the pole was driven so deeply that it held firm. Bill leaned forward and drove the left hand pole deep, moved onward, and pulled the right hand pole loose—to drive it into the soil farther ahead, and advance another yard.

The center of the pit he avoided. Like an old man walking

with two canes he moved around the rim, yard by yard. One pole was always buried as deep as he could thrust the point to hold him erect. Sweat runneled through the ash that coated his face. The great chest commenced to pant before he was halfway around the pit, but though his progress was slow, it was steady, and he did not slip.

At last he managed to reach out and catch the end of the broken lava flow. He hauled himself up to solid ground, hurled the two poles out of sight, and caught up the spear which the sentry had discarded.

"Don't you try that stunt, kid!" he called back warningly. The booming voice was lowered to a whisper. "You'd get tired! Stand by and trust to us! You'll see or hear from us soon after sundown—by dawn at latest."

The boy gulped and nodded.

Bellow Bill strode down the black lava trail, his eyes searching the bush for an ambush. Thus far he had heard nothing from Clipper.

BEFORE HE had covered half the distance to the beach, however, he became aware that a body of men were moving up the trail. The savages were calling and shouting to one another, and the nervous tension of the voices belied the words they spoke.

"Tari is not afraid!"

"See, Kooamua, Tari is not afraid!"

"We will all go with Tari!"

"Yes, we will all go!"

Bill hurried to a point where he could look down the trail for fifty yards, and hid himself in the brush. A Papuan advanced, step by step, and stood staring, his feet braced to run, and his spear waving as though every leaf concealed an enemy. This, Bill inferred, must be the brave Tari. Behind him were fully a score of savages, huddled together, spears waving like grass in the wind. When they came up to the leader, they stopped. When Tari advanced fifteen feet beyond them he stopped.

They were convinced, with the utter certainty of superstition, that they faced an enemy whom their weapons could not harm, who could not only kill with a blow of the fist, as they had seen for themselves, but who could strike them dead by a touch.

Yet they advanced. Even the terror of the pit could hardly have driven them against a *tupapaku*—a savage fears an unknown death ten times worse than the fate he has seen—but nevertheless they were obeying Clipper's orders. Bellow Bill gave a grunt of admiration, for the savages, and for the mastery the trader had achieved. Clipper himself was not present. Once sure of that, Bill sprang from his hiding place, and with a thunderous shout charged down the trail.

The Papuans scattered like sparrows. Tari, courageous to the end, clung to his spear, but he raced down the path with leaps a rabbit would have envied. The others stumbled over themselves to scramble into the underbrush. The path where they had stood was littered with spears and wood knives. Bellow Bill could have killed half a dozen men. He charged ahead without so much as striking at one. Clipper had remained behind. At the beach, therefore, or in the bungalow, was the only enemy worth encountering.

On the steep path the pearler covered the distance to the sea quickly—though not quickly enough to overtake Tari, whose yells, uttered every few yards, were Bill's best guide. Near the beach, however, Bill turned into a side path, guessing from its width that it led from the native village to the bungalow. The surmise was correct. There was no grove of palms around the bungalow. He caught a glimpse of the rusty sheet iron roof while dense jungle surrounded him, and swiftly formed the plan of charging up the veranda and facing the trader's revolver with his spear.

But it was not Clipper who confronted him. The path ended in a sunlit space, like a lane, about fifteen feet wide which led to the right and left. Directly in front was a hedge of green thorns, higher than Bill's head, and so thick that he could not see through it. Behind this rose the bungalow roof.

The pearler hesitated, uncertain which way to turn. In all the South Seas he had never seen a bungalow defended like this one. Even the narrow open space had not been cleared away in order that the breeze might help to keep the bungalow free of insects, for the outer edge of the lane was also formed by a thorn hedge. Whether an intruder turned right or left he was trapped between green walls through which not even a dog could have forced its way. He was forced to circle the bungalow before entering it.

Bellow Bill had had more than enough of strange paths, and traps. His hot blood cooled. He listened, drawing upon all his bushcraft to make sure no one was behind him. He thought not. There was not a sound from the bungalow, either, and the hope of obtaining firearms lured him on. He chose to turn to the right, and advanced slowly, prodding the earth in front with the point of his spear, watching for the trigger of a set gun, and alert for the smallest break in the green wall of the hedges.

HALFWAY AROUND the bungalow he came to a gate in the inner hedge. It was also formed of thorn branches, dried brown since they had been cut, and lashed to a framework of poles. The gate was ajar—and through the gap Bill caught a glimpse of the paint-smeared face of Haupu, the witch doctor.

It was a glimpse only. Instantly Haupu ducked out of sight. But the gate remained ajar, though a push would have closed it.

Had Haupu been stricken with panic? Fleetingly Bill weighed the chances. That painted face had not been frightened, but vicious and eager. Few natives are good shots, but if Haupu had a gun—and there were undoubtedly plenty of guns in the bungalow—he could hardly miss the man who pushed the gate open.

Bill turned on his heel and retreated. Once in the shadow of the jungle he breathed more freely. That double thorn hedge had been planted for a purpose not solely connected with defense. A single hedge would have been protection enough, and Clipper had too firm a hold over his Papuans to need walls of thorn. Bill swore under his breath. Clipper's mind worked deviously, and the lack of physical courage which made him hide constantly behind his natives only made him the more dangerous. Meanwhile, however, Nick's approach to the island must be made safe. Bellow Bill turned toward the sea.

The beach, when he stepped upon it, was deserted. Even Tetio's body lay where it had fallen. The sails of the sloop, however, which was moored near the water's edge about three hundred yards from the pearler, had been hoisted and flapped in the trade breeze. Over the rail Bill glimpsed a woolly, bushy head.

As he looked a rifle flashed from a porthole. The bullet sped by him with a long-drawn hiss before he heard the flat *crack* of the shot.

With a heartfelt oath Bill jumped back into the undergrowth. He damned the caution, or the cunning, which had induced Clipper to leave most of his natives ashore while he patrolled the waterside—ready to cut off Bill's escape with Tom, in the event that the pearler had succeeded in releasing the boy, and also, as Bill reflected grimly, ready to intercept Nick Atterson.

Clipper did not possess the physical courage to risk a hand to hand encounter, but that circumstance only made the devious and scheming intellect of the trader the more dangerous. Nick must be warned somehow, or he might come blindly sailing into the point-blank range of Clipper's rifle.

There were half a dozen outriggers drawn up on the beach— rude boats hollowed from a single log lashed parallel to prevent them from capsizing. All were equipped with triangular sails braided from coconut leaves, but their speed was distinctly problematical compared to that of the sloop.

Nevertheless, Bellow Bill shrugged. By helping the sails with a paddle he could shove an outrigger along pretty fast, and if he could lure Clipper far enough out to sea the trader could not fight by trickery. Nothing was to be gained by waiting for sundown, and Nick.

Bill burst from the bush and sprinted across the sand toward the largest outrigger.

Bullets whined around him and showered him with sand while he shoved the heavy craft into the water. He bent low, paddling directly away from the rifle, fairly lifting the outrigger from the water with each stroke. When Clipper exhausted the magazine Bill hoisted the braided sail and set a course as close as possible to the wind. The schooner was not in sight. Nick was at least ten miles offshore, and behind Bill a single native whom he recognized as the courageous Tari was trimming the sheets of the sloop to give chase.

CHAPTER V

SEA STRATAGEMS

WHILE THE HEAVIER sloop was getting away from the beach Bill gained more than a hundred yards. For the first two miles he was under fire, but even his broad back offered no easy target to a marksman who must shoot from a heaving deck. Clipper's best shot only punched a hole in the braided sail more than a yard over Bill's head, and the trader soon elected to save his cartridges for closer range.

During the first two miles, also, the outrigger gained on the sloop. Thereafter the relative position of the two remained unchanged—which may have puzzled Clipper, but which made Bill grin. Though the pearler continued to paddle, he calculated the amount of effort that went into the strokes to a nicety.

If he tired, Clipper was close enough to gain three or four hundred yards and shoot him.

But Bill did not tire. The shores of Terror Island were ten miles astern. Three miles ahead he made out his own schooner, hove to with only the peak of the mainsail hoisted. His great voice boomed across the sea like a trumpet call.

"Nick! Ahoy, Nick! Hoist all sail! Bring the wind on your port quarter, old-timer, and crack on! Steer for my voice!"

Far away the peak of the mainsail ran up to the masthead as the ears of the blind man caught the command. With a sail area far greater than that of the sloop the schooner turned before the breeze. Bill paddled with all his might to intercept it, bellowing words of guidance. Once aboard the larger, faster, and sturdier craft, he hoped to get between Clipper and the island.

Clipper saw the trap. The sloop jibed and ran for the shore before the wind, but if the trader hoped to escape while the schooner paused to pick up Bill he was soon undeceived. Roaring to Nick to crack on, the pearler paddled directly into the schooner's path. The great dog bayed a welcome. Bill stood up, caught the bowsprit as it stabbed over his head, and swung himself onto the deck as the bow of the schooner crushed the outrigger and rolled it under water.

"Is Clipper near?" Nick shouted. "Did you find Tom?"

"Yes to both!" Bill boomed. He seized the wheel, and under his expert handling the gurgle of water under the bow grew louder. "Your kid's fine, though Clipper had a devil's mess fixed for us!" he shouted jubilantly. "Get below with the dog, old-timer, where a bullet can't find you! Toss me up a shotgun and an iron belaying pin! I'm going to run Clipper down, and Lord! how I want to get my paws on the slimy devil! I'm a mean, wild *tupapaku* after its meat!"

Even so early in the race the eye of a sailor could judge that the schooner would overtake the sloop at, or nearly at, the shore of the island.

Nick stared ahead with a fierce wistfulness, and loosened the buckshot pistol in his belt. "I want to help," he pleaded. "I'll lie on the deck, and hold Puck down beside me. It's a good dog. I've sat here guessing where the sun was and imagining all sorts of hells. I can tell you, Bill, to-day has been the first since Joshua when the sun stood still in the heavens. Don't order me below!"

"Lie down, then!" Bill rumbled. He pushed the man and the

dog to the deck behind the cabin skylight. "Hells? I hung to the roof of one, and that kid of yours snatched me out. There's a level-headed youngster, Nick. 'Stay and wait for us,' I said, and he stayed without a whimper. Clipper left him with an old woman and with nothing but water to drink, Nick.

"Once Clipper is scuttled we can get him out with a couple of hundred feet of rope."

"Thank God!" Atterson growled into his beard.

IN A low, rumbling voice that scarcely rose above the slap of water against the schooner's hull Bill told in detail all that had occurred since dawn. The shore of Terror Island drew near. The gap between the ships had dwindled to a few hundred yards. Clipper's rifle began to crack. Holes appeared in the schooner's jib and mainsail, and a splinter flew from the mast, but Bill only crouched on the deck.

After a dozen shots the trader must have recognized the futility of long-range fire. Abruptly the sloop changed course, slanting along the shore instead of heading directly toward it. By shifting the rudder so that the schooner would have cut across the angle Bellow Bill might have gained rapidly, but he only grinned.

Every trick of the South Seas was at the pearler's finger tips. He continued to steer over the same water through which the sloop had passed, and changed course at the same point. Sure enough, when he looked over the side he observed that he was now sailing just inside a hidden coral reef. Clipper had attempted to lure him where the schooner would be wrecked.

Both boats threaded through bosses and hidden knife edges of coral. Rarely was the water beneath the keels more than thirty feet deep. The shore was close at hand, but to land through the reef was impossible.

"Stand by for a ram, Nick," Bill warned. He held the shotgun by the grip, like a pistol. As he spoke the sloop unexpectedly tried to come about, was caught aback by the breeze, and turned her side to the schooner's bow. Behind the rail at the point where the collision would occur rose Tari.

Clipper was invisible. He neither exposed himself nor fired. Beneath the jib Bellow Bill caught a glimpse of Tari's face, ashen with fear and dogged with purpose. The native stooped— and the two vessels struck with a crash that drove the schooner's bow deep into the sloop's side.

Bill charged forward. As he leaped to the sloop, Tari tossed an anchor over the rail of the schooner, locking the two boats together. Bill knocked the native sprawling with his fist. The sloop's deck was empty. Too late the pearler noticed the wire which ran across the planks, leading from the open companion-way over the side. A detonating wire—dynamite—and Clipper was swimming toward the shore.

The deck of the sloop heaved and burst beneath the feet of the pearler. The roar of the explosion was like a blow on the head. He was thrown high into the air and splashed into the water, half stunned, momentarily paralyzed by the shock. Splintered planking rained down upon him. Bill let himself sink, from weakness as much as choice, and then struggled feebly toward the surface.

Tari rose beside him. Bill caught the native by the woolly hair. The man was unconscious, either because of the explosion or from Bill's punch. The sloop was a shattered hulk, already sinking to the water's level. The bow of the schooner was blown open. The stern was high, and the deck slanted sickeningly. It would sink too—bearing down the gold—into thirty feet of water.

Bill groaned. A child could bring that gold to the surface again. Grimly the pearler trod water, holding up Tari with one hand. Now was Clipper's chance to strike. His stratagem had succeeded; the explosion had robbed Bill of weapons and the advantage of position. Well beyond the ring of scattered wreckage Clipper was swimming strongly toward the shore. He had dropped the detonator with which he had exploded the dynamite, but over his shoulder was the rifle. He swam with the stock above water. Once on shore he would have easy targets.

CHAPTER VI

THE TERROR

BELLOW BILL WAS too shaken by the explosion to overtake Clipper in the water. There was, however, or should be, a faster swimmer at hand. The pearler shoved Tari toward the sinking schooner.

"Nick!" he called. "Sic the dog on him, Nick!"

There was no answer, and no barking. To a rifle duel between a poor shot like himself, temporarily able to find shelter behind the schooner's rail, but soon to be left floundering in the sea, and a reasonably accurate marksman such as the trader, Bill could see but one end. Nevertheless Bill hauled Tari across the rail, scrambled over the tilting deck, and dove down the companionway.

The cabin was full of water, but the rifles were in their proper place in the rack. A few strokes enabled Bill to seize a weapon. He swam to the companionway and scrambled out, throwing himself down behind the skylight where he had left Nick. Clipper was already running out of the shallows, shaking the water out of the action of his rifle as he went. Bill did the same.

He was the first to fire. He missed, but the shot made Clipper turn and run across the beach for the shelter of the jungle. Bill rested the rifle on the skylight and drew bead on the retreating back. He was sure he had the sights notched. He remembered not to jerk the trigger, which was his besetting fault. The bolt snapped before he was conscious that he had fired, but the only sound was the click of the firing pin on a primer spoiled by salt water.

Clipper broke into the jungle. His return shot smashed through wood and glass close to Bill's face. There was a pause, which Bill sensed instinctively was wrong, a brief break in rhythm as obvious as though a bass drummer had missed a beat, and then a second shot high over Bill's head.

"Bum shells in your gun too, eh, Clipper?" he rumbled. He had nothing but leaves to shoot at, and only six rounds left in the magazine. God alone knew how many shots that meant. Bill held his fire. He had been so sure that Nick and the dog had been killed by the explosion that he had not glanced to seaward, but in the silence a splashing sound behind him made him turn.

No wonder the dog had not barked! Puck held the collar of Nick's coat in his teeth. The head of the blind man lolled forward. The dog was straining to hold the nose and mouth above the surface, and though the animal swam powerfully, the weight of the big man was so great that progress toward the boat was by inches.

"Good boy!" Bill boomed. He slipped over the rail and drew Nick to the ship. Instantly Puck began to bark. From the shore a bullet sang over Bill as he raised his head too high.

"Good boy!" Bill repeated. "Now—go sic him! Get him, boy—get him!"

Puck barked furiously and put both paws on the rail to climb out beside his master.

"No, no!" Bill commanded in desperation. "Not here! There—on shore, Puck!" He pointed across the skylight, but Puck only barked the louder.

Nick's head stirred feebly on the wet planks, across which the sea was beginning to creep. "Sic him!" he whispered. "Go far, Puck—far!"

Puck pivoted in the water. His lips drew back in a snarl that bared two-inch fangs. Like a brown torpedo he swam under the stern of the schooner and headed for the land.

"I heard a shot. Clipper'll kill him!" Nick whispered feebly.

FROM THE jungle the rifle cracked. Water leaped up less than a foot from the tawny brown head that drove toward the beach as though towed by invisible rope. Puck no longer barked. The mastiff breed is silent in battle. Into Bill's mind flashed the vision of the bared fangs at which Clipper must be peering over the foresight. As the trader aimed he must be wondering whether or not the cartridge would explode. That doubt was not easy on the nerves of a man who preferred that others face his enemies.

The thought came in a flash, as quick as a firing pin can fall on a damp cartridge. Bill rose on his knees, head and shoulders above the skylight, and opened fire on the green wall of the jungle to cover the advance of the dog. Two shots crashed into the leaves without a reply from the trader. Bill levered out a spoiled shell, and fired until the magazine was empty. Still no reply. Had Clipper found the nerve to wait till Puck leaped for his throat?

The dog was dashing through the shallows. He crossed the beach in three great bounds and plunged into the jungle—without drawing a shot!

"By the blue hells, Clipper ran!" Bill thundered. "When he missed the first time he ran!" The pearler dug his fingers into Nick's shoulder and held his breath, all ears.

For five, ten seconds—silence. Then a rifle shot and the blast of a shotgun that blended into a single report, a scream of human terror, cut off at its shrillest and hard upon it, a savage yell that changed from rage to a squeal of pain, and abruptly ceased.

"Two guns—and two men!" Bill exclaimed. "That can only be at the bungalow, and Puck got them both, I think!"

Out of the jungle, loud and triumphant, came the ringing bay of the dog. Nick lifted his head and whistled. Again there was silence, but this time a minute passed, and no Puck emerged from the jungle.

"I don't like that!" Nick whispered. "Puck would come to me if he could drag a leg!"

"There were two shots, and yet Puck didn't bark as though he had a bullet through him," Bill scowled. "Let's go see, Nick."

The schooner was sinking under their feet. Tari had recovered consciousness. Bill kicked him into the water, pulled Nick's buckshot pistol from his belt, and lifted the blind man onto his back. The three swam ashore and crossed the beach, with the Papuan slightly in the lead.

"Follow the dog's trail, and keep moving," Bill commanded menacingly.

Tari shuddered.

"Are you the *tupapaku* still, or did you send your spirit into the dog?" he muttered sullenly in Melanesian.

"Me one fella damned big *tupapaku*. Plenty big enough one fella man, one fella dog," the pearler rumbled gratingly. "You go ahead, or me be cross along you."

Cross, in *beche de mer*, is a very strong word indeed. Hurricanes occur because the spirits of air are cross with the sea; a murderer explains that he was cross with the victim. Tari closed his eyes slowly, and turned to follow the trail with feet that dragged. The bruised leaves and broken branches which had been left by the passage of Clipper and the dog were plain enough even to Bill, and yet after a surprisingly short advance Tari stopped dead.

THROUGH A break in the trees Bill saw the rusty iron roof of the bungalow. It had been nearer than he thought, and he ceased to wonder how Clipper had reached it ahead of the dog.

"Go on!" he ordered.

Tari faced him, much as he had stood at the rail of the sloop to toss the anchor. The dark face had the same dirty ash color.

"No!" he refused, and slowly shut his eyes. "Bush fella go here, he fall dead. Big curse all along here. You cross along me. Clipper cross along me. All the same, savvy? Clipper say, 'Tari, you throw one fella anchor, or I make you walk to see me at house.' I know I fall dead. I throw anchor, savvy?"

"Sounds like bad medicine, somehow, though it isn't too clear," Nick muttered. He whistled for Puck, and bent his bearded face to listen. The jungle was like a green tomb.

"Go on!" Bill ordered inflexibly. "If you don't I'll throw you into the pit up the mountain. That's the curse on the island."

Though the threat was a bluff, Bellow Bill knew that Tari

would accept it at face value. Nevertheless the savage did not budge.

"No curse in pit. Only a devil," he insisted stubbornly. "Haupu put curse on you. You change spirits with dog—and look!" Tari stepped aside, pointing to the ground beyond. In the center of the trail, half hidden by a low bush, lay Puck, stone dead.

Bill knelt by the dog coolly enough, but as he examined the coat of the animal a cold wind blew on his spine. Puck had not been killed by a bullet. A buckshot had pierced one ear, and there was a lump on the great head which might have been raised by the butt of a rifle or a shotgun. These injuries were trifling. The dog's muzzle was covered with blood, but it was not his own. Most strange of all was the fact that though he lay in the trail, headed toward the sea as though he were obeying the summons of his master, his lips were retracted in a blood-curdling snarl of such unearthly ferocity that Bill was startled. Puck had snarled when he started after Clipper, but nothing to approach this.

The bungalow and the gap between the encircling thorn hedges where the sun shone were about fifty feet ahead. In the jungle the shade was cool—clammy cool.

"Nick, here's Puck, dead without a mark," Bill breathed. "I swear I don't like this! I was near this place before, and didn't like it then! Clipper's done for, I'm sure, and the savages are in the hills. That explosion on the sloop would be the last straw for them. But Tari here has more courage than most, and if he'd rather be tossed into that pit than go on—"

"Let me examine Puck," Nick answered, raising sightless eyes. "I trained him, and know him, Bill."

"Look him over while I go ahead," snapped the pearler. "I'm going into that bungalow. I'll be damned if I'll be outdone by a dog or scared by the mumbo-jumbo of a painted savage!"

Bill was turning away when Nick, reaching upward, caught and held him by his trousers.

"As you said, there was something. Something killed Puck," Nick insisted. "Wait!"

"Yeah, and the only way to find out is to go and meet it!" Bill boomed. He jerked his leg free.

"Puck had courage, Bill," Nick said softly. Bill halted, his under-lip out-thrust. "I don't need more courage, Bill," Atterson went on, more softly still. "I can't get to my son alone, despite all you've told me. I don't care to lose another brave friend. You don't mind if I class you with Puck, do you?"

"Not me!" Bill muttered.

The jungle was very still.

NICK TOUCHED the dog's muzzle. His fingers lingered on the fixed snarl of the lips, and passed on to the coat.

"Puck's coat is full of thorns on one side," he said.

"That's natural!" Bill grunted. "The hedges are thorny, and so is the gate."

"These thorns didn't scratch. They are driven deep into the flesh—on one side only," Nick reported gravely. He picked a thorn from the fur, very carefully, and held it up. "Can you see traces of poison, Bill?"

"No!"

"It was there," said Nick. "Tell me, isn't there something odd about Puck's muzzle? I can feel that the muscles are rigid as iron, but—"

"The snarl's horrible, like nothing earthly."

"Then the poison that's been wiped off the thorn by the fur is a kind that produces tetantic convulsions. The smile of strychnine, Bill. It's a symptom. This poison can't be strychnine, though. It must be deadlier still if so small a dose killed a magnificent animal like Puck so quickly." Nick rose. "I wouldn't go into that bungalow, Bill," he urged gravely. "A deadly poison is there, and a means to use it."

"But Clipper may be only badly bitten. Unconscious or lying low."

"That's just it!""

"And if he crawls out while we're bringing Tom down the trail he'll ambush us yet," Bill boomed. "In I've got to go, Nick!"

The blind man stood motionless. Slowly he nodded, and sighed. "Yes, I guess so," he whispered. "But not at a run, Bill. Not recklessly."

Bellow Bill grinned. He reached for fine-cut, but his fingers left his pocket empty. Watching where he set his feet, he moved to the gap between the hedges and turned to the right. He had been this far before, with Haupu's malevolent eye upon him. So far he was safe.

The gate of dried thorn branches was still ajar. A grayish film covered the withered leaves and the bristling thorns. That might be dust, and might not. Clipper had rushed through the gate with a savage dog at his heels. Had he failed to close it in time—or didn't it close?

"Not recklessly, huh?" Bill muttered. "Nick, for once I'm glad you're blind."

The pearler walked to the jungle, broke off and trimmed a heavy pole. He loosened the pistol in his belt, seized the pole in both hands, and dashed at the gate. It was low. He pole-vaulted high above it and dropped on the far side, jerking the pistol clear.

Nothing happened. He stood in a narrow compound of bare earth, facing the open door of the bungalow. Across the threshold Clipper lay on his back, with Haupu tumbled across him. Their throats were not pretty to see. A thread of blood had trickled as far as the top step of the veranda. Puck had done his work well.

From the compound inside the thorn hedge the mechanics of the gate were revealed. A sapling was lashed to act as a spring and hold it ajar. From a pulley in the center of the gate a flexible wire ran to a stake and back to the bungalow. Bill pulled the wire. The gate swung shut, and opened again. Anything entering at that instant would have been cut by the thorns.

Bill scowled. His vaulting pole was outside, and he did not care to walk through that gap, though the space was wide enough if a man were careful. He stepped to the hedge and tore away the sapling spring, which he used to poke the gate wide open.

With his jaw set he returned to the house. Stooping over the bodies across the threshold, he lifted down the hanging lamp and sloshed half the kerosene across the floor. He struck a match and tossed it onto the oil. In ten minutes the bungalow would be a furnace, consuming all that lay under the sheet iron roof.

The remainder of the kerosene he used on the dried thorn branches of the gate, pausing to watch till the poisoned thorns were burning well.

"Okay, Nick!" he boomed. "They're dead, and I've set the place afire. Cremation is a cleaner funeral than that pair deserve, and the best antidote for scattered poison." The voice deepened to thunder. "You fella Tari!" Bill roared. "Go get one fella rope! Me no cross along you! Me no cross along any your brothers! Me go bury dog, put up big stone to hold down spirit of *tupapaku*, savvy?"

"Me savvy!" Tari yelped. His voice was shaking, but he proclaimed proudly, "Me never have fright along you! Tetio dead, me one fella chief now! I go!"

Nick appeared in the gap between the hedges, feeling his way with his feet.

"We'll have Tom down to the beach by sundown," Bill hailed. "With the natives to help me I can raise the schooner and the gold, and use planks from the sloop to patch the bow. It'll all be easy—now that this place isn't Terror Island any more!"

JIB-BOOM CHARLIE

Why had Jib-boom Charlie, beach comber,
suddenly turned into a South Seas pirate?

CHAPTER I

AN EMPTIED ISLAND

"GONE!" IT WAS a shriek of discovery. Profanity followed, shrill with rage.

"Mille tounerres! Cochon! The pirate, the species of camel, the offspring of pig and mule, the—"

The torrent of words might have been endless, but, though it was clear that some Frenchman had lost something, the time was dawn and Bellow Bill Williams had not finished his sleep.

"Shut up, out there!" he called in the deep voice that rumbled like surf after a gale.

"But she is gone! Not a rattle of the anchor chain, not a sound from the engine. Pirate! Rat! Thief!" howled the Frenchman.

Bellow Bill opened the thatch of the native hut with a sweep of one huge tattooed arm, and thrust out head and shoulders. Bill was broad as a barn door, and tattooing covered him from neck to waist, and from wrist to armpit. Six feet three in his socks, two hundred and twenty pounds of sea tested muscle, with curly, coppery yellow hair and blue eyes that gleamed with the fun of danger, the South Seas knew no more experienced pearling skipper, nor a greater adventurer.

Nevertheless a man must sleep, and to Bill's drowsy eyes nothing about the island and harbor of Onamatu looked altered. There was the same half circle of palm trees, with the gray dawn sky above and the blue-gray sea below, the same whitewashed British Residency on the knoll, the same godowns, in tin of all stages of galvanizing and rust, the same thatched native houses.

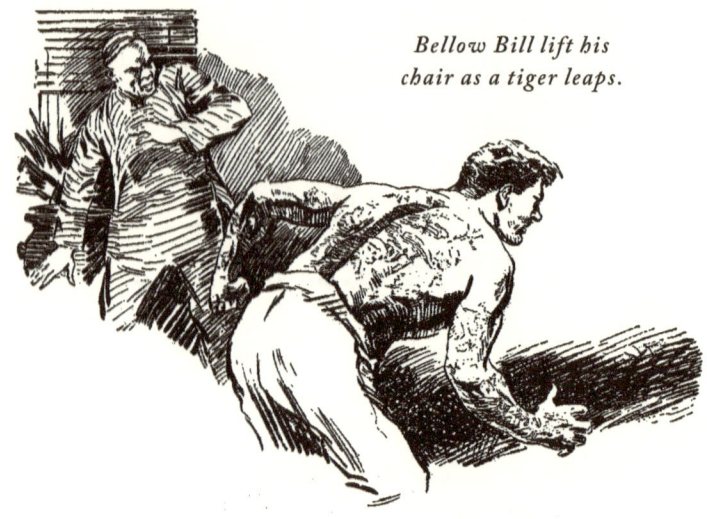

*Bellow Bill lift his
chair as a tiger leaps.*

"Hell, you just forgot to draw your boat far enough up the
beach, and the tide took it!" Bill rumbled disgustedly. "Go look
for it out by the reef, before I slap you like a mosquito!"

"Forgot—!" The little Frenchman stopped, his mouth wide
open. "But thousand thunders, it is the oil launch, my boat!" he
exploded. "Of steel, *m'sieur!* A hundred tons, with a thousand
gallons of kerosene and six hundred of petrol that I sell from
island to island! With two anchors I moored her, and—look—
gone—*volé*—evaporate!"

Bill looked. The oil launch was a new and valuable vessel. The
night had been much too quiet for a ship to go adrift unaided.
To steal a vessel and sail her onto the high seas is piracy. Men
are hanged for it. Nevertheless—

"There was troubled waters," Bill grinned.

"M'sieur?"

"And somebody wanted to pour oil on 'em!"

"M'sieur, you jest!" snapped the little Frenchman bitterly.

"Honest?" Bill boomed. "But you're quieted down, ain't you?
Now go report the piracy to the Governor. It's his business.
Anyway, go somewhere's else, savvy?"

The Frenchman scowled. He was starting to move away, but

He seized the gun and fired in one motion.

there was to be no more sleep that morning for Bill. Down the beach a fat and elderly Chinese came on the run. Wu Chang was an important merchant and pearl buyer. He was dignified even for a Chinese, and normally so slow of speech and unruffled in demeanor that his very wink seemed deliberate. For Wu Chang to run augured catastrophe.

"Allee gone, Bill!" he burst out in a quavering sing song as he recognized the big skipper. "Allee your shell, allee your pearl!" The smooth yellow features, normally so bland and expressionless, quivered with shame. "Wu Chang no could help!" he wailed. "Hab got padlock, hab got sently! Maskee! Lock is cut! Man is hit on head! Wu Chang velly solly. Nevel happen beflo'oe—"

"Steady, Wu," Bill rumbled "I know you're straight, old-timer. Thieves that can lift a couple of tons of pearl shell between sunset and dawn have never happened before, for a fact. Don't apologize."

The pearler's left hand strayed to his hip pocket, and he filled his cheek with fine cut chewing tobacco, rolling the quid from side to side. Bellow Bill had stored his season's take in Wu Chang's godown. His loss, he estimated, amounted to more than five thousand dollars. The fruits of nearly a year of his labor had been snatched out to sea, probably aboard the Frenchman's oil launch. The loss was heavy—but a little grin appeared on Bill's lips, and flecks of gold began to dance in his blue eyes.

Bellow Bill was reflecting that he had been robbed by a master hand. He could not have engineered a more daring and colossal theft himself. It was hard to decide which was the greater feat—to get a ship under way noiselessly or to load tons of shell aboard unobserved.

"Some one wishes to make buttons, *peut-être,* or play the—how you say—shell game?" interpolated the Frenchman nastily. "You laugh now, *hein?* It is a joke, no! The pirate, the thief, the—"

"Shut up!" Bill boomed. He stared until the eyes of the smaller man dropped, and then grinned broadly. "Give credit where it's due, Captain—and run along! I'm going to the Governor myself, and I can't stomach a chattering monkey like you this early in the morning."

The Frenchman opened his mouth angrily, took another look at Bill—and remained silent, his mouth open. With a shrug, as though he had shaken off an annoying fly, the pearler turned on his heel and started along the beach toward the Residency, walking slowly in order that Wu Chang could accompany him at the usual sedate pace of the Chinese.

"YOU GO see Govelno' in pants? No shoes, no shirt?" Wu chattered, scandalized.

"Yep. McGirk won't care," Bill boomed. "Terry McGirk is a roughneck at heart, if he is the second son of an Irish lord. Whisky and a horse race and a good fight are his meat, as you can tell by the red face and the hairy neck of him. Did your guard at the godown see the men who knocked him out?"

"No see," Wu reported.

Bill nodded and shifted his quid. "In the gang we're after there must be an A-1 sailor and a bunch of damned strong active men," he announced cheerfully. "There aren't so many that fit that description on Onamatu. While I'm talking to McGirk you toddle off, Wu, and find out who is missing since sundown. Get all your nephews and cousins on the job. Comb the island, and report to me at the Residency, savvy?"

"Can do velly quick," the merchant agreed. He turned toward the cluster of tin godowns, while Bill strode on.

The Residency was close by. In order to save time when Bill reached the fence, which was built of lumps of brain coral, he raised his voice in a shout that was audible for a mile.

"McGirk! Ahoy, McGirk! Wake up and have some fun!"

The answer should have been a hoarse roar from within and the sight of a red face and a tousled gray head poking through the door onto the veranda. Instead there was silence, a moment's delay during which Bellow Bill vaulted the fence, and then the almost stealthy appearance of McGirk's young English secretary.

Malcolm Ashley-Preston—he insisted on the hyphen and the title of Mister—habitually dressed and acted as though he were Chargé d'Affaires at the British Embassy at Paris or London instead of a clerk to the rough and ready Governor of a frontier outpost. He was well knit and muscular, pink cheeked and flaxen haired, and he loved red tape—which meant that he was not loved himself by the pearlers and traders with whom he had to deal, and by Bellow Bill in particular.

Ashley-Preston frowned at Bill's naked, tattooed torso and the dirty duck trousers which were his only garment with a distaste which was meant to be cutting.

"His Excellency can't see you," he announced in a clipped accent.

"Then he'll tell me so to my face!" Bill boomed impatiently, and strode up the steps. The pink cheeks of the secretary whitened with anger, but he stepped aside—just in time to save himself from the indignity of being shoved out of the way—and followed Bill within, walking on tiptoe.

The pearler went straight to the screened veranda where

McGirk slept, thrust the curtain at the door aside—and halted, so suddenly that Preston bumped into his back.

The veranda was empty. There was a six foot rent in the mosquito netting. The clothing which McGirk had taken off the night before lay scattered over the floor where he had dropped it. On each side of the room the cords which had supported his hammock hung limply from the hooks, cut off clean with a sharp knife, but the hammock and the Governor were gone.

"His Excellency has been kidnaped," said Preston precisely. "I trust that since you've learned the circumstances through forcing yourself in where you weren't wanted you will keep the matter secret until I can take steps." The secretary paused, for Bellow Bill had turned, grinning broadly. "I fail to perceive what you find amusing!" Preston added indignantly.

"You would," Bill rumbled. "To be so damned serious about everything as you are must be tough. You can't see things in any proper kind of proportion. Here's a gang that steals a ship, and a cargo, and the Law—in the person of Terry McGirk."

"And that's funny?"

"Not any," Bill purred. "That's serious to the extent of one thousand pounds to me, and Terry's my friend to boot. But just the same I can grin to think of the way Terry'll cuss the gang for forgetting his pants!"

CHAPTER II

A DIFFERENT SLANT

THE GRIN FADED. "Luckily they forgot to scuttle my schooner, too," said Bill thoughtfully. "We'll follow them in that."

"I have already cabled the proper authorities," Preston contradicted stiffly. "The British Empire does not need your assistance or advice—"

"Steady! That's just language you're talking. The Empire boils down to a secretary who has a chance to prove he got the gimp to get his boss back, and a Yankee pearler called Bellow Bill Williams that wants to help. A cable," Bill went on, "won't do any good. All it means is that in ten days a gunboat arrives here to investigate. Meanwhile my shell is sold, and the thieves scattered to hell and gone with the dough. What did they say in the note they left?"

"Note?"

"Of course they left a note! Kidnapers have to!" Bill boomed. Preston was white to the lips. He backed to a chair and sat down.

"In the absence of McGirk I am in charge," he said. "My duty is to carry on. Hold court. Issue clearances to the shipping—" He choked and swallowed nervously. "A cable to my superiors is what the regulations require."

"I've known many British officials, but never one to hide behind the regulations in a crisis." Bill's great voice was hushed. "Are you afraid to follow?"

Hatred gleamed in Preston's pale eyes. "To follow means McGirk will be killed," he answered. "And furthermore," he blustered, "I don't want your help, can't you understand?"

"Damned clearly, though not the reason," Bill rumbled. "Then there was a note?"

"Yes!"

"Where is it?"

"In my pocket, where it stays!" snapped Preston viciously. "I'm in charge, and I don't show an official paper to a damned tattooed Yankee sea tramp!"

Bellow Bill merely leaned forward, his huge arms on his knees.

"More language," he remarked. "It's no use to try to get me sore, Preston. McGirk's my friend, and I've a thousand pounds at stake. You're right that I'm an American citizen, and that's just the point. This won't be a chase into the bush, beyond the law. It's a pursuit on the high seas. If I catch that oil launch, and board her, I'm a pirate too, unless some official is with me to make the act legal.

"That's why I've got to have you with me. I can't send a cable that will start a gunboat moving. You can. I can't libel a ship, and refuse her clearance papers. You can. Together, you can trip these thieves with law and your precious red tape if they stay at sea, and I can knock 'em on the head if they take to the land. While we work singly, neither of us is half as effective." Bill smiled persuasively. "Try to forget that I'm a roughneck, and that we haven't liked one another too well in the past," he urged. "I wish you'd let me read that note."

"I won't!" Preston snapped. His face was white as chalk. As he spoke he moved close to McGirk's chest of drawers, and the tone he used ended argument. Will had clashed with will, but though Bellow Bill realized an ultimatum had been delivered, he remained seated, frowning slightly.

The pause lengthened. In the tense silence the faint scuff of felt slippers on the veranda, the scratch of a finger nail at the front door, were audible.

"Come in, Wu!" Bill boomed without turning his head.

PRESTON MADE a nervous, angry movement, but it was too late to interfere. At the inner door Wu stopped short. He glanced at the two white men, at the broken screen and the dangling hammock cords. He had, however, recovered his calm.

"Thlee men gone," he reported. "Ev'lybody else Wu can find. But not Jib-boom Charlie."

"Huh? But Jib-boom's been a beachcomber twenty-odd years!" Bill boomed. "He's sleeping it off somewhere, Wu! Why, Jib-boom doesn't weigh a hundred and fifty pounds, and he's sixty if he's a day! He doesn't even own a boat, much less sail one! As long as Jib-boom has a bottle of squareface a day and some one to recite Shakespeare to he doesn't ask anything more of life!"

"Jib-boom not dlunk yeste'day," retorted the Chinese, unmoved. "Moa and Kula gone, too."

"That's different," Bill admitted. "But still—"

He shifted his quid. Moa and Kula were the biggest and ablest natives of Onamatu—and the most prosperous. Bronzed, black mustached, laughing giants who could bring up shell in twenty fathoms, and weather a hurricane in an outrigger canoe. Able to move tons of shell between dark and dawn, able to get an oil launch under way silently as a ghost—but with no reason to do so.

Except that Moa and Kula were brothers-in-law of Jib-boom Charlie. Had that harmless, amusing old reprobate, with the white head and beard and the sharp crimson beak of a nose thrusting through the whiskers suddenly gone berserk? Jib-boom had been educated once, and neither gin nor idleness had ever completely quenched the spirit that twinkled in the bleared blue eyes. Beachcombers in general are a sorry lot, but Jib-boom had never been sordid—only content with his remittance, his native wife, and his gin.

What his motive could be was a problem, but there might be one spark of the old fire left in that frail physique, and a gentleman, however deeply sunk, is capable of crime on a scale that men less highly organized cannot hope to match. Two bronzed giants, animated and guided by the brain of an old man with nothing to lose—

"**MUST BE.** Nobody else gone," said Wu, poker faced.

"Well, if it is we've got a simpler job," Bill rumbled. "None of the three can navigate except by dead reckoning. They've got to dispose of the shell and the oil launch fairly near by. Where's a trader crooked enough to handle a deal of that sort, Wu?"

"Lee Sin. Him Chinese, but plenty gamble'l fo' plenty profit."

"Yep, Lee Sin," Bill boomed. "Three Finger Sweeney in Tahiti might take it on, too, but he's a thousand miles farther away. Lee Sin is the most likely fence, and we'll tackle him first. How about it, Preston? Do I get to see that note now?"

"No, you're too reckless. You'd get McGirk killed trying to save him," snapped the secretary.

Bellow Bill's face warned him. He moved quickly, but not quickly enough. Preston pulled open the top bureau drawer, snatched out a revolver, and fired as his finger touched the trigger, all in one motion. But Bill left his chair as a tiger leaps—one instant motionless, the next in midair. His hand was on the gun as it exploded. He twisted it from Preston's fingers and caught the secretary by the throat.

"Damn you, you shot to kill!" Bill thundered. There was a smudge of burned powder on his cheek. "You white-faced fool!"

"My duty—here," Preston panted. "Won't be abducted—too!" He was shaking from head to foot. Bill shoved the gun into the waistband of his trousers, spun the younger man around, and pulled a smudged piece of paper from his pocket.

> To Whom It May Concern:
> I don't care whether I live or die. For God's sake remember that, and don't follow me. Neither McGirk nor any one else will be injured if I'm let alone, but rather than fail in what I must do I will kill myself and every one around me ten thousand times. For God's sake don't think of me as Jib-boom Charlie. Under that name there was nothing I wanted. The man I am now is a different person.

"Jib-boom means it," Preston gasped. "He's gone mad as a dog, and he'll kill McGirk if we catch him. It's McGirk I'm thinking of!"

"That's what Jib-boom wants you to think, all right," Bill retorted. "But if you take that letter at its face value, do you think McGirk is safe in the power of a man in that frame of mind? I don't. Suppose Jib-boom decided that he'd succeed quicker with McGirk's throat cut. He'd cut it."

Preston was stubbornly silent.

"And why did Jib-boom steal my shell?" Bill rumbled. "He can't sell a ship, and he doesn't ask for a ransom, observe. He wants the dough he can get by selling the shell and the oil, which can't be traced—and he's determined he shall sell 'em. Why does Jib-boom suddenly need money, and how was he able to persuade Moa and Kula to help him? A native never sees the necessity for much cash. Jib-boom is desperate, all right; but he's not crazy."

"He is!" Preston repeated. "I warn you I won't help you! You can carry me off by force, but I'll fight you every step of the way! I'll escape—"

"Pipe down. I'm sick of language," Bellow Bill grunted. He turned his head toward Wu. "Have my schooner sailed around to the other side of the island," he ordered. "I can't take Preston through the town by the nape of his damned neck, but he and I are going to interview Lee Sin. I've got to have an official with me—even if he wants to blow me full of holes!"

CHAPTER III

THE MADMAN

BELLOW BILL TOOK Preston's arm under his own, as though the two were the best of friends, and walked him through the rear of the Governor's garden into the bush. After a few steps the secretary realized the futility of attempting to resist a man twice as strong. Arm in arm the pair crossed the island, and waited hidden in a thicket until the schooner was sailed around to them. Within an hour they were at sea.

Once aboard, Bill merely locked the arms chest and put the key in his pocket. Preston shrugged. Without a weapon he could not possibly overpower the pearler, but throughout the ten-hour sail to Nuahua, where Lee Sin had his godowns, he preserved a frigid silence which the questions, the taunts, and even the threats of the pearler were unable to break down. Upon several points Bill wanted enlightenment. He did not get it. Preston's attitude merely became more and more a puzzle.

At Nuahua Bill anchored off the windward side, and slipped into the little cluster of thatched huts from the rear, as unobtrusively as possible. A glance revealed that the oil launch was not in the harbor, but nevertheless a feeling of excitement was in the air. No canoes were fishing at the reef. No loafers were drowsing in the sand. Everyone was indoors. The gabble of a large group of natives, in vehement argument, rose and fell.

"Aren't there any white men in this place?" Preston demanded.

"Lee Sin don't encourage settlers," Bill grunted. "They might be witnesses. The only white man here is Yesterday Clark. He's so deep in debt to Lee he has to keep his mouth shut, and he's usually drunk. Every time you meet him he has a long story of how he would have been rich—yesterday—if something different hadn't happened to-day."

With sure instinct the pearler led the way to Lee Sin's trading room and bar. At a casual glance the place seemed empty except for the clerk in attendance, a heavy-set and surly Chinese who leaned on the counter as silent, and ugly, as a gargoyle carved from yellow wood.

After an instant, however, what had appeared to be a heap of dirty clothing tossed in the corner stirred. A white man sat up, unshaven, red eyed, miserable from a hangover.

" 'Lo, Bill," he moaned. "Always around when hell pops, ain't you—you half ton of tattooed beef."

"Hell's sure to follow mixing gin and *kava*," the pearler boomed genially. "What misery are you drowning this time, Yesterday?"

"The Irish Sweepstakes was won by a rank outsider," groaned the derelict. "The horse I backed finished fourth, and nobody but a fool would have backed the winner." Yesterday made the explanation almost mechanically. "You're from Onamatu," he added with more animation. "Are you following Jib-boom?"

"Has he been here?"

"Has he!" The bleared eyes snapped. "He's gone to cut the Governor's throat!"

"Where!" Bill boomed.

"Oh, somewhere out to sea."

YESTERDAY CLARK held his head in his hands and groaned. Talking hurt. "He sailed in with the oil launch about noon. The natives all started yelling, and the noise hurt my head. I didn't think I could move, but I dragged myself down to the beach— and damn it, Bill, if I didn't forget about my hangover for two solid hours! McGirk was lashed to the foremast with a gag in his mouth, and Jib-boom was dancin' around him, mother naked, an' wavin' a knife.

" 'Five hundred guineas gold for ransom, or I'll cut his throat!' Jib-boom was screamin', over and over." Clark paused. "He was mad, Bill. Blind, ravin' mad. Why, he swung the knife that close to McGirk's face I was lookin' to see a nose drop! Nobody dared paddle out to stop him—and the only gold in Nuahua owned by a dirty Chink!"

"Jib-boom was alone?" Bill rumbled.

"He didn't need any help," Yesterday retorted. "He was screechin' as loud as you could yell yourself, Bill. So I went to Lee Sin, and told him he'd have to come through with the brass. McGirk would pay him back, I said. The old yellow devil didn't want to pay, but I'm white, ain't I? I made him!"

"How?"

"I'd have shot him!" said Yesterday. Bellow Bill glanced at the trembling hands, and smothered a grin behind a huge, tattooed palm.

"Right you'd have been to shoot, Yesterday," he agreed. "So Lee Sin paddled out with the gold—all by himself, eh?"

"That's what he did—though damned if I see how you guessed it!" Yesterday retorted. "He threw the bag of gold onto the deck. Jib-boom grabbed it and poured out the coins. Lee Sin shouted for him to cut McGirk loose, like he had agreed. Jib-boom began to laugh—shriller and shriller till it was enough to turn your blood cold. Then he got the oil launch under way and sailed out to sea, leaving Lee Sin cursing."

"Jib-boom got under way alone?" Bill rumbled. "That isn't possible!"

"I know it, but he done so!" Yesterday retorted. "Well, maybe there was some one below decks, but there was no one but Jib-boom and McGirk in sight. What's the difference? Jib-boom's got McGirk, ain't he? He's mad as a March hare, and he'll kill him, won't he?"

"That's what I told you!" Preston whispered fiercely.

Bellow Bill shrugged huge shoulders.

"Tell Lee Sin to come here!" he boomed at the clerk.

"Lee Sin no can do. Him sick," the Chinese refused.

"Then I'll see him in bed!" the pearler thundered.

The slant eyes narrowed. For an instant the clerk was silent, weighing the chances. Then he vanished through a curtain, like an ugly ghost.

Bill caught Preston by the shoulder and dragged him to the opposite side of the room.

"Give me your word of honor to stay here till I come back!" he whispered rapidly. "Lee lives underground in rooms hollowed out of the coral, and he ain't here alone, or sick, believe me! He won't touch you here! You're an official, and neither Yesterday or the natives could be kept quiet if Lee gets rough in the open. I don't want to drag you underground, but I can't have you running back to Onamatu on my schooner."

Preston licked his lips. The dead white pallor had returned to his face.

"I promised—that I would never break my word," he whispered. "I won't have you bind me—in that way."

"Lee's back room is no place for his enemies, and I mean to call him a liar to his face," Bill warned.

"I prefer to be there—free to act as I see fit," Preston retorted stiffly.

The curtain parted.

"Allee light. Lee Sin see you now," the clerk intoned.

WITH A wave of a huge tattooed hand Bellow Bill motioned Preston to go first. The pearler followed, walking on the balls of his feet, the great shoulders thrust forward, as a wrestler walks to the center of the ring. The clerk led them down a flight of eight steps into a long corridor, with white sand underfoot and the walls and ceiling hidden by curtains and strips of printed cotton. There was no break in the wall coverings to indicate how many doors the curtains masked, but scarcely half way down the corridor the clerk pulled a strip of cloth aside.

"Lee Sin!" he intoned.

Preston and Bill entered. The clerk vanished, leaving the door curtain open.

The room into which the pearler advanced was about twenty feet square. The wall curtains and ceiling cloth were of yellow cotton. The furniture consisted of low stools of black teak-wood carved in Chinese designs, and low tables with carved legs and black marble tops. At the largest table sat Lee Sin, dressed in a black nankeen coat. His arms were folded, and he stared at a jade cigarette box placed in the center of the table before him. Bellow Bill was reminded of a black spider in a yellow web.

"Nice, cool room. The air's good and fresh!" he boomed.

"Velly nice," Lee Sin agreed.

"Curtains are a swell idea, too," the pearler rambled on. "Half a dozen hatchet men can stand behind them and never be noticed, eh?"

"Me no savvy," whispered Lee Sin without looking up.

Bill pushed Preston slightly behind him, and an arm's length away.

"Me, I savvy," he grinned. "We old-timers don't mind a little trouble to reach a profit. I stand to lose a thousand pounds, Lee."

"No savvy. Not your ship Jib-boom have got."

"Ah, but he had my shell. Until you bought it," Bill purred. "You wouldn't pay five cents to keep McGirk's throat whole, Lee. He's experienced and he's honest. You'd make money a lot faster under a younger official."

"You have cigarette?" Lee whispered.

"Nope. Nor doped liquor, either," Bill grinned. "It was a

swell act you and Jib-boom put on. A madman gets the Governor. That's a yarn to travel the length of the South Seas. The new-chums will be too busy telling it to think it over. For it's an act. You'd have been willing to pay five hundred quid to be rid of McGirk—and but for one thing, I believe that was what you—or some one—was trying to do."

"You clazee," said Lee Sin.

"Moa and Kula wouldn't abet a killing," Bill rumbled. "Even if a young official wanted promotion bad enough to hire a killer and was shrewd enough to prepare the defense of insanity in advance. That's the angle I'd have worked on if Moa and Kula hadn't lifted my shell—and maybe they were tricked, and maybe swiping the shell was a blind."

PRESTON SHIFTED his weight and Lee Sin seemed to freeze rigidly in the carven chair.

"If that theory is wrong," Bill purred, "then that 'ransom' was a means of paying Jib-boom for my shell in a way that couldn't be explained. If Jib-boom had stolen a ship and cargo and been found with five hundred quid you both might have had some explainin' to do. But not now. You paid the money as a public-spirited act, Lee. And he took it—because he was mad as a hatter. It was a smart stunt—but me, I savvy!"

"You wantee tlouble!" squeaked the Chinese. "What you wantee?"

"I want you!" Bill boomed. "Since you're the guy that put up the dough, you are coming on board my schooner and pilot me to the place where Jib-boom cached that shell you bought at half price. Or if it ain't shell you bought, you're coming so that the police won't have far to look for you when McGirk's body is found!" The great voice dropped. "Somebody figured McGirk's friends were dumb," Bill purred. "Or afraid to step into the center of the web—where most men wouldn't come."

Slowly Lee Sin's head moved. He looked at Preston, and at Bill. Behind the wrinkled mask which was his face his mind reached a decision. Slowly he reached to the jade cigarette box and removed—one cigarette. As it was revealed between the clawlike yellow fingers a knife came flying through the door at Bill's chest.

Ready though he was, the missile came too swiftly to be dodged. Bill knocked the flying steel aside with his bare hand. Like a rat Lee Sin dove under the heavy marble table. Through the doorway rushed three hatchetmen with long knives.

Cornered, unarmed, Bill must have seemed an easy victim. Like a flash he crouched behind the table. It was too heavy for an ordinary man to lift. The hatchetmen yelled in triumph, and divided, right and left to take him on both sides—and with a ponderous swing the table rose in their faces. For a split second Bellow Bill held it poised—both hands on the edge, his knee crooked under the top. The hatchetmen saw his savage grin, the blood that spurted from his wounded hand along the black marble. Then, edge-first, Bill tossed the table on their feet.

Two were caught, and fell screaming. The third leaped back, just avoiding the top as it slammed to the floor. With a roar, Bill charged—and as he sprang forward withered old Lee Sin, crouching at his feet, tripped him.

Bill fell flat and hard. For a split second the wind was knocked out of him. He was heaving himself up, yet for an instant his back was a target for a knife. The hatchetmen jumped forward—and so did Preston! They met over Bill's body. With bare hands the secretary snatched at the descending steel—and the stab aimed at Bill's heart opened his forearm to the bone. Preston reeled back—but before the hatchetman could raise the knife again Bellow Bill seized him around both knees, slammed him to the floor, and rolled upon him.

A huge fist fell like a sledge hammer. There was a brief struggle, a flash of steel, and Bill rose, gasping, the red knife gripped in his fist. Lee Sin squealed as the pearler seized him by the throat and jerked him upright.

"You don't get it yet!" Bill snarled. He held the Chinaman

between his body and the open doorway, like a shield. His eyes darted around the hangings that concealed the walls.

"That was a swell chance to get away you had, Preston," he growled. "If you'd stood still I'd have been split like a shad. Pull some of those curtains down and tie up your arm!"

"The door—open—run before more—come!" Preston gasped.

"Not up that corridor while that ugly clerk is hiding behind a curtain somewhere," Bill boomed. "Lee Sin ain't got an army!" He shook the Chinese viciously. "Tell that clerk to stay where he is!" he threatened.

Lee Sin obeyed in a rush of Chinese. "Shell no hab got!" he squealed. "Pay cash, no get shell yet. Go find Jib-boom quick— quick—"

"Shut up till I tell you!" Bill rumbled.

"Jib-boom go to Neura Island—"

"And you'll go to Neura Island and see him or your throat won't hold water!" Bill promised grimly.

THE CURTAIN which Preston had torn down revealed nothing but a wall of coral. With a strip of the cotton cloth he had managed to stanch the flow of blood from his arm.

"Rip down the ceiling cloth, too," Bellow Bill ordered coolly. "The air here's too fresh to come through the corridor."

And indeed, as the ceiling was torn down a short ventilating shaft was revealed. Bill dragged a small table beneath the opening and stood upon it, holding Lee Sin in one arm and still careful to keep the old man between the door and himself. The hatchetmen caught under the table eyed the pearler in vicious silence—not daring to make a sound lest he jump down and finish them with the knife, yet ready to squirm out and resume the fight if he were careless, or slipped.

"I said you had a fine chance to escape—considering you tried to shoot me yourself," Bill rumbled. "Why didn't you take it?"

"Oh, you were tripped and I jumped," snapped the secretary, irritated by the question and the pain of his wound. "I didn't study it all out, damn it. You had them licked, and you were tripped and it wasn't sporting, that's all!"

"All except that you're okay at bottom—when you *don't* study things out," Bill rumbled. "That bein' so, tear off a strip of that cloth and climb out on my shoulders. When you're topside, pass me down the cloth for a rope. I'll climb out with Sin here—and of course you can beat it to my schooner and leave me down here if you like."

The secretary flushed. He tore the cloth angrily, and climbed up over Bill as though the pearler were a tree. Nevertheless as soon as he was up he dropped an end of the cloth back into the underground chamber. Bill took the knife in his teeth and held Sin with his wounded hand. With both feet and one hand he climbed with astonishing speed, as a sailor can. He was out of reach before the hatchetmen could lift the heavy table off their legs and interfere.

"Thanks," he grunted as he emerged into the open air, and added, after a significant pause, "Partner." The ventilation shaft was concealed by a thicket of pandanus at the rear of Lee Sin's store. Bill set the Chinese down and reached to his hip pocket for fine cut.

"That's as close a call as I can remember," he admitted. "It would have annoyed me to be done in because of a rack of skin and bone like Lee. I figured he'd duck when the fighting started. My error."

"Did you figure on the table?"

"There's always something," Bill rumbled. He shifted his quid. "Of course, you're mixed up in this case yourself, somehow, Preston—though not to the point of double crossing me. You might amount to something as a man yet."

"I don't know what you mean," snapped the secretary, suddenly frigid and precise.

"Well, you don't have to trust me," Bill admitted. "I had to find out whether you were yellow, or if you were engineering the whole thing. You aren't."

"If I did trust you there's nothing that could be altered," said Preston hoarsely. "I swear there's been nothing that I could do—not since the beginning—but go along. Jib-boom's—*mad*."

"So?" Bill reflected. "Lee Sin was too quick in telling me where Jib-boom was, too. And I'm not going to underestimate that Chink twice."

CHAPTER IV

JIB-BOOM KEEPS HIS WORD

NOTWITHSTANDING BILL'S SUSPICIONS, Lee Sin had blurted out the truth. Neura Island was the rocky tip of a volcanic peak which thrust itself a hundred feet or so above the sea. Treeless and hot as a stove lid, it possessed a long and narrow harbor formed by a break between the cliffs. For a criminal it had the advantages of being close to Onamatu and Nuahua, and the disadvantage that the narrow entrance made the harbor a trap.

Bill sailed between the cliffs an hour after sunrise. The oil launch lay anchored in the center of the harbor, in deep water more than two hundred yards from the nearest shore. The dugout stolen at Nuahua was gone, but on the forward deck Jib-boom Charlie was laboring with a winch to get the cargo out of the hold. As Bill caught sight of him he was dumping a basketful of pearl shell over the side into the water.

He knew Bill's schooner. At a glance he must have recognized the three men on board, and realized that escape was impossible. That white head tilted back slowly. The bearded lips parted.

"Go-o back!" he howled. The utterance of the two words stretched into seconds. *"Bel-low Bill! Go-o ba-ack!"* It was a wail, long drawn and mournful, that made the pearler's scalp tingle.

"You hear? He's mad! For God's sake—" Preston whispered.

"I'll go back with McGirk!" Bill roared. "Where's he? Where's

Moa and Kula?" The schooner kept sliding across the smooth harbor water.

Aboard the launch Jib-boom ducked behind the rail while Bill could count ten.

"Get down! He might shoot!" the pearler was rumbling, when Jib-boom reappeared—unarmed. He merely held a box of matches in his hand, which he lifted high, without saying a word.

But around the launch the water was suddenly streaked with purple and crimson. From invisible vents in the steel sides poured a flood of oil that spread around the launch in an ever widening circle which advanced to meet the schooner almost as rapidly as the schooner closed in. Bill's eyes started from his head. Six months' supply of kerosene, the Frenchman had said. Dozens, hundreds of gallons, pouring from the tanks—and still leaving dozens, hundreds of gallons aboard.

Deliberately Jib-boom struck a match, let it blaze an instant in the still air—and blew it out.

"Put the schooner about, Bill, or I drop the next on the oil!" he called. His voice was different—quick, and hard. Any pretense, any play-acting of madness, was finished. "Go back, or it'll be corpses you find when the fire burns out!"

Lee Sin cried out in terror, for the oil slick was almost under the bowsprit of the schooner. Preston leaped up and dashed at Bill, aiming a roundhouse swing at his head. Mechanically the pearler blocked the blow.

"He means it! I told you! Back!" Preston panted. Frantically he strove to put the wheel over, gripping the spokes and punching at Bill's face. Over his shoulder Lee Sin kicked and clawed. With a sweep of a huge arm Bill sent them both sprawling.

Jib-boom Charlie misunderstood. The second match sputtered and fell.

From the sea flame leaped to meet it. Flickering tongues of flame reared themselves like the heads of snakes around the launch and writhed outward, dying as they burned through the film of oil to the water, leaping forward as the fuel was renewed, but rearing ever higher, ever hotter. On the launch Jib-boom threw his arms across his face and staggered to the hatchway.

"You murderer! You damn hard-headed, thick-witted louse—" Preston screamed at Bill.

The pearler threw the wheel hard over. The schooner turned. None too quickly. At the wheel the breath of the fire could be felt.

"Take her, mister!" Bill boomed. "I mean sail the schooner, you fool!" he thundered as Preston continued to curse. "McGirk's in that hell trap! Beat the fire out of the harbor, and come back when it dies!" The pearler leaped down into the cabin before Preston could rise. He was back on deck, a Winchester carbine in his hands, before the secretary had the wheel. In two motions Bill took the rifle apart, hurled the stock into the sea and leaped after it.

"You can't swim that far—over or under water!" Preston shouted as he rose.

"Sail the schooner! I pay for my mistakes!" Bill thundered. The advancing fire was close to his head. Still gripping the rifle barrel he ducked under the surface. For a minute, two minutes the secretary stared into the thickening inferno of flame and smoke. There was no more sign of Bill.

PRESTON SLUMPED against the wheel, but only to straighten himself. His face was whiter, older; drawn as though it had felt the fire.

"If I were just worth it!" he ground out through clenched teeth, and put the schooner on her course. It was Bill's epitaph—and yet, during those two minutes, Bellow Bill had breathed twice. He was still swimming under water toward the launch. The rifle barrel which he poked to the surface when he needed air had escaped Preston's eye.

The expedient Bill adopted in the emergency was desperate, but it was neither new nor an inspiration. In every lagoon in the South Seas little native boys amuse themselves by lying under water in the shallows and breathing through a bamboo tube. In a flash Bill had remembered and decided to take the risk, but he was finding the bore of the rifle a narrow orifice through which to fill his lungs, and there was the danger of drawing down a breath of flame.

He had, he judged, about three hundred yards to swim. That required, roughly, three hundred strokes. He counted them, swimming strongly, without haste. When he wanted air he turned on his back and let himself float slowly until he was close to the surface. He poked up the butt of the rifle barrel, holding his tongue over the muzzle—exhaled, which started his body sinking, and then gingerly sipping at the air, testing the temperature with his tongue. If it burned, he tried again a little farther on. The oil did not burn in a sheet, but in shifting patches.

He kept alive, but when the count of strokes reached two hundred and fifty he was close to exhaustion. The sight of the anchor chain of the launch, slanting downward, was welcome as though it represented safety. With the last of his breath he swam to the iron links and hauled himself up hand over hand.

Above the water the iron burned his fingers. The touch of flame on his wet skin was like the scald of steam. The deck, when he tumbled over the rail, was hot to the touch. The paint on the sides of the launch was beginning to burn, but as yet the ship itself had not caught fire. Bill took the rifle barrel from between his teeth and gripped it like a club. He ran to the hatchway and swung himself into the cabin below as an acrobat swings from a trapeze.

At the far end of the long cabin table sat Jib-boom. His head was bowed upon his arms, and a revolver was held loosely in his hand. He glanced up in utter amazement and lifted the gun. Bill hurled the rifle barrel. Jib-boom ducked. Headlong Bill dove the length of the table. One huge hand was outstretched to knock the revolver aside, but in that split second Jib-boom swung the muzzle, not at Bill, but backward at his own chest. Bill struck the old man's elbow upward, but that only altered the path of the bullet as the gun exploded.

Headlong, Bill slid into a thin, wasted body that was suddenly limp as a loose string. The bearded head lolled back over the rim of the chair, the eyes closed, the lips still parted with surprise.

Bill gulped. The violence with which he had collided with Jib-boom was suddenly so futile, so brutal. This little, wasted out man had not been crouched, gun in hand, to fight like a cornered rat. He had been sitting, quietly, indomitably, holding a gun only in order to save himself the torture of the fearful death that his own hand had set blazing.

By instinct the pearler ripped open the ragged shirt to expose the withered chest. The blue mark of the bullet was low. The wound was mortal, even though Jib-boom still breathed.

"Ahoy! McGirk!" Bill croaked in a voice that was a mockery of his usual booming tones.

There was no answer. Bill rolled off the table. To search the oil launch below decks took less than a minute. The staterooms, the engine room, the galley and lazarette were empty. McGirk, Moa, and Kula were gone, and in the hold were only a few bushels of pearl shell.

CHAPTER V

THE MAN WHO WAS

BELLOW BILL COULD look defeat in the face. He was sick at heart and his lips were grim, but he wasted no precious seconds in regret. He ran to the engine room and got the launch under way, dashed on deck and slipped the anchor chain, and steered the launch hard and fast aground on the rocky edge of the harbor. Flame still surrounded the boat. To attempt to save her was useless. Indeed, the oil tanks were liable to explode at any second, but nevertheless Bill collected blankets, a water cask and a bottle of brandy before he returned to the cabin, slung

Jib-boom over his shoulder, and leaped from the bow of the launch onto dry ground.

On shore he carried the old man just far enough to be out of the blast of the explosion. Laying him in a hollow of the rock with blankets wrapped around him, Bill set about coaxing back the spark of life which still flickered. Warmth, repeated doses of brandy, and a dash of water in the face succeeded at last. Jib-boom opened his eyes.

He grinned at Bill weakly.

"I did it!" he breathed. "Almost—got me. Not—quite."

"Aye!" Bill boomed. "Man, you're dying! Where's McGirk?"

The eyelids fluttered.

"Figured—on dying. Easier than jail—or asylum. Had to be one of—the three."

Bill thrust the brandy bottle between the teeth. Again the eyes opened.

"McGirk?" whispered Jib-boom dreamily. He tried to grin, but the effort was too much. "Put him in cave ashore—there." The eyeballs rolled to the right. "Tied him—not tight. Free himself before schooner got back."

"And Moa and Kula?" Bill boomed.

Jib-boom smiled this time. His eyes were open. The energy that comes to the dying was lifting him up, but he would not speak. Significantly he shut his mouth tight, and closed his eyes. Brandy had no more effect. For a minute or two more he continued to breathe, slower and slower, but his teeth remained clenched, and his eyes closed. The bearded face was determined—and self satisfied. Jib-boom died triumphant.

Bellow Bill pulled up the blanket and started to look for McGirk. There were dozens of caves in sight, and he was walking toward the largest and nearest when Preston came scrambling over the rim of the hill that blocked the view toward the sea and ran recklessly down the steep slope.

"The schooner's anchored and Lee Sin's tied up safe!" he

yelled, reading Bill's thoughts. "I saw the launch start for shore. Did you save him?"

THE PEARLER pointed to the heap of blankets. Preston dropped beside it, panting from the run, and white as a ghost.

"You—you shot him?" he demanded hoarsely.

"He shot himself," Bill rumbled. "But whatever he was doing, he put it across. McGirk's ashore here somewhere, bound and gagged. Moa and Kula are gone. In the dugout, I guess, and with the five hundred pounds, I'll bet! They don't need it themselves," Bill growled vehemently. "They are taking it to some one, Preston, and damned if I can think of whom, or why! Damn this mess anyhow! The shell was unloaded at Nuahua. That was why Lee Sin was so quick to tell me where Jib-boom had gone. Anything to get me away so that ugly clerk of his could raise the shell and put it into his godowns.

"Damn it!" Bill rammed a fistful of fine cut into his cheek. The enormous quid seemed to relieve his temper. Slowly a grin spread across his face.

"Jib-boom beat me," he rumbled. "He was little and he was old and he'd drugged his brains with twenty years on the beach, but in the pinch he coppered me every step of the way. He stood *me* on my ear for twenty-four hours, and at the end he grinned at me. 'I figured to die,' he said. 'Death or jail or an asylum, it had to be one of the three.' That was the kind of stuff that was in Jib-boom Charlie, and I called him a drunken bum. Moa and Kula are taking that five hundred pounds where he wants it to go, and as for Jib-boom, he'll get a native funeral—stuck in a hole with his head between his knees—and the whole South Seas will call him mad! Mad! He was no more crazy than I am!" Bill boomed. "It's a damn shame, when nerve and courage are as scarce as they are. Though I guess Jib-boom won't care!"

Through the outburst Preston had crouched by the body without moving a muscle.

"I do, though," he said in a strange tone. "I've said he was mad, but only to protect him. You see, Bill, Moa and Kula are taking the five hundred pounds to me. I think I'd rather have my father properly buried and—respected."

"Your what?"

"Quite so. I'm Jib-boom's son," said Preston precisely. "Does it seem impossible? We tried to make it seem so. He drank a little more after I was transferred to Onamatu, and I became pukka official. Both leaning over backwards, so that any chance resemblance between us would be discounted. It was his idea. He insisted that to be known as his son would ruin my career in the South Seas."

"That's true enough," Bill rumbled. "But still, I don't get this. Why the five hundred pounds?"

"Because the Prestons are gamblers. It is simple enough—to tell. Father was a captain in an English regiment. When I was a baby, about six months old, he took part of the mess funds to bet on a horse. He thought it was a sure thing, but the horse lost. He was cashiered, and the family sent him out here. That I was transferred to the same island was simply an unfortunate coincidence. Though, fortunately, my father wore a beard.

"I," Preston continued precisely, "was given five pounds by McGirk to cable to a bookmaker to be placed on the Irish Sweepstakes. The horse was a rank outsider, and I decided to take that bet myself. I put the money in my pocket, and the horse won—at 100 to 1. Father's horse lost. Mine won. The result was the same. I paid McGirk his bet out of the consulate funds, but the monthly audit was coming. I had to have five hundred pounds, and it just didn't exist. So I went to father and said I was going to run away."

"And he told you to stay?" Bill rumbled.

"For three days—no matter what happened," said Preston precisely. "Nothing did happen the first day, except that father sobered up. Before dawn on the second he came to me with that note you read. He had kidnaped McGirk, and had the pearl shell loaded. He warned me that if I didn't keep quiet he'd go to jail anyhow. He said he would kill McGirk rather than see his son travel the path he had taken. He would have done it! And—and the rest you know."

"And why don't you take the five hundred?" Bill rumbled.

"Because I'd rather be a beachcomber than live a lie!" Preston blazed. "To sit and hear filthy tramps call my father a madman, and have to say, 'Yes, he was.' It isn't decent. I'm not worth it! I've got the right to decide what I want! The Frenchman's ship is insured!

"You can raise your shell and squeeze the full price out of Lee Sin! No one's hurt but me."

"And Jib-boom," said Bill deep in his chest. "I asked you how you were mixed into this case at Nuahua. You wouldn't say then, and I don't see that you got any right to throw away what Jib-boom's done now. He decided what you were worth, and I'm thinking he was right. This time you didn't act on impulse."

PRESTON SHRUGGED impatiently.

"Moa and Kula would do anything to aid a kinsman to help a son," Bill added thoughtfully. "That's Polynesian morals. They won't talk. But Lee Sin guessed. Remember that it was *one* cigarette he pulled out of that box? It was me he wanted killed—figuring that he had a hold over you. Maybe your father had to tell him the truth. Maybe he guessed. Anyway, if you had taken that five hundred pounds he'd have blackmailed you until hell would have been a relief!"

"You see? Then I was right!"

Bellow Bill shifted the enormous quid.

"Yep," he nodded. "Jib-boom wouldn't have done much for you by getting you out of debt. Not if you were the guy you were twenty-four hours ago. But you ain't. You kept a knife out of my back and you're standing on your own feet. It'll be tough to hear tramps callin' your father crazy, but that was how he wanted it. And they'll just be tramps, and you can bury him in his own name."

"Because Lee Sin can't blackmail you over five hundred pounds he is supposed to have paid as a ransom for McGirk as long as the pearl shell is in his godowns," Bill smiled. "He's a dirty thief, and I aim to leave my shell with him and keep him a dirty thief—with his mouth stopped, savvy?"

"You mean you'll give me a thousand pounds?" Preston exclaimed.

"Yep, I mean I'll finish the play of Jib-boom's hand," Bill rumbled. "If you think that's queer you've learned damned little about me.

"Jib-boom paid, and I'll deliver. Come on, let's find McGirk and listen to him roar! Gagging an Irishman after stealing him away from his pants is too damned much. McGirk will be fit to be tied!"

THE WRONG MOVE

*They didn't know Bellow Bill, if they thought he'd
stand for being shanghaied in a Chinese coffin*

CHAPTER I

CHEN FU ADDS A PIECE

CHEN FU OWNED and directed a gambling hell, along with many other enterprises less openly conducted and more criminal. Yet he himself played no game save chess.

Day after day he sat in a small alcove overlooking the main floor of his establishment, but concealed from the players by a screen of gilded wood backed by curtains of faded and dusty crimson silk. To his ears rose the muffled thump of dice and the rattle of roulette, the slap of cards from the poker tables, and the click and murmur of *mah jong*. By turning his head, he could watch through a slit in the curtain the bartender and the dealers of a dozen games.

In his veins ran the gambling fever that is the heritage of the Cantonese. Yet those who entered the alcove to whisper reports of other enterprises, scattered through the pearl islands east of Cape York, invariably found the old man with a chess board across his knees.

His opponent was an even older, more withered Chinese in a black coat; a man who had the gentle face of a scholar, whereas Chen Fu's features possessed the sharpness of the fox. The games between them were incessant. Were pearls to be pirated around Thursday Island? Was wool or opium to be smuggled? Could a planter with a crop coming into bearing be driven from his land? Was there a place where a trader could make a legal profit, and no trader there?

The wrinkled fingers of Chen Fu hovered over the ivory

*Everybody dodged the
big pearler's rush.*

chessmen while he listened to such propositions. He would
move a piece—and offer money or ships or men or advice.
Whatever he said, and whatever bargain was agreed upon, the
black-clad scholar remembered word for word. They were brain
and memory, and the most prosperous freebooters in the South
Seas owed allegiance to the pair. Chen was shrewd. He knew
how far to venture, and with whom. Even at the chess, he won
more often than not.

He was winning as usual, seated alone with his familiar, late
one afternoon, when a booming voice drowned the sounds of
the gambling room. Chen Fu turned and peered through the slit.

"The big pearler with the voice of a dragon, he who is tattooed
from shoulder to wrist and from neck to waist, is back," he said.

"Bellow Bill Williams," reminded the scholar in a whisper.
"He is honest, or you would make him rich."

"He is drinking whiskey—half the bottle of whiskey before
he sets it down," muttered Chen. "Yet his step is steady, and
his eye bright! Now he will play stud poker—and he will win,
because he is not afraid. Then he will drink more whiskey, and
go back to sea."

"Men seek profits, and monkeys fun. But which do the gods call the monkeys?" the scholar paraphrased maliciously. "It was Bellow Bill who killed your kinsman's hatchetmen."

"My kinsman pitted a pawn against the queen," Chen growled.

He moved a chessman, almost at random.

"When a tree grows big enough to shade a garden the wise farmer cuts it down," he added.

"But if the tree grows on the land of another, the farmer can only bite his thumbs," whispered the scholar maliciously.

He moved, also, and exchanged a bishop for Chen's queen.

"You will lose," the scholar remarked dryly, "because you were thinking that fewer pearls come from the north, and fewer smugglers need our help. The tree that shades us grows, and the farmer is even now building a high wall which we cannot cut down."

"*Aie!*" Chen Fu agreed.

He hardly seemed to notice the loss of the most important piece in the chess game. He lifted a wall phone, and spoke softly to the bartender on the floor below. Then he bent intently over the board.

"My mother's—!" gasped the scholar in consternation.

He leaped up and ran to the peep hole. Concealed behind the bar, the bartender was shaking a pinch of white powder into a glass of whiskey. The boy set the glass by the huge, tattooed hand of the tattooed giant, who was well over six feet in height and two hundred pounds in weight. And with the toss of a curly, coppery-blond head, Bellow Bill downed the drink, too intent on his cards to look at it.

INSTANTLY THE pearler was up, with a roar like a roused lion. His chair was hurled back. One mighty heave sent the poker table flying, the players sprawling before it. Ten men could not have stopped his rush at the bartender—but knock-out drops work swiftly.

Half-way across the big room, Bellow Bill swayed, stumbled to his knees, and slid gently onto his face.

Like buzzing flies, the Chinese attendants gathered around him, lifted him up and bore him through a side door.

"*Aie!*" shrilled the scholar. "What have you done? When the drug wears off he will not leave one stick of this place together—nor your pigtail on your head!"

"Honored uncle, it is your move," said Chen Fu, placidly.

The scholar fumbled with the pieces.

"But you dare not kill him!" he shrilled. "Even the police know he is honest! That he would spit in your face—"

"That is true," Chen Fu muttered regretfully. "Each man moves in his own way. The paths of the rook and bishop cross—but they cannot move together. And yet I needed a man who was honest—and unafraid." He smiled slightly, and taking advantage of the scholar's blunder, he moved a pawn into the king row. "Give me back my queen, honored uncle," he commanded.

When this had been done, Chen said:

"I shall not hurt Bill. But it came to me that we could send the opium by another schooner, and that *he* might go north in the big box, in the opium's place."

Amazement drained the scholar's face of blood until it was the color of ivory long buried in earth.

"And then?" he gasped.

The face of the gambling proprietor was bland.

"One cannot foresee the end of the game; only the moves," said Chen Fu placidly. "Both games were lost—and see! I have brought back the queen onto the board!"

CHAPTER II

THE BIG BOX

BELLOW BILL WILLIAMS awoke with a splitting headache. He lay in darkness; he smelled the bilge water of a ship's hold; he felt the plunge and heave of a schooner sailing closehauled in a moderate breeze.

The sensations were too vivid to be a nightmare, but they made no more sense than a dream—unless he were the victim of a practical joke. Bill recalled Chen Fu's place, the taste of the last drink, and the expression of the bartender as Bill started after him. The joke was a damned poor one, and the men who had played it were going to find that out—pronto. With an anger sharpened by the racking pain in his head, Bill raised himself and collided with something padded but unyielding, four inches above his nose.

Frantically, he lashed out with arms and legs.—He was in a box.—No! He was in a padded coffin! He was being carried out for burial at sea!

Bill's courage was as hard as his muscles. Cold sweat broke out on his forehead, yet he made but that one convulsive movement. By an effort of will so great that it was physical as well as mental, he changed a yell of horror into a strangled grunt. Every muscle was rigid, yet he forced himself to lie still.

He was in a coffin, but why was the coffin in the ship's hold?

At sea, dead men are buried from the deck; not shipped to some other spot. Besides, Bellow Bill had no home to be shipped to. If he had been judged dead, the people who had carried him where he was had gone to a great deal of unnecessary labor.

Moreover, if this was a coffin he was lying in, why could he breathe so easily, and smell the bilge so strong? His rigid muscles relaxed. With his fingers Bill commenced to feel the sides of his prison, inch by inch. He was confined in something the size and shape of a coffin, and lined like a coffin, though the lining felt more like a cotton quilt. There was a pillow under his head, but it was lumpy and uncomfortable. Bill explored—and touched—first the blade of a heavy knife, and second the barrel of a revolver.

The box was too narrow to permit him to grasp either of the two. Again he lay rigid. Weapons had been provided; but hardly that he might commit suicide, unless he became utterly panic-stricken. Otherwise, the gun would have been put into his fingers. He had been armed, which implied that he was expected to fight, but that conclusion still made no sense.

Though Bill had enemies in plenty, none of them, as far as he was aware, were also enemies of Chen Fu's. In fact, the contrary was true. Bellow Bill had often aided the officials in the South Seas, and the criminals never. The puzzle was unsolvable, but he felt around the inside of the box with renewed confidence. Eventually he discovered an iron knob. When he pulled on this, he heard the lid of the box slide open an inch or two. Reaching upward, he enlarged the gap until he could sit up.

As he rose, his face scraped against sailcloth, but there was no weight upon the canvas. An old sail must have been tossed over the box to conceal it. The darkness was still absolute, from which he inferred that the sun had set, since the hold of a schooner is seldom light-tight. Bill had matches, but first he reached for the fine cut chewing tobacco which he carried loose in his hip pocket.

He chewed slowly, extracting the full measure of solace and

enjoyment from the quid. That was typical of him. He stopped wondering why he had been shanghaied; he stopped guessing about the destination of the schooner and the character of her skipper.

All of these things would be important—later. For the next half hour they were immaterial.

Here he was, almost certainly without the knowledge of the skipper, and probably unwelcome to the crew as well. And so what? He might be compelled to work his passage, merely. He might find himself involved in some highly nefarious enterprise, and in order to save himself he might be forced to aid it, with all his strength and his vast experience in the South Seas. Anything he planned in advance, as likely as not, would be wrong. Therefore, he must not plan; he could only prepare. Bill thrust the quid under his lip and struck a match. He was no longer excited or tense. He had a job to do, and he was even able to grin at the rather grisly humor of his predicament.

THE FAINT light revealed a schooner hold such as he might have seen in a thousand ships. There was very little cargo, so little, in fact, that it could not be that the schooner was engaged in legitimate trade. Planks and wooden billets used for dunnage littered the lower deck, and Bellow Bill also marked an iron-shod handspike which had been left in the hold for stowing or shifting cargo.

There were two exits. The main hatch in the deck overhead was battened down. The crew must open this before he could climb out, and while he was climbing out he would be at their mercy. On the other hand, he could easily overpower any sailor who climbed down. The thing was fifty-fifty.

The other possible exit was the cargo port, a door built in the side of the schooner and held shut with iron dogs. This he could open, but it led to the sea; and though he might reach up, catch the rail and climb over the side, he would be likely to make some noise which would attract a sailor to the spot. Bill would be as helpless as though he climbed out of the main hatch, and he would leave behind him an open port which might fill the hold with water.

He struck another match, and examined the big box he had just left, hoping that he might find a letter which would give him a hint. There was nothing. The box was obviously of Chinese workmanship, probably designed to smuggle aliens into the United States or Australia. Bill grinned. He needed no further evidence that Chen Fu had tossed him into this mess.

The old chess-playing crook had evidently expected him to get out by himself.

Bill concealed the knife and revolver under his coat, picked up the iron-shod handspike, and began to pound mightily on the side of the schooner. The sound of the blows reverberated through the hull—and under the cover of the noise, the pearler opened all the dogs on the cargo port except one.

For ten minutes he made racket enough to wake the dead. But nothing happened.

He shifted his attack to the main hatch then, and pounded so hard that the tip of a handspike splintered a plank. Still there was no response from the top side.

Bill ceased, suddenly. Had he been sent out to sea on a derelict, with the helm lashed? The idea was illogical, but vivid. He listened, and among the noises of the sea heard a new sound— the rasp of a bit boring through the deck, close to where he stood.

That was all. But Bill was almost relieved to learn he was not aboard a flying Dutchman.

"AHOY! OPEN the hatch!" he roared in the great voice that boomed like surf.

Scrith—scrith—scrith went the bit. No other answer.

Then, with a snap of splintering wood, the drill broke through the three-inch deck planks into the hold. Instantly it was withdrawn.

"No, I won't open that hatch!" rasped a voice on deck. But it was not addressing Bill. "What the hell difference does it make to us who it is? We know who it *ain't*, don't we?"

"It's Bellow Bill Williams!" thundered the pearler.

"He says he's Bellow Bill, and he roars enough like a bull to be telling the truth," rasped the voice.

It was an edged and sneering voice. Never before had Bill disliked an unseen man to the same degree. He fingered the revolver—but the deck planking would take most of the force away from a bullet.

"Give me the funnel and the bellows, Moa," rasped the voice. "We ain't done this in too long, anyhow!"

Bellow Bill moved swiftly away from the auger hole. He heard the wheeze of a bellows—and instantly a sharp whiff of burning sulphur was forced into the hold. The place was being fumigated—to kill rats!

With an oath, the pearler whipped off his coat. The cold-blooded deviltry of the deed infuriated him. They knew who he was, and they didn't ask a question. They were just going to keep on pumping in the gas until his skin was burned out of his throat and lungs—until he choked, turned black in face, and died!

Bill wadded the coat around the handspike. He could plug the hole, temporarily.—*Temporarily!* Then they would knock out the plug, or bore another hole! And gradually the hold would fill with those biting fumes. As yet, the sulphur only made a smell.

Bill unwound the coat from the iron-shod club. He had a better use for it than that.

"A rat, am I, hey?" he bellowed, knowing the men on deck could hear. "Okay!"

CURSING SOFTLY, he stumbled across the hold to the big box and ripped out the quilted lining. He dragged the sail to the side of the schooner, close to the cargo port. He hoped they could hear him stumbling around, and that they would believe he was seeking an exit.

He lifted the revolver, and fired—at the sound of the pumping bellows—and then, in five slow, evenly spaced shots, he emptied the gun. He hoped that first bullet had stirred them up, and that they would believe the other five had been aimed the same way. They'd be wrong, of course, for with the muzzle held against the side of the schooner, Bill had sent the last five bullets crashing through the planking, blowing a ragged hole about an inch in diameter.

Swiftly, he put his lips against this orifice, and sucked in fresh air—for already the fumes in the hold were making him cough. Grimly he touched the single dog that held the cargo port shut. He would turn that—but not now; not while they were waiting for him.

He grasped the handspike and attacked the bulkhead that separated the hold from the living quarters of the schooner. He might have broken through—the first blow, struck with all his strength, cracked the thick oak planks. But they would be waiting for him to stick out his head. Between his own strokes, he could hear a hammering somewhere aft in the schooner. That puzzled him, though he put the sound down to more deviltry.

Little by little, he let his assault go feebler. The sulphur choked him. He coughed more and more.

The blows of the handspike now would scarcely have cracked a box. They ceased—only to begin again with the frantic, aimless hammer of a dying man.

Bill's coughing, the harsh gasps torn from his great lungs, were not assumed.

He was half strangled when he let the handspike slip through his fingers, wrapped the coat and the quilt around his head, flung himself down with his lips against the bullet holes, and drew the old sail over his body.

Some of the sulphur fumes seeped through. He shut his eyes against the smart. At least, he was breathing fresh air, and he believed he could hold out until long after those on deck believed him dead.

Rat, was he? Well, those who corner a rat had better make

sure that they kill it! An immense, cold rage filled him—against a man with a nasty voice, another called Moa, and a chess player named Chen Fu.

CHAPTER III

THE NOOSE

THE RUSH OF the water along the sides of the schooner drowned every other sound. Bellow Bill could only guess when the bellows ceased to force gas into the hold. He endured a pain that seemed to press under his eyelids and into his eyeballs; he had a throat that was like sandpaper.

He tried to remember how long a sulphur candle burns. He had fumigated a hold hundreds of times himself. You lighted one of the sulphur candles; closed the hatch, and went away. In the morning, you opened the hatch again.

In time, these devils would cease plying the bellows. In time, there would again be but the one man at the wheel who was awake on the deck of the schooner. That man would know when Bill flung open the cargo port. His nose would warn him, if his ears did not, but he would not be able to leave the wheel instantly. When he did run to the rail, over the open port, Bill planned to be elsewhere. He visualized every projection along the side of a schooner which would afford a handhold. He could get aft—if he could see.

He was in dread lest the fumes were injuring as well as torturing his eyes, and that fear ended Bill's endurance at last. He breathed deep and leaped up, throwing off the quilt and the old sail. He wrenched back the last of the dogs, pushed the port open, and swung out on one of the doors, as a child rides a swinging gate.

His eyes were still tight shut when he crashed against the side of the schooner. Had they failed him he would have climbed the rail, but through streaming tears he managed to locate the scuppers—small, oblong slits cut through the rail at the level of the deck, to permit sea water to run off. They were three feet apart, and they offered no more than a finger hold; but for Bellow Bill's steel-sinewed fingers that little sufficed.

Like some huge gorilla, he swung himself aft. Though the rushing sea tore at his feet, which dipped at every roll, he was not shaken loose. With an amazing speed, he went the length of the schooner without showing so much as his head above the rail. Though he saw the man who had been at the wheel, when the latter leaned over the rail, the sailor looked downward, at the cargo port, instead of aft.

"Peltz!" the sailor yelled, *"Peltz!* He ain't dead! Get up here!"

Bellow Bill swung under the stern, located with his feet the preventer chains on the rudder, and let himself slip into the water, seizing the chains and letting the schoo'ner tow him. The overhang of the stern concealed him, and the salt water cleansed his eyes. For an expert swimmer, that spot was safe, since he could not be shot at from the deck. Later, he would reboard the vessel; but at the moment, two men were looking for him, guns in hand, and when he rushed them he preferred to have the revolvers back in the holsters at least.

"I say! Who shanghaied you?" came a whisper.

It was faint—almost drowned by the rush and gurgle of the water—but the shock of hearing a whisper at all almost made Bellow Bill let go of the chains. No one could see him here! There was no possible way....

He looked up. No one was leaning over the taffrail, but underneath the stern itself, not two feet from his head, what should have been an immovable glass dead-eye was an open hole which framed the pale blur of a face. How a man could cram himself into that tiny compartment under the stern, and how he could have unfastened the dead-eye flashed through Bill's mind while his hand was flashing to his waist for the knife. He struck—and the face dodged, escaping the steel.

"**OH, I** say!" came the whisper—excited, protesting, and barely audible. "I'm shanghaied myself, y'know! Didn't you hear me pounding when you did?"

"Shut up!" Bill rumbled.

For there was talking on deck.

"—you'll damn well go down, sulphur or no sulphur!" snarled the voice Bill hated. "You're at sea now, Moa, I'll have you know! I'll see Bill's body, or by the Lord, I'll heave to till I find it floating!"

"There's no time to waste! If he did jump overboard, he must drown! How can he make shore, across the barrier reef?"

"He must have choked in that hold, too, but he didn't!" snarled Peltz. "You damn sheep-stealin' landlubber, Bellow Bill Williams's name is a byword! He's *known* at sea, lemme tell you! An' Smiler Peltz ain't takin' chances with tykes like *him!* Leave the wheel in the becket and get below! I'll hold the deck with my gun till you find him!"

Bellow Bill listened, but Moa made no further protest.

There was a thump as Moa started to raise the hatch. Bill raised himself till his lips were close to the pale blur of a face in the dead-light.

"How many of them are there?" he rumbled.

Whisper he could not, but he could lower his voice until the growling sound deep in his chest was pitched in key with the gurgling water.

"Just two. Moa and Peltz.—I say!" the answering whisper was excited and eager. "I'm John Harris, of Sydney, you know—the heir."

"I don't know; besides, what of it?" Bill rumbled. "Make some kind of noise. Pound on the door—yell for help."

"But they'll see I got the dead-light open—with a spoon. They wouldn't even give me a dull table knife to eat with!"

"Yeah, I hope they do see it," Bill growled.

He could hardly repress a grin. Harris was a kid, proud of himself—and indignant.

"Don't stop them from shutting it, either," Bill added. "They've got to shut it, or they'll sink when the wind changes. Yell bloody murder, buddy. We've got to get that damn sure-thing player of a Peltz excited.—Damn the guy that invented guns! I'll bet that bozo's sitting aloft, waiting patient for me to stick my head up so that he can pop it!"

"But I *want* the schooner to sink! They'd have had to let me out!" Harris retorted. "And if I yell, they'll find you!"

"Don't you ever obey orders?" Grim laughter rumbled in Bellow Bill's chest. "You yell, buddy. Make believe you're scared. It won't hurt you. Or I'll go and get myself shot, and when you sink this boat you'll have fifty miles to swim, startin' from a locked room!—Let you out?—Peltz? You're thinking of another sort of skipper."

"Oh, all right!" Harris whispered disgustedly.

His face disappeared from the dead-eye. With fists and feet, he hammered on the door; and the scream he uttered was so shrill, and so long drawn out that Bill winced. Only a dying horse, or an utterly terrified woman, can put that maddening quality into a scream. It was hard to believe that a man could do it—especially a man who didn't believe in the idea.

"Ay-eeeee—eeeee!"

On and on, shriller and shriller, till Harris's voice broke. A gasp for breath, and then a choked, despairing wail.

"Sinking!" Harris yelled. "We're sinking! Oh, God, look at the water!—Let me out!"

Bellow Bill took a better grip on the rudder chains, and lifted himself close to the dead-eye, the knife poised. He heard the click of a lock, the thud of a blow.

"Shut up!" Moa snarled. "Leak, eh? Huh! You wanted one!"

"Don't kick me!" Harris sobbed.

"No?"

Three measured thuds, and silence.

"Whew!" Moa snorted. "Cheap London soft-belly! Where the hell's the dead-eye?—Oh!"

And in the opening under the stern appeared, not a face, but the heavy circle of glass!

BELLOW BILL was as quick. His knife did not make a thrust, but a whipping circle. The blade grated on the glass, and slashed around upon the fingers which held it. Moa screamed and dropped the dead-eye. Bill drove the knife through the opening as far as he could reach, but the blade met nothing. Within the schooner there was a brief grunting and thrashing. On deck, Peltz demanded sharply what the matter was.

"I say! I've his gun!" Harris's whisper, exultant and triumphant. "I laid doggo, and snatched it when he lifted his hands!"

"Pass it out!" Bill rumbled fiercely.

"Oh, but I say—"

"Then lock the door, you damn young fool!" Bill roared, with all the power of his lungs.

The chance for surprise was gone, tossed away by an over-zealous and inexperienced kid. With the knife in his teeth, Bill caught the taffrail and swung himself onto the deck. He expected a shot, but Peltz had evidently been too cold-blooded to rely upon the uncertainties of marksmanship at night.

The slide of the cabin companionway was thrown back, and the light of an oil lamp beat upward.

From below, there was a burst of revolver fire—shot after shot. Grim-lipped, Bill leaped from the darkness down into the light. He landed in the cabin like a cat. No man alive could have located Peltz quicker, where he stood backed against the cabin bulkhead, revolver in hand. A cat could scarcely have whirled quicker than Bill, or made a greater spring. The pearler hurled himself across the cabin like a living spear with a knife tip. And he knew in that split-second both that he was a split-second too slow, and also that Peltz could not save himself either.

No bullet could stop Bill's lunge. The knife drove through Peltz's body. Bill crashed against the bulkhead, and the skipper toppled upon him. Blood deluged the pearler. For an instant he was not aware that the blood was not his own. Peltz's revolver lay on the deck beside him. Bill had not seen the blaze of powder; had not heard the shot. *Peltz had not fired!* And there had been time for Peltz to shoot.

In a daze, Bill stood erect, mechanically feeling his body for a wound. The pearler stared down at the lifeless body. In addition to the gash of the knife, blood welled from a bullet hole in Peltz's chest. He had lost his chance because he had already been shot through the lungs.

Under the stern a door opened. Moa staggered into view—a swarthy, powerfully built half-breed, but dressed in the ducks of a white man instead of the Melanesian *lava-lava*. Against his back Harris, fair-haired and crimson with excitement, held a smoking gun.

"Peltz fired through the door and I fired back!" he crowed.

"That so?" Bill rumbled.

Annoyance struggled with amusement.

"Then go get a bucket and a swab and clean up this mess, kid," he said. "You've had your beginner's luck. From now on you're the deckhand."

"But I say!"

"*You listen!*" Bill contradicted. "You came so near grandstanding me dead that I can't start in too soon to teach you to leave something to the other guy!"

CHAPTER IV

SPIDER TO FLY

MOA SAT AT the cabin table. His right hand was bandaged, and his lips were locked in stubborn silence. Bellow Bill pushed back an empty plate that had been piled four inches high with slabs of bread and slices of canned corned beef half an inch thick.

"We could make him talk, but why bother to get rough?" he rumbled. "I'll take an observation of the stars and find out where we are. By morning, we'll be back in port. Then we'll turn him over to the police on a kidnapping charge, and that will settle him."

Harris squirmed in his chair.

"To-morrow will be too late for me," he said. "If I don't take active charge of my grandfather's sheep station by to-morrow at noon; I forfeit my inheritance under the will. I say, I'm not objecting to your plans, Bill!" Harris added hastily. "But I can't possibly reach the station from the port in the time that's left—and you know, the coast is inaccessible from the sea, what with the barrier reef and all. I've just been shanghaied out of ten thousand acres of good Australian land. It's gone and all that, and so I'm not beefing about it! Only Moa is an under-overseer, and he taught me to ride when I was a nipper. I know who bribed him to shanghai me, and why. But it's really very little satisfaction to me to put Moa in quod. He's just a pawn, y'know!"

"Whose pawn?" Bill boomed.

"Oh, my cousin's. Named Harris, christened Ben. You couldn't possibly understand, unless you were an Australian from the back blocks yourself. You see," Harris declared with perfect candor, "my great grandfather was a convict—transported and all that. He went into the Never-never country when any one could have ten thousand acres for the asking; and three generations of Harrises made a sheep ranch out of the bush. It was bally hard, and out in the sun and the dust and the smell of sheep dip, we wanted to prove we weren't scum—that we were just as good as the men who'd stayed in England. We were, y'know. But we fair wanted to make them admit it.—But you can't understand!"

"Your *cousin's* pawn?" Bill rumbled, as softly and heavily as far-distant thunder. "And what does that make me? Go on, buddy. I'm from the States, but maybe I'll savvy."

"I was the fourth generation, and I was the Harris that got to England. Ten years ago that was. I was but a little nipper—with something to show." Harris's fair face glowed reminiscently. "I showed them," Harris said. "I spent more money than some. I took prizes others wanted. And still others I jolly well punched in the nose, because that was all they could understand. All grandfather wanted was letters from me that told every detail. Every time I made a good showing, he increased the size of my monthly draft. It was his triumph—the family's triumph, y'know. He'd never been in a town bigger than Melbourne. He'd never seen the inside of a cabaret or a university. And yet he got more of the old bounce out of hearing what I did than I got in the doing."

"The checks got larger and larger," Bill purred. "Doesn't that strike you as strange, with the price of wool on the toboggan?"

"Why—er—the clip might have been larger," Harris replied vaguely.

"Unlikely!" Bill grunted. "But perhaps your grandfather showed your letters to Chen Fu?"

"Who?" Harris demanded, open mouthed. "I say, what are you leading to?—Show family letters to a Chinese? Bally nonsense! Grandfather wouldn't have a Chink on the station!"

BELLOW BILL glanced at the swarthy face of the under-over-seer. Moa's features were wooden—too wooden. He knew who Chen Fu was. Bellow Bill could see, and he was uneasy.

"Your grandfather died?—Suddenly?" Bill rumbled.

"I say, will you please let me explain!" Harris snapped. "Not at all! He was sick for weeks, though all the time he was sure it was nothing serious. The actual news was unexpected, of course. I'd just time to catch a steamer. Real Australians, you know, hate absentee landlords in England. The understanding was that when Grandfather died, I must come back at once and manage the ranch. His will give me only thirty days, so I wouldn't have time to hem and haw. Of course," said Harris candidly, "I did want to stay—rather. But ten thousand acres was too much to give up. My cousin Ben must have thought so, too. For when I reached the port—with just twenty-four hours left to get to the station—Moa was waiting for me with the car. He suggested a drink to celebrate, and the next thing I knew, I was crammed into that compartment aft."

"Did you drink in a Chinese gambling house?" said Bill.

"I drank out of Moa's flask!" snapped Harris. "Are you hipped? You keep trying to involve Chinamen in my affairs! Don't you see that if I fail to fulfill the provisions of the will, Ben gets possession of my property? I might go to law, claiming that I was shanghaied, but Ben would have money to fight the case, and I wouldn't. He's stayed on the land and I haven't. He's likely to win, or enjoy the income of the estate for years, while the case dragged along. Whereas if he cut my throat, questions would be asked. There'd be lots about me in the papers. But I could disappear like—like—"

"Like a tattooed old roughneck pearling skipper," Bellow Bill chuckled.

He shifted his quid and continued to address Harris.

"I thought you were kidnapped," he said, "but you haven't the money to pay a ransom, so that's out. I can see why your cousin would prefer to have you alive, but I can't see why he wants two sheep stations. Financially, a station to-day is nothing but a pain in the neck. Yours managed to pay dividends, and that's miraculous. Two men—strangers—get shanghaied on the same schooner. Me they try to kill at the drop of a hat, though they were aware that some one would know who murdered me, and when." Bellow Bill stared at Moa with narrowed eyes. "The case is too complicated for us, kid," he rumbled, "and so we'll go back to port and lodge a complaint of attempted murder against Mr. Moa here; then we'll go to law to recover your station."

"Without money?" Harris snorted.

"No, buddy," said Bill softly. "With all the cash you need— supplied by an old chess-playin' Chink named Chen Fu. Chen's interested in you. That's the one thing that's clear. Don't ask *me* why! I'm going to ask *him*—by dawn to-morrow. *And I'll find out*—eh, Moa?" Bill bellowed, sudden and loud as a clap of thunder.

"Yes!" rasped Moa. The wooden mask of his features broke suddenly. His lips twisted into a snarl like that of a wolf who feels the jaws of a trap close. "Chen will hang me, and send the constables to put your cousin and my brother in jail. Chen will catch them red-handed, without even a warning, and then he will laugh and give you your worthless land!"

Moa leaned toward Harris with vicious, savage delight.

"Did you think that wool paid for the drafts you got?" he sneered. "You fool! The price of wool was in the paper every day, and you thought the clip was larger!—Opium paid the drafts! Stolen pearls and smuggled aliens! Your grandfather, your cousin, my brother and me are the biggest fences in Australia! We've taken the cream of Chen's business, and so he hates us!"

"Supplanted Chen? How?" Bill roared.

Moa flung himself back in his chair, exhausted by his outburst.

"There's a channel through the barrier reef, in front of the station," he snarled. "I'll pilot the schooner in before noon to-morrow—if you choose!"

CHAPTER V

NEEDLE'S EYE

TO RIGHT AND left, surf roared over shallow reefs of coral. A mile ahead was the low line of the shore, grayish-green under the morning sun. Beneath the bow of the schooner a narrow ribbon of smooth water twisted erratically toward the land.

Harris had chosen, and Bellow Bill had acquiesced.

Forward, Moa pointed out the course. His arm swung like a weather vane. At the wheel, Bellow Bill exerted all his seamanship. The bowsprit followed Moa's arm as though the two were actuated by a single will. The pearler no longer wondered that this channel was not shown on the charts. Rather, the marvel was how the secret had been discovered, for no sane sailor would have thrust his ship into such a narrow lead, with a two-mile wide belt of surf thundering around. Despite his skill, Bill expected at every instant to feel the keel scrape on the coral. He was not quite sure that Moa had not elected to drown rather than rot in jail.

And if the schooner reached a harbor, what of Harris and himself? A channel through the barrier reef was like a rat hole in a granary that was otherwise locked and guarded. No coast guard patrolled the barrier reef. The constables ashore watched for contraband along the routes which led into the interior, and not along the roads which skirted a coast supposedly without a harbor. Though this channel was too crooked and too narrow to have any commercial value, to thieves it was priceless.— And thieves would be certain to guard the secret as something beyond price.

Bill glanced at Harris. The lips of the younger man were bloodless, and stubbornly set. The pearler both admired and pitied him. With one savage speech, Moa had smashed Harris's ideals and his pride in his family. The kid had rocked to the blow, but instantly he had elected to fight back.

Seek Chen Fu's aid and betray his cousin to the police Harris would not. To give up his rights to the sheep station and disappear was a step that he refused to consider. The station was his. By his grandfather's will he had become the head of the family. He insisted that he would go on, assume his inheritance, and act as the master. Stolen goods should flow through the Harris station no longer.

How would he stop the flow? John Harris did not even attempt to answer that question. He had no plans; only determination and courage. His cousin, Bill pointed out, had shanghaied him in order to force him to join the others, and to be in a position to get rid of him in case he refused.

Yes, quite so. And though Chen Fu might be anxious to rid

himself of dangerous rivals, he would be indifferent to the fate of Harris, personally. The Chinese had been careless enough about the risk Bill ran, hadn't he?

Yes, quite so. Nevertheless, blood was thicker than water. Did Bellow Bill want to leave the schooner before it entered the channel? He could row away in the dinghy. Some passing ship would pick him up.

Bill had greeted that suggestion with rumbling laughter. He was aware that courage, unless backed by experience and craft, would only put Harris into an unmarked grave. He had not saved the younger man to let him throw himself away. Nor did the pearler care to be a cat's-paw for Chen Fu. The scowl on Bill's face was not caused wholly by the perils of the tortuous channel through the reef. He had been played with. He was embarrassed, and he was angry, which made him doubly dangerous.

BY THE time the schooner came within a quarter of a mile of the shore, Bill had decided that Moa's pilotage could be trusted. Very soon they would cease to thread through the reef and would enter the deep, calm, safe waters of the lagoon which lay between the coral and the beach.

Moa, at that moment, was signalling to put the wheel hard up. With a tight-lipped grin, Bill spun the spokes—hard down! The schooner crashed against a hidden reef, and while the masts were still vibrating from the shock, Bill whipped out his knife and slashed through the main sheet and the halyards. The boom swung outboard and snapped at the gooseneck as the schooner pounded on the reef. The falling sails buried the deck.

"Oh, but I say!" Harris gasped.

Moa came running aft—to stop short, and glance in desperation at the surf to port and to starboard. Bellow Bill had drawn a gun. He was taking careful aim at the buckle on Moa's belt.

"You ain't useful any more!" he boomed. "Get down below!— Follow him, Harris!"

The two descended to the cabin, covered every step by the gun. No sails hid the deck of the schooner from the shore.

Bellow Bill crossed the deck erect, cat-footed, grim. The sight of his face as he swung down into the cabin made Moa shrink.

"But why?" Harris mumbled in horror. "Why do you have to kill him—now?"

"That's up to him!" Bill boomed. "Moa, have you got that flask that Harris drank from?"

The muscles of the under-overseer's throat worked convulsively. He managed to nod.

"Get it!" Bill commanded. "And drink it—all of it!"

Moa moved to obey like a man already drunk. The drug was so powerful that he was unable to finish the draught before he swayed and collapsed. Bellow Bill snatched the flask from his hand as he fell, knelt beside him, and raised his eyelids to examine the pupils. Moa lay with only the slightest rise and fall of his chest to indicate that he lived. Bill nodded in grim satisfaction.

"There'll be no more trouble with him for hours," he rumbled. "And so.—Can you take orders, Harris?"

"I—think so!"

"I can knock you out," Bill rumbled. "I'd have knocked him out—with a belaying pin—if he hadn't been willing to take that drink. But drugs and discipline are safer than a knockout, and they last longer."

The pearler drew his revolver and fired twice into the deck, with a distinct pause between the shots.

If possible, Harris's eyes stuck out further than ever.

"But I say! Are you balmy? What do you want?" he mumbled.

"From you? Nothing. Don't speak—and don't move," Bill boomed. His face was cold and hard as bronze. "That'll give you practice."

He turned on his heel and ascended to the deck.

THERE HE first swung the dinghy into the water. Next he carried out of the hold the big box in which he had been shanghaied, and tumbled it down into the cabin. Last, he cut three large squares of canvas from the sail and provided himself with a coil of rope. He moved without haste, for he knew that he was being watched from the shore. He hoped he was being watched closely. Just one thing Bill hoped had escaped observation—the fact that Moa had been pointing for uphelm when the helm went down.

In the cabin, Harris was poking gingerly at the big box. For the first time, Bellow Bill let a dancing, reckless twinkle creep into his eyes. Harris appeared to be relieved.

"You realize," the pearler boomed abruptly, "that we can't row ashore without giving the men who may be waiting for us a dead, cold drop? Therefore—all this. I ain't crazy, buddy. I'm just getting ready to fight, with a chance to win."

Harris frowned.

"This schooner can't be floated easily or quickly," Bill explained. "Some passing ship is going to see masts where the masts of a wrecked ship couldn't possibly get to, according to the charts. There'll be a report, an investigation by the coast guard; and within a week at most this channel will no longer be a secret. Then the flow of contraband stops."

"But I say! That's clever!"

"The bozos ashore will think it's something else," Bill boomed curtly. "Take a look at your gun, and make sure it's in damned good working order."

While Harris complied, the pearler wrapped Moa's unconscious figure in canvas, leaving the feet exposed, and lashed the bundle with rope.

"You see," he purred, "it'll look as if Moa steered me wrong and wrecked the schooner. Therefore, I took him down here in the cabin and shot him."

"But you didn't!"

"Don't he look like a corpse?" Bill boomed. "Stick that gun under your shirt where it will be handy, and lie down in the big box. I'm going to cover you with canvas and put Peltz in on top of you. *He's* dead enough!"

Involuntarily, Harris recoiled.

"Lie underneath—" he gasped.

"Lie under a stiff and make believe you're one, too!" Bill boomed. "That's orders, buddy! You see, I'm supposed to have taken you down here and murdered you, too. Because I figure that was what your cousin Ben would want me to do, once the secret of the channel was discovered."

Stiffly, Harris climbed into the big box. He repressed a shudder when Bill laid Peltz upon him. Yet for several seconds he did not speak, and in the end all he said was:

"It'll be a bit hard to lie still."

"Aye-aye, buddy!" Bill agreed. "And it's hard to put your life in another man's hands, too. But at least you won't be shot in cold blood as you walk across the beach, and a corpse that jumps from a coffin waving a gun is—surprising. Use your head, and listen for a cue from me. Then jump up, run for the thickest brush, and hide. You know the country. You ought to be able to remain hidden, and in a day or two no one will stop you from taking charge of your station."

"But I say! How about you?" Harris protested through the canvas.

"Oh, I'll have a gun in each hand." Deep, reckless laughter bubbled in Bill's chest. "I don't think they'll shoot till they find out what I've got in the big box. And afterward—I'll be looking for trouble, you see!"

CHAPTER VI

SUN—AND SAND

BELLOW BILL STOWED Moa's canvas-wrapped body in the bow of the dinghy, letting the feet stick up to be identified. The big box with its double load he balanced across the stern sheets, and took his place at the oars.

He was forced to row slowly, for the little boat was loaded

almost to the water's edge, and to swamp, or to jar the box off the stern, would be fatal. As he pulled away from the schooner, the beach lay yellow and empty under the sun, and though the hair rose on the back of his neck and his heart hammered as he approached the land, he did not look around until the dinghy grated on the sand. He must not appear nervous.

As a matter of fact, he wasn't. The suspense merely keyed him to concert pitch. If they shot him, they shot him. In every campaign there is bound to be one step, one moment, of pure gambling risk. There is no use in worrying how the dice will fall. Bellow Bill merely wondered whether he would have a chance to show his stuff.

That he was allowed to land was in his favor. Turning, he saw—one man, waiting alone, half way between the shore and the dense, gray-green underbrush. A scout? Bill thought so. The beach was fifty feet wide. The man appeared to be unarmed. A tangled golden beard concealed his features. He was middle-aged. His complexion and the set of his shoulders had a definite resemblance to those of John Harris.

"Are you Ben Harris?" Bill boomed confidently.

"Aye, mate.—And who the hell are you?" The tone was bitter, impersonal.

Ben's eyes were on the big box. He scowled.

"Name's Williams. Peltz's new deckhand," Bill boomed. "And damn me, mate! I've never have signed on if I'd known the cargo! I'm like to swing!"

"Aye, you've played hell!" was the bitter retort. "Don't lie, you Chink-loving bush-loper. Peltz never had a deckhand. I know what you are. Take those stiffs back and dump them into the hold. Then burn the schooner, and them along with it. After that, come back and get yours—and I hope to God it's a rope at the last!"

For an instant Bill's blood was ice. So he wasn't to have even a chance? So Ben Harris was another Peltz, who played sure? Bill's huge tattooed hands closed on the revolver butts at his belt.

Ben hoped he would get a rope. Why "hoped"? Ben could knot it round his neck!—"Chink-loving"? The big box was obviously Chinese, and yet—

"Light a fire and burn a ship. Sure!" Bill roared. "Have them find charred bodies in the hold? Not me, mate—and that's flat! We'll stick them in the ground ashore. And as for swinging"—Bellow Bill drew both revolvers—"we'll see about that!"

He paused, watching the underbrush.

"Peltz double-crossed you," he added. "He was going to let Harris go free—in return for a deed of gift to the station. Moa got wise and shot him, but I guess Moa decided Peltz's idea was good, after thinking it over. He ordered me to come about and go back to sea—and I guess you saw what happened! There was nothing in that for me, so I gave it to them. I didn't figure you'd care.—And now get your mates out of that brush!" The roaring voice rose to thunder. "I know they're there. Are they too yellow to shoot it out with one man?"

Ben Harris smiled bleakly, and half turned.

"I wouldn't have cared—much," he muttered. "Though I just wanted to put the screws on the young fool." He raised his voice. "Well?" he called questioningly.

OUT OF the bush came the dry, throaty chuckle of an old man who seemed to be well pleased. Bellow Bill's guns wavered. In a flash, he knew part of the answer.

"That was well done, Bellow Bill!" called Chen Fu softly. "Let us talk no more of ropes and bullets, but of gold."

The old Chinaman thrust the foliage aside and stepped out on the sand, his black-clad secretary at his elbow. Chen Fu was so pleased that he was shaking hands with himself in his wide sleeves.

"The queen," he chuckled to his chess-playing companion, "is a mightier piece than the knight or the rook. I never doubted it would be you who swept Peltz and Moa from the board; and throughout the South Seas, all men know that Bellow Bill never asks to see his profit in advance."

"Oh, aye?" Bill purred. "What's the spider doing out of his web, Chen?"

"The spider hoped that the wasp would bring home a fat fly to another web," Chen explained softly. "I thought that you could remove Peltz. But what would you do here, with him?" A long-nailed forefinger pointed contemptuously at Ben Harris. "He is a fool who chanced upon a valuable secret. But he's no match for me—or you. The thing was very simple: I had promised him opium. I brought it—and seven men. The knives of my men were at his throat before he was aware that he had reason to fear me. He should play chess." Chen Fu chuckled. "The king is not dangerous, except when other pieces prepare his attack. And so I will put the screws on a young—pawn. To whom I intend no harm."

"I don't get you. The game's ended," Bill boomed.

He wondered swiftly whether Chen counted his secretary as a man or not. Probably not.—In that case, there were seven tough Chinese in the bush to be dealt with.

"For you, Bellow Bill," Chen Fu chuckled softly. "You played well, but I was not deceived. Men move according to what they are, whether the men be flesh or ivory. The eagle bites—but not like the snake. And *you* did not murder John Harris.—Peltz? Yes!—Moa? Perhaps.—But never the lad. For he would have been shot only through fear, and you have never been afraid, Bellow Bill."

Bill caught his breath. Chen's shrewd, wrinkled face mocked him, banishing any idea of bluff.

"You are right, Chen," he rumbled. And added more loudly, lest there be a movement in the big box. "And yet John Harris— is dead. Men are as they are. Yet they blunder. And I blundered. I wished to frighten Moa, and he read in my face the death that he would have given me if he had held the gun. When I swung below, he snatched the other revolver I wore in my belt. I shot him, but he pulled the trigger and Harris stood in the path of the bullet." Bill shrugged. "Afterward, I tried to profit by an accident.—I did not expect you here."

The sun burned down upon the yellow sand. Little waves lisped at Bill's heels as he stood beside the dinghy, staring across the big box at Chen. Chen's beady black eyes searched the pearler through and through.

"Look for yourself!" he boomed. "Dead men will—wait."

Chen smiled shrewdly, and spoke in Cantonese. A burly hatchetman shouldered out of the underbrush and crossed the sand toward the boat.

Bill smiled slightly. Seven minus one left six.

"Suspicious, Chen?" he mocked. "There is no need. I'll help your man."

HE STEPPED to the bow, lifted out Moa with one hand, and sent the canvas-wrapped figure rolling across the sand.

The effort made Bill stagger. He lurched against the dinghy, at least pushing it a foot backward toward the sea by a thrust of his hip. Bill was grinning, and his eyes danced with golden flecks. With both hands, he lifted up Peltz so that all might see the gaping wounds, and dropped him carelessly—into the bow, where Moa had been.

"A living shield is better than a dead one!" Bill boomed.

Inwardly he blessed John Harris for his fortitude.

The hatchetman had stopped six feet away. Bill caught the canvas that covered young Harris, and swung it into the air with a wide flourish toward the hatchetman's face.

Behind the flying canvas, Bellow Bill leaped. A huge tattooed hand closed on the hatchetman's throat; another gripped the sash at his waist. With a terrific heave, Bill swung the man into the air, whirled, and slammed him bodily down into the big box.

"Hold him there, Harris!" Bill thundered, and dove headlong for the stern of the boat.

With a roll and a twist he was crouched in the shelter of the hull.

"Plug him if he moves! Not unless!" he ordered Harris.

Rifles cracked in the undergrowth. Bullets whined around the dinghy, but they flew high. Instinctively, the marksmen tried to spare their comrade in that first fire. Bellow Bill caught the stern of the dinghy and braced his heels in the gravel. Only for an instant was he exposed. With one long, steady pull, easy for his vast strength, he drew the dinghy off the sand and dropped beside it again—into water that was knee-deep.

Reaching upward, he tipped over the big box, and knocked the hatchetman senseless with the butt of a revolver as he came tumbling out. Next, Bill caught young Harris by the collar. Bill threw himself on his back in the shallow water and kicked furiously with his feet, swimming with the dinghy as it drifted toward the sea.

Chen Fu screamed with rage. At sea was the schooner, with another dinghy, provisions and water, that offered a safe means of retreat. And the beach was empty of boats! Shrilly, the old voice cackled orders.

A volley sent splinters flying from the dinghy. With high-pitched yells, the Chinese charged, firing as they ran across the beach and plunged into the shallower water. There were six of them, but Bill uttered a satisfied grunt.

"Keep your head down, Harris!" he boomed. "We've got to get the dinghy out, buddy! That's the job!"

Bill rose himself in water that was now waist deep, to fire over the stern. He had never been a good shot. He scarcely aimed, but blazed away into the thick of the charge. One man pitched forward on his face at the water's edge and lay still. A second dropped, howling, to clasp his shin in both hands. The other four dashed into the water.

Bill ducked under the surface and swam back to meet them. A pearler and a deep sea diver, he was as much at home under water as a shark, and his knife was more terrible than a shark's teeth. The foremost Chinaman screamed horribly, and toppled over in a swirl of water that was suddenly red. The second saw a huge dim shape swimming at his legs; he yelled Bill's name, and turned to run. Before he had made two strides, however, the knife overtook him. The others waited for no more. In mad panic they splashed for the beach.

For a moment they ran alone. Then Bill, seeing no more legs beneath the water, sprang up and gave chase. One Chinaman still clung to his rifle, but his eyes were tight shut. And the crack of a revolver as Harris opened fire lent the man wings. Screaming, he crossed the beach and plunged into the bush, heedless of the thorns. His comrade was not a yard behind.

BEN HARRIS still lay in the sand where he had thrown himself at the first shot.

Chen Fu was in flight, like his Chinese gunmen, but the transition from victory to defeat had been swift, and his old legs were not equal to the emergency. He slipped in the soft sand. The black-clad secretary, with a courage and loyalty that did him credit, was trying to lift him when tattooed hands caught both by the pigtails and bumped their heads together. They dropped, half stunned.

Bellow Bill shoved the knife back into his waistband and picked up the nearest rifle. He covered Ben Harris. John Harris was already wading ashore.

"Well, Ben?" Bill thundered.

"I don't give a damn whether it's the Chinks or you or him!" growled the blond-bearded man. "I'm dusted out!"

"Yep!" snapped Bill. "And lucky at that! I ought to drill you for hiring a squid like Peltz. But you're just wooden-headed, I guess; and I'm just your cousin's partner. He'll want to let you go. If—"

"If what?" Ben growled, for Bill was grinning down at Chen Fu, who now blinked up at him, half dazed.

"—if you'll show me where this one put the opium he said he brought," the pearler finished grimly. "Ben, I'd advise you to turn King's Witness. If you help to put this old chess-playin' devil where he belongs, I think the authorities will let bygones be bygones. And as far as you're concerned—"

"But I say! Can't we keep the whole mess quiet?" the younger Harris interjected.

"This quiet?" Bellow Bill swung an arm at the stranded schooner, and the bodies on the beach. "No, buddy. You can save your family, but damned if you can whitewash 'em! You run your station, and the talk will die down in time. It always does, unless a man tries to be too smart. Eh, Chen?"

"No can be too smart," the old man contradicted with a firm, gentle dignity. "I play a game, and I lose. I smuggle opium forty years, and I go to jail over a paltry twenty tins. All right!"

Chen touched the base of his pigtail with a wry grimace. "From the classics you have learned wisdom, honored uncle," he remarked to his secretary in Chinese, and added, in English, "but not because I was too smart, I said to him, 'I have added a queen to the board'; but you not only move every way—too far and too fast, like a queen—you jump, too.—Next time, I know—I get out of jail some day. I play more chess. But next time, I say to bartender, 'There comes Bellow Bill. Give him very best whiskey; nothing more, nothing less.'"

ABOUT THE AUTHOR

THE TROUBLE WITH writing an autobiography is that you begin to ask yourself, "Why?"—and no reason is discernible. I was born in Medford, Massachusetts, on the 23rd of March, 1895, and so qualify as a Yankee even among Yankees. When I was a kid I was captain of a baseball team and played third base, instead of pitching, which shows unusual restraint. The trouble was I could throw an in, but not an out, and what's a pitcher without an out? Exactly. A third baseman.

Nothing else happened until I graduated from Columbia in 1916. I was a Fellow in English (maybe that was prophetic) but, as the event turned out, no scholar. I wanted to write a history of Sunday newspaper sections, all about the "Yellow Kid" and "Why Girls Leave Home," but the professors chose a newspaper that had been out of print for two hundred years. To disturb a literary corpse so remarkably quiescent seemed a shame, so I got a job with a trade exposition, which is a combination of circus and business convention, and when that was over, with the New York *Globe*. I was and am the worst salesman in the world, and was trying to sell advertising.

Then the war, which landed me eventually in command of a sub chaser. Getting there I wore every uniform in the navy, missed getting to France on the *Noma* in May, '17, because a bosun's mate thought my name was Sperry—I've never felt so low before or since—just had brains enough to get off the ship before they coaled her, and ran down the dock with my gear wrapped up in a blanket, and that bosun's mate bawling at me to come back and work.

Ralph R. Perry

Stayed at sea during the war, and for a year afterward. Saw fog and ice and France, finally; got shot at in mistake for a sub, and learned something of seagoing from Captain Hugo Osterhaus, who finally decided I could be trusted with a deck watch while we ferried the A.E.F. across the Western Ocean.

Late in 1919 the navy, in peace time, became dull. There were more merchant seamen with ten years' experience against my three than there were berths, so I came ashore. If I'd saved my pay everything would have been swell, but I never could make more than two successive passes in craps. Jobs weren't to be had in 1920, so I began to write. Didn't quite starve, but was pretty glad just the same to land an editorial job in the summer of '21. Four years later I quit to write fiction, and here I am, with a hundred stories back of me, and more interested in writing than ever. Some people think any grandmother could go to sea these days, and five hundred yarns wouldn't demonstrate the contrary too strongly.

Avocation? Building up a run-down Connecticut homestead. There's stone walls to lay, wood to cut, and painting and carpentering *ad lib.* Pleasures—going somewhere far off. Loading the Underwood and my wife into the car or onto a boat, and seeing how people do things two thousand or ten thousand miles away.